Lorraine
I hope you
low politics, even if
not the high finance!

NEMESIS

[signature]

Trigger Warning: This book contains sex,
violence, foul language and corruption.

NEMESIS

The dog-eats-dog world of high finance and low politics

SAM BELL

Matador
Unit E2 Airfield Business Park,
Harrison Road, Market Harborough,
Leicestershire. LE16 7UL
Tel: 0116 2792299
Email: books@troubador.co.uk
Web: www.troubador.co.uk/matador
Twitter: @matadorbooks

ISBN 978 1 80313 225 9

British Library Cataloguing in Publication Data.
A catalogue record for this book is available from the British Library.

Printed and bound in the UK by TJ Books Limited, Padstow, Cornwall
Typeset in 11pt Jensen Pro by Troubador Publishing Ltd, Leicester, UK

Matador is an imprint of Troubador Publishing Ltd

AUTHOR'S NOTE

When Nick de Carteret meets Tselmeg Yusupov he doesn't know whether to love or hate the Oligarch (soon-to-be President) from Kuikbakhistan. All Nick does know, with the visceral certainty of an abused child desperate for validation, is that he needs to be the best- and very rich. But Yusupov knows a bit about abuse, and when loved ones start dying, Nick realises it's crowded at the top, and the sweet scent of wealth and power soon turns to stench.

Nemesis is set in a pre-crash 'Wolf of Wall Street' world, where greed rules supreme. Various people eminently more experienced and better qualified than me, have told me that in today's super-regulated financial world these excesses will never be seen again.

But when only money talks, the law has no teeth and morality takes a back seat, what's to stop it?

Nemesis, what's yours?

Nemesis is dedicated to all you driven people out there who make the world go round. When you meet your nemesis, whatever form that takes, may you choose the high road of decency and not the soft option of vanity and greed.

My heartfelt thanks go to all my family and friends who responded to my constant pestering. You have no idea how helpful you were.

My particular thanks go to my daughter Emily Graham, unbelievably efficient editor, publisher, website designer and overall creative spark. You are one in a million.

PART ONE
RESURRECTION

1

My eyes opened. I wished they hadn't.

The unfamiliar surroundings alarmed me.

I was in hospital, that much was plain. But it was entirely beyond my powers to reason or remember why.

I must still be dreaming.

The nightmares had been bad enough, but a stubborn, angst-filled voice kept telling me reality was worse.

I scoured my memory, but mind and body both ignored my bidding.

My eyes alone obeyed. I swivelled them frantically, searching desperately for the cause of my impairment, but if there was any clue, it was beyond what remained of my faculties to grasp it.

My body seemed intact.

I struggled to dredge up anything to connect this mummified corpse with my own self, but waves of drug-induced torpor rolled over me, dampening any attempt at lucidity.

I fearfully rejoined my dreams.

2

A faceless hag tugged at my arm. I could sense others behind her, in that ill-defined and borderless infinity that dreams possess, none wishing me well. A dog barked.

Some power directed them; something malevolent, resentful of my very being. The puppeteer who pulled the strings. I could sense him fleetingly, in the background, and our souls seemed each to acknowledge the other. There was a strange and worrying connection between us, a duplicitous attraction that bound us, a pastiche of love and hate, good and evil, greed and fear.

Which, of all the demons, tormented me now, I could not tell, but she persisted with her yanking, like a dog with a bone.

"Mr de Carteret, Mr de Carteret…"

My eyes opened, and I was instantly transported, from one distressing unreality to another.

A kindly nurse leaned over me.

"Your supper," she smiled, adjusting a tube which disappeared under a plaster, into my wrist.

An orderly wheeled in a tray with pills and bottles, managing to spill only one. He lingered, and I caught his eye. He looked away. He was familiar, whether from my dreams or from that previous existence that kept wrenching me back to it, I could not tell. My pulse raced.

The nurse tried to soothe me and adjusted my sheets. She almost managed to hide a fleeting look of pity.

I had always disdained pity, even feared it, and now I tried to counter it with words.

But they stuck, stillborn, in my throat. My brain commanded, but my voice would not obey. I began to panic. What had happened to me?

The nurse put her hand on mine.

"The doctor will see you shortly," she soothed. "He will explain everything."

She wrongly interpreted my look of terror.

"If you are suffering, blink your eyes."

I kept them firmly open. I needed my full senses, and anyway, I felt no pain, at least none physical.

"I'll get him now," she decided. "I'll only be a minute."

No sooner had the door closed behind her, than it reopened slyly, giving the clumsy orderly unwelcome admittance. Checking the room quickly, he came to my bedside.

He stared brazenly at me, with a knowing smile that mocked my incapacity.

"You need to be careful, Nick," he whispered, caressing my throat with a gentleness that threatened more than any violence. "They always say that hospitals are dangerous places."

There was a knock on the door.

My nurse re-entered, followed by the doctor. Dismissing the orderly with an unknowing smile, she gestured at me.

My state of agitation was even greater now than when she had left me, for reasons she could not have known.

"You have to calm down, Mr de Carteret." The doctor put his hand reassuringly, as he thought, on my shoulder.

"You had a stroke and now have what we call locked-in syndrome. I am afraid there is little we can do for the moment."

I did not find that particularly reassuring, and upped my blink-rate.

"Be patient, Mr de Carteret. Modern medicine is capable of wonderful things, and you have all the very best facilities at your disposal here."

He waved his hand around the room, and put his iPad under

one arm in a gesture of closure. "So, for now, I am afraid, all we can do is let nature take its course."

He whispered to the nurse, and left quietly. After a peremptory patting down of my sheets, and with a kindly smile, she excused herself, almost apologetically.

I was so terrified I wanted to weep, but even that seemed beyond me.

3

Time passed, as I meandered in and out of opiated consciousness. People came and went in both worlds, some seemingly familiar. As far as I was aware, my would-be aggressor was not among them.

The only constant was a nagging certainty that my current predicament was merely an epilogue, and thus if I were to survive, a prologue to other, more critical dilemmas. The worst possible revelation came when I recognised the source of all my ills, my puppeteer. One night (for all my dreams were darkest night to me) we finally came face to face, my nemesis and me.

The encounter set my pulse racing so fast it that it brought the nurses running.

For suddenly, it dawned on me: the malevolent being who appeared to orchestrate my persecution, was none other than a dark reflection of my own true self.

As memory started to trickle back, I realised that the terror of my nightmares was going to prove far less troubling than the unanswered questions of full consciousness. I trusted neither, and began to dread both.

One sentiment that utterly failed to return, was any glimmer of happiness.

So, when I heard the words, "Your wife is here to see you, Mr de Carteret," my emotions overcame me. It was almost a relief to know that I really could still cry.

Anastasia peered nervously round the door and, seeing my delight, but mistaking it for distress, ran to me. Bringing her face close to mine and smiling bravely through her own tears, she kissed my lips, and while I could feel little, I did sense the love.

"Thank God you are conscious," she whispered. "It has been two weeks."

She placed a photo of our one-year-old daughter on my bedside table. "Chloe sends a big kiss."

She laid her head on my chest and stroked my cheek.

We lay together for a few moments, but unfortunately for this brief interlude of loving calm, my Nasta was no actress. She stood up, and a cloud of fear and worry scudded across her face, quickly overshadowing the sunny uplands of affection that had preceded it.

"What have you done, Nick? They tried to kill me." She held her hands together, wringing them gently, hoping for reaction, but getting none.

"And what do we do now?" She stood and waved her hands around the hospital room, slowly bringing them together in a gesture of hopelessness directed at me. "With you like this?"

It was a question I could not answer.

4

Anastasia had been sitting on my bed for less than five minutes, when two hospital orderlies, whom I did not recognise, came in, pushing a wheelchair. I knew something was wrong, and blinked as rapidly as I could to warn her.

It was not enough.

The alarm in my eyes got through to her, but induced entirely the wrong reaction. She held my hands, turning her back on the new arrivals, trying to soothe me.

"Calm down, Nick, please calm…"

The men obviously knew their business, and she slumped onto the bed after what appeared merely a light touch to her neck.

For the second time in as many minutes I found myself staring into eyes which were dark with emotion.

The voice was quiet, the accent faint, the evil intent all too clear.

"Your choice is simple, Nicky, my darling." The term of endearment served only to accentuate his malevolence. He leered at my lover.

"You are going to come up with our money." He rubbed his finger and thumb together slowly.

He paused, undoing Anastasia's top button for effect, and peering down her cleavage.

"And Danny is going to have fun with your girl until you do."

They dumped her body roughly into the wheelchair and pushed it towards the door.

As he left, he turned, the door ajar.

"Sorry about your little problem, Nicky," he shrugged, nodding at my useless corpse. "But you know Tselmeg… He really didn't like what you did to him." He shook his head. "He wants his money back."

He let the door close behind him.

5

I had never experienced a migraine before.

I had one now. I could not have conceived of such pain; all I could do was suck it up and blink.

My memory was returning slowly, and it brought little comfort. Quite the reverse.

I looked around again, as far as my eyeballs could swivel, to check I was still in that carnal world I had built for myself; a world of improbable deals, beautiful people and beguiling half-truths.

There didn't seem to be any angels hanging around playing harps, so I assumed I was still mortal.

It had all been going so well…

I closed my eyes, hoping for relief. Instead, the nightmares flooded back, so I opened them again quickly.

My head was getting worse.

And now Anastasia was in the grip of Tselmeg Yusupov, my sometime business partner.

I would have paid him back…

It had all been going so well…

Until this happened.

I closed my eyes again, and cried silently, but Danny returned to haunt me, and they opened of their own accord.

"What have you been doing, Mr de Carteret? You really must calm down."

The nurse mopped my face carefully.

"I see that your wife left you a photo. So pretty. Is that your daughter?" She was trying to soothe me, and failing olympically.

I was blinking fit to bust. Surely, she would give me something for my exploding head.

The doctor came in, and the nurse gestured at me.

"You must calm down, Mr de Carteret," he reiterated ineffectually. "As I have already explained, you have to be patient. We are doing everything we can, but the body takes time to recover from this kind of trauma." He looked at me over his glasses. "You are likely to be with us for some time."

I did not find any of this particularly reassuring. The pain in my head was unbearable.

He nodded at the nurse, who came towards me with a large syringe.

If it had not been for Anastasia and Chloe, I would have gladly succumbed to whatever they were intending to give me, but the memory of her being wheeled off to meet Tselmeg Yusupov made me crazy.

The pain was so bad, I wanted to scream.

And suddenly, some passageway in my brain unscrambled.

"*Fuck!*" I bawled.

The shock on their faces made me think my language had offended them. The excitement that replaced it told me otherwise.

I wanted so desperately to warn them about Nasta's abduction, but such refinement was, as yet, beyond me.

So, I stuck with "*Fuck! Fuck! Fuck!*"

They seemed to like that.

PART TWO

FROM SMALL BEGINNINGS...

6

I am not a bad person.

I have just always felt the need to prove that a boy who never had a father, and wished he didn't have a drug-dependent prostitute for a mother, could go out and make a success of his life.

I had a few things going for me: looks for one, a quick brain with a rocket-fuelled memory, and not a scruple in sight.

Everything else, I made up as I went along.

It worked pretty well.

I had a few jobs after I left school, but the lack of any decent exam passes didn't help. My friend, Bobby Jones, got me my lucky break.

Bobby was actually my only friend. Still is, apart from my dog, Scrapper. All the others, especially my siblings, had let me down.

Bobby and I met when we were fourteen.

It wasn't pretty.

I came back from school, and there he was in bed with my mother.

My bed.

I didn't blame him; she was attractive in a funny way, if you ignored the hopeless look in her eyes, the unkempt hair, and the scars down her arms, where she had been injecting herself since God knows when.

But some things are sacrosanct, and my room is one of them.

Bobby was quick, and he was out of my bed, and my mother, faster than you would believe. I remember being impressed, but nailed him one anyway as he grabbed his clothes.

"Who the fuck are you?" he asked, circling me warily, managing to get his underpants on, while my mother stumbled into me. I was too embarrassed to admit the facts.

"Friend of the family."

He laughed at that derisively and almost KO'd me when I charged him, howling like an infuriated animal.

I won't bore you with the details, but that scrap was epic, and we fought each other to a standstill. I managed to get him out of my room, so we trashed a couple of the others instead. To be honest, you couldn't really tell. My family wasn't too house-proud.

After about ten minutes we were both exhausted, he on the sofa, and me supporting myself against the wall. I had cracked a tooth of his, and blacked both his eyes. I think he had broken my ribs. I hurt all over.

As we panted, eyeing each other angrily, my mother walked in, completely naked, with his wallet, and threw it back to him, light of a few notes, which she tossed on a table.

With great aplomb she tightened a belt around her arm, lay back with her legs wide open beside him, and stuck in the needle, as if this was normal. Unfortunately, for me, it was.

We both turned away.

She closed her eyes, apparently fulfilled, and one of my sisters came in.

Showing little surprise at the scene, she raised her eyebrows appreciatively at Bobby, and relieved her mother of some of the notes she had so recently acquired.

"Any milk in the fridge, arsehole?" she asked, as if nothing else mattered, aiming a kick at my foot.

Bobby looked at me, aghast.

"You live here?" he questioned.

"That's my mother," I replied, with as much insouciance as I could muster, nodding at the sofa.

She started to snore.

"Holy shit," said Bobby, with genuine astonishment, his eyes swivelling back and forth between us.

And with that we both fell over laughing. It was a painful experience for me, as my ribs hurt like hell. But we couldn't stop.

We have been laughing together ever since.

Who needs family?

7

Bobby and I got to running errands for some local people and the old folks' home; shopping for them, collecting doctors' prescriptions, walking their dogs and such things. It kept us out of mischief, and we made a bit of money on the side, short-changing them when possible, and taking an 'introduction fee' from Mr Ahmed at the local shop for pushing business his way.

We probably shouldn't have tried to sting Ahmed for protection, even though we were fit and strong for our teenage years. His five sons beat the crap out of us.

Two of his daughters tattooed 'I love Ahmed' on our stomachs.

It hurt like hell, and while the witches in my own family had made me pretty wary of the entire female race, that tattoo hammered in the final nail. I kept mine as a lesson to remember. Bobby got rid of his.

The only good thing to come out of our rootless existence was Scrapper.

I found him on a garbage tip one day in early January. He was some kind of terrier. I could just make out a plaintive whimper coming from a pile of dirty rags. He was barely breathing, but he was a survivor, like me, and we took to each other straight away. He tried to bite me in a perfunctory kind of way, but I could see he didn't mean it. I looked him in the eye and recognised a soulmate. At least my family hadn't thrown me out with the rubbish, as his obviously had done, once their Christmas euphoria had hit the necessities of everyday life. I wrapped him up in one of the cleaner rags for warmth, and took him home.

Scrapper grew fast and, while he would defend me and Bobby to the death, he was a friendly soul if you treated him right. He was a good judge of character, and I took him everywhere.

He was also quite a good-looking little terrier, so we managed to charge a few stud fees for his family-planning services. Unfortunately, he was inclined to offer those same services pretty generously on a freelance basis, so that put a bit of a dent in our stud-farm projections.

"Dogs always take after their owners," Bobby informed me, and I didn't have much of an answer to that. Scrapper and I certainly had a lot in common.

The years passed, and we were drifting through our lives without much purpose, other than getting laid.

The odd jobs we picked up weren't doing anything for me, and I began to get itchy.

My sisters had always made it very clear to me that I was a worthless arsehole, who would never do anything with his life. My mother was in no position to gainsay them. Deep down I knew I had talent, and I was desperate to prove them wrong. But every night, in my dreams, they taunted me for some unspecified, but life-threatening failure.

By day, they introduced reality to those nightmares, inventing failings if none came to mind, mocking me roundly in front of their friends, daring me to do anything 'useful', and threatening me with retribution from the local street gangs, who were their real family. Only Scrapper stood up for me, and I returned the favour. They tried to take it out on him, and kicked him if they could, but he was quick and often managed to retaliate, so they mostly kept their distance.

The next night those nightmares would return, enhanced and magnified in an awful and ever-growing vortex of torment and angst. Whether asleep or awake, I was haunted by terrifying harridans who pursued me, always deriding my uselessness and waiting to pounce on me from the darkness of their hidden lairs.

I began to run.

In my dreams, I ran towards the light of some unspecified triumph which would justify my being, and thus make my existence worthwhile.

Waking to the reality of failure, I began the single-minded, uncompromising pursuit of anything which would validate my worth; to the world at large, and to the whole sisterhood out there, whose gender had conspired to scorn me.

Whatever life held in store and wherever it took me, I knew that I had to be the best, whatever the cost. Anything less would prove them right.

8

Ironically, as I grew up, the ladies seemed to go for me, without asking too many questions. That suited me, and I soon began to realise that the worse I treated them, the more they seemed to like it. Bobby and the other guys were always hanging around with their tongues hanging out, and I could see the girls stringing him along and feeding him shit, until they found something better. Once I realised the way to play their game, they started flocking to me like bees to honey. I made my hive as welcoming as possible.

But with the treatment I had got from my mother and sisters, not to mention Ahmed's daughters, there was no way I was letting them get too close. I gave them their dose of nectar and sent them on their way, all loved-up and teary-eyed. Each notch on my bedpost hammered another nail into the coffin where I kept the memories of those who had tormented me in my early years.

I told Bobby my strategy and showed him how it worked, but somehow his heart wasn't in it. I guess he didn't have sisters.

"Keep wafting on," he would say, whenever something didn't quite turn out right. That was what Pippy Nightingale had told him when the old bruiser had sold him an electronic gizmo which was supposed to unlock car security systems; 'Pippy's Magic Wafter'. Of course, it was just a piece of junk, and didn't do anything of the sort.

Bobby had paid good money. But you didn't screw with Pippy or his boys. So, he just did what Pippy said and 'kept on wafting'.

He learned a good lesson and tried to pass it on to me. But I wasn't much of a student in those days.

So, we kept floundering around keeping ourselves amused, if not in any way fulfilled.

It was Bobby who eventually set us on our path.

"Forget the building site, Nicky mate," he insisted, one evening down at the pub. "They are looking for messengers at Davenport's. I signed up today."

He punched my arm playfully.

I had heard of SJ Davenport, a posh Yankee investment bank. I must admit I never thought about working there. Why would they want me?

But I wasn't exactly overwhelmed with other options.

"I'm in, Bobby. What do I need to do?"

It wasn't much, and I did it. The following Monday, I was there at six in the morning.

They even fitted me up in some fancy suit with SJD in gold letters on the jacket. I set up a basket for Scrapper in the mailroom.

9

I knew I was going to get on well there that very first day.

I was sent up to deliver a package to one of the partners, a Len Olebiowski.

"Just leave it on my desk," whispered his secretary, eyeing me frankly. I smiled and made a mental note.

Olebiowski's door was open, and he was in full flow.

"I warned you, Simon. Nobody goes behind my back in this bank."

Simon didn't get further than, "But…"

Olebiowski obviously wasn't a listener. "And how many times do I have to tell you, I don't give a flying fuck for your goddammed scruples." He spat the word out viciously. "You can't afford them. If you won't take advantage of a golden opportunity when it comes along, you're never going to make it at Davenport's. I am just saving time and effort for both of us."

"He was a client…"

"Get the fuck out of here, you little arsehole." There was a scraping of furniture and things began to turn violent. "Don't tell me how to do business. I warned you once, and you didn't learn."

Simon came out fast. I think he had assistance from Olebiowski, who was still shouting at him from inside.

"Anyone who wants to stay at Davenport's learns first time round, or not at all. Angie has your paperwork. Now, I have work to do."

The door slammed.

Angie passed him a document and a pen, and showed him where to sign.

"The settlement's good," she smiled. "Nick here will help you clear your desk," she said pointing at me. She handed me a black binbag.

The fight had gone out of Simon. I had heard the phrase 'dead man walking'. That was what he was.

Angie's intercom bleeped.

"Has that fucking package arrived?"

Angie took my delivery in to her boss.

They were both already moving on to bigger things.

I took Simon to his desk, and helped him clear his belongings into the bag.

In the elevator, he began to come out of his shock and started to babble at me.

"I can't fucking believe it. Only last month he told me I was on track for the 'D-club'. I remortgaged my house for an extension on the basis of that, as my wife's pregnant."

I actually thought he was going to cry.

"What the hell am I going to do with a baby on the way, and no job? That motherfucker." He hit the wall hard, and I was glad to see him beginning to fight back.

He looked me in the eyes. "You need to get out of here. It's a shitty place. How long have you been here? I haven't seen you before."

I explained it was my first day.

He looked excited. "Then you should walk out right now. You can't believe the things that go on here. It's shit."

The doors opened in the basement car park. He looked round for prying ears, and whispered to me.

"I won a really big currency deal with Mitsushotu." He seemed proud, and I played the part of the impressed junior, although I didn't understand what he was on about.

"New client for the bank. A big one, and it was mine alone." I didn't like the way he seemed to be reliving past glories. He needed to move on. Everybody else had.

"Old Elbows was over the moon, as he could see a big chunk of extra bonus coming. Then he got greedy."

He looked round again, and put his binbag down beside a new Porsche. I didn't think it would fit.

"And nasty. Can you believe what he wanted me to do?" I was interested to find out, so shook my head.

"He wanted me to warn him when Mitsushotu was preparing to make a big currency purchase.

"The first time, I did just that, only to see the price spike the day before Mitsushotu went in. I thought that was funny, so I asked my mate on the prop desk, and he confirmed that it was Elbows who had told them to do the trade."

I was lost, and looked it.

"He was front-running my client, you idiot. Using the insider information I had given him…" He looked at me, exasperated that I wasn't catching on. "…to make a profit for the bank at the client's expense."

Simon was beginning to sound a bit like his boss, but sort of in reverse. "That's fucking illegal. It's robbery. And the way he manages things, it goes straight into the dark pool and most of it from there, directly to his bonus." He slammed his fist onto the Porsche's roof.

I could see he was not going to get over this easily, and that would not be good for him. I didn't understand the details, but reckoned Olebiowski had been right to fire him.

He looked aghast. "He earns over twenty million, for Christ's sake. How much more does he need?"

He watched me angrily for any reaction. I raised my eyebrows, wondering what a twenty-million paycheque might look like.

Simon was indignant. "I can't work in an institution where people behave like that. It's just not the right place for me."

I looked at him, and shook my head sadly. "No, it probably isn't."

We just managed to stuff his bag into the Porsche.

But it's bloody perfect for me, I thought to myself.

10

Angie turned out to be a sweetie, and we had some pretty hot sex on our first date.

"You have gorgeous eyes, you know," she told me, putting the soundtrack from *Evita* on repeat and joining me on the sofa in her sparsely decorated flat.

I wasn't used to compliments, so I changed the subject. "Haven't heard this music for a long time."

"Like it? She's my idol, Eva Peron."

I wasn't quite sure what to say to that, so I nodded and just let her continue.

"Poor girl from a broken home in the backwoods of Argentina, spots a man who's going to succeed, goes out and grabs him and then helps him realise his dreams."

She looked at me with a grin. "My kind of background; my kind of lady. Should have been black, though. We need punchy role models. Love the music, too."

Pausing and almost closing her eyes, she asked quietly, "What are you looking for, Nick?"

I felt slightly uneasy with such, for me, unprecedented intimacy. I always worried that if any girl got to know me well, she would soon recognise me for the guttersnipe I really was, or worse, reveal herself to be just like one of my sister-bitches. So, I normally tried to get straight down to business, without getting too chummy. This one didn't seem like the others; certainly not like my sisters, but she was getting a little too close for comfort.

So, I leaned over and kissed her. I was relieved to feel her respond with gusto, and we were soon busy, exploring bodies and shedding clothes.

When we were both ready to roll, I carried her to the bed. It didn't last long, but I think she enjoyed herself as much as I did. It somehow felt right.

In the mellow glow of afterburn, I asked her about Olebiowski and all the rest of the players at Davenport's. She didn't need any encouragement on that score, and the floodgates opened; she was good at pillow talk, and I can tell you those pillows needed to be fucking fireproof.

She gave me all the lowdown and, as she did so, I slowly realised that the big guys at this bank were exactly who I would have wanted for a father.

"Are you telling me your boss can earn more than twenty million?" I whispered incredulously, trying to get confirmation of what I thought might have been jealous ranting from Binbag.

"Easy." She nodded with the assurance of someone who has seen the evidence first-hand. "And sometimes much more than that." She looked very proud. I imagined she got some sweeteners out of it all.

"But he earns it. Believe me, they all earn their way at Davenport's. To get to the top, they have to work their way through the ranks, and you saw what happens to the ones who don't make it. They don't call him 'Elbows' for nothing."

I nodded, remembering Binbag's moaning.

"That young guy, Simon, was good, actually," she continued. "Bright, tough, he never stopped working and brought in some great clients. He drove his team hard, and was on track. But, of course, you have to play by the fucking rules."

She was getting animated now.

"He just lost the plot," she complained. "I ask you, Simon was keeping his clients to himself, and not giving Olebiowski a chance to front-run them. Who the hell did he think he was? Certainly not a candidate for the 'D-club.'"

Talking about the bank obviously turned her on. She kissed me hard and rolled on top of me, straddling me and staring down into my eyes, her rock-hard nipples caressing mine.

"What's the 'D-club'? Is it like Partner?" I asked, although I thought I already understood the difference.

"Not quite. When you make the 'D-club', they decide to trust you, and suddenly you find you're on the inside. Until then, you eat shit every day and every night, and you lick the plate for more, if you know what's good for you."

She seemed to enjoy the thought, and began to fuck me slowly and lasciviously. It felt bloody good. I groaned quietly, and I can tell you that was a first for me.

"How's it feel to get screwed?" she giggled. "I can tell you it won't feel so great coming from Len Olebiowski."

She continued her simultaneous verbal and physical assault.

"You don't have a life. It belongs to Davenport's twenty-four-seven every day of the year. And then suddenly you are in the 'D-club' and everyone trusts you." She whimpered and threw her head back. I wasn't sure if it was me or the thought of the 'D-club' that did that to her. Probably the latter.

"Then it's your turn to test out those coming behind you, because the better they are, the bigger your bonus is going to be. You don't want any weak links, do you? You have to be able to trust them with your life. So, shit rules."

She was grinding her hips against mine and moaning. Suddenly she stopped, looked at me, and whispered "You want a shot at it? You're too good for the mailroom. I mean it, I can get you in at the bottom. You would probably make the 'D-club'."

That was music to my ears, and we were both pretty steamed up by now.

I turned her on her front, lifted her buttocks, and sent her on her third trip to Valhalla. I was pushing her face into the pillow, so the neighbours couldn't hear her sounding off.

But she was a fighter, and she struggled free, panting "He wants to bring someone in, on the bottom rung, to learn the business."

She paused, and I could feel her appraising me in that forthright way she had done the first time we met, although this time the judge and jury were located firmly between her legs. That was fine by me.

"Someone in his image, who knows how to play the game. Someone he can trust."

She yelped, as I thrust again.

"Someone like you."

That really turned me on, and before long, her neighbours were actually banging on the wall. We didn't give a shit. All I could think about was the 'D-club'.

11

By ten the next morning, I was beginning to wonder if Angie was running the place.

First, I got a welcoming call from the 'onboarding' team, followed in quick succession by HR. They gave me a numeracy exam which was fairly easy, as was some kind of reasoning test. A few of the other bits were impossible. There were a bunch of forms to fill in and sign.

Next came 'talent assessment'. A rather pale-faced creep ignored me for several minutes, before finally looking up from his computer.

"Len Olebiowski is sponsoring you, so if you get past him you're in. If not, you're finished here."

He looked back at his screen.

"Judging by these, I suspect he'll throw you out before you get past the door."

That was comforting. I got the feeling Angie hadn't got to this one, which didn't wholly surprise me. He didn't look her type.

He handed me my file and pointed at the door. There was no 'good luck' or anything.

By the time I got back to Angie's desk, Olebiowski was waiting for me.

"Is that delivery boy here yet? What the fuck is keeping him so long? Couldn't he find the up-button?"

Angie winked at me and whispered. "Ignore all that. Stand up to him and just go for it." She took my file and smiled, mouthing, "Like last night."

I was glad I had made an impression.

I knocked and went in.

Olebiowski was behind his desk.

"Angie tells me you want to be a banker."

Some papers on his desk had his full attention, and he didn't look at me. I thought they might be my test results.

"Why?" he asked, looking up. "It's a shitty job."

Best not to lie to this one, I told myself. He was eyeing me carefully now, like a spider weighing up its web-entangled prey.

"I want to join the 'D-club.'"

A smile flickered across his face, and he looked closely at me, giving nothing away. I had no idea if that was what he wanted to hear, but it was the truth.

"Did you fuck my office manager last night?"

I wasn't expecting that. I was on dangerous ground here. He could probably tell from the way she had spoken about me, but he might be testing my loyalty. It could be against the rules for her. Anyway, in my book it was none of his business.

I told him that.

Olebiowski narrowed his eyes.

"Everything's my sodding business in this bank, you little arsehole. How your shit comes out is my business, where you are at three on a Sunday morning on your holiday is my business, and who you are screwing, and where and how you do it is definitely my fucking business."

He was completely under control, and it was a masterclass in disciplined aggression.

"Especially who you are screwing."

He was waiting for my response.

I was actually quite angry myself, but I took a leaf out of his book and remained calm, leaning slightly towards him.

"I won't shit, leave my mobile off, or screw anybody or anything that gets in the way of joining the 'D-club.'"

This kind of talk came pretty easily, what with the way I came up through life, so I looked him straight in the eyes and held his gaze. I thought I saw him waver.

He changed tack abruptly.

"Your friend, Bobby Jones."

The surprise in my eyes must have been obvious, although I controlled myself quickly.

"He's applied as well."

He rolled his pen between thumb and finger, looking at me with a cold smile.

"You need to do something for me. I will take you on board on one condition."

He was enjoying this. Perhaps he was repaying me for my disrespect.

"Angie is going to call him in here now, and I want you to tell him in front of me that you made the grade."

He hesitated, weighing up his next move. I was ready for anything. Almost anything.

"Then you tell him he's only a shitass delivery boy, and to get the fuck back to the mailroom where he belongs."

Bobby had not applied yet. I was sure of that. I had intended to get him in once I was signed up.

"He's my greatest friend."

He shrugged.

"So?"

My anger was in danger of getting the better of me, although I realised he was playing me.

"I don't think he has applied, although I was going to suggest he did. We'd work well together."

He opened his mouth, but I was too quick for him.

"Is that how the 'D-club' treats old friends, Mr Olebiowski? If so, Davenport's isn't the place for me."

It was a big risk, but that's how I am with Bobby. We could always find something else. We bantered and argued a bit, but my feelings for him were the closest I had ever come to love.

I held Olebiowski's dismal glower with difficulty. This bastard was hard to read.

"You're not in the flaming 'D-club', Mr de Carteret."

There was a long and, for me, agonising silence while he checked his mobile.

"But with a lot of luck I think you could be. Welcome to Davenport's. I'll have a look at that friend of yours. See what he's made of."

He held out his hand and I took it, feeling elated.

He was stronger than he looked, and he caught me off guard, crushing my hand and almost breaking it.

Anger rapidly replaced euphoria, but I was buggered if I was going to show him the pain I was in.

"Just remember that God's work here at Davenport's is totally dedicated to improving my bottom line. Nothing else counts. Until and unless you get into your famous 'D-club', you screw everything and everybody who gets in the way of that, including your mother, your best friend, your clients and your new fuckbuddy." He nodded towards Angie.

"Understood?"

It suddenly dawned on me that Len Olebiowski didn't differentiate too fastidiously between the bank's and his own bottom line, and I was pretty sure that he hadn't stopped screwing his mother just because he had joined the 'D-club'.

I was going to learn a lot from him.

12

I didn't have much time to worry.

Angie handed me a laptop and a page of joining instructions for an 'on-boarding' course in the New York training centre.

"It started today, but you'll have to catch up. Your boarding cards are on your mobile, and the course reading material is on this laptop."

She suddenly looked worried, realising how little she knew about me.

"You know how to use a laptop? I'm good with spreadsheets if you need any help."

I laughed. "I learned that young, if nothing else. Bobby and I made some money hacking bank accounts."

I wasn't lying. She looked a bit taken aback, as if not sure whether to believe me.

"But I'd certainly like some help with the spreadsheets."

"Good luck," she said rather stiffly. I saw Olebiowski in his doorway, watching us.

* * *

I got a text in my hotel room from Bobby, telling me he was catching the redeye and joining me in the morning. So, he had passed Elbows' inquisition. As if I would doubt him. He and I knew how to deal with people like that.

The course was dynamite; heaven had come down and landed in my motherfucking lap.

If I was to say I learned more in that two-week stint than I had in the rest of my life, it wouldn't be an exaggeration. We got an overview of all the bank's operations, and I really liked what I heard, especially the trading desks. It was just like the horses, and I was damn good at the horses.

I couldn't quite understand the rationale for trading on behalf of clients when you had a posh-sounding 'Proprietary Desk' to trade for yourself (well, strictly speaking, for the bank).

I didn't see why anyone would want to make money for somebody else, be they a 'client', or whatever the fuck. But they told me that was what banks did, so I kept my mouth shut.

Bobby and I argued long and hard over that point. Bobby liked the idea of using other people's money to make a 'turn', as he put it, while they took all the risk.

"Makes sense, Nick. You have a little slip-up…" he paused knowingly, and shrugged. "The client loses out, and you still take your commission and keep wafting on."

I suppose he had a point. I had always been more of a risk-taker and couldn't understand why you wouldn't want to take all the profit for yourself. Slip-ups are for losers, like Binbag.

"Jesus, Bobby, if you really don't want to back yourself fully," I raised my eyebrows, as I always did when I thought he was being too cautious, "you can take out an option against your own trade. Heads I win, tails you lose. You can't fucking fail."

I was pretty sure that after a half-day session on options trading, I knew all there was to know about this business. I felt it in my bones.

"For Christ's sake, you can even go short, and make money when companies go down. Can you imagine if you could do that on the ponies? This bank has thought of every way to make money, and I know a winner when I see one. Trust me, Bobby."

Bobby was wavering. He never went for broke, like I always did. But we worked together well and, just occasionally, I admit that his more restrained approach had kept us out of the shit.

For me it was too late. I was already dreaming about my first twenty-million paycheque.

13

On our return, I was co-opted onto a research team looking into investment opportunities for the prop desk. I had expressed a strong preference for that side of the business. Bobby had not listened to me and he was doing client relationship management, or CRM as he liked to call it.

My client relationship management had usually involved kicking out some arsehole who had tried to short-change my mother. Bobby told me this was different, but I didn't want any more of that shit.

In the late afternoon, a tall, not unattractive girl, but with hard gimlet eyes, came over and handed me a file marked Mitsushotu. I remembered that was Binbag's client.

"I want you to take these forecasts apart for me. They are based on a copper price of $7000. Redo them for me based on $5000. I think that could break them."

She looked happy about this.

"You know I just joined as a prop trader," I pointed out, giving her my best smile. We had covered spreadsheets on the course, but my skills were quite basic. There were lots of nerds around who could do that. I waited confidently for her reaction.

"You'll manage," she replied, fixing me with those cold eyes. "If not, then you won't be here long. I need it first thing tomorrow."

That worked well, I thought to myself. I needed to focus.

After looking through the papers for a few minutes, I could see my way to some of it, and got going.

By early evening, I was making real progress, and it was all beginning to fall into place. I just needed something to link the prices to various assumptions. There had been a 'macro' we had learned on the course, but my notes were sketchy.

I turned to a guy with specs at the next desk, who was buried in his screen.

"Can you remind me how to work that macro which links research details to various outcomes?"

He didn't even raise his head. "Fuck off, arsehole. I'm busy. If you can't work it out for yourself, you shouldn't be here."

I looked over to see if he was actually one of my siblings in disguise. I started to get out of my chair to give him a bit of 'CRM' treatment, but thought better of it.

Be nice for the £20 million, I whispered to myself.

"Wrong time of the month?" I asked him. He tried to ignore me, and went back to playing with his computer.

"Nice wrist action," I continued, not wanting any of his shit again. "Get a lot of practice?"

He looked decidedly uneasy, so I thought he had probably got the message.

I remembered Angie's offer of spreadsheet assistance and texted her. She sounded keen, so I started to pack up.

As I passed 'arsehole's' desk, I kicked his chair, and he swung involuntarily round to face me.

Overkill has always been my weakness, but I don't like having the piss taken. I relieved him of his laptop, pulled out the battery and threw them both hard in his bin. There was an ugly cracking sound.

"My project!" he yelled, but I shoved him gently back into his seat.

"Call me an arsehole again, arsehole, and I'll disconnect your battery too."

I don't think he had ever had anyone treat him like that before. I left him spinning gently.

14

I explained to Angie where I was with my spreadsheet when I got to her flat. Scrapper jumped up to his, by now normal, place on her sofa. She rubbed his ears and gave him a little dog biscuit. He wagged his tail happily.

"Payment up front, please," she whispered, unbuttoning my shirt.

I don't normally pay up front, but Angie's idea of compensation was different from most people's. I paid in instalments, and it was absolutely no burden. Quite the opposite.

I would make an advance payment, and then she would work wonders on my copper prices. Then she would want some more recompense, and so it went on. By three in the morning we were ready for some sleep, and Mitsushotu was bankrupt.

"Everyone on the course was complaining about these exhausting 'all-night sessions'. I think I like them."

"Different terms and conditions," she giggled.

"You really know your stuff," I said admiringly.

"You're not bad yourself," she replied, nodding.

"That too," I laughed, "but I was meaning the copper prices. Where did you learn all that?"

"Long story," she responded, pensively.

"Want to tell me?"

She looked at me and stuck her chin out, in that way I was coming to know quite well, as if rising to a challenge.

"I started in the back office here. Systems analyst. I had a first in computer studies and was producing a lot of special reports, and doing projects for people. Especially Elbows Olebiowski."

I looked surprised.

"I was good." Somehow, that was no revelation.

"I had to be." She smiled. "My mother warned us what life would be like growing up 'on the wrong side of the rainbow', as she put it. She was right. I always fought hard against it, and often landed up angry, sometimes with a bloody nose. It was only when she told me on her deathbed, 'Get over it, Angie. Just remember, you're black and you're the best. It's nothing less than the truth, so believe it.' I've always tried to follow that in life. It works for me."

"Sounds like a great mother," I said, enviously.

"She was… she was."

After a few moments' silence, during which, I suspect, we were each reliving our very different childhoods, I asked "What happened with you and Elbows?"

I was interested to see what the relationship was between Angie and Olebiowski. I admit, I was hoping it was purely professional.

"I managed all the systems for a particular project of his, not unlike this project of yours, but covering a major client of his co-head of Investment Banking, Simon Rutland. We didn't tell Rutland."

That was a name I hadn't heard before.

"We didn't even give him access. Rutland had been sole head of IB until Olebiowski pushed his way in. Really old school. You know the kind of thing, Eton, Oxford, country estate."

She put on her smartest accent. It wasn't very good, but I got the idea.

"Tough, but not in Olebiowski's league."

A frown crossed her brow, and my interest was piqued.

"Anyway, Elbows shorted Simon's client massively, and when the price of platinum tanked suddenly, he made an absolute fortune. Rutland hadn't even seen it coming, with the way I managed the data for Elbows."

She was talking very quietly, as if someone might overhear.

"The client went bust. Rutland was really pissed off, and he went for Olebiowski's jugular."

She laughed ruefully, and I could see where her sympathies lay.

"Unfortunately, he couldn't even find out where it was."

She screwed up her face in distaste.

"If he even had one. It wasn't attractive and there was blood all over the trading floor."

She blew her cheeks out. "I was playing piggy in the middle with those two. And that is not somewhere you want to be at Davenport's, whatever your colour."

She looked at me urgently, wanting to make sure I understood fully.

"I mean it. The traders took sides, and the normal arguments and little spats became full-blown physical fights. There were leaks to the press, and it was all getting totally out of control. The chairman called them both in to clear the air."

She turned me on when she was so intense like this, but she brushed my hand away.

"Finally, they put it to a vote at the board. When all was said and done, Olebiowski was bringing in the business, so it was pretty much a foregone conclusion."

She looked sad.

"That was the end of Simon Rutland's career at Davenport's."

She put her hand out to me.

"Len Olebiowski took over as sole head of IB, and he asked me to help manage all his systems. That was easy, and I was soon running his office for him."

I watched her face, as it went through various contortions, but I knew better than to interrupt.

"You can't believe what he pays me, and I never work weekends. That's good for me."

We both knew she was justifying herself.

I started with the question that had been bugging me.

"Did you and Elbows ever…?"

But she saw it coming, and shook her head, putting her finger to my lips.

"Are you kidding? I had better taste than that." She laughed. "Until now."

15

We were quite a threesome in those first few years.

I did the work, Angie ran the ship, and Elbows took the money.

That's how it works in banking. I was fine with that, and I made sure Angie was too. We didn't starve.

Scrapper even put on weight, but he and Elbows were always a bit wary of each other.

That came to a head one day. Elbows would often wander into my office on the phone to one of our joint clients. I listened in on his speakerphone and scribbled down any suggestions on his pad, to ensure he was fully up to date with all the latest developments. On this occasion he was concentrating on a particularly complex deal I had been running. He was trying to read my notes, and tripped heavily over Scrapper.

"You fucking little dog," he yelled, landing a kick in the little dog's ribs. Scrapper yelped, and hid under my desk.

The rib was actually broken, and after that occasion he always gave Elbows a wide berth. I think the client did, too, which suited me, as I became his main port of call for a good chunk of business.

I made the 'D-club' in record time. Even Elbows was impressed. Angie too, although not surprised, she told me proudly.

I hummed *Evita*'s anthem, 'Don't Cry For Me, Argentina', at her. She laughed a little wistfully. Making the 'D-club' was changing my horizons. I think Angie could see that, even if I couldn't.

Olebiowski asked me to lunch one day shortly after, and we went to some fancy Japanese restaurant.

I knew this end of town like the back of my hand by now. I had taken Angie a few times to dinner, and I often went out with clients and colleagues to the bars and lap-dancing joints. It was a hell of a lot easier now I had a car and driver, Jimmy 'The Wheel'.

Jimmy looked like a nightclub bouncer, which was okay by me. He was also the height of discretion, which was even better. He absolutely loved Scrapper, who took pride of place on the front seat, and all three of us bonded straight away. Jimmy rode shotgun for me with a devotion which wasn't wholly a result of how well I looked after him, over and above the pittance he got from the bank.

"Yes, boss, no, boss, three bags full, Mr de Carteret," he would laugh when I told him our next port of call. But he was well in with the cops, and if anyone gave us any trouble, he turned nasty, extremely quickly. That wasn't a pretty sight, and most people backed off pretty fucking quickish.

To be frank, I constantly worried I would bump into my mother or sisters doing a turn in one of the clubs, or one of my brothers minding the door at a posh eater. So, I always kept my head down, in case I ran into anyone I knew.

Nicky de Carteret, someone would say in my dreams. *What the fuck is a prick like you doing in this place? Come to see Mummy?* I would wake in a sweat, usually shaking Angie by the throat, until she could calm me down.

It never happened, but I always had the feeling I was just one step ahead of disaster. That's what kept me moving along so quickly. When your past's hounding you, you keep on running; it doesn't matter where. You just have to keep ahead of those demons.

"Here's to success." Elbows raised his glass, bringing me abruptly back to the present.

"You made it, Nick," he grinned proudly, appearing to take the credit himself.

"Thanks to you, Len," I responded dutifully, chinking mine against his. I knew what floated his boat, and to be fair to him he had covered my back most of the time.

"But the 'D-club' isn't everything," he continued, stuffing an enormous king prawn into his mouth and spattering mayonnaise everywhere.

I knew that, but said nothing.

"Next step for you is partner." He looked at me. "And then, who knows?"

Who knows indeed? I thought, pointing at a gob of mayo on his chin. Most people didn't draw attention to any of his social failings, but I was trying to learn the rules myself from scratch. His shortcomings were a direct reflection on mine, so I took it personally.

I also liked to challenge him occasionally, and these little matters of etiquette constituted a safer field of combat than most others for that particular activity.

He looked angrily around, and a little waiter rushed up with a clean napkin. Elbows snatched it and gestured dismissively, without looking at him.

I smiled at the little foreign guy. I knew where he was coming from; just trying to make his way; paid nothing and treated like shit. I had been there too. I winked; he nodded, and smiled back appreciatively.

"You have the talent, and you can hold your own," continued my lunch companion. "But if you really want to make the big-time, like me…" He literally puffed out his chest.

I want the big-time, I thought, holding his stare, *but not like you.*

"If you want to get to the top, you need to stop talking like a barrow-boy." He counted off one finger as I narrowed my eyes, taking in carefully what he was saying.

"Stop dressing like a fucking pimp." He frowned at my wide lapels and grabbed his wine glass, waving a thumb and finger at me.

He took what I thought was much too big a swig for a place like this.

"And you need to marry something smart."

That did raise my eyebrows.

"Look the part, Nick, work your balls off, and learn to fit in.

Take a leaf out of my book." He tapped his nose, positively glowing with self-satisfaction.

Nobody seemed to know about Len Olebiowski's background, and I am sure he encouraged that, but I recognised the look of a driven man. I could see the demons behind him, and shivered involuntarily.

I studied my boss objectively, and had to admit that he looked, spoke and dressed the part, even if his table manners sometimes let him down.

I hadn't met his wife, but rumour had it she did the same, although they didn't spend much time together. He was either with clients or with his Brazilian mistress, whom he had set up in a smart Kensington apartment.

"Then we can really hit the big-time."

I noted the royal 'we'. But I was past being part of Len Olebiowski's team.

Now it was my turn.

16

Bobby was moving up the client side and, if anything, we were closer than ever. He was going places, and I knew he would join me in the 'D-club' before too long.

We discussed the markets every day, and we saw eye to eye on most things. When one of us expressed a strong opinion, the other took note and acted on it. We were much more than the sum of our parts.

He had a couple of clients that he warned me off, but, for the rest, I relied on him to tell me when they were looking to do a big trade. When he did, I would put the 'prop desk' in ahead of them, so the bank made a guaranteed profit and the client a bit less. This front-running was strictly forbidden at Davenport's, and they had some Chinese wall arrangement, but me and Bobby went back way too far for shit like that.

Bobby kept me down to earth. Always had done, him and Scrapper. That's why we were such perfect foils for each other.

I came up with all the interesting angles and ideas to turn us into billionaires (although to be fair, he did get us into Davenport's); he tried to keep me grounded with what he called 'good sense and moderation'.

I would retort that he suffered from small balls and a lack of imagination, and that he should have been an accountant.

He would laugh and remind me of all the times I had over-reached and got us into the shit, starting with Ahmed.

"For Christ's sake, just hang in and play by the rules, Nicky," he said, one evening in a bar we often frequented.

"You made the 'D-club', you're tight with Elbows, and you're shacked up with Angie. Just keep bloody wafting on, mate. What the fuck more do you want?"

"I want the £20 mill paycheque," I whispered.

"You're like a spoiled brat," he murmured, smiling sadly. "It's always the same, ever since I first met you."

He looked at me with concern.

"You're not the only person in the world with a fucked-up mother, you know."

I decided to ignore him.

"Or a coven of abusive witches for siblings."

Bobby always knew which buttons to press. I breathed deeply, just managing to keep my focus.

"I'm going to get that paycheque soon," I persisted. "I'm going to be the best there is, and £20 mill seems a good place to start. And that's all it is, mate: the start. The big-time will follow, sure enough."

He held out his hands towards me in frustration, almost knocking over his glass.

"That's a whole load of shit, Nick. You're good, yes, bloody good, and you can go all the way, but you always push the fucking boundaries before they're ready to be fucking pushed. Can't you ever be satisfied?"

He was looking at me with a pained expression.

"Every time you get what you want, you just take it and come back for more. You don't even enjoy it. For fuck's sake, learn when to stop. It's crazy and it'll be your downfall. And don't expect me to be there to pick up the pieces."

"Thanks for the advice, mate. I'm listening." It was at times like these I realised how much I valued and relied on him.

I shook his shoulder gently with my right hand, and I think we could both feel the bond that held us so strongly together.

"I *am* playing the game, Bobby," I insisted. "I'm bloody wafting on, just like you say. Elbows told me exactly what to do, and I'm doing it." I was aware that I was justifying myself, but felt the situation called for it.

"Suits from Savile Row." I fingered the lapels of my exorbitantly expensive new two-piece.

"Learn to talk proper." He raised his eyebrows disbelievingly as I tried out my new posh accent.

"Hook up with some society bitch."

He laughed at that. "What about poor Angie?" he asked, only half in jest.

"Make partner," I continued, ignoring that. He raised his eyebrows and nodded slowly.

"You can be a partner too, Bobby," I added, and I meant it. He waggled his head, in that way that Ahmed used to do, when you asked him a question he didn't know the answer to.

"You're definitely going to make it," I asserted. "We're going to rule this place, you and I."

Bobby shook his head slowly, although he looked slightly happier now that he could see I had a strategy.

But I hadn't finished.

"However, Elbows missed one major step on my ladder."

Bobby looked at me quizzically.

"His job."

Bobby held his head in his hands, closed his eyes and muttered, "Oh, fuck."

He peeked out at me between his fingers, and I could see he was laughing.

I held out my hand, and the relief I felt when he guffawed and took it, was almost orgasmic.

He was shaking his head slowly, but the smile wouldn't go away.

"You're fucking crazy, Nicky. Always have been and always will be."

The smile vanished.

"I just hope to God you don't live to regret it."

17

I got used to the new suits (although not the price), and slowly got rid of my cockney twang. That was easy; I was good at accents, and I began to notice a subtle difference in the way people reacted to me. Elbows had been right.

We made a couple of killings on the trading side, and things were good.

Olebiowski called me in one day, and he looked excited.

"I've hit paydirt for you." He looked pleased. I assumed I was getting a handout for the two recent deals I had completed, and was thinking about the new Ferrari. I was wrong.

"Mary has come across your future missus," he said, without emotion.

Mary was his wife. I had never met her.

"Lord Abercrombie's daughter." He could see the look of surprise on my face.

"Don't sweat it. Father talks like you used to, made his money in plastics and gave a lot to the Conservatives."

He pulled out a photo.

"Debs is attractive and ambitious. Calls herself The Hon Deborah Champney. No idea where that came from. Believe me, her dad's no hereditary peer."

I took the photo, and the strong brown eyes held my gaze. I found myself nodding.

"But she knows everybody worth knowing, and I can see exactly where she's headed. She'll do you perfectly."

He was rubbing his hands, as if he was marrying her himself.

I was feeling a bit queasy, not the least because Elbows was starting to treat me like the son he never had time to have. But I knew he was heading for a big tumble. I could feel it in my bones; mainly because I was doing the pushing.

"Be at San Martino's at eight. Look your best. Mary has given you a big write-up."

I was, and she had. Deborah was gorgeous, in a slightly 'confectionary' kind of way. I liked that, and couldn't wait to undo the wrapping.

The meal went well. Elbows and I hinted at big deals; Mary was all over me, and I was at my attentive best. I had learned that women like a man who listens, so I had learned to listen.

Mrs Olebiowski frightened me. Her smile was radiant, but the eyes gave her away. There was no joy there, just cause and effect. When she wanted something, she smiled, and, I imagine, she usually got it. I didn't want to be there when she didn't. I looked at Elbows and thought I understood him a little better. But it was too late for remorse.

"Why don't you two head off to that new Revolution club? We old folks have to go home." She laughed and squeezed her husband's arm in a way which could easily have been mistaken for warmth. He called for the bill, but I had already settled up. Deborah liked that.

I was attracted to Debs in a funny kind of way. She knew when to laugh, although I don't think she had a sense of humour.

She certainly knew what she wanted, and liked my shop talk. I steered pretty clear of family, hinting passingly at country living, dogs and private schools. She drooled over my photo of Scrapper.

"He's so sweet. I can't wait to meet him." I hoped Scrapper would repay the compliment. He was quite binary about people; he would either jump straight on your lap, or bite whichever bit of you first came in range.

"I'm buying a little town house off Sloane Square," I lied. "Haven't had time since I joined Davenport's, but I think the time's right."

She looked impressed, and I realised that particular plane was now going to have to be landed. I had seen a couple of places advertised.

"Or, do you think I should get a penthouse?" I wanted to make her feel part of this decision.

She took my arm and nestled closer.

"The town house is good," she purred. "Just don't go too near Victoria. And make sure there's a double garage."

I realised we were made for each other, although I took an involuntary look around the room. They always tell you never to look a gift-horse in the mouth, but I don't take anything for granted. I always check for Trojans.

18

Things went well.

I got my town house, and Debs came with it. She made a great fuss of Scrapper and set him up with a fur-lined basket, which was all the inducement he needed, although I felt that, like me, his motivations weren't solely altruistic. To be fair to him, he was getting a bit arthritic.

We were married in style. She didn't even wait to get pregnant. There were a couple of snide comments in the press about plastics and bankers, but Debs' father hadn't made his fortune by letting people get away with crap like that. He and I saw pretty much eye to eye. I was taking his daughter off his hands, and I laughed at his jokes, which Debs had never really understood. Her dowry comprised her address book. That's what he told me and that was fine by me.

Bobby was my best man. Thank God, my family didn't turn up. To be honest, I didn't know if they were dead or alive. I rather hoped the former.

Business was great. Elbows and I were a team, and the deals flowed thick and fast. He kept me in on everything. But he was taking home the big paycheque, so I didn't return the favour.

It was tough for Angie, I suppose. One minute, we were an item, and I was spending most of my time in her apartment. The next, I had my Chelsea town house and Debs moved in with a bump.

"You'll always be my Evita," I told her.

She was silent for a few seconds, then she shook her head and stuck her chin out as she always did when challenged, and said quietly, "Actually, I'm beginning to think I'm more like Piranha."

She saw my puzzled look.

"Peron's sixteen-year-old mistress who was thrown out on the street when Evita arrived."

She started to leave, but turned back.

"Perhaps one day, Nick, you'll find someone to love, who isn't called Nick de Carteret."

That made me think, even if I didn't completely follow her.

"Because that's the only way you'll be able to stop running."

That I understood.

"Look after Scrapper." She closed the door.

* * *

Debs knew everyone. She not only put me on the map, I think she had drawn the bloody thing.

Deals started to come to me, like bees to a honeypot. I wasn't complaining. A few came from left field, but I didn't turn anything down, or anyone.

Debs got pregnant again, almost before she was out of hospital with our firstborn, Rupert. It didn't stop her networking on my behalf. I liked that.

The only blot on the horizon was when I had to put Scrapper down. His arthritis had begun to make his life a misery, and the vet said it was the kindest cut.

"Let's get a proper family dog," suggested Debs, with, I felt, unnecessary enthusiasm. "Like a Labrador." She had begun to realise that Scrapper's affection for her was only cupboard love. If the supply of biscuits and treats ran out, he would get pretty frosty.

But, for me it was the end of an era. I shed a few tears at his graveside, and thought about life.

In the end, we compromised.

Debs found some highfalutin, moronic, overbred, golden retriever approved by the Kennel Club. It spent most of its life going round in circles with its tongue hanging out.

I found another Scrapper, this time not off a garbage heap, but from a family whose terrier had got knocked up by some type of pit-bull. He reminded me of Scrapper, and we hit it off, right from the start. I called him Snapper. I thought it was appropriate. He often lived up to it.

Olebiowski almost dug a sense of humour out of somewhere.

"The partners have decided to take pity on you." He looked serious and, for a minute, he had me fooled.

Then he actually laughed. It was rather scary.

"They have decided that your family is growing so fast, you need some emergency assistance."

He paused for effect, but now I was with him.

"Congratulations, partner."

He tried to give me a man-hug, and to be fair, I think it came from the heart. It was a bit awkward. Neither of us had much practice at hugging.

I was looking over his shoulder at his office layout. I had a few changes in mind. That racy little interior decorator girl, who Bobby used, would know what to do.

I drew away from him, in case he thought my hard-on was for him.

19

"I am looking for a business partner."

Tselmeg Yusupov was an ugly bastard, but that didn't worry him at all. It didn't seem to worry his girlfriend either. They were both from a little country called Kuikbakhistan which, I found out later, snuggled somewhere between Russia and Mongolia.

I think Debs was a bit taken aback. The man must have had perhaps a couple of years on me, but he looked older than that due to the deep scars across his face, which added to an already sinister aura. They looked like old knife wounds, but I thought it better not to ask. He had been introduced to her by a distant, mutual friend, who had gone to boarding school with him in the UK.

I have to say, Yusupov didn't look much like a public-school boy to me.

My wife hung onto me, which was unusual. I put it down to her hormones, although I think our dinner companion had something to do with it.

He gestured for the girls to leave. His bitch moved fast. It took a raised eyebrow for Debs to get the message. She looked at me, and I could see concern in her eyes. She kissed me on the way out.

I decided to go on the offensive. "What can you offer us, Mr Yusupov?"

He laughed. His eyes didn't. He leaned towards me.

"Do you want to be rich?"

He didn't wait for an answer. He could probably tell.

"Perhaps the question you should be asking is what *you* can offer me." I didn't like the way he smiled as he said that, but I also leaned forward and spoke quietly.

"I can offer you all the resources of a major international investment bank. So, let me ask again…"

He cut me off.

"Do you speak for Davenport's? I thought Len Olebiowski ran the show there."

He was testing me.

"He does for now. But if you want to deal with Davenport's, I'm the future there."

I realised I was fast-tracking my career projection, and I was going to have to back my words up with some heavy action. But if this guy was what he appeared to be, then he was the wormhole to my future.

"OK then, Mr de Carteret, let's say I take you at your word. I will need confirmation of that. But let me put my proposition to you, just in case you are correct."

He looked right though me with such godforsaken soullessness that I shivered, and I thought I already knew what godforsaken soullessness looked like.

It left me with the icy certainty that, if I failed to keep my end of any bargain, the result would be terminal.

"I have one billion dollars to put at your disposal."

His gaze did not waver.

"I want you to invest it for me, based on the likely future positions…" he emphasised the word future, "… to be taken by your bank's prop desk. I will pay you ten per cent of any profit I make as a result."

I was having difficulty breathing. This complete stranger was willing to hand me a billion big ones to front-run the bank's prop desk, which was already, thanks to Len Olebiowski and me, tailgating its own clients. It was a kind of musical chairs, with me taking ten per cent of the profit I could make on Yusupov's money, and about half that on the prop desk trading.

I decided it was better not to clarify what would happen if the chairs ran out.

"Twenty-five," I said without thinking.

He looked at me, and I thought I saw approval. It was very hard to tell.

"I am the wormhole to your future," he whispered. "Fifteen per cent."

I didn't like the way he seemed to have plucked the very words out of my mind, but, when he held out his hand, I felt compelled to shake it.

20

I had to move fast.

As it happened, Elbows signed his own death warrant.

I had the office next to his by now, and he would come into mine when he wanted to be sure nobody was listening. Things hadn't always been going his way, I was making sure of that, so he was being especially careful.

Snapper growled at him viciously from his basket in the corner. I'd never forgotten those broken ribs that Elbows had given Scrapper and, as if by osmosis, Snapper had taken on his predecessor's feud. Elbows scowled back.

He looked worried, and spoke quietly.

"We need to get Roger Biggar on side."

Biggar was a pain in the arse, who had recently made it to the top of the main financial regulator. His rise up that greasy pole involved writing up a lot of meeting notes over the years and keeping his nose clean. So, effectively doing nothing; which suited us fine.

I couldn't help thinking he would have been the shitty little sneak at school who ratted on the big players. He seemed the type. Never looked you in the eye, but always seemed to be watching.

"He's beginning to ask questions about our trading patterns. I don't like the way he is headed. Someone must be putting him up to it." Elbows actually looked concerned.

He didn't realise that it was me who stood more to lose than anyone if the fucking thought police started to get on our backs. Yusupov would not appreciate having Biggar nosing around. I could see my wormhole slithering back into outer space.

"Weren't we talking about him taking up a senior advisory role with Davenport's when he retires next year?" I queried.

I remembered Elbows mentioning this and getting informal approval from the chairman only a few months ago. If we could sign him up, we would lean on him to keep us out of the limelight until then, and use his contacts at the Regulator, once he was on our payroll.

"Correct," he nodded. "But that's in the future. Right now, he wants to meet with the compliance people and review our Chinese walls. I swear somebody's putting him up to it."

I said nothing.

Nor did my face.

"Girls or boys?" I asked quietly.

Elbows was on my wavelength immediately.

"Girls, big boobs," he whispered with a smirk. "I had dinner with him at Long John's last month, and he couldn't keep his eyes off them."

I thought I noted a more than professional interest, and stored that little gem away on my own mental hard disk, filed under 'Worms'.

* * *

The evening was totally surreal. We took Biggar to dinner at the Klimax Club, a strip joint where Bobby had connections.

Obviously, we had dinner companions, and all three had great knockers. Too big for my liking, but I wasn't sampling the menu. Biggar was in heaven. So was Elbows, it should be said.

The girls were pros. I know that sounds pretty fucking obvious, because that, of course, was why we'd hired them. But they were bloody brilliant; consummate performers at the very top of their game. I took my hat off to them, and in other circumstances would have taken everything else off as well. But this was business.

To be fair to him, the little rat tried his best to control himself, but a succession of opportunities was provided to look down and then, as the alcohol took over, to manhandle their hardware. He just managed to restrain himself until after the brandy when, offering a token resistance, he was led off to a VIP suite we had reserved.

I turned with relief to Elbows, but his head was buried so far down the other girl's chest it would have taken a stomach pump to extract him.

She looked at me questioningly, and I nodded and gave a thumbs-up.

Before too long, she was leading him off to another suite which, thank Christ, came free just at the crucial moment.

My girl was feeling left out, and fondled my crotch, but I was in no mood for games. I called Bobby's mate, paid her off, and went with him to the hidden recording room.

I won't bore you with the grimy details, but Biggar provided enough material for a full-length porno movie. He was like the proverbial rat up an extremely conducive drainpipe. We had action shots from every conceivable camera angle. God knows where they hid the bloody things, but every time he rolled over, I had to turn away, half-expecting to hear a yell as a macroscopic lens went up one of his orifices.

At a secret signal, the girl stood up, effortlessly warding off his now feeble attempts to pleasure her and, carefully picking up her underwear, left discretely.

Biggar was sobering up rapidly, and when I went in with some of the more lurid still-shots of their activities, I could see by the horror of revelation on his face that he was mine.

I always believe in kicking a man when he is down. When else do you get the chance? The best thing was that he didn't even realise he was being kicked.

I passed him the contract I had drawn up, giving him an extremely lucrative consultancy with the bank. I had not filled in the start date. I showed him where to sign, and his drunken look of resignation rapidly turned to one of greed when he saw the remuneration. I gave him his copy in a Davenport envelope. Little did he know.

"This contract can start whenever you want it to, Roger," I said, trying not to sound condescending.

It was difficult, as he was stark naked, and still dripping.

21

Elbows was looking slightly guilty the next morning, and very hungover, but when I showed him a couple of Biggar's photos and a short video clip, a devious smirk spread across his face, banishing all thought of physical or emotional discomfort.

"The sanctimonious, two-faced, little arsehole," he muttered happily. "I've got him. Did you show him any of this?"

I nodded. "I also gave him a 'Senior Advisor' contract. That'll keep him off our backs."

That brought him up short and, in a moment, the old Elbows was back.

"Have you lost your motherfucking mind?" he demanded, looking round in case anyone could hear. He hadn't cottoned on yet that my office was fully wired up. By me.

I could see the cogs whirring.

"You signed that contract on behalf of the bank, and on the basis of a chance hearsay conversation I told you I had with the chairman, where he expressed provisional approval for it?"

His eyes were drilling into me.

"Six months ago?"

It was rather pathetic really. Not so long ago he had been running the show. Now I was so far ahead of him, I had to give him time to catch up before I applied the *coup de grâce*.

"If that contract hits the headlines, we'll all be indicted for corruption, and Christ knows what else, and you'll be in so much shit your fucking children won't recognise you."

I realised he was having to hold himself back from calling his buddy at the BBC at that very moment, to hit the newswires, seeing this sudden opportunity to destroy me.

I decided to give him enough rope to rip his head off.

So, I said nothing.

The bile tumbled out of him. He couldn't help himself. All these months of being outmanoeuvred by his own protégé, and now his chance to get even had apparently presented itself on a plate.

Last night's alcohol and sex may have provided a catalyst, but whatever started it flowing, the malice vomited out of every nasty little creephole in what passed for his soul.

He was coming for me now, stabbing his finger at me, and curling his lip.

"And that's exactly what you deserve, you little cocksucker…" He was nodding his head. "After all I did for you."

I thought he was going to hit me. I didn't even bother to flinch. If he had lived with my family, he wouldn't have troubled to waste his energy. He was up close now, and I could feel his breath on my cheek. I puckered my face up in distaste. He didn't smell good. He must have downed some of that cheap Kuikbakh brandy as well.

That really got him.

"I taught you everything you know, you motherfucker. But ever since I promoted you, I have fed you everything, while all you have done is work against me and try to bring me down."

I couldn't really argue with that.

"Well, now it's my fucking turn to fuck with you."

I admired the depth of his vocabulary. Bobby would have been proud.

"I'm going to call a board meeting for tomorrow morning," he spat. "And you can say goodbye to Davenport's, and a career in the City."

He turned and started towards the door, but spun back to me with an afterthought.

"Unless you count the Old Bailey." He almost laughed at his own joke, but before he could reach the door, I pressed the remote control, and a screen slid down behind my desk.

"I should have a look at this before you call your board meeting," I suggested quietly.

As the video medley of both him and Biggar rolled, the expression on his face went rapidly from surprise, through anger, to horror.

"You fucking Judas," he managed to whisper.

But it was when the young Asian ladyboy came in naked and gave him a blowjob that I thought he might actually cry.

I was relieved to find I wasn't going completely soft. Thinking of Yusupov helped a lot.

"And if you think I signed that contract myself, then you really would have to admit that you did a lousy job of teaching me everything you know." I laughed at his look of bewilderment. "It's not my writing."

He opened his mouth, and I probably sounded bored when I whispered, "No fingerprints, physical or digital."

He looked deflated.

"Except for an old contact, who has a string of convictions for forging documents."

Fear replaced deflation.

"And yours."

His cheeks turned sheet-white, and I thought for a moment he might keel over. But he recovered enough to head for the door, hissing through clenched teeth, "You haven't heard the last of me, you fuck."

* * *

Tselmeg rang me when Elbows' resignation and my promotion hit the wires.

"Tell me where to deposit the funds."

He never wasted words, when actions were better.

We had prepared for this, and Bobby had set up a private client account for the purpose.

Luckily, compliance wouldn't be getting too much grief from Biggar's stiffs, since our little evening out.

I gave Yusupov the details, as the phone was clean, and he read them back carefully to me. Neither of us wanted anything to go astray, and it was better not to leave any written or email trail.

"You have complete authority over the funds, Mr de Carteret. I know you will look after them."

He put the phone down, and I did consider whether I was getting in over my head.

But only briefly.

Grab what life gives you with both hands, I had always been taught. *One round the neck, and the other by the balls, if you want to hang onto it.*

I had a feeling that Yusupov had learned that too.

My balls tried that disappearing act they sometimes pull when you hit cold water or a brick wall.

22

There are certain major turning points in your life. Good and bad.

The moment Yusupov's funds were transferred was one of those points in mine.

It was so fucking simple, I couldn't believe why nobody had tried it before.

Probably, I supposed, because the world had never previously witnessed the juxtaposition of three people in positions of such power, with a billion dollars to play with, and the combined moral compass of a blind Venetian whore.

Bobby was into the occult, and said the planetary signs were favourable. The last time I heard him say that was when we decided to sting old Ahmed for protection. That didn't work out too well, but I crossed my fingers and hoped that his star-reading had come on a bit since then.

To be honest, nothing really changed that much. Bobby continued to let me know when there were big client deals coming up, and I made sure the bank's prop desk was in there just beforehand to front-run them, cleaning up some of the profit.

The only new twist was that I put Yusupov's cash to work, just before I tipped off the prop desk.

We made out like bandits. Which was what we were, when you looked at it objectively. Bobby and I didn't see it like that. We were the good guys.

I occasionally thought about Elbows. He had, after all, done a lot to get me where I was, and I hadn't exactly repaid the favour. Quite the opposite. But, before I could begin to get too maudlin,

I recalled Scrapper's rib that he had broken, and reminded myself that he had been ready to shop me to the board if I hadn't played my cards just right with Roger Biggar. He'd died by his own sword.

We barely heard from Yusupov. I billed him quarterly from an account I had set up in the British Virgin Isles, on a trip I had made there a couple of months previously.

I remember thinking at the time, that if the general morals in the BVI were anything near as lax as their banking regulations, then I very much doubted there would be any British Virgins left out there.

There was the odd complaint at Davenport's that the rise in the prop desk profits had stalled, but it was pretty marginal. My guys on those desks were no slouches, and they still did well.

I made a presentation to ExCo, and then the full board. They clearly credited me with much of the trading room profits, and also the new Yusupov account. They definitely didn't want to dig too deep in case anything came up which might need looking into.

Digging too deep wasn't a character trait much in evidence on the board and senior management at Davenport's. It wasn't considered part of their role. Unless their bonuses began to slide.

That suited me fine.

The bank's IT systems were such shit, that Angie was able to exclude Yusupov's account from the reports comparing Davenport's own-account trading with the client deals.

23

Time flies when you're enjoying yourself. One summer, Debs and I took the children to a little place outside Saint Tropez.

I was enjoying a quiet beer on my own at one of those chic bars on the beach, checking my emails and admiring the girls.

Debs was taking the children to lessons in tennis or swimming or some other godforsaken exorbitant pastime she insisted they had to master, like kite-surfing, for Christ's sake. They weren't actually interested, but she wanted them to be seen in all the right places, so she dragged them there anyway. The trouble was, they weren't really interested in anything, apart from their social media accounts. Coming from my background, that lack of drive was a constant source of irritation, and they seemed to be growing up without me. In truth, four had been about four too many for me. I always left the house by six, before they got up, and was never home before eleven what with work, dinners and the occasional night out, so I suppose I was partly to blame.

Debs herself was getting a bit heavy and complained a lot. Her dwindling sense of humour (she didn't start out with much), and increasingly sporadic sex drive, wasn't encouraging me to rush home early every evening. In my more honest moments, I did ponder which was cause and which effect.

On the business front, life was good. Bobby and I were like glue. I had just received my first bonus of more than twenty million. That was on top of my Yusupov loot in the BVI account, so anything I wanted I could buy. As a result, I was looking to broaden my horizons; I needed another challenge in my life.

Yusupov paid up on time and never gave me any hassle. Of course, he was getting complete payback on his investment about every eighteen months, so that would have been stupid.

And he wasn't stupid. Arrogant, opinionated, devious, greedy, unscrupulous, and alarmingly psychotic. But not stupid.

Bobby told me that I shared most of those characteristics with the Kuikbakh, and backed up his case with a few quite picturesque examples; so, I suppose it wasn't surprising that Yusupov didn't aggravate me as much as my feckless children and cumbersome wife.

Apart from one thing.

"You are learning quickly, Nick," he would say, whenever we had dinner together. "I like a quick learner."

Then he would give me one of his patronising smiles and sometimes even a pat on the shoulder. One time he raised his glass and we drank an old Kuikbakh toast which can be roughly translated as, 'The pupil who breathes his master's every breath, may some day hope to wear his hat'.

But I didn't want his hat. I wanted his whole fucking wardrobe.

As he put his glass down, he told me, "I chose you because my contacts told me you were one of the best bankers in London, Nick, as well as the most ambitious."

He looked at me with a penetrating stare. "But they also said you were too greedy ever to be Top Gun."

That made me think long and hard. But, having come through the maelstrom of my early childhood, and survived, there was nothing, nobody, in this world, or even the next, that was going to stop me from reaching the very highest pinnacle of success. And that included Tselmeg Yusupov: especially him. In fact, it was Yusupov himself, above all others, who I really needed to topple to achieve fulfilment.

Finally, I found my voice. "Your friends were wrong, Tselmeg. One day I'm going to be the best of all, so nobody will ever look down on me again."

We sat there eyeing each other like rutting stags, but we both knew whose antlers were the sharpest.

He smiled and raised his glass again, narrowing his eyes in concentration. "You have given me good returns on my investments, Nick, and credibility with your people, but I have a lot more to accomplish. Stay with me for the ride and you will realise your dreams." I knew he was right. It was the only reason I was there. We drank together to wealth, health, and the confusion of our enemies.

A stunningly well-filled bikini sashayed past, bringing me back with a jolt, to the beach. I ordered a second beer, and resolved to stay with Yusupov 'for the ride'. I agreed with myself to let that ride last no longer than it had to; just until he had taught me everything I needed to take his place.

In the meantime, I promised to get myself a little love nest in Mayfair, a replacement for Debs, and a 'Roller' with tinted windows.

24

Anastasia was a headhunter when I met her. A bloody good one. And gorgeous; petite, full of bounce and energy, tough when she needed to be, with dark flashing eyes, a throaty laugh and a quick riposte.

She only really had one failing, and it was a serious one.

She wouldn't sleep with me.

I was looking for someone to head up the prop desk as my management duties were taking too much time. Making sure that everything ticked over nicely, without any pieces running off down the wrong track, was becoming a full-time job.

"What can I do to persuade you to let me do this assignment for you, Nick?" she asked, rather ingenuously, I thought.

"Sleep with me," I replied, with a grin.

She laughed and tilted her head, giving my cheek a pinch, as if to let me know she was running this particular show.

"I am sure I would enjoy that, Nick, as much as you would." She laughed sexily. "But I understand that both my competitors, Susan Boyd and Marigold Struthers, have already slept with you, and we can't all do the assignment, can we?"

Shit, her intelligence is good, I thought to myself, holding her gaze.

"Yes, I know most of what's going on," she smiled at me, as if reading my mind. That made me think a bit.

"That's why I am so good." The way she said it left just enough doubt in my mind as to what she was good at.

We had reached an impasse.

"I will make you a deal." Her eyes were smiling now as well, and I could see she liked doing deals. A woman after my own heart.

"You pay my entire fee up front and I will find your Head of Proprietary Trading." She paused theatrically. "And if we are both happy with the result, you can take me out to dinner."

I moved forward to close the deal, but she held her hands up.

"No commitment, Nick. If I enjoy dinner and feel like it, I may sleep with you. That will depend on how we get on."

There was no way I was not going to get on with this one. I smiled and shook her hand.

She found my head of prop trading, and he was world-class.

So was she.

25

With a decent guy to run the desk, I could focus on driving the business, and, at the same time, sorting my life out. I got a Mayfair apartment, and set up Anastasia there. She loved Snapper, and spoiled him rotten; he returned the favour. She knew the way to both our hearts.

She generally tried to keep me level-headed. But, with all that success, it was almost understandable that I began to bury my head pretty far up my own arse.

I really began to believe I could do no wrong.

Perhaps I should rephrase that; I began to think I was invincible.

On the few occasions I took my head out from that dark place, I realised full well that I was not the Angel Gabriel.

After all, I was double-dealing my wife with Anastasia; I was double-dealing Anastasia with a couple of girls on the trading floor; I was shafting those girls by reducing their bonuses if they weren't on call when I needed them. And there were a few others; nothing serious.

Then, of course, I was taking the piss out of our clients by front-running them on the prop desk; and I was screwing the prop desk, tailgating them with Yusupov's little fund, and taking fifteen per cent off him for the pleasure.

The only person I wasn't screwing was Bobby; and Snapper, of course.

"What do you want out of life?" Bobby asked me one day, after his clients had left us alone in our favourite lap-dancing club.

The question surprised me, especially coming from him. The answer was pretty fucking obvious.

"What do you mean?" I asked, not sure where the conversation was leading.

He turned to me and raised his glass.

"You made it, Nick. You made it big. Now you need to think of yourself a bit."

That completely flummoxed me.

Who the fuck did he think I spent my entire life thinking about? My Fairy Godmother?

I told him that. He could see my confusion, and nodded.

"You're the talk of the town, mate. 'Poor boy, from broken home, makes head of IB at the blue-blood City Institution, Davenport's. Beautiful society wife, four lovely kids and millions in the bank. The guy's a legend.'"

I was nodding. I still didn't get his point.

"Don't you see, Nicky? You've got to the stage where the deals, the money and the girls are driving you, rather than the other way around. You're on a treadmill. You're losing touch with your own soul, mate."

Bobby had always been a bit into the supernatural. He patted my arm, and gave me that sympathetic look, which I had seen a few times recently. I didn't like that. I didn't need anybody's sympathy, even Bobby's.

"You don't laugh any more, Nick. Tell me, how much of a kick do you get from screwing the bank every time you do a deal for Yusupov? How much satisfaction do you get fucking those kids at the bank? Or Rosie over there?"

He gestured at one of the lap-dancers who did me a turn every now and then. I didn't think Bobby knew that. I must be getting careless.

He put his hand on my shoulder and stared at me balefully.

"Money and power completely control your life now, Nick. I don't think you get real pleasure from anything, anymore. We never laugh like we used to. You are just completely focused on the next deal; the next girl – before the last one's even gone home."

There was a horrible nagging truth to what he was saying. It was true, I wasn't getting as much fun out of life as we used to, when things were simpler. But I couldn't help myself. I just had to keep moving forward, stay ahead of that pack of demons, which I could feel just a couple of steps behind me.

He could see that he had hit home, and he listened to my protestations with sadness in his eyes.

When I had finished, a pained expression clouded his face.

"I'm resigning from Davenport's, Nicky." He put both hands on the table in a gesture of finality.

That was like a bullet to my heart. My best friend was abandoning me.

"I've been headhunted to lead the wealth management business at Willow's Private Bank. But, the truth is, I just can't stand by and see you destroy yourself."

I think my mouth was hanging open, because the miserable expression on his face got worse.

"Holy shit, Bobby," I finally managed. "You can't do that to me."

"I'm doing this for myself, Nick," he corrected me. "But it is also for you. Someone has to make you see the light, before the whole show goes up in smoke, with you as the firelighter."

I was speechless, and felt numb.

"I'll always be there for you, mate," he continued. "I just don't want to be at the bank when it all goes pear-shaped. And it will do, one day, sooner than you think."

I downed my drink and called Rosie over for another.

I managed a forlorn, "Good for you, Bobby. I really hope it works out for you." I meant it, but I was pretty dazed, and wasn't quite sure what I was feeling. I was wondering where it had gone wrong, and sensed my demons circling for the kill.

We would still be friends, of course, but it was going to be tricky running the bank, and all our little games, without him.

We buried ourselves in small talk, while I tried to recover my equilibrium.

After a few drinks I just about succeeded, and it was almost like old times. We relived the highlights and laughed like young kids. It was a feeling I hadn't experienced for some time.

I texted Jimmy, and we took Bobby home, on the way back to Anastasia's.

We embraced drunkenly, and I tried to persuade him to change his mind, for the umpteenth time.

Bobby had never been one to change his mind, once it was made up. I admired that.

"Just do two things for me, Nick," he said, as Jimmy opened the door.

I thought I knew what was coming.

"Look after Anastasia." He patted my arm.

That was easy, as I had every intention.

"And don't fuck with Yusupov."

My face probably told him that he had read my mind. He always had that knack, did Bobby. It was a bit scary.

26

Bobby saved my life that evening.

He was absolutely on the button. I had, indeed, been preparing to put one over on Tselmeg Yusupov. I hadn't worked out all the details yet, but I just didn't see why he should take eighty-five percent, when I was doing all the work.

In retrospect, I reckon it would not have gone well for me. What I already knew about Yusupov should have told me; what I found out later, confirmed it.

So, I decided to keep muddling along 'for the ride', as Yusupov had suggested, and make do with what I had.

For now. My time to topple him would come. I needed to be patient.

I kept the girls on the trading floor and in the clubs busy, although Bobby had been right; I didn't enjoy it like before.

The deals and the sex seemed to merge into one another.

I ticked off each conquest as another notch on my bedpost, or bank account; but there was little satisfaction anymore. I had stopped keeping count a long time ago, and deep in my heart I knew that gratification was not only out of reach; it was actually stretching away from me, far out into the distance.

I was beginning to frighten myself.

I saw even less of Debs and the kids, although I was still going through the motions with them. My youngest, Lottie, in particular, kept on at me to come to her school plays and her parties. I managed a few.

Anastasia was my rock. She could read my moods, and always

knew exactly what to say and how to react. Sex was good, of course, but she drew me out of myself, and helped me to begin to understand the complex workings of my own mind. For the first time in my life, I almost welcomed that, although there was a part of me that just wouldn't give in. I was hard-wired to my past, and it wouldn't surrender without a fight.

She would wait up for me when I worked late. One evening, after a full day culminating in a client dinner, I arrived home, tired.

She gave me a kiss, and presented me with a glass. "Here's your whiskey. Anything to eat?" I shook my head. She took a sip of her customary gin with ginger ale.

I slumped into a chair by the kitchen table and took a swig.

"You look knackered," she said, pushing my shoulders gently forward onto the table and massaging my back. It was bliss.

"Do you know why I fell for you, Nick?" she asked quietly.

"My money?" I suggested. She laughed, and pinched me viciously. "That would never be enough to warrant putting up with all your foibles.

"No, apart from those hypnotic eyes, I think I was fascinated by the contradiction between your all-consuming drive to succeed, and such vulnerability. I couldn't understand how two such opposing characteristics could co-exist in the same person."

I couldn't argue with her assessment. "It was my upbringing," I muttered, glad that my head was buried in the tablecloth.

"Like mine, I suppose," she agreed.

I turned to look at her, but she pressed me back down and kept up her gentle kneading. "Was yours so bad?" I asked.

"No, nothing like yours. My parents were lovely, and I adored my two little brothers. My father ran Mother's family brewery business. He was so enthusiastic and had such great ideas; it was expanding really fast." Her hands were suddenly still. "Until it went bust." She was silent for a few seconds, and I knew better than to interrupt.

"He was wonderful, my dad, always joking. Our lives were a

social whirl. I think he probably had the odd affair, but Mother seemed to forgive him. Then, one of the big international drinks conglomerates, Bovingtons, made a bid for us." She started massaging gently again.

"Mother's family didn't want to sell. They thought they were too posh to be involved in actually running it, but they liked the cachet of having their family name all over the local pubs. Father knew Bovingtons would play hardball and got a wonderful offer from them, but the family would have none of it."

I pulled my chair back and she came round and sat on my knee.

"You see, he wanted to succeed, my dad, and he was good at what he did, but that just attracted the attention of the big boys." She looked at me sadly. "When things turned really nasty, he just didn't have the strength. He turned to drink and would just moan endlessly about the nasty tricks that Bovingtons and their backers were pulling. In the end, he crashed the car in my first term at university." She inhaled with a slight sniffle. "They all died, Dad, Mum and my brothers. He was drunk and I always wondered if he didn't do it on purpose, to escape."

There was a tear in her eye, and I hugged her hard.

"Two years after university, I started my own headhunting business. I wanted to succeed where my father couldn't, you see. I haven't done badly." She smiled ruefully. "I just wish they'd all been here to see it."

27

Business trundled along, and I transferred Yusupov's funds to Willow's. Bobby persuaded me that it would be good to put some clear water between my prop trading and the cash I was using to front-run them. He was probably right.

The Davenport board made a bit of a stink about losing a major client like that, but they needed me more than I did them. I kept my head down, and they got over it.

It was just like before, except cleaner.

My challenge was to identify someone senior in the wealth management business, to keep me posted on their proposed deals, so I could continue to front-run them. I was beginning to make headway with a couple of young bloods, but in the end, Angie came up trumps.

"You didn't go out and snare that guy just so you could blackmail me, did you?" I asked her, only half-joking.

"Not blackmail, Nick." She smiled enigmatically. "Just a fair deal for my input. I'm going to need Bobby's commission plus a hundred basis points."

She was right, of course. She was providing the critical info to make all our wheels go round. She was the only person at the bank, apart from me and Bobby, who knew anything about Yusupov and his fund, and what we were doing with it. I had inherited her from Elbows when he went, so she also knew a lot of the shit we'd been pulling, across the whole organisation. She held all the cards.

She proffered her hand and I had little choice but to shake it. I had always admired Angie, and I really shouldn't have expected anything less from her. Her mother had done her proud.

Before too long, the stream of insider info from our wealth management arm actually began to increase. I felt a tinge of perplexed jealousy at the thought of what she must be doing with her new love-interest to keep the pillow talk flowing.

She was rather like me in some ways, and I found that worrying.

She also insisted on an utterly outrageous increase in her already exorbitant salary, on top of the money she was now making on Yusupov's account. I had to admire her for that.

She invited me round for dinner one evening and proudly took me through a spreadsheet she had produced to track all the historical trading related to Yusupov.

This document is dynamite, I thought to myself, looking at her in a new light. It was just the kind of analysis that, by 'selectively improving' their systems, we had ensured the bank couldn't put together. Compliance and internal audit would have a field day if they ever got their hands on it.

It did show that we continued to make Yusupov up to fifty per cent return on his money every year, after commission.

That only reinforced my sense of injustice.

Angie could see where I was coming from.

"You've done him really well," she said quietly. "Do you think he knows that?"

I looked around involuntarily.

This wasn't the kind of conversation I felt I should be having with anyone except Bobby.

"Look after that shit." I stared at her, nodding at the offending document.

She shredded it, returning my gaze meaningfully.

"Just make sure you look after me," she retorted.

"I will, Angie. I promise." I meant it, and not only because of what she knew.

She smiled.

28

Understandably, Angie wanted a move. As head of IB I managed to get her a senior position in the IT group. She was too bright to be sitting at a desk organising my diary, even though she also helped keep my management information as I wanted it. She had, of course, been on the systems side before Elbows had hijacked her. We gave her a big leaving party and the warmth with which everyone spoke about her and treated her spoke volumes. It made me feel guilty.

The bank found me a good replacement PA, although it wasn't quite the same.

There was something missing. My life was becoming just too routine. I needed something big to get my teeth into.

Bobby had always told me to have patience and, funnily enough, I was taking even more notice of his advice since he had left Davenport's. I missed him at the bank, but we saw each other regularly outside the office. He was doing well at Willow's. Of course he was.

Bobby's patience paid off in the end.

After sitting on my hands for a couple of months, I got a sniff of a possible mega-deal. An old client of mine, World Trading Fuels, a big US oil producer and trader, had its eye on a Gulf outfit, MahdiGas. I had been pushing them together for some time.

It was common knowledge that MahdiGas had some stratospheric, market-changing oil and gas reserves, which they showed no signs of tapping into.

I kept the deal red-light confidential, and did all the initial legwork myself.

When the markets got news of it, MahdiGas shares would go ballistic.

I didn't want anyone else taking advantage of that ahead of me.

We put half of Yusupov's fund into MahdiGas.

And with all the rest of the Kuikbakh's funds as collateral, we shorted the oil price big-time. Highly leveraged, with minimum margin call. It was a low-risk punt. As soon as the market got wind of this deal, the price of oil would hit the basement.

Then, I just sat back and waited for paydirt.

Bobby and I went down to the club to celebrate.

"What did I tell you, Nicky?" he chortled. "Patience is the best virtue in the world."

"You could even be right," I laughed, not totally convinced.

I could tell that he was at the communicative stage prior to inebriation, when we all tend to become genially philosophical. I wasn't sure I was in the right mood, but he waded in anyway.

"You're becoming more and more like Yusupov every day, you know," he said with a twinkle in his eye. "In fact, I reckon you look a bit like a slightly prettier version of him, but without the scars." He 'framed' my face theatrically with his fingers, giggling quietly to himself. "Not sure what it is exactly, but the similarity's there somewhere."

"That's not a compliment, mate," I said, trying to laugh it off.

But he wasn't finished with me.

"You're following along behind him on the 'rich' list. Everything going to plan on that front." He put both thumbs up. "Only trouble is, you're also tracking him on the 'dick' register. And that's not a compliment either, by the way." He smiled, but I could see he was serious.

"Christ, Bobby," I retorted, just managing to camouflage my anger behind a guffaw. "I thought we were here to celebrate, not to get depressed."

"That's what friends are for, Nick." He looked at me affectionately. "To stop you from turning into an arsehole."

I called one of the girls over. I needed to clear my head.

"You've already made your fortune, Nick, and I haven't done too badly either, for a street kid. We're all going to make a killing out of this MahdiGas deal. Why don't you just sail off into the sunset with Anastasia after that, and bid good riddance to Yusupov and all that he stands for?"

I shook my head, feeling my heart beginning to thump. "You don't understand, Bobby, it's not just the money." I pulled him towards me, my hand round the back of his neck. "It means more than my life to me. I feel it down here." I smacked my stomach with an open palm. "The only way I can survive my past and outrun my demons is to be the best ever."

I suddenly felt calm.

"Right now, Tselmeg Yusupov is bigger than me. I am going to change that. I can't stop myself. Don't try to make me. I'm going to break him."

Bobby looked worried. He put his hand on my shoulder. "You know I'll do anything I can for you, Nick. I've always told you that. But, Christ, mate, good luck with that one." He was shaking his head sadly. "That guy's the Devil incarnate."

29

"You're so distant, Nick."

Debs had waited up for me. I hated these heart-to-heart sessions. Especially as my cupboard-full of secrets seemed to be getting a little overcrowded. I had so many 'committee evenings' and 'client dinners' that I barely saw her. I had to keep my wits about me just to keep my various calendars apart.

I think she knew my fidelity wasn't in the John the Baptist league, but she just ran with it. Her dad was no saint, so she didn't have high expectations.

She had no idea about Anastasia. Let alone Chloe. Christ, no. She wouldn't have appreciated that.

"This stuff doesn't grow on trees, Debs," I said, gesturing round the room. "You want a big-time banker for a husband, then absence pretty much comes with the territory."

"But the children never see you," she whined. "Lottie, at least, is persistent enough to get some of your attention, but the others…" She was shaking her head gently. "They just don't feel they have a father."

"I will try," I muttered, and for a minute I meant it.

"I am arranging dinner with Petra Marinelli. I talked with your PA, and we put next Thursday in your diary," she smiled.

"Why's that?" I asked. Anastasia had wanted to go to the theatre that night. But Petra was the chancellor's right-hand woman in the Treasury, and Debs knew her way around those corridors.

"She is looking for someone in the banking world to be on a finance and banking committee, but also to advise her informally and introduce foreign governments into the right parts of the City."

I perked up. This sounded fucking high-octane interesting.

My eyes lit up. I couldn't help myself. She laughed.

"You have a date," I laughed, nodding my head involuntarily.

I gave her a hug, but any spark had long since gone.

"I have the biggest deal of all time coming off, and perhaps after that, we can all go on holiday together?"

She smiled happily, and I think we both believed it for a minute.

30

The connection with Petra Marinelli put a rocket up my career, not that it had particularly needed one.

Contacts like that, of course, were the main reason old 'Elbows' had hooked me up with Debs. Pity for him, he didn't reap many of the benefits.

I admired Petra. She had fought her way up the dog-eats-dog world of high finance and low politics, navigating astutely through the minefields of backbiting and paranoia which are present wherever real power is to be found.

I did my level best to help her return the compliment.

I had mixed success in that regard.

She never really liked me. I tried putting the moves on her, but that failed too. I suppose ours was a normal business relationship. We scratched each other's backs, but made sure we washed our hands thoroughly afterwards.

She got me on the Banking Ethics Committee. One or two people didn't seem to appreciate that, but we gamed them without too much hassle.

The committee worked well for me, as I got a heads-up as to what tricks were coming under scrutiny. I could also point the finger at some of my competitors.

Petra was regularly on the phone to me for advice, and I produced some research pieces for her. Our compliance team at the bank dreamed up most of these, and I just gave them a couple of tweaks.

I began to introduce senior lawyers and accountants to

government and of course received payment in kind. My network was getting to be so premier league that I could see the day coming when even Debs would be redundant.

Then I started to use my international Davenport contacts to introduce Petra to a few ambassadors and finance-oriented politicians, initially around Europe, and then further afield.

I didn't introduce her to Yusupov. I wasn't sure he had the right whiff about him for her particular circle.

Not yet.

So, it was an unexpected cloud on my extremely sunny horizon when a note came out of the blue from the head of my research department. His extremely well-argued analysis covered World Trading Fuels and MahdiGas. It set out, in some detail, all the factors which had led me to take such extreme positions on both MahdiGas and the oil price. But it also pointed to a few factors which could move both prices in the opposite direction. For a moment the note made me doubt my own intuition.

I felt a bit weak, but I put in a ceiling on the oil price, just in case things didn't work out, and a floor on MahdiGas.

31

I was in the office by seven the next morning.

Life was pretty much under control, and the excitement was back. The MahdiGas deal was almost complete.

Debs was happy.

So was Anastasia.

Angie was doing well in her new role. That reflected well on me as her sponsor.

I had a good new PA.

I felt quite relaxed.

So, it came as something of a shock when Bobby rang.

"Those fucking towelheads," he screamed down the phone.

It was coming up on my screen now.

'Revolution in Saudi Arabia. King assassinated, and Islamic clerics take over. Western embassies evacuated by special forces, with some loss of life.'

I checked the news. I could feel myself panicking and tried to keep calm.

"Sell MahdiGas, and close the oil position," he yelled, controlling his panic with difficulty.

At least he was still thinking straight. But it wasn't Bobby I was feeling sorry for right now.

Bobby had to face his board, and a rap on the knuckles.

I answered to Yusupov, and he didn't bother with knuckles.

Fuck, I had only put a very high ceiling on the oil price, thanks to my research head; and a sub-basement floor on MahdiGas.

"I'm on it," I shouted and slammed down the phone.

I tried to raise Konrad, who did my Yusupov trades for me, but all the lines were busy. I ran down to his floor and grabbed him by the neck. He was panicking.

"Sell the fucking MahdiGas," I screamed, and I held onto him while he looked at his screen.

"You're out already. It triggered the floor," he gabbled, pointing at the screen.

I was looking round for my commodities dealer and saw her also freaking out, hammering at her keyboard with one phone under her arm and another in each ear.

The place was utter turmoil.

"Are you sure it's totally closed?" I yelled at Konrad, and only when he nodded, did I push my way over to commodities.

I gave the girl there the same treatment. She was in complete meltdown.

I almost had to throttle her, to discover the same situation. The ceiling I had belatedly imposed, had kicked in. I had lost a fuck of a lot of Yusupov's fund, but it could have been even worse, if not for my research head.

Only when I was satisfied that we had closed both the positions, did I go back up to my office.

I felt sick.

My mobile buzzed. It was Bobby.

"Did you offload?" he yelled.

"Too late," I murmured.

I looked at my screen. I wished I hadn't, and began to feel distinctly ill.

We had lost exactly two thirds of that part of the fund we had put into MahdiGas.

But that wasn't the half of it.

With the low margin call I had so painstakingly achieved on the commodities deal, the $500 million we had put in was currently $750 in the red.

We had turned Yusupov's billion-dollar asset into an overall $600 million liability.

Settlement was in three days.

"Fucking Arabs," I muttered, as I slid gently to the floor.

For some reason, a fleeting vision of Debs, the children and Anastasia flashed across my mind. They were all wearing black, and were glaring at each other across an open grave.

My grave.

Chloe was crying. Nobody else was.

Oh, fuck!

PART THREE

REPOSSESSION

32

"A Mr Yusupov to see you, Mr de Carteret."

I had surprised the doctors and made a startlingly good recovery.

The right arm wasn't great, and I walked with a slight limp. They said that, with therapy, I would be almost as good as new.

The bank had kept me on as a 'Senior Advisor'. No more management duties, which was good and bad. Good, because the in-fighting and whingeing had been driving me berserk; bad because I had been able to decide before, pretty much unilaterally, what shit went down and who got paid for it.

The brain functioned like new. Words didn't always come out exactly right, but as long as I kept calm, most people couldn't tell that the man behind my desk wasn't still a Master of the Universe.

Keeping calm, however, wasn't always straightforward.

Debs decided that she had had enough of my loose interpretation of our marriage vows, and my lack of interest in our children. She hired the most aggressive divorce lawyer around and went for my jugular. The children were right behind her. I hadn't seen any of them since their one visit to see me in hospital.

Nasta had been released before I had returned home. Danny's little kidnapping had been his own idea, apparently. He had tried to rape her once. She led him on a bit and, when he dropped his guard, she hit his head so hard with a metal doorstop they had to take him to hospital.

To say that Yusupov had been pissed about us crashing his fund, would be a masterly understatement. But, Bobby persuaded him to provide Davenport's with sufficient collateral to secure a loan. They used that money to 'top up' his investment account at Willow's, until I was back in action.

Yusupov had made it very clear that Bobby's and my continued existence depended on some stellar returns.

Now he was here to discuss things, and I didn't much like the look on his face.

"I am sorry about Danny's behaviour, Mr de Carteret. Mistreating women is not my style," he assured me quietly, after he and the still-bandaged Danny had walked past my secretary without waiting for an invitation.

Frankly neither of them looked too sorry. Blood-curdlingly vengeful would be a better description, and my blood duly curdled.

I considered pressing the emergency alarm button under my desk to call security. I didn't reckon it would help much, so opted to wait. I say I 'opted', but frankly, when Yusupov was involved, you didn't 'opt'. You did what you were told.

They sat down, leaving an ex-boxer type scowling at the door, which he closed behind him, having pushed my PA outside before doing so. Snapper raised his hackles and slunk towards him, teeth bared and growling menacingly. I was slightly comforted to see the big thug take a wary step back.

"However, I am sure you will understand that our arrangement will have to change," Yusupov continued, with such civility you might have thought he was discussing the weather.

Danny smiled evilly. I swallowed.

"You have managed to turn my billion-dollar fund into a $600 million liability." Anger flashed across his face, to be replaced immediately by that unblinking, soulless stare, which is common to many predators in the animal world as they circle their prey.

He held up his hand before I could interrupt.

"Which your loyal friend, Mr Jones, persuaded me to refinance, giving security over my assets, pending your return."

The message was clear.

"Now you have returned, Mr de Carteret…"

There was a long and pregnant silence, which I was at a complete loss as to how to fill.

Yusupov saved me the trouble. "I need my assets back, Mr de Carteret."

He tailed off, leaving me in no doubt from the look on his face, that if he didn't get them back fast, his own style would be considerably more direct, and less fallible, than Danny's.

I played my only card, and pulled out Angie's latest spreadsheet. While not looking quite as rosy as the first time she had shown it to me, it demonstrated quite clearly that overall, I had made more than $700 million profit for him, ex my commission and even after the losses from the recent little debacle.

"That's a good return for the years we have worked together, Tselmeg," I said as firmly as I dared.

He leaned forward, and the boxer took a step towards me in exact harmony with him. The threat could not have been clearer. Snapper growled.

"I think you are making a common fool's error, Mr de Carteret." It was clear we were not on first name terms anymore. "And I do not like fools."

I opened my mouth, but thought better of it.

"Never confuse income with capital." He was becoming quite venomous, and it was all I could do to hold his gaze.

"How much are you worth to me now, Mr de Carteret?" he asked, in what turned out to be a rhetorical question.

Before I could suggest twenty-five per cent, as we now needed to make up for lost ground, he answered himself.

"I paid you well for your efforts, and you failed me. However, someone who loses my entire fund, and turns every dollar into an IOU, is not worth very much. I suggest we settle for zero until you have made back my losses. Then we will renegotiate."

He, and the smirking Danny, rose as one. I could see that he was genuinely beginning to lose control of his temper. His scars were vivid red. I am no wimp, but I was terrified.

He placed his hands on my desk and drew his face very close to mine.

"I repeat, in case you had forgotten. You lost me all of my capital."

He held my chin with one hand. The touch was gentle; the threat was not.

"They tell me you are a star in your industry, Mr de Carteret. Let that star shine bright."

The boxer opened the door for them, and Yusupov walked towards it. He turned, before exiting.

"Or it will be extinguished."

33

Davenport's was delighted to have such a prized client back. There was also 'my' loan, which of course was in his name. He placed a small amount of additional funds with our wealth management business. Compliance moaned about 'money laundering' and 'provenance', but cash talks.

Yusupov had signed a guarantee for the loan and had given some oilfields as very generous security. I had no idea that he had any oilfields.

Of course, compliance couldn't know that he had my personal open-ended guarantee for all capital and interest. Nothing in writing; Tselmeg Yusupov didn't work like that. We both knew that if I didn't pay him back and start earning premium returns again, financial security would be the least of my worries.

And so, we all set off again. Only this time it was my neck on the block. I could not afford to lose any more of his money. I needed to use every trick in the book, and so I leant heavily on Angie and the information she was screwing out of her new lover in wealth management.

Angie tried to insist on two per cent for herself. I explained that could only happen once we had made good the losses.

I began to realise that it wasn't only the Kuikbakh who was holding my balls between the blades of a pair of rusty sheep-shears.

Angie was in way too deep for her own good. And for mine. She knew every detail of our operation and could have held me to ransom at any time.

"You'd better look after me then, Nick."

I couldn't really argue with that.

The compliance team wanted to 'Know their Client'. But this client wasn't too fucking keen to be known, and he passed them over to me, having given me an open-ended power of attorney.

They balked at that, initially.

But this was no time for games, and I slowly got them to see things his way. I had to get rid of one guy, Alan Jones, who was too smart to be in that department anyway.

"I have no option but to take this to Mark Davies," he shouted, when I fired him.

He was really pissed. I could see his point. He was only doing his job.

Mark Davies was the new head of IB. A bright guy who, I felt, could do a good job. Not quite ruthless enough, and far too straight. I had mentored him on his way up, so he was mostly friendly.

But I didn't really want him getting involved in this. He could easily take this compliance nitwit's side.

I debated with myself into the afternoon and, eventually, I decided to let Yusupov know. I called him on the emergency number he had given me.

This was a fucking emergency.

Yusupov was not happy.

"Are you still able to run my affairs at Davenport, Mr de Carteret?" he asked quietly. "Because, if not, then perhaps I need to find a more competent banker."

He paused.

"In any event, while you flounder around, I have dealt with your problem already. Mr Jones has just had an accident. A cement truck unfortunately, could not stop at a traffic light. These things happen."

And with that he put the phone down.

I felt numb. Not in any way due to the demise of Mr fucking Jones. He should have known better than to cross me.

It suddenly struck me; Yusupov had my phones wired.

And my office.

I desperately tried to remember if I had given him any cause for concern.

Or anger.

He didn't sound too friendly.

I took one of my pills.

* * *

After that, the show kept on the road pretty much as before, and we were making some inroads into the loan. I was working my arse off. So was Angie.

But Yusupov wasn't the philanthropic type. He wasn't going to reinstate any commission without me earning it. Not much I could do about that. Frankly I had a full-time job making sure I remained indispensable. I didn't want any cement trucks following me around.

After a couple of weeks of particularly heavy activity, my PA put dinner in the diary for Anastasia and me, with 'Mr and Mrs Yusupov'.

"He wants you to invite Petra Marinelli and her husband. Shall I get her on the phone?"

I nodded. The girl seemed to take orders directly from Yusupov now.

I had a vague feeling that I was slowly, but surely, losing control.

34

I was surprised to see Yusupov had the same girlfriend as before. Especially as my impending divorce was all over the tabloids. It did not seem the right way around, somehow.

That was in no way to denigrate her.

Quite the opposite. She was monumental, with a million-dollar smile, legs like a camel and humps to match. I like camels.

"You have met Irina, I think," he assured me.

She smiled, and I made to peck her cheek.

That was obviously not on the cards. The ex-boxer, standing behind his boss, shifted his stance. I pretended I was adjusting my collar.

Tselmeg seemed not to notice.

But I was getting his measure.

He noticed everything.

"This is…" I started to make my introductions, but he ignored me.

"Anastasia, how lovely to meet you. Danny told me you are a dangerous woman."

He pretended to duck, his face all smiles, but the implication was lost on nobody.

He grasped both her shoulders and kissed her three times; the last one, proprietarily, full on the lips.

Nasta looked at me warily.

"Ah, here is Petra."

Petra Marinelli walked across the room, ushering her husband attentively to our table. The old man (he must have been twenty years her senior) relied heavily on a stick, as his left leg was noticeably shorter than the right.

Yusupov got to his feet and just held himself back enough to allow me to do the introductions.

Then he took over.

I had to admit, the guy had what it takes. You didn't have to like him, but he sure as hell got your attention.

You would have thought he had started the world's first charity for politicians' invalid spouses, the way he fussed over Petra's disabled husband.

More likely he had added to their number, I thought to myself.

Yusupov positioned himself between Petra on his right, and Anastasia. Old man Marinelli and I filled in the gaps.

He came straight to the point.

"Mrs Marinelli," he paused. "May I call you Petra?"

He continued, without waiting for a reply.

"I want to help you finance some of the infrastructure projects your country so badly needs."

He had a way of making the UK sound like a Third World banana republic.

"You may consider my funds, together with those of my associates, to be limitless. In return all I want is a small equity stake and a one per cent real return on the debt."

Petra wasn't used to this kind of table talk, but she smiled and said her team would be delighted to meet him tomorrow to discuss details.

But Tselmeg Yusupov hadn't got where he had by playing to other people's rules.

He produced a letter with a flourish.

"This letter provides you with an irrevocable commitment up to five hundred billion sterling."

The look on Petra's face said it all. This, for her, was like manna from heaven. Very cheap and apparently limitless funding, without having to rely on the markets.

"If the arrangement works for both of us, then more is available."
He looked at her and smiled. "Considerably more."

"As you say, your team can sort out the details with my associates, any time."

He waved his hand, and I realised he was referring to me.

Nasta squeezed my knee and looked at me questioningly.

Dinner went surprisingly well after that.

Petra Marinelli was like putty in his hands. Her husband looked slightly non-plussed, but I don't think he had much of a say in the scheme of things.

As he left, Tselmeg whispered in my ear, "Thank you for the introduction, Nick."

I had never heard him thank anybody nor, recently, refer to me as Nick. Both novelties worried me.

"I have reinstated your fifteen per cent commission. Tomorrow, you will see some interesting developments."

35

It was all over the news.

'President Armenov of Kuikbakhistan dies in his bed, at eighty-three.'

I should not have been surprised to see that I recognised the photo of his successor.

It was Tselmeg Yusupov.

Nor, in view of that fact, should the rumours have surprised me about the manner of his predecessor's demise.

I got an invitation to Yusupov's inauguration in the capital, Szchymkent. So did Petra; and the Chancellor; and the PM. Tselmeg was on a charm offensive. The UK seemed to be the primary object of his intended affections. I wasn't too sure why. His schooling here had not been a happy time, and he wasn't any philanthropist. But it certainly opened up a vast horizon of possibilities for me, and I wasn't going to complain about that.

He sent his jet for us. It was just Petra, Anastasia and me. I think the PM wanted to be seen to be suitably grateful for this new source of financial opportunity, while keeping some appropriately diplomatic distance.

The official instatement ceremony was impressive. Military parade, which gave pride of place to some ultrasonic missiles with nuclear warheads, a formal religious service and a state dinner in the evening.

The new president made a long statement at dinner, promising to use his country's oil wealth to upgrade infrastructure, improve education and healthcare, while eliminating poverty. "I promise you all..." he looked round the room at the gathered dignitaries, both local and foreign, "that the corruption which plagued my predecessor's regime, and which so disadvantaged the honest hard-working Kuikbakh citizens..."

He looked round the large table again, and spread his hands wide in a gesture which I recognised from my own efforts at obfuscation.

"... will be seen as a relic of a distant and unpleasant past."

The table erupted in applause, fuelled more, I felt, by the excellent imported French wine than by any serious belief in what he was saying.

I had heard similar speeches from politicians across the world, and I knew them for the bullshit they always were. But at least I stood to make a cut on his various projects and good works, so I drank up and smiled.

Tselmeg's eyes met mine for an instant, and his childlike look of pleasure at the raucous applause and adulation slowly disappeared, to be replaced by that neutral, thoughtful smile, which never ventured further than his tightly pursed lips. I clapped my raised hands and proffered my glass. A real smile flickered momentarily, before he continued his speech.

"I also undertake to use that wealth to finance similar projects, in those countries which have shown themselves to be supportive of my country's development and philosophy."

He smiled at Petra.

She looked happy. She caught my eye, and raised her glass to me. I returned the compliment.

I knew what she hadn't found out yet. Yusupov was a bit like Elbows. They both confused their sponsoring institution's resources with their own. Petra would soon find out that what was good for the UK was very good for Kuikbakhistan; and very good indeed, for Tselmeg Yusupov. If there was any conflict, then she would quickly find all that goodness disappearing down his trouser pocket.

I understood that. It was pretty much my philosophy, too.

After dinner the guests slowly filtered away. Yusupov and his aides were very attentive, and made all the big wheels feel good about themselves.

I was duly flattered that he sought me out as I was escorting Anastasia towards the exit.

"Thank you for coming, Nick. And for bringing the lovely Anastasia." He kissed only her cheeks this time. The wine and Christian-name terms had the intended effect, and I gushed about the opulence of the occasion, and the prospects for Kuikbakhistan with such a forward-looking president.

"Nick has been a great help to me," he addressed Nasta with a smile, but in that hard, matter-of-fact tone of his. I remembered only the hardness from a few weeks earlier. But that was then, and things were apparently changing.

"I want him and his friend Bobby to help run my bank for me."

He wasn't waiting for my response.

He looked directly at me now. "The Bank of Kuikbakhistan. I look forward to seeing you there at one, for lunch tomorrow. I will send a driver."

I didn't know much about banking in Eastern Europe, but I had heard that BOK was one of the oldest central banks in existence, known for being a bit quirky. Its charter, for instance, specifically forbade foreigners on its board. Things were obviously 'modernising' fast in Tselmeg Yusupov's country. I had a nasty feeling the previous president had been the first to suffer that experience.

Anastasia looked at me with a mixture of pride and concern.

36

I got the full treatment at the bank.

Yusupov sent his apologies, but the rest of the board was there, and they had all the best silver out. The food and wine were surprisingly good. I imagined that the previous chef had been 'modernised', as well.

The country's president was ex-officio chairman. His deputy, Bolat Karimov, was charming and, I assumed, suitably malleable. He, like his boss, had been part-educated in the UK, and had some of the famous public-school polish. Not too much wood under the wax, I thought to myself.

Over the brandy, the executive committee gave us a PowerPoint presentation. Reading between the lines, my suspicions were confirmed. Until very recently BOK had been a sleepy and bureaucratic organization.

Modernisation would have been apocalyptic – 'Tselmeg style'. The entire executive team, along with most of the board, had been binned. A boutique Russian investment bank, well known to Yusupov, had been acquired. The executive committee, who now ran the bank, was entirely from there. Some of the old board had been kept on for appearances.

The bank was embarking on a rapid expansion of its international operations, and especially its natural resources, commodity finance and derivatives businesses.

I got the distinct impression that a large part of the country's oil and mining revenues had found their way direct to BOK without passing 'Go'. Perhaps someone had been deemed to have missed a repayment by the new bank management. Or perhaps they had simply reached their own deadline.

I assumed that those same oilfields, which Yusupov had given as security for his loans from Davenport's, were closely linked to BOK. Probably also being given as security for anything else that came up. I knew his style by now. 'What's yours is ours; what's mine is mine.'

"We are honoured to have Mr de Carteret with us today," gushed Karimov.

There was a polite round of applause from the old guard. A reserved nod of the head from the ExCo guys.

"Our president holds Mr de Carteret in the very highest esteem." More applause.

"The president has offered Mr de Carteret the position of head of our London operations, and I understand he has accepted."

He came over to shake my hand, and handed me an envelope.

Now, in my book, Yusupov had simply told Nasta last night that he wanted me and Bobby to run the bank. I didn't remember accepting. Of course, I hadn't turned it down either and, in Yusupov's book, that was tantamount to the same thing. Realistically, we both knew that my cash tills had been ringing loud enough to pass for a full-blown acceptance speech.

I opened the envelope as unobtrusively as I could under the table. The waiters came round with coffee, which helped camouflage my enthusiasm.

I scanned through the terms of the offer, which had been signed by Yusupov.

Any reservations I may have had flew directly out the window and into the warm Szchymkent air.

The bank was guaranteeing me a minimum of £20 million per annum, for two years. He certainly understood how to press all my buttons. He even knew the figure I had dreamed of in my early days, and which I now took to be the threshold of a good year.

If the bank and I exceeded our targets, I reckoned I might even make nine figures.

Holy shit! Try as I might, my face said it all.

Karimov saw my expression and carried on smoothly.

"Mr de Carteret will be staying with us for a few days, to review our operations, in preparation for his esteemed colleague Mr Robert Jones, who will be running the operations here in Szchymkent."

This obviously didn't come as any surprise to the assembled company. It was a bit of a shock to me.

"Mr de Carteret and Mr Jones went to school together." They all nodded wisely, as if perfectly understanding the secret shibboleths of these strange faraway schools, where their country's president and their bank's deputy chairman had been educated together. Probably just as well they couldn't tell the difference between Yusupov's alma mater, and the sink estate where Bobby and I had just about learned to write and add up.

"President Yusupov has every confidence that Mr Jones will accept the generous offer that Mr de Carteret will convey to him on our bank's behalf."

So that was it. All I had to do was persuade Bobby to pick up sticks and move out here to this godforsaken dump; to run a bank whose ethics would make Elbows' and my own scams seem like some cuddly little ploy cobbled together by a double-act of Jesus Christ and the Prophet Mohammed.

He saw the dubious look on my face. I couldn't hide it. But he didn't bat an eyelid.

"The offer, of course, will be sufficiently attractive to persuade Mr Jones to accept."

I didn't like the sound of that. I could see immediately that I was being asked to aid and abet these guys in disposing of the last vestiges of my only friend's honour and self-esteem.

I sensed a fleeting shadow of a sentiment I had managed to submerge completely since childhood: shame. Not a happy feeling, and it brought horrible memories flooding back.

Of my family.

And Bobby, in my bed with my mother.

I looked down at the document, clenched firmly in my hand under the table, for reassurance.

After a short pause, I raised my glass.

The port was excellent.

37

It shouldn't really have come as any surprise when I met up with Bobby on my return to London to find that he was in love.

Nor, that the object of his affections was an extremely beautiful Eastern European called Marina, who had seemingly appeared out of nowhere.

I was impressed. Yusupov's henchmen had done their homework. That was going to save me some persuading.

I did have a fleeting moment of unease for my old friend. We were in with the sharks, and this girl looked remarkably like rubby-dubby, but Snapper gave her a sniff and didn't growl.

I reminded myself that Bobby was an adult, and this was business, so I buried my concerns. Once Bobby saw a paycheque, I suspected he wouldn't worry too much about his new girlfriend's provenance. And of course, he would find living in Kuikbakhistan a lot more attractive with her there to warm his bed.

She gave every appearance of being genuinely hooked on him. He was totally smitten.

I would watch out for him, I promised myself.

"Nick has just come back from Szchymkent," Bobby crooned to his new paramour. "He was attending the president's inauguration."

She looked suitably impressed, although I was fairly sure that was old news to her

"It is lovely in Szchymkent, isn't it?" she laughed, with touching affection.

"Marina wants me to meet her family," Bobby informed me. "She says Kuikbakhistan is beautiful in the summer."

They kissed and giggled like teenagers.

I assumed she hadn't told him it was mostly thirty degrees below in winter. I didn't want to spoil her pitch. Or mine.

She smiled at me.

I gave her my 'Watch out for my best friend' look, and I got the feeling she understood.

I thought it might seem all a bit contrived if I blurted out that I had an offer for him that would make his job at Willow's seem like charity work.

I needn't have worried. Marina came right out with it.

"My Uncle Bolat owns a bank out there, and they are looking for an international executive to run it for them," she stated, looking at me innocently as if this was a routine occurrence. "They think Bobby is exactly what they need."

This was my moment of truth. Should I tell him she was a plant? A nice juicy one, and perhaps one who, with luck, could make him happy. But still a plant.

I opted to follow Snapper, and give her the benefit of the doubt. I would talk to Bobby later. He was exactly the right guy for this job. He just didn't know it. This was the big ticket he deserved.

Marina would persuade him.

I reckoned she pretty much already had.

38

"What do you think, Nick?"

Bobby and I were in one of our favourite bars, a couple of days later. Marina had gone back home, and would come back to pick him up the following week.

This was my chance to make sure that at least he was going in with his eyes open. Love can do funny things to a guy like Bobby.

"Marina, or the bank job?" I countered.

"Both," he said.

I took a big swig of my beer.

"How did you meet her?" I asked, to give myself time to think.

"She came to Willow's to invest some of her uncle's money. Apparently, he had given her my name."

Christ, I thought, *these guys are way ahead of me. They aren't leaving anything to chance.* They had obviously seen the doubt on my face when Bobby's name was mentioned at the board meeting, and had just gone right ahead and taken things into their own hands.

From the point of view of getting on with the deal, this was definitely a good thing. But a thread of apprehension flitted across my mind. If they thought anyone wasn't up to the job, they just went right around them; like they had just gone round me.

"What's bugging you?" queried Bobby solicitously.

I thought it was best to get things out on the table, and this seemed as good a time as any.

"They asked me to run their London office."

I wasn't quite sure how he'd take that, as he had already left Davenport's to put some distance between us. But a smile lit up his face.

"That's fucking brilliant," he said and clapped his arm round my shoulder. "They want the top team, and they've got it. We're back in business. Marina's uncle assures her you've mellowed."

I wasn't quite sure how to take that. First, I was sure I hadn't mellowed. Pretty much the reverse. And second, I realised that Marina and her uncle were running this show now; for better or worse. One more front for me to keep a watchful eye on.

He ordered more drinks and raised his glass. "Waft on, mate. What did I tell you? Just keep bloody wafting on."

I returned his toast and gave him a hug.

One of the girls came over and sat down beside Bobby.

I had rarely seen him turn one down before, when celebrating. He declined politely.

We chinked our glasses together.

"The cash will be phenomenal," I told him flatly. He didn't look surprised.

"I reckon, in a really good year, I could make high eight figures."

That really got his attention.

"And you will be running the whole show," I added. "I'm only running London."

"Holy fucking shitsville," was all he could say, so I thought it was a good moment to give him some of the downside.

"I reckon you may be asked to put down some strange shit by these guys," I ventured. "They are no angels, and they certainly won't pull their punches."

"Like some of the shit we did at Davenport's?" he asked quietly, opening his eyes wide in a parodied gesture of innocence.

"Could make some of that stuff look almost tame," I nodded gently.

We looked at each other, and I think there was a little bit of me that was disappointed to see that Bobby was failing this particular integrity test.

Of course, I myself was well past that stage, but somehow, I didn't like to see my friend treading the same slippery path. Frankly,

I wasn't sure he had the balls to make it work like I did. He was a straightforward kind of guy when it came to the crunch.

"I can handle that," he stated flatly, and I knew the argument was over.

I tried one more approach. I would feel better in future if I had pointed out all the pitfalls to him.

"Living in Kuikbakhistan will have some drawbacks," I persisted. "Like the weather." I drew my arms around me, feigning bitter cold. It gets down to minus forty in winter."

I looked at him.

"Most of the winter."

"I'll have Marina," he retorted, dismissing my point out of hand. "And if what you say about the remuneration is right, I should be able to get myself a decent place to hole out."

I realised that Bobby was completely hooked. Marina had set the ball rolling, and the prospect of serious cash, together with the opportunity to run his own show, while she waited for him at home, had sealed the deal. Anything I did to play devil's advocate was simply alienating him.

"I think Yusupov may have planted her on you," I blurted, without really meaning to.

A look of hurt flashed across his face, followed by one of determination.

"I'm going to make this one work, Nick. I know it's easy for you getting the women – and the cash. They both just flock to you. But this is my time. I can feel it."

What was I going to say? He was arguing my case for me, and I reminded myself again that he was a big boy who could look after himself. He screwed my mother when he was fourteen, and left me at Davenport's to go into competition at Willow's. He knew how to stay afloat when the water rose.

And perhaps he was right. Perhaps this really was his big chance. Mine, too.

"Anyway, she can't be a 'plant', as you so kindly put it. Her father opposed Yusupov, and died recently. She thinks the regime might have had him bumped off. She's no fan of theirs."

I put my hand on his shoulder. I had said enough.

"I think you're absolutely right. And, whatever happens, Bobby mate, I'll always have your back."

We had a couple more drinks and, for the first time I can remember, we both turned down all opportunities to interrupt our celibacy. Bobby with more conviction than I.

Our world was changing. I was moving up a gear, and Bobby was going to hit the bigtime.

39

Bobby's feet barely hit the ground after that.

He signed a contract that was similar to mine, with a $5 million relocation allowance. He liked that. So did Marina.

As far as I could tell, she really was Bolat Karimov's niece. Frankly, Yusupov and his mates had the country so well sewn up, she could have become that person, even if she hadn't been before.

Anyway, it was Bolat who gave her away at their wedding, which happened almost immediately, since she fell pregnant straight away.

I was Bobby's best man. Nasta was there, and we filled the bank's plane out to Szchymkent with a few of our, mostly single, friends and banking colleagues.

The Kuikbakhs certainly knew how to party.

There were a lot of very attractive, and mostly unattached singles, of both sexes there, together with much of the country's social elite.

The latter kept themselves pretty much to themselves, apart from offering heartfelt wishes for the happy couple's health and happiness.

The former mixed in enthusiastically. Some worked for the bank already. It was a prestigious institution now that their president was behind it, so many of the others were keen to join them. They spared no effort to ensure that our guests were made to feel extremely welcome.

As a result, some of our people suddenly decided they would be keen to stay on in the country. Bobby and I had to shoehorn them back onto the plane on the Monday, considerably the worse for wear.

We opened the London branch with quite a fanfare about a month later. A few of those same young Kuikbakhs came over for the inauguration party. I chatted with some of them, and they sang the bank's praises. They were obviously part of our unofficial recruitment effort and were keen to spread their message round the London financial, and social, scene. They were extremely persuasive, so Bobby, Anastasia and I gave them every assistance, including introductions to all the best bankers we knew. Before long, we were getting extremely well-qualified applications to join the bank, and both locations were flying.

Yusupov seemed happy when he passed by on his way to a reception and dinner in his honour given by the Chancellor. Anastasia and I were going with him. I had, of course, arranged the connection. Well, actually it had been Debs. She had, after all, been my wife at the time and she had married me 'for richer or poorer'. I had married her for the 'richer' bit. We'd both come out ahead, and I'd moved on.

"Bobby is very happy with his team at head office. What about you, Nick?" asked Yusupov.

He didn't wait for a reply, he just saw the look on my face and turned away, nodding gently.

Our chairman was long on rhetorical questions.

40

Dinner with the Chancellor was a triumph.

A triumph of new-world plain speaking over old-world diplomatic obfuscation; of abundance over need.

The Chancellor and his advisers made very clear their eagerness to benefit from Kuikbakh largesse. Clear, in that very British way which, to most normal people, appears as though they are not remotely interested, let alone eager.

The Kuikbakh president made it all too fucking clear that his largesse was up for grabs. In fact, he waved it about wantonly in front of his hosts' noses, like a tart with a grumpy pimp.

Every time anyone mentioned a particular infrastructure project, Yusupov, who was seated between the Chancellor and Petra Marinelli, would put a term sheet for finance into one of their proffered hands and try to shake hands on the deal, then and there.

"We are very keen to help our British allies modernise their wonderful old, war-damaged Victorian infrastructure," he would say, trying to invoke the camaraderie of the two World Wars, while showing his appreciation for that long-gone era of history when Britain actually did rule the waves. In truth, the nineteenth century was the last time Britain amounted to anything remotely Great, in his not-so-humble opinion.

The Chancellor and his team very quickly learned to keep their hands in their pockets, which slowed the meal down a bit.

"I think we should leave that to our team in the morning," he would laugh, trying not to shake a proffered hand without causing offence. You could see the longing in his eyes.

Each document offered more than the amount required, on apparently very beneficial terms, through special-purpose vehicles set up specifically in order to keep it off the government books. As always, you had to admire the Kuikbakh. He had done his homework. Actually, Bobby and I had done most of it for him.

"But surely, we can agree in principle, Chancellor? I believe in the old English tradition: My word is my bond," he smiled, spreading his hands in supplication.

"My advisers will sort out the details later, with your people," he offered, gesturing at me.

"Mr de Carteret and his colleague, Mr Jones, are rapidly putting the Bank of Kuikbakhistan on the map. They have managed to recruit a number of top bankers, both here in London and for our head office in Szchymkent."

"Yes, I have been hearing about that," nodded the Chancellor, looking at me uncertainly, trying to recall if he had uttered any word which could be held against him as representing his bond.

"Very impressive. You are making some of our local institutions sit up and take notice."

"We are here to do business with you," whispered Yusupov.

I found myself nodding.

Outside, after dinner, Yusupov was sanguine.

"They will take up most of that finance. Trust me."

I didn't generally, but I was with him on this one. In fact, I would have taken bets on him being right.

I had to admire his animal cunning.

"You British are so easy to read."

He smiled at me, as one of that naïve and gullible race.

"I can see it in their eyes. They are desperate to get these projects started, without adding to their own debt," he was shaking his head.

"For most of it, we won't even ask for their guarantee," he chuckled, in that pleasureless way of his. "That way they can keep it completely off their books."

I could see that would be extremely attractive to a government like ours, trying to live beyond its means.

"No guarantees?" I asked. "Really?"

"Do not fear, Nick. I never fail to recover my investments. Those who benefit from my largesse always pay me back with interest," he assured me, adding quietly, "That is the price of their survival."

The threat could not have been clearer. The clarity of the message shocked me.

He moved on, without pausing for breath. "You westerners are so reluctant to improve your countries. In Kuikbakhistan, when we want a new airport we just go ahead and build one."

He clicked his fingers, as if bringing one to life. We both knew that was actually happening in his capital, as we spoke.

"And when my friends in the UK want one, then I just try to help them as best I can."

He emphasised the word 'friends', in a way which contradicted the meaning.

"Why on earth can you Brits not drag yourselves into the twenty-first century along with us?" he continued.

Perhaps because we have too much democracy, and not enough oil, I thought sadly to myself, beginning to imagine myself in his position of absolute and unconstrained power.

He smiled again. He seemed to be getting a kick out of these displays of financial and diplomatic muscle.

I knew where he was coming from. I had to admit, all this power was pretty fucking intoxicating. I had always found it so. If you had enough power, you were sure as hell not going to go short of cash, or sex for that matter. And right now, I could smell the power oozing its way over towards me.

I looked at him with renewed admiration and thought of all the times he had proved himself to be way ahead of me. I was learning fast, and this guy was still the master.

But my time would come.

41

Bobby and I were in heaven.

Well anyway, that bit of it reserved for guys like us.

We were running *The Bank* in town, which was making all the waves in the financial world.

It was soon accepted that, to get into BOK, you had to be so fucking smart your shit came out in algorithms; to last your probation period, you needed the physical constitution of an ox; to make it big you needed all that, neatly wrapped up in the hide of a dinosaur.

And when you made it through all that crap, an Elysian Field of blissful opportunities opened up to you.

I decided to institute the old Davenport 'D-club' system, for those who were definitely on partner track. Yusupov liked that, and took an immediate interest. He understood the importance of restricting our inner circle to those top performers who bought unreservedly into our philosophy; and getting rid of the rest.

I am not sure Bobby completely grasped it. He paid lip service, but when push came to firing squad, his trigger finger usually needed greasing. It didn't matter too much. I was running wing-man for him, and I did what was needed. I didn't always tell him.

To make the Club, you had to be fucking your best friend's grandmother on a regular basis; and charging her for the pleasure. Figuratively speaking, of course. Scruples were off limits.

That's why we called our clients 'grannies'. They were the ones who were usually getting screwed.

Most of the strategy was my idea. The board wasn't complaining.

Anastasia came up with a few good ones, as well. We were a tight couple, and we saw eye to eye on most things.

Of course, my eyes saw a few more sights than hers did, mainly down at the Klimax, but also with some of the new BOK recruits. They all understood how to get on in life, and who was I to deny them some top-class training?

We started with the old Davenport scam, pre-trading our clients. At least I didn't have to double up by jumping the gun on my own prop trading team, now that I was working for Yusupov. So, it was pretty fucking easy; and pretty motherfucking profitable.

One morning I was in the shower, thinking of the day ahead.

Nasta looked at me through the glass shower-door.

"You always know what you want, Nick, don't you, and you're strong enough to get it, unlike my poor father. You manage to keep one step ahead of your rivals, as you pick them off one by one."

She scrutinised me carefully. "Except Yusupov. You haven't worked him out yet, have you?"

The truth of her words made my chest tighten involuntarily, as I grabbed my towel.

"But you will, my darling, you will. I can feel it." Her confidence was important to me, and I leaned down and kissed her.

Talking of Yusupov always made me focus, and a sudden thought struck me. I needed to use every trick in every book, and one tome I hadn't even opened was Yusupov's finance minister. He was running a fixed exchange rate, which he had a habit of altering quite creatively, normally just before the oil price fluctuated. It always took the market by surprise.

I had a quick word in Bobby's ear, and suddenly we were plugged into the Kuikbakh government's financial strategy. We hid it well, under a barrage of complex derivatives, but the upshot was that, just before the Kuikbakh exchange rate or interest rates moved, or if Yusupov was going to say anything interesting to the press, we got in first and made a killing.

It was fun when you got used to it.

42

As often happens in life, one of our most profitable business ideas came from out of the blue.

Some family firm in Scotland, Duigald & Sons, was trying to build a name for itself, selling tweed clothing, whiskey and smoked salmon in America. When they got into problems, they came to me for more finance. I could see there was the makings of a good business. I just couldn't see the couple of public-school twats, who were running it, turning that into reality. I had been on the lookout for a situation like this, as I felt it could be a real money-spinner. Now I had found it, I was keen to be the one to champion it. I liked Yusupov to know that I was the main source of new ideas and thus profits for BOK.

My opportunity soon came. Yusupov, Bolat and Bobby were all at the business dinner that we always held before our ExCo meetings in London.

Yusupov had spent the early part of the evening ranting about the bad press he was getting in the UK.

"I provide them with all the finance they need, and still they treat me like a pariah."

"It's just politics," I assured him, as I always did.

"Do they not understand that I have a group of rebels in my country? If I do not bear down hard on them, they will only increase their terrorist campaign, and more innocent people will die."

I looked at Bobby, who took a less flexible stance with his chairman than I chose to do. He always managed to rile Yusupov, and I was worried where that might lead. I could see the warning signs as he began to get restless. I decided to pre-empt him, by raising my new idea. I knew it would go down well.

"There's money to be made out of good businesses which are badly run," I told them, going on to outline the situation with Duigald & Sons.

Yusupov and Bolat nodded; Bobby looked at me with that slightly wary expression which meant he thought I was crossing the boundaries of decency.

"I'm talking metaphorically, Bobby," I assured him. He shrugged, but I could see he wasn't wholly convinced.

"They're only a bunch of public-school twats, who were born with silver spoons shoved up their arses."

That just about got him onside. He didn't like anyone whose privileged existence arose from accidents of birth. He felt you should make your own way, through hard work and graft. I did, too.

"They like anything shoved up their arse, don't they, those public-school boys?" asked Bolat, laughing. That got Bobby going, but Yusupov didn't look too amused. Of course, he was a product of one of those schools.

Bolat remembered suddenly, and looked slightly relieved to see that Yusupov wasn't taking any notice. He was in his own little bubble. As always, he was just working out how to make something out of nothing.

"Under UK law there is an arrangement called 'pre-packing,'" I continued. I knew this would be right up Yusupov's street.

"I have heard of it," he murmured, immediately interested, all thoughts of human rights banished for the evening.

"When a business gets in trouble, its assets can be sold to the highest bidder quickly, to avoid it collapsing completely," I explained, glossing over the details. "Without paying off the creditors."

"So, if any of our banking clients get into problems, could we set up a company to take them over cheaply?" he asked, his mind whirring almost audibly.

"Absolutely," I replied, realising we were completely in tune. I would explain the legal requirements to him later, not that he would be too interested.

"Call in their loan," he directed quietly. "We need a team to take control of businesses like that."

Dinner didn't last long after that. Yusupov was thinking too hard to make conversation comfortable.

* * *

The next afternoon, all the ExCo members were seated round the boardroom table.

A secretary handed out copies of draft minutes.

Yusupov often liked to have the minutes printed before the meeting had actually taken place. We would then add a few things from the meeting itself, if anything important came up. In that way he ensured that the bank ran along the lines he set for it. We would debate anything we didn't understand and, very occasionally, raise concerns or opinions. Mostly, the drafts were signed unaltered.

The first point (following the peremptory acceptance of previous minutes and apologies for absence), dealt with the UK infrastructure finance.

The loans would all be channelled through BOK. We discussed a few technical points, and the issuance was duly authorised.

We then went briefly through all the various facets of the bank's business. It was all pretty routine.

"I have one more topic," declared Yusupov.

I looked down at my papers.

"I felt it better not to record this in the minutes," he continued, looking at me and Bobby.

"I have been looking into the feasibility of putting some of our weaker clients into pre-pack insolvency." He looked round the room but seemed to miss me. I had known that he would want to focus on this kind of manoeuvre in a big way. It resonated closely with what he had already done with much of his own country's major businesses – i.e. stolen them.

"You mean, like I suggested last night for Duigald & Sons?" I asked pointedly, hoping for some recognition, but quickly grasping that there would be none. This was his baby now. I don't think he even heard me. A little knot of anger and resentment tightened in my stomach.

"I have instructed our lawyers to set up a company called Curzon Asset Management. It will deal with all those businesses we are going to 'pre-pack.'" He beamed smugly. "Any businesses which cannot service their loans will be acquired by Curzon."

"Any questions?" he asked, looking round the table.

How the fuck do you have the nerve to walk off with my brainchild without any thanks or even acknowledgement? I wanted to ask, but I saw the expression on his face and swallowed my words. He wasn't in receive mode.

Bobby never bothered to hide his dissent. I couldn't decide whether he was braver than me, or just not so greedy.

"I am worried we run the risk of tainting our reputation." He was the only one who ever openly disagreed with the pre-printed minutes, or in this case, with Yusupov's wishes.

You could see the chairman didn't like that. "Curzon will be completely separate from the bank," he said in that quiet voice, which managed to convey such menace.

"The Kuikbakh connection will be obvious," persisted Bobby, raising his voice slightly. I had never seen such stubborn disagreement at ExCo. Nor had anyone else. The atmosphere was distinctly awkward, and I looked at Bobby with a warning frown.

"Then I suggest that you and Mr de Carteret set it up so that it is not obvious," he hissed, the formal use of my surname taking me back to earlier, less pleasant days.

"Hire the best people to run it, and get your…" he paused for a second and I thought he was going to swear. That really frightened me, but he controlled himself with difficulty, and continued, "…lawyers to make it work."

He got up abruptly and, with a withering look round the table, walked out.

The ExCo meetings always finished when Yusupov exited.

Bobby and I made our excuses, and headed to the pub.

"I can't believe he just did that," I moaned, the knot in my stomach twisting slowly.

"Steal your idea, you mean?" replied Bobby. "I'm surprised you're even surprised. That's what he excels at. Walking off with your ideas, and pocketing other people's assets. Two birds with one stone."

He shrugged and shook his head at me. "But what really worries me is that, if we overplay this one, it will ruin the bank's reputation along with yours and mine."

"We'll only do it in exceptional cases," I assured him.

"That's the way most of the major infrastructure in Kuikbakhistan disappeared into his pocket," moaned Bobby, and he was right. But after a couple of beers, and a reminder that his plane would soon be taking him back to Marina, he quietened down. She had miscarried, and he was desperate to see her.

I put my arm round him. Bobby would always be my mate. He was also a bloody good banker. I needed both of those, right at that moment.

43

Anastasia hired a couple of very accomplished venture capital guys in London and Szchymkent for Curzon AM, and they went out looking for young businesses with potential. We incorporated Curzon under a nominee company, based in my old friends, the British Virgin Islands. Our lawyers assured us there was absolutely no trail to connect it to the bank, ourselves, or Yusupov.

Just for good measure, I hired a firm of private detectives who specialised in that kind of thing, to see if they could find out who was behind it.

They drew a blank. Even Bobby was happy with that.

When the Curzon boys identified suitable targets, they tipped us off at BOK, and we went round and offered them finance for whatever they needed. It usually wasn't much, and hardly anybody else would give them anything (certainly not on the kind of beneficial terms we were offering).

Soon, new clients were coming to us in droves.

There was always a common theme: over-optimistic business plans, and onerous financing agreements, pushed on them by a range of greedy advisers.

The business owners worked their butts off. I almost felt sorry for them.

Once the companies had taken our money, we kept a close eye on them, as we could see, even if they couldn't, where the risks lay.

Often, they couldn't pay even the first balloon payment, which we built into our loan agreements, once the introductory rate had expired.

When they ran out of options, we just 'pre-packed' the business and replaced top management.

And who were we to complain, when the insolvency guys accepted that the only way to keep the business trading was for an immediate transfer of assets to Curzon Asset Management?

We sometimes let the owners retain some equity, if we felt they were worth keeping on as minority shareholders. They were so grateful it almost brought tears to my eyes. And, of course, they worked with renewed gusto.

To be fair, most of them managed to scrape by without us. I never really understood how. And some who didn't, got refinanced by other institutions.

But a good trickle of companies found their way into Curzon. With a change of focus, and often some new management, they prospered.

"I can't believe how our UK legal system makes it so easy," griped Bobby. "All that hard work, and then we can put these poor fuckers into liquidation and take them over, just because they over-estimated how quickly their companies were going to grow."

I cradled my glass, and nodded thoughtfully.

"What the hell were their advisers doing?" he fumed.

"Bigging up their client's potential probably, to increase their own fees," I replied, recognising the technique, as that was pretty much straight out my own training manual.

It was Bobby's turn to agree.

We both began to look at these voracious consultants with new-found admiration. I would have liked to sign them up to work for the bank, or at Curzon, but that would have given our game away.

Luckily, the bank was growing so damn quick, that the clients we actually ditched in this fashion made up only a tiny proportion, and thus didn't make any major waves.

The Kuikbakhs simply followed the UK's lead. Kuikbakh corporate law virtually mirrored the UK template. Nobody could complain about that. Of course, their interpretation of it was slightly more lax. But that's what happens in frontier economies.

Bobby didn't like it, and he continued to make his feelings clear to me. I tried desperately to keep his doubts strictly between us. I didn't always succeed.

The Curzon guys came up with another, completely legal, scam. They looked for asset-rich companies and acquired them with loans from BOK, secured on those same assets. In that way, the company paid the full costs of the acquisition, and we extracted any remaining profits as dividend. What more could you ask for?

What with the bank's explosive growth, I just about managed to keep Bobby onside. The evolution of his own finances helped of course; along with Marina.

Truth be told, he hadn't really stood a chance. Nobody could have turned down the inducements put under his nose. Fuck it, nobody in their right mind would have wanted to.

Now, he was in too deep to go back. I sometimes felt bad when I woke up in the night and thought of him out in that godforsaken place, slowly selling his soul.

But he was getting the important things in life: lots of successfully completed deals, approbation from those who mattered, a warm bed and more money than he could have dreamed of, with all the benefits that come from that.

I promised myself that I would always be there for him, if the shit ever hit his fan. Mostly, I tried not to think about it.

All in all, I had to be pretty happy with life.

So was Yusupov. That made things easier.

But Bobby finally passed his breaking point.

We 'pre-packed' a business belonging to one of his old friends, John Barney.

When the bank almost immediately got it firing on all cylinders without him, John started to holler. With a bit of help from Marina, Bobby got over it quicker than I had been expecting.

Until John's wife left him, and he killed himself.

PART FOUR

FRIENDS DISUNITED

44

The bank's AGM was held at head office in Szchymkent, with Yusupov presiding. The boardroom was easily big enough. After all, the bank was only quoted on the Szchymkent stock exchange, and while there was a smattering of shareholders present, I couldn't see any who weren't old friends of the president.

Bobby gave a quick rundown on results and progress to date, all of which were dazzling. Nobody asked any difficult questions.

Niceties, such as the directors' remuneration, were nodded through without a murmur.

The statement issued to the press could best be described as flamboyant. But then, so were the results. Everyone involved was doing very nicely.

Afterwards, the board retired to the dining room for a congratulatory lunch. The mood was ebullient.

During coffee, Yusupov rose to his feet. There was immediate silence.

"Thank you, gentlemen," he started quietly, looking round the room and nodding almost imperceptibly at each board member in turn. He knew how to work a room.

"A magnificent first two years under our new management."

That was high praise indeed.

He then singled out Bobby, as I had asked him to. He took my advice on certain specific matters like that. Yusupov understood how to motivate people, which was good, as unmotivated people did not do well in any of his institutions.

I was keen that Bobby should remain in his good books, rather than landing up under one of his new motorways. I felt responsible for my friend, especially after the recent loss of his friend John Barney. But, I couldn't stop him becoming a lot more open in his criticism of the bank's tactics, and that worried me.

Bobby looked chuffed, and managed a smile. But I could see he wasn't totally happy.

Yusupov went over the main areas of business he wanted to develop. He especially liked the pre-pack scam.

The particular facet of it that he liked so much was, of course, the ability to put a potentially healthy business into liquidation and take it over, under what he described as 'that pre-pack procedure we have created, on the advice of our magic circle lawyers in the UK'.

He liked that 'magic circle' bit and smiled benignly... well, at least he smiled.

Yusupov found this procedure almost too good to be true.

Many of the major Kuikbakh businesses had already been brought under his control.

But, when he mentioned some of the UK and European businesses that he now envisaged getting his hands on, I made a mental note to have a word with those 'magic circle' lawyers. They needed to make sure that he had some inkling of the limitations to their particular brand of sorcery.

I was responsible for the UK operations, and I could see that he had every intention of pushing 'pre-pack' liquidations to situations where not only the regulators, but also the police and fraud squad, would begin to squeal.

What Yusupov had in mind could easily blow the lid off our hard-earned sheen of respectability.

And in the UK, I was going to be first in the firing line. I felt a bit hot, and groped for one of my pills.

It was at that moment that Bobby put his hand up.

I mouthed "Not now" at him, but he had the bit between his teeth, and I could see he was pissed.

"I am also truly delighted at the way our business has been

going." He smiled at Yusupov, although there was an unfriendly edge to his voice.

Yusupov was no dummy, and his eyes narrowed, the lids lowering like a rattlesnake's in a sandstorm.

"However, I feel I have to take issue with some of the excesses of the pre-pack processes we are party to." He reached for his glass and took a swig of water.

There was complete silence. Now, everyone could see what was coming.

"You may all be aware that my good friend John Barney committed suicide recently."

Yusupov crossed himself, and some of the others followed suit.

"He did so, directly as a result of the despicable treatment his company received at the hands of Curzon Asset Management. A company not, I believe, entirely unknown to all of you."

He looked really angry now, and I realised this was make or break time for Bobby. Not to say for our friendship, and probably quite a bit more.

I rose to my feet and put my hand up when he tried to interrupt. His years of playing second fiddle in our relationship took their toll.

"What my friend Bobby is trying to say…" I raised my hand again, as Bobby barged in for a second time, "… is that we need to be very careful how we develop the Curzon business."

I chose my words extremely warily. I knew I was walking on hot coals.

"Bobby has suffered the loss of a close and dear friend, and is understandably upset. Also, his wife has recently suffered a miscarriage." I was playing every card in my hand. There was a slight ripple of sympathy, from all except Yusupov.

"However," I continued, "the point remains that while the 'pre-pack' procedure is often carried out in the UK with the full complicity of the law…" I could see Yusupov nodding, "… business in the UK relies not only on the regulators, but also, on the integrity of the players, and of course the quality of the advisers, to ensure that all transactions are fair and equitable."

I could see I was losing Yusupov.

Bobby couldn't help himself and butted in, his voice raised. "And if anyone has any doubts in the UK, they can always resort to an impartial and impregnable legal system, backed by a law-abiding police force for full redress of any injustices suffered." He banged his fist on the table.

Yusupov was now seething.

"I hope that Mr Jones is not impugning the integrity of my bank," he raged.

Looking directly at Bobby, he threw the red wine from his glass in an angrily measured sweep across the white tablecloth, and then smashed the empty glass against the silver candelabra in the middle. Bobby covered his face, as shards of glass flew around him.

"Or my country."

For the first time since I had known him Yusupov was losing control of his temper. His face was white; his scars a rich crimson.

He flung his napkin towards Bobby, and walked out.

Lunch was over.

45

I pushed Bobby into a taxi, and gave the man his address. I needed to talk to him with Marina there, too. I wanted to see exactly where her loyalties lay.

"That little cunt," he ranted.

I held his shoulders firmly, closing the glass partition so the taxi driver wouldn't hear his president being slagged off. That amounted to treason in Kuikbakhistan, and informers were everywhere. Not that Yusupov was in any doubt as to Bobby's feelings about him.

"I'm going to fucking kill him."

"Don't throw it all away, Bobby," I pleaded. Because that was what he was doing.

We arrived at the house, and the door was opened immediately by one of his people, who must have been watching out for us. Bobby stormed in, throwing down his things on the hall floor. He poured himself a drink and offered me one.

I shook my head.

"Just go with the flow, Bobby. Keep wafting on, as you yourself always say. If you carry on like this, you'll land up in one of his prisons. Believe me, you don't want to go there. We can sort this out, but please, just trust me."

I was holding his arm, but he shook me off angrily.

"The guy's a fucking crook, Nick. He doesn't give a shit about you or me." He was shouting now, and Marina came in, looking worried.

"He's just using us to build his empire. Fuck, he's using the British government, too. There's no limit to his ambition. Look at the cash he's pouring into all those infrastructure schemes. And if any of those don't go entirely to plan, he'll land up owning them too. Fucking little shite."

Marina was looking at me with real concern.

"I agree that we need to rein him in a bit, but we're riding on his coat-tails, Bobby. Just remember that. Look at all you have here."

I waved my hand around his plush sitting room.

"Look at your paycheque the next time you have any doubts. Look at how people treat you now. Yes, we need to keep him under control, but, for fuck's sake, don't throw it all away for the sake of a couple of lousy failed businesses. We're using him, Bobby. Think of it that way."

I tried my 'honest Nick' stance, arms held wide open, as if to embrace him. But he'd seen that one too many times. Both from me and Yusupov.

"You're as bad as he is," he whispered. He was shaking his head forlornly, now; he polished off the whiskey and refilled his glass.

Marina took his drink and put it down on the table.

She held both his hands, and I could see that there was a real bond between them.

"Tell me about it, Rob. What's happening at the bank?" she demanded anxiously.

Bobby proceeded to spell out systematically his worst fears about what Yusupov was intending to do, both in his own country and also in the UK.

"And Nick is right behind him," he finished, with a venomous look at me.

"You must be careful, darling," whispered Marina. She was obviously worried for her husband. I was really happy to see that she seemed genuinely to care for him. She knew what her uncle and his crowd were capable of, and she obviously didn't want to see Bobby fall foul of them, as her father had. She clung to him desperately, willing him to give way.

"Nick?" She looked at me for help.

I was torn. I admit that I couldn't bring myself to contemplate throwing everything away that I had built up so painstakingly. I could see that under some interpretations (and frankly Bobby was invoking the very worst of these), the bank's activities were crushing a few fragile shells and treading on a few vulnerable toes. But that is how business works. The strongest learn to win, and those who don't have the skill and intelligence to succeed, or even a stomach for the fight, lose out. Evolution. That guy Darwin had worked it all out, studying some stupid birds in the middle of the Pacific Ocean. Survival of the fittest.

Which brought me back to Bobby.

Marina was calming him down slowly. She kept shooting me worried looks as she did so.

He eventually sat down on a sofa and she poured him another whiskey. I was relieved to see it was a weak one. He was rapidly regaining his composure.

Marina glanced at me and mouthed 'Go', with a fleeting smile to reassure me.

Bobby looked at me, and I could see the storm had passed. His expression was a mixture of penitence and confusion.

"I'm sorry, buddy. I over-reacted. I couldn't stop thinking about John, the poor fucker. Or our baby." He looked at Marina and held his head in his hands for a second. But then he got up, and I could see him fighting to get himself back under control. He took a deep breath.

"I know only too well that we're all in this together. I'll apologise to Yusupov in the morning. I'll explain how close John was to me."

I felt we were probably past the stage of 'Sorry, mate, I didn't really mean it', but I nodded approvingly, anyway.

A look of anger flashed across his face, and I thought we were off again, but Marina stroked his brow, and he was calm.

Then an unfathomable sadness took possession of him, and its intensity was such that I could almost feel it physically. He started to weep. I had rarely, if ever, seen that happen before.

I went over to him and hugged him hard. He appeared to cheer up. "Sorry, mate," he sniffled.

Marina accompanied me to the door, and I kissed her on both cheeks. It was the least she deserved.

"Call me if you need anything," I whispered. "Anything at all."

If anyone was going to get him back on track, it was her. I needed her to stay strong.

"He will be fine," she declared, with a hardness I had not seen before. "We will sleep, and he will do what is best."

She was obviously going to stay strong enough, I thought. A little flicker of doubt crossed my mind. On which side was that strength going to settle?

46

The next morning, by the time I got to the bank, it was as if nothing had happened. It was surreal.

Bobby was at his desk. Yusupov was sitting opposite him, cradling a cup of coffee, and they were discussing bank strategy like two old soldiers-in-arms.

Which is sort of what they were.

Except, last night, I could have sworn they were on different sides.

Yusupov's good humour was frightening, for someone who had so recently been an eruption-in-waiting. Frightening, but wholly in character. Controlled aggression. The control had been fraying at the edges a bit recently, and I had worried yesterday that he might lose it completely.

I wasn't quite sure where that would lead.

And I didn't particularly want to find out.

But the control was back.

I wondered, in passing, how the president of the country had time to show so much interest in BOK. But, as he looked up with a smile, I realised this was his little piggy bank; a pension scheme so fucking bountiful that to call it gold-plated would have been to debase it.

Bobby's behaviour was even more worrying. Last night he had gone from rabid fury, through clinical (almost suicidal) depression, to schoolboy-like contrition, all in the space of an hour.

And here he was, treating last night's adversary like an old buddy who had just saved his life.

I judged Marina with renewed admiration.

The presidential chauffeur-cum-bodyguard was looking at his watch apprehensively. His boss had a busy day, and he needed to get him on the road.

Yusupov got up slowly.

"Bobby and I have been going through some of the bank's assets which need performance improvement measures." He handed me a sheet with a list of names.

"He will fill you in. Some are in the UK. Make sure he gets your full cooperation, Nick."

And with that he was gone.

I looked at Bobby questioningly.

When the door closed, all I could think of to say was "Are you ok?"

Bobby nodded. "Marina made me see sense." He saw my expression and held his hands up.

"Ok. I was pissed off. Still am, if you want to know. But I can handle it."

He shook his head slowly.

"I just can't stop thinking about old John."

He focused again, and I looked down at the piece of paper Yusupov had handed me.

"Holy shit," I whispered, reading down some of the names. "Ekivastuz Energy; Kuikhkommertsbank. These are big fucking businesses, Bobby. I know they're struggling, but are you happy you can just 'pre-pack' them? There's going to be a lot of flak flying round here."

"Yusupov wants the Curzon boys to get their hands on them, and this is his home ground. So that's what's going to happen." He shrugged and gave me a rather wan smile. "I don't suppose it matters much to him, whether I help or hinder him."

There was an edge to Bobby's voice which I couldn't pin down; a jumbled fusion of surrender and defiance. It worried me, and I looked around the room to remind him that the walls had ears.

I turned the page on Yusupov's paper.

"Holy fuck, Bobby." I couldn't stop myself from shouting. Some of the team outside looked up hesitantly.

"Harbour Oil." I went on down the list, quietly now. "Greensleeves Engineering. That's one of the UK's main frackers. He's going to start a fucking war if we're not careful." I almost wanted Yusupov to get that message.

Bobby looked at me, and last night's forlorn look had returned.

"That's your list, Nick. I'll manage things here, as best I can. I know what needs doing. Marina will help me. But the UK businesses are your baby."

He looked at me, and for the first time since I had known him, I couldn't read him.

"Are *you* ok, Nick?" He flung my words back at me in an obvious challenge, suddenly full of defiance again.

Some of last night's anger was returning.

"You got us into this, Nick," he blazed. "I'll keep my end up here. But remember, we're in this together," he nodded at me, and suddenly he was his old smiling self. "Till death do us part."

47

My flight back couldn't take long enough. I didn't want to arrive.

I went over all that had happened, trying out every conceivable interpretation of Bobby's state of mind

Yusupov was, as always, crystal clear. He wanted to get control of most of the remaining worthwhile assets in Kuikbakhistan. Unfortunately for me, he was also now eyeing up some major UK ones as well.

I couldn't say I hadn't foreseen the possibility. He had chosen his targets well. Harbour Oil had made some silly exploration gambles, and the current oil price wasn't helping. Rumours had been flying around about its finances, but it was still a FTSE 500 business, and all hell would break loose if we played too fast and loose with it.

Greensleeves Engineering was the big white hope of the UK fracking industry. Not solid yet, but it carried the aspirations of the UK energy sector. Obviously, it had suffered at the hands of the green protesters and countryside do-gooders, but it was bound to succeed eventually; it was the only short-term path to UK energy self-sufficiency and if its temporary demise was ever traced back to Yusupov – and through him, to me…

I felt queasy just thinking about it, and swallowed one of my pills.

But then again, I reminded myself, I was going to make a personal killing out of this, when Curzon got its hands on them.

I made it to the office, just in time for the credit committee meeting.

"The meeting is in the new boardroom in the basement, Mr de

Carteret," smiled the receptionist, gesturing at one of the messengers. "Jonny will take you there."

Jonny directed me to the lift, which went down two floors to what had, only days ago, been largely unused storage rooms. There was a lot of renovation work, with Kuikbakh-speaking workmen excavating, putting in new walls and plastering, while others were installing some complex-looking wiring, covering it with plush finishing touches.

We walked along a wide corridor into a small reception area, and he pressed a button beside the door.

"Please stand in front of the camera, sir." He pointed to where I should position myself.

A red light blinked three times.

"Good morning, Mr de Carteret," intoned an electronic voice. "Please look directly at the blue dot on the screen."

There was a buzz, the lock clicked, and the door hissed open.

I went through and was in the anteroom outside the boardroom.

A secretary ushered me through into the credit committee, which was in full flow.

I normally chaired the meeting, but they had been told I would not make it back in time from head office. A Kuikbakh girl, who I knew only too well, Inzhu Alani, was running the meeting and she had obviously been briefed by her bosses. And I didn't mean Bobby.

"Are you happy to sit in as a spectator on this one, Nick?" she asked without blinking. "Mr Yusupov said you wouldn't be joining us."

That sounded altogether too final for my liking.

She seemed pretty sure of herself. Until very recently she had been taking my instructions lying down.

On the boardroom table.

I really went for her sultry good looks. They reminded me of Ahmed's daughters, and I enjoyed getting a bit of my own back.

Now she was taking orders from a higher power, and the

dynamics of our relationship seemed to have moved onto another, not altogether welcome, level.

"No problem, Inzhu," I agreed. I thought there might be benefits in watching developments at this particular meeting, without having to sign the minutes.

We quickly came to 'Impaired assets'.

"We have two major additions to the non-performing list," said Inzhu quietly.

I knew what was coming.

"Harbour Oil, and Greensleeves Engineering."

She looked across at the young Englishman who was the relationship manager for both of these. I felt sorry for him. His banking career was about to take a dive from the high board; and the pool was empty.

He shuffled a few papers nervously.

"Harbour Oil is a FTSE 500 business…"

"Was," interrupted Inzhu.

"Even if it has fallen out of the FTSE, it is still an important UK business, and we need to be careful how we are seen to deal with it," he soldiered on. "It's constantly making the news."

I admired his spirit. Inzhu didn't.

"We don't run our bank on charity, James. The rumours are everywhere. Can they repay us?" Her feelings on that were obvious from her tone of voice.

"They are going through a bad patch at the moment…" James held his hand up to stop her interrupting again.

He had my full respect now. Like the captain of the *Titanic*.

"Some unfortunate blank test-drilling off the Falklands, and a rig team abducted off the Somalian coast. Of course, the current oil price is not helping their cause…"

"Can they repay us?" Inzhu ignored James and was now addressing the chief risk officer, another Kuikbakh.

He replied briefly, in their own language, and Inzhu simply made a cross on her meeting notes.

She turned back to James who was looking thoroughly scared, as his two main clients headed for the scrap heap.

"Greensleeves Engineering."

She looked down a summary sheet and gazed questioningly at him.

"They don't look solvent to me, James." It wasn't a question, but James was a game one.

"They have had a lot of trouble with the Green lobby, but they now have licences for three exploration sites in Hampshire and Dorset."

"Do they have any proven reserves?" asked Inzhu quietly.

"It doesn't quite work like that," smiled James, making the mistake of patronising her.

"I take that as a no," she replied quietly, turning to her CRO again.

I had to admit that she was turning me on the way she was managing this show. I wondered if we might have time for a little aperitif before lunch.

After another brief conversation between the two Kuikbakhs (the exact meaning of which was beyond me, although the conclusion only too clear), she put another cross in her notes and turned to me.

"Of course, we will need your sign-off, Nick," she smiled, with a hint of enticement.

"Could I have a minute with you alone?" I replied, as nonchalantly as I could.

She looked at me with those dark flashing eyes, and nodded slowly.

"That will be all for today," she directed. The others got up and left.

I moved on her quickly, pushing her onto the table, but she put her hands on my chest, sitting upright, her eyes an inch from mine.

"Things are changing here, Nick," she smiled confidently.

Whatever else may have changed, I was relieved to see that same lustful look in her eyes.

"Mr Yusupov has promoted me to deputy general manager of the London office."

"Congratulations," I breathed, grabbing her.

"I report directly to him now."

That brought me upright. The look on my face made her smile. I couldn't tell whether in sympathy or amusement.

"To Yusupov?" I echoed lamely.

"So, I won't be taking orders from you anymore, Nick," she whispered sexily, confusing the hell out of me.

"But first would you sign this?" She leant across me and pulled one of the papers out of her folder.

It was a letter to our solicitors, instructing them to proceed with an order in bankruptcy against Harbour Oil and Greensleeves Engineering. It had already been signed by Yusupov as chairman.

"Holy fuck," I muttered.

"Only when you've signed it," whispered Inzhu, nibbling my ear.

"What if I don't?" I probed.

"Then neither Mr Yusupov, nor I, will be very pleased with you," she breathed, continuing to chew my ear. She knew she was driving me crazy.

I persuaded myself, pretty quickly, that the letter would be effective whether I signed it or not; whereas I was going to need to change my trousers if I didn't.

I took out my pen.

Inzhu was quick. She stashed the letter with my signature and had our clothes off in a blur. She would have made a great pickpocket I thought, mentally checking the contents of my jacket for anything incriminating.

I gently lowered her head, but she shook it, and lay back on the table.

"My turn, Nick," she panted, pulling me down on her.

Of all the girls at the bank Inzhu was the one who really got my juices going. I think she felt the same way.

As she came, she hammered her fists on my shoulders, and

shouted a couple of expletives in her native tongue. I thought the entire bank would hear us. I looked round and covered her mouth with my hand.

"You want everyone to know how much fun you're having?"

"Don't worry," she moaned, pulling me back onto her and draping her legs over my shoulders.

"I told you things were changing round here."

"You already said that," I said giving her exposed buttock a slap. She yelped.

"Yusupov has had this room soundproofed."

And probably fully wired up, I thought to myself, involuntarily brushing a hand through my hair and looking round for cameras.

"He's decided to run his new business from here."

"What new business?" I asked, not sure if I wanted to know what business of Yusupov's would require a soundproofed, secure room.

"His import-export company. It's called 'Bakhtu Basics'."

"What does it deal in?" I asked.

She shook her head. "No idea."

I could see she was lying.

48

When BOK made a move, we didn't hang around. That was how Bobby and I worked. It was also how Yusupov did. That's why, most of the time, we all got on so well.

However, Bobby and I always had a very firm set of red lines we wouldn't cross. Those lines may have been way further down the track than many people would have chosen; some would say out of sight, but they were there.

Yusupov didn't understand the concept of red lines.

That's where it all started to go wrong.

So, when the senior partner of Anstruther & Gough, our magic circle law firm, rang me personally to say he was worried about the 'latest developments', and I had to admit to him that I was too, we both thought it was time we had a quick coffee on neutral territory.

James Gough had a withered left foot from a sporting accident in his youth. He was absolutely charming. He was also volcanically bright; an extremely dangerous mix in the wrong hands. The success of his sixth-generation family law firm was a testament to his talents. I really liked him. I think he returned that sentiment, but he was always the first to disapprove of any devious activities. He disapproved quite a lot, but we still managed to work well together.

"Good morning, Nick. Coffee?"

James was never one to rush things, and we talked about the usual bullshit, from the weather to the results of his football team, until I was almost jumping up and down with impatience. Snapper loved James, who always gave him a biscuit, but he could feel my tension and kept humping his leg, and whining.

I think that may have helped push things along because finally, he came to the point.

"I am a little worried about this instruction I have received from your head of legal." He handed me a document which I immediately recognised as the one I had signed under 'duress' on the boardroom table.

"And even more so, if you tell me you have your doubts about this course of action." He looked at me and raised his eyebrows. "Although your signature is at the foot. Together with Mr Yusupov's."

There was a pause, as he examined the document carefully. "That is your signature, Nick?"

There was no point in bullshitting. I nodded.

"I had no choice, James," I said quietly. Not strictly true I suppose, but Inzhu had certainly made a sufficiently forceful case at the time, for me to be able to square the partial truth with my, admittedly rather pliable, conscience.

"You realise there will be a violent reaction to a foreign bank pulling the plug on two quite…" he paused, as was his style, "… shall we say 'newsworthy' British companies?" He raised his eyebrows at me.

"I am very well aware of that," I replied forcefully. "Not least because I am the head of that bank's London office, and most of the 'violent reaction', as you put it, is going to land up on my doorstep."

The truth of my own words brought a clarity to the situation that I had not fully appreciated until then. James often seemed to do that for me.

"The other communication I have received, which is relevant to this case, is from Curzon Asset Management."

Our eyes met, and I knew he could see that Curzon was a name I was familiar with. Of course it was.

"They have put in an offer to acquire all the assets, in the event that either of the companies is put into receivership. Currently the best offer we have. I see you recognise that name, Nick," he said, his eyes narrowing slightly.

"Curzon has a very complex ownership structure." He was looking intently at me, and I shrugged and put on my best poker face. "So complicated, that we could not identify the beneficial owners, although I believe they are registered in the BVI."

That was probably no surprise to either of us.

"I am a little perplexed as to how they came to be aware so quickly that both these companies might be put into receivership," he continued warily. "I don't suppose Curzon is in any way related to Mr Yusupov, Nick?"

If I hadn't been expecting the question, the expression on my face would have told him all he needed to know. As it was, I just managed to portray a sufficient touch of surprise to allay his fears.

"Not that I know of, James," I managed, raising my own eyebrows. "I have heard the name somewhere I think, but I can't remember exactly where."

After a long pause with our eyes locked, he nodded almost imperceptibly.

"Because if Curzon is successful in their 'pre-pack' acquisition, and any link with Mr Yusupov becomes public, I personally, would not want to be located in the UK if I had any connection with Kuikbakhistan."

He pushed Snapper down gently, his message clear.

"Does your bank wish me to proceed with this order in bankruptcy, Nick?"

I considered for a second whether this might be the moment for me to come clean and make a total break with all things Kuikbakh.

But, then I thought of the bonus I had agreed with Yusupov on completion.

And my carried interest in the soon-to-be revived Harbour and Greensleeves…

I nodded, and made myself as clear as possible.

"Go ahead, James," I instructed him. "We are virtually the only creditor, apart from a few small suppliers. This Curzon outfit seems to want them, so get that 'pre-pack' completed as fast as you can. My bank can't be looking backwards when their customers screw up."

49

There were a few pithy comments in the financial press, over the following days, about foreign banks ruining solid British businesses. My twitter account took a beating, and there were a few reporters camped outside the bank, not to mention my house.

Mostly, I ignored them.

I had to appear on a few news programmes, and I got pretty adept at doing my 'honest Nick' routine for them.

It was all beginning to calm down, as I had predicted it would.

The creditors' meeting to approve the 'pre-pack' was set for Friday.

On Tuesday afternoon, I got a call from James Gough.

"Good morning, Nick," he started, and I was preparing myself for the normal niceties, but he cut straight to the chase.

"I thought you would like to know that we have a better offer for Harbour Oil and Greensleeves Engineering. The insolvency administrator is very keen, and is advancing the creditors' meeting to tomorrow afternoon, as he feels time is of the essence if he is to keep the businesses trading."

"Who is it from?" I asked, and the panic in my voice was probably evident.

"Netherby Investments." He paused. "Does that name ring any bells, Nick?"

The truly frightening thing was that it didn't. It was probably some group of Brits trying to hang onto the family jewels. There had been a few rumours.

"Never heard of them," I whispered, not wanting to hear myself admit it. "But that doesn't change things. BOK is still the major creditor, isn't it, James?"

"Absolutely," he replied. "The only significant one. And yes, you are right, you could choose whichever offer you prefer."

I let out a relieved sigh.

"However, I should tell you, their offer is significantly higher than Curzon's, and they are also offering to give the original shareholders some equity."

"What the hell are they doing that for?" I shouted.

"I assume, with a view to keeping on the existing management team, who they obviously value," he replied. "And not completely ignoring public opinion.

"You can see the headlines, Nick. 'British-backed consortium bails out Harbour and Greensleeves, after they were bankrupted by the Bank of Kuikbakhistan.' It has a good patriotic feel about it." James obviously sympathised with this Netherby outfit.

"Who's behind this outfit?" I asked.

"I had been hoping you might be able to tell me that, Nick," he replied, obviously doubting my previous denial.

I could see I was going down in James' estimation. Either he felt I was so fucking stupid I would forget I had just denied knowing them, or he thought that I was an out-and-out liar who would change his spots in the space of a single conversation.

"Can you find out?" I asked.

"We can certainly try. But, if their tracks are as deeply buried as Curzon's, we may find that difficult. Especially in the timeframe available."

"Well give it a fucking good try," I suggested, hoping that my profanity would give his task the necessary impetus.

"I will report back to you," he said, frostily. "You may want to ask your Kuikbakh friends if they have anything to do with this, Nick." He paused. "Either Netherby or Curzon." He put the phone down.

I rang Bobby immediately and relayed the information.

Bobby didn't sound at all surprised. It was almost as if he was expecting it.

"You do realise this means Curzon won't get control of them?" I shouted. "The administrator is going to allow this fucking Netherby outfit to take it out from under our noses."

"So, you mean Yusupov won't get control of Harbour or Greensleeves, Nick," he said, too quietly for my liking. "Will that keep you awake at night? I expect you will lose out a bit, won't you? As for me I have a large grin on my face, just thinking about it."

I will admit he was right. I was thinking of my bonus and carried interest spiralling down the toilet, and I wasn't thinking too straight about anything else.

"Do you have anything to do with this, Bobby? Please tell me you don't," I whispered, suddenly realising that he might actually be behind it.

There was a long pause, and then he said in hushed tones, "I don't stand to benefit, if that's what you mean, Nick. Frankly, I've made enough to last me and Marina two lifetimes. I have you to thank for that. I don't need any more."

He paused for effect.

"Nor do you."

I was hardly hearing him.

"If you don't stand to benefit, then who does, for fuck's sake?" I asked, in exasperation.

"John Barney's son, Charles, is the major shareholder in Netherby. I helped him put a bid together. He's an oil man, and he has just the team to make both of them work. In fact, he knows the founders and management of both companies, so he's the perfect white knight for them. He's going to make the millions that John should have done, if fucking Yusupov hadn't come our way."

I was speechless. Mainly at the thought of my financial loss, but also at the danger that Bobby was putting himself into.

"BOK is virtually the only creditor, Bobby. The bank can insist on Curzon getting the thumbs-up, even if it doesn't appear to be the best deal for us. I intend to place the bank's vote for Curzon at the creditors' meeting tomorrow."

There was a long pause.

"Bobby?"

"I think you've forgotten who is the bank's CEO, Nick. I've already instructed both the administrator and James Gough, that the bank's favoured bidder is Netherby."

"Are you fucking crazy, Bobby? Yusupov will make sure that Curzon gets the deal. For Christ's sake, see sense. You'll be dead meat, Bobby. He'll put you through the mincer and sell what comes out, vacuum-packed in one of his supermarkets."

There was a poignant silence, only broken by my breathing.

"Only if you tell him, Nick."

My breathing stopped.

"You wouldn't do that, would you, Nick?"

50

In times of stress, I have always found that sex is the best solution. Often, the only one.

And right now was such a time. I was shaking like a leaf, and popped a couple of my pills.

Our latest plans were going up in smoke, and the only way I could avoid that was to warn Yusupov.

If he ever found out that Bobby was behind the Netherby guys, my friend would be a goner. Yusupov didn't like traitors.

This was a dilemma. A pretty fucking major one.

I called Inzhu, but she was out, and none of my other regulars were available, so I headed down to the Klimax club to clear my head.

I took two of my favourites into a VIP room, and they started on a raunchy pole-dancing routine. They turned each other on almost as much as they did me. I think they swung both ways, and that was fine by me, as long as they didn't get too carried away to swing back again when I needed them.

As they gyrated over and into each other, I downed a couple of drinks.

My mind was racing.

Bobby was being an arsehole. He had always had that tendency. He lacked staying power when things got tough. Anastasia told me it was a decent quality, but I couldn't see that. Of course, her father had been like that. Starting something big and then not finishing it off; how could that be decent? Fucking idiotic, more like.

This time, he really was playing with fire.

And he had put me in one mother of a quandary.

I had two simple choices.

I could let Bobby fuck up our deal with Curzon, and allow his friends to run off with Harbour and Greensleeves.

In which case, it could be curtains for me and Bobby if Yusupov found out how it happened. Which he would.

Or I could warn Yusupov what was coming, so he could get the board to overrule Bobby. In which case, it might well be curtains for my buddy. But I would keep him out of trouble. He was, after all, doing what he thought was right.

Misguided, but right in his book. Surely, Yusupov would understand that? I would fight Bobby's corner. Together we would be ok.

I'm not sure I was wholly persuading myself.

My head was spinning, so I ordered another round and moved in on the girls.

It has always amazed me, how the execution of some basic bodily functions, after a few shots of alcohol, can bring clarity when you are faced with even the biggest disaster. A thought meandered across the back of my mind that perhaps the booze was doing more clouding than clarifying, but I swatted that one away without difficulty.

I set about the girls as if they were the cause of all my problems. They were very appreciative, and as I was pleasuring them every which way and back, I remembered what Bobby had said to me.

"I've made enough to last me and Marina two lifetimes. I have you to thank for that, Nick. I don't need any more."

I think he had mentioned something about me having made enough as well, but that was silly. The past was over. What mattered was doing the next deal; more money in the bank; more notches on my bedpost. I could never get enough of those. I wasn't in the mood to stop now, even if Bobby was.

Suddenly, my decision was made for me. I shooed the ladies out of the VIP room and called Yusupov.

He would just be getting ready for the day. I hoped I wasn't going to ruin it. I needed to find out what he knew about Netherby and try and cover for Bobby. Was it my duty to tell my chairman, if he didn't already know? I would see how he reacted when we spoke.

The phone rang, and his house secretary answered. She put me through.

"Yes?" he said in that neutral tone, which could mean absolutely anything.

I breathed in.

"Good morning," I said, to give myself time.

"No, it is not a good morning. It is a very bad morning, when the CEO of my bank decides to collude with his friends and act in complete opposition to the best interests of all our stakeholders."

That really floored me. He knew already.

I thought I had better cover myself, and got it all out quick.

"I was just going to say that Bobby thinks the bank's best interests would be served by accepting a new offer for Harbour and Greensleeves, from Netherby Investments."

I hurried on, before he could interrupt.

"I wanted to warn you, so the board could consider our options."

I added, as forcefully as I could, "Bobby only has the bank's best interests at heart, Tselmeg. I can assure you of that. The bank will benefit, as the Netherby offer is considerably better than Curzon's."

"For who is it better?" he asked coldly.

Before I could reply, he did so for me. "Not for me. Not for you. And, I can assure you, not for Bobby either."

"I know," I admitted with feeling, totting up my bonus and potential carried interest, which would run into hundreds of millions assuming the two businesses flourished under the tender mercies of Curzon and Tselmeg Yusupov. As we both knew they would.

"We will deal with Bobby, as we deal with anyone who throws our largesse back in our face," hissed Yusupov. "You and your friend continue to underestimate me, I see. But thank you for telling me.

I am interested to see that your own loyalty to an old friend can be so easily overcome with the prospect of a few millions. I hope your loyalty to me, as your benefactor, will not prove to be so fickle."

He put the phone down.

51

Things happened too fucking quickly after that. I rang Bobby immediately, to tell him that Yusupov was onto him. There was no answer, either on his mobile, or at home. The bank hadn't opened yet. I tried Marina, but got the message service.

I considered sending Bobby a warning text. But if Yusupov had got to him and had his mobile, that would be suicide. My altruism didn't stretch that far.

I went home. Nasta was asleep. I didn't feel like waking her.

I tried Bobby again in the morning, with no better luck. I did manage to speak to his secretary, who said he had a planned meeting out of town. She hadn't spoken to him, but was due to do so later.

There was nothing for it, but to wait. I had plenty to do.

James Gough rang me just before twelve.

"Netherby has pulled out, so that leaves the field open for Curzon," he informed me, his tone uncharacteristically cold.

"How's that?" I asked, with a nasty feeling I already knew.

"Apparently their CEO, Charles Barney, has contracted Ebola, somewhat out of the blue. They do not believe he will survive."

"My god, how awful," I blurted out, not managing to inject enough surprise in my voice to satisfy either of us. Barney and Bobby had been playing with fire, and although I had not foreseen this, the reality was so obvious I should have known it was coming.

There was a long and uncomfortable silence.

"Apparently, he had never been near an Ebola-infected country. His team are perplexed. I don't suppose you know anything about that do you, Nick?" he breathed. "Nothing to do with your friend Yusupov?"

"James…" I started to explain, but thought better of it. I was not sure I had the words to convince him. My priority was to warn Bobby.

I left him with a curt, "I have to go."

I rang Bobby's mobile again.

He answered immediately.

I could hear Yusupov in the background.

Bobby sounded nervous.

But he was alive.

I heaved a sigh of relief.

"How is it going?" I asked him urgently.

"Yusupov's not happy," whispered Bobby. "He discovered my connection to Netherby. You didn't tell him did you, Nick?"

"No," I assured him. "He found out himself. He was always going to, Bobby. You need to be more careful."

"Thanks for that, mate," he murmured gratefully. "I just got carried away with thoughts of old John. Guess I wasn't thinking. Anyway, he seems to understand where I'm coming from. I didn't expect that, Nick. He says he admires strong leaders, who stand by their friends."

"He never ceases to surprise me," I agreed, wondering whether Yusupov's assertion was aimed disparagingly at me.

"Netherby had to pull out," continued Bobby. "Charlie is really ill. Can you make sure he's got everything he needs, Nick? I'll pay for anything. I feel responsible for that family. They've gone through a lot of shit, and most has resulted from dealing with BOK." He sounded drained of all emotion. At least he wasn't having one of his anti-Yusupov rants.

"Of course, mate. I'm here for you, Bobby. Anything you need, I will do it. I mean anything, mate."

"Thanks. Have to go," murmured Bobby wistfully. "Wish me luck. I love you, mate."

I had never heard Bobby say that before and it worried the shit out of me.

"Hang in there, Bobby," I said, willing him to do so.

52

Nasta woke me from a deep and troubled sleep. She handed me my phone, which was ringing loudly, with Bobby's 'Oranges and Lemons' call-sign.

"They tried to fucking kill me," he screamed. I could hear the sound of honking horns and I realised he was hands-free in his car.

"Where are you?" I shouted back, my pulse racing, as I jumped out of bed.

"I was on my way into the bank, when some bastards jumped me at the lights. Tried to pull me out of my car."

I heard squealing of tyres, punctuated by expletives from Bobby.

"Have you lost them?" I asked, feeling totally impotent.

"Managed to slam the door in his face and took off. Lost them for the moment."

He screamed at someone, and there was a lot of hooting.

"What the fuck do I do now, Nick? Yusupov wants me out of here. And I thought we were over that. He seemed ok, after we thrashed it all out."

"Have you lost those hitmen?" I repeated.

"Think so," he said, sounding calmer.

"Can you get a flight out?" I pondered.

"He'll have an alert out for me," replied Bobby. He was sounding desperate.

"I'm going to try the back roads to the border."

"Bobby, if Yusupov had wanted you dead, he would have done it quietly, when you met at the bank, or at home. He doesn't hang around."

Then I had a thought.

"Where's Marina?" I asked.

"She's meeting me on the outskirts of town in twenty minutes."

I was trying to tie up loose ends, like a blind man scrabbling on the floor for marbles. I still wasn't sure whose side Marina was on.

To be completely honest, I was playing with the idea that Yusupov wasn't the one behind this attempted kidnap. In fact, I was praying he wasn't.

I didn't believe he would dispose of either me or Bobby. We were his face of western respectability, although I had never in my wildest dreams thought Bobby and I would be that to anyone. Which made me realise how far we'd come; or perhaps, how low we'd fallen.

"Are you sure its Yusupov who's behind this, Bobby?" I asked.

"Are you fucking crazy, Nick? Who the fuck else do you think might be behind it? Santa Claus?"

I persisted. "What about Marina, for instance? Didn't her father oppose Yusupov before he came to power and disappear? Are you sure she's with you, Bobby?"

That was probably a mistake, but I needed him to consider all the possibilities. I wanted to make sure he was playing with a full deck.

It really got to him.

"For fuck's sake," he screamed.

There was a brief silence, and then he spoke quietly and slowly.

"I have been worrying that I've lost you, Nick. Marina has been saying so for a few months. Now, I know she's right."

"I'll talk to Yusupov, and make him see sense," I offered lamely, wanting to take back my doubts about Marina, while at the same time, making a mental note that she was bad-mouthing me to Bobby.

Bobby wasn't listening to me anymore.

"He's hooked you, Nick, hasn't he? You have so much skin in his game that you can't think straight. How much do you stand to make out of Harbour and Greensleeves? A few tens of millions in bonus…?" He paused. "Or do you call it commission, for enabling Curzon to 'pre-pack' them?"

He was in full flow. "And then the 'carried interest' when Curzon ramps them all the way up the FTSE. How much is that worth to you, Nick? Are we talking millions or billions? I don't think you can tell the difference, anymore. I am out here trying to stay alive, so you can carry on making money you don't even need. Fuck it, Nick, he's got you hook, line and sinker and you just can't see beyond the walls of the gilded prison he's buried you in, can you? You're as bad as he is."

I had to admit that he had something of a point. There was nothing I wouldn't do for Bobby, and I was going to talk urgently with Yusupov to make him relent. Or find out who was behind all this, if it wasn't him. But as long as I could keep everything ticking along on track, I was going to make so much goddam cash that I would be able to have whatever the fuck I wanted, wherever the fuck I wanted it.

I had to admit, that was certainly clouding my view.

"Bobby, I am going to talk to Yusupov straight away, and get all this sorted out. He's president of the country, for God's sake, and I swear he's not behind this. He will get his security people out to you, to escort you back."

"Don't tell him where I'm heading, Nick," Bobby screamed at me. "Don't tell him that I'm meeting Marina." His voice was breaking, and it was wrenching at my heartstrings.

"In fact, don't tell him fucking anything at all. I wish I'd never met you, Nick."

The phone went dead, and I felt Anastasia take my hand. She hugged me, and I don't think I had ever been so grateful for some human warmth in my life.

Those few last words that Bobby spat at me had brought my entire life flashing past me, like a drowning man going down for the third time. Which was, perhaps, what I was doing.

If my only friend could curse me like that, what point was there in resisting the waves that pulled me down? I felt despair.

"Who do you trust, Nick?" asked Anastasia. She would have heard the whole conversation, as she sat up beside me.

She looked at me and took both my hands, searching my eyes with a heartfelt smile, which invited me to offer up all my darkest secrets.

"Who should Bobby trust?"

We sat there in silence, with that pregnant question holding our whole world in the narrow space between us.

My brain began to function again, and I pulled my thoughts back from the desolation that tried to overwhelm me.

"I don't think he has any option, other than to trust Yusupov," I replied, trying to let go of her grip.

She wouldn't release my hands, or my eyes.

"Was Bobby right, Nick my darling? Can he trust you, or has he lost you to Yusupov?" She opened her eyes wide, inviting me in. "Have you sold your soul to him, so all you can see is the wealth that oozes from his every pore?"

I felt a flare of anger that she could accuse me of such disloyalty.

But her eyes and hands would not release me, and I felt again the desolation of a dying man, who knows he is failing.

I took a deep breath.

"Nasta, I swear to you, Bobby's only hope is with Yusupov. He is in the man's own country, and he will never get out of there if the president doesn't want him to. Marina's father was a rebel. She must be following in his footsteps."

"Are you sure?" queried Anastasia. "I thought you admired her."

"I did, but Yusupov showed me a security file which was pretty damning."

She raised her eyebrows and shrugged, as if just about giving me the benefit of the doubt.

"I trust Yusupov." The words came out, somehow without my guidance. I didn't know if they were true, or not. I just knew that they had to be, if my life was to be worth anything.

And if Bobby was to survive.

I picked up the phone.

Yusupov listened in silence, as I outlined what had happened and pleaded with him to send his security guys to save my friend.

"Tell me you're not behind this, Tselmeg," I whispered. "Bobby has been a great CEO, and BOK wouldn't be half the bank it is, if he hadn't been running it. You owe him that."

"I can assure you, Nick, that I have nothing to do with any of this. Bobby and I ironed out all our differences, and I have every confidence that he will go on to raise my bank to even higher levels."

I sighed with relief.

"This is a rebel gang, who have been agitating for independence for years. Kidnapping the British CEO of my bank would give them wonderful publicity for their cause. I will have them dealt with. Where did you say Bobby was headed?"

I felt the whole weight of the world on my shoulders at that moment. I was willing myself to believe that Yusupov was with us. As long as he was, then the Kuikbakh security services would be Bobby's salvation. If not, his death.

There was silence.

"Trust me, Nick. Have I not given you everything you ever dreamed of? Trust me in this, above all."

"He's headed by road to the border after he meets with Marina on the outskirts of town. That's all I know."

"Thank you, Nick. That is all I need. I will see to it that your friend is safe. We need to be quick. As you know, Marina's father was one of those rebels. He died in their cause. I had hoped she would not follow him. I was obviously wrong."

53

Anastasia and I followed what little news emanated from Kuikbakhistan, over the next few hours. There was not much. Of Bobby, there was nothing.

I could follow his progress on the smartphone app which linked us. He made a brief stop on the outskirts of the capital (I assumed to hook up with Marina), and then headed for the border.

Whether in Marina's embrace, or on the floor of her henchmen's vehicle, I could not know.

A few miles short of the border, he stopped again. He appeared to leave the road. After a few minutes of seemingly aimless meanderings, the phone came to rest.

I rang, but it didn't answer. I sent him a text, and one to Marina. There was no reply.

"They are hiding from Yusupov's people," declared Anastasia, hopefully.

"For God's sake, just survive, Bobby," I whispered.

We waited for half an hour, and still there was no movement.

We were beside ourselves. We had no way of knowing what was happening.

Finally, my phone rang. It was Yusupov, on a video connection. I took heart from the openness that implied.

I was wrong to do so.

"I am so sorry, Nick," he said, and the face on my screen did actually look contrite.

"What happened?" I probed, looking for any sign of deceit.

"My SWAT team got there at the same time as the rebels, who

arrived with Marina. There was a shoot-out. I am afraid that Bobby didn't make it."

I was in shock, my ears ringing.

"Are you telling me Marina was with these people all the time?"

I thought I saw a hint of embarrassment. Not a sentiment that came readily to him.

He nodded.

"I told you, her father was one of their leaders, until his death. We were watching them, but I am afraid they outsmarted us."

"Did any of the rebels survive?" I asked, hoping we may be able to get the truth out of them somehow.

He shook his head.

"So, we just have to take your word for it, Tselmeg? Is that what you are telling us?" shouted Anastasia.

I pulled the phone away from her, but I was also getting angry, as the realisation slowly dawned on me that Bobby was dead, and I had no idea who was responsible.

Apart, of course, from me.

I could see a flash of anger on Yusupov's face also.

"I hope my word is good enough for you, Nick, after all I have done for you. Even if not for your wife."

I held his gaze, realising, as usual, that he was holding all the cards. I was willing him not to be lying, but my faith was fraying at the edges. The truth was not going to come out of this one easily. I would just have to seek it out for myself.

"Perhaps you had better decide, here and now, Nick. Because if my word is not good enough for you on something as fundamental as the death of your oldest friend and his wife, then I have no doubt that you will not want to continue working at my bank."

He looked at me with that inscrutable, neutral glower.

"And indeed, I would not want you to. Choose now, Nick. I will completely understand, if you decide you have had enough. You have plenty of cash to retire comfortably. So, choose your path. Are you with me, or against?"

My mind was in turmoil.

Anastasia looked at me without expression, waiting for my decision.

I could feel my lips moving, and I heard the words flowing, although I could swear, I was not their author.

"Count me in, Tselmeg. I am with you."

54

Kuikbakhs take the death of their loved ones very seriously. And Bobby had become one of them.

The country was given a holiday for the memorial service, and Yusupov flew over most of the bank's UK management to attend it. The ritual was pretty impressive.

Of course, it was also fully charged political circus. A show of establishment solidarity.

Yusupov gave a stirring eulogy for Bobby. But he just couldn't stop himself merging it into a diatribe against the separatist rebels. His hate for them was visceral. His grief for Bobby less obviously so.

As I stood up to give my own homage to my old friend, I passed Yusupov. He shook my hand, and put his arm round my shoulder, in a gesture which the congregation would have taken for genuine sorrow and support.

As our eyes met, I had to admit I had no idea whether they were right, or whether I was in fact embracing my friend's killer.

His eyes appraised me candidly, as a flicker of a smile appeared. He squeezed my arm and motioned towards the lectern, where I was to put my friend to rest.

Again, the gesture was eloquent.

To the assembled dignitaries, it spoke of the all-encompassing care that their president offered to those he backed. To me, his eyes gave a different message. They said 'You are still mine. My golden honeypot holds you in its sweet embrace. It holds you so tight, you do not even want to discover who killed your friend. In case the truth might turn that nectar into venom.'

As my mouth spewed out the words I had prepared to honour Bobby, I looked down on my physical being, as if from above. I watched, as the speaker intoned the words which I, myself, had written. The speech was good. But it was hard to tell if it came from the heart.

"And lastly, Bobby would have wanted me to thank our benefactor, Tselmeg Yusupov and indeed, the entire Kuikbakh people themselves, who have welcomed him, and me, and our families so warmly into their country and their lives."

I looked up, feeling my complete self again and stared at Yusupov, who was still smiling.

I paused and looked around. There was that utter silence, which occasionally makes you wonder if some higher being is passing overhead.

"He would also have wanted to hear me say that whatever it takes, and whoever it affects, I will use every resource and power at my disposal to avenge his death, and to punish those who slaughtered him in the prime of his sweet life."

Yusupov nodded his approval, but his smile had vanished, and his eyelids narrowed, all emotion banished.

55

Our car took us back to the hotel and the driver parked cautiously in a VIP area in the basement car park. We went to our rooms, collected our things and checked out. We had opted for a commercial flight. "There is no way I am accepting a ride in that man's plane until we find out whether he killed Bobby and Marina," Nasta had declared.

As the lift doors opened in the basement we could see our car, parked and waiting for us. I turned towards it, raising my arm to hail the driver, but as I did so a large man in a dark hoodie almost knocked me over, slamming my briefcase out of my hand. My heart was pounding, and I desperately searched for escape options. I was reassured to see Nasta untouched and climbing into the back of the car.

Far from harming me, my 'aggressor' held a hand out to prevent me from falling and apologised profusely, in heavily-accented English. He brushed a couple of marks off my suit, where I had scraped the lift door.

Recovering my equilibrium, both physical and mental, I smiled back at him and reassured him that I was fine.

He stared intently at me and as the doors closed, I could have sworn I heard him whisper, "Take care of it."

My senses now completely alert, I climbed in beside Nasta and closed the door. The driver confirmed our flight details and we set off at her sedate pace. As she did so, I felt something in my pocket, and, feeling its outline gently, I recognised it as a USB memory stick. Remembering my warning from the lift, I let it drop back into the protective darkness of my pocket.

Nasta had obviously seen my brief encounter, but took it to be an everyday collision between scurrying travellers. "You're getting clumsy in your old age," she said, patting my knee comfortingly. I was relieved at her inference, and hoped any other prying eyes had come to the same conclusion.

I decided not to tell her about my souvenir until we were safely home. If, by any chance, airport security were on their toes, and if, as I suspected, its contents would not meet with Yusupov's approval, it would be better for all concerned that Nasta's surprise at its discovery should be genuine.

I tried to put it out of my mind.

56

I remained on edge for the entire trip. I was desperate to see what the mysterious gift in my pocket would reveal, and equally desperate that nobody else should. It was burning a hole in my jacket.

I tried to bury myself in work. Nasta asked why I was keeping my jacket on, and I snapped at her. She was, as always, tolerant and tried to comfort me with happy reminiscences. When that failed, she kissed my cheek and went to sleep.

We made it home in the early evening, and only when we had crossed our portal and locked the door behind us, did I begin to relax.

"I'm not getting old or clumsy," I informed her with a reproachful smile. "That guy who almost knocked me over by the lift at the hotel…" I pulled the memory stick out of my pocket. "I assume he was one of the rebels. He gave me this." I held it up for her to see. "He told me to take care of it."

Nasta stared at me. "I thought you were a bit tetchy on the flight. Thank God security was lax; and thank you for not telling me," she whispered, giving me a hug. "We have to run it right now."

I fired up my laptop and plugged in the memory stick. We sat down, not knowing what to expect. She held my hand.

Marina appeared immediately. She was standing against an indeterminate white background, looking straight at the camera.

"Bobby, my darling. If you are watching this, then I am in a better place." She paused. "I love you more than I can say, and the past few years with you have been the most blissful of my life. I am only sorry if I have not been able to leave you with a child of your own." There was a slight catch in her voice but, with a deep breath, she continued. "I have been supporting the resistance all this time, as my father did before me, and especially after that foul creature Yusupov assassinated our wonderful President Armenov. I think you sympathised with our feelings about Yusupov, seeing all the deceit, corruption and robbery going on at your bank, as well as in the country at large. I could not tell you, as I did not want to implicate you in any way. I hope you can forgive me." She sniffled. "If you are alive and well, then I beg you, pack your things and leave this godforsaken country. You have more than enough to live on and you will not be safe once I have gone." She looked imploringly at the camera, and it brought a tear to my eye. I could see Nasta was gushing tears.

The picture stayed focused, and Marina's face took on a desolate look. She said quietly, "If you are not watching this, then you too are gone, and may the Good Lord forgive me for what I have done." She crossed herself and the screen went blank.

"Oh my God," sobbed Nasta, hugging me. "I can't bear it. They were so happy together."

Before I could respond, the Kuikbakh national flag filled the screen and a female voice started in excellent English.

"Mr de Carteret, I am so sorry that your friend Bobby Jones has died. May he and Marina Sultanov both rest in peace. Marina was a martyr for our country. She very recently offered to approach 'The Pig', Yusupov, with an offer to broker a peace deal. We would not let her put her unborn child and husband in such danger, and another patriot was chosen. Yusupov knows that his time is coming, but he turned us down, laughing at us, even though we offered him free passage with all the wealth he has already stolen from us. The man will never be satisfied; he always wants more." There was a pause and Nasta shook her head at me in disbelief. Then another deep, male voice with a strong accent took over.

"I am afraid that 'The Pig' could never accept the criticism that your friend directed at him. Do not blame yourself; they could not have escaped, it was all too sudden; but now, watch how your friends died. May they rest in peace." There was a brief pause, as if in respect, punctuated only by Nasta's sobbing. He continued quietly, "And may Tselmeg Yusupov rot in the furthest depths of hell. We hope you will help us speed his journey."

There then followed a grainy video, probably from a drone, of a car careering down country roads through the bare hills of northern Kuikbakhistan, followed by a group of four-wheel drive vehicles, firing sporadically at their quarry. After a short while, the car lost control, whether from speed or a bullet it was hard to tell, and it was immediately surrounded by uniformed troops. Two bodies were dragged from the car and, whether dead or alive, the soldiers raked them both with bullets. The bodies jerked and writhed, like string dolls, directed by their twisted puppeteer.

The dolls were Bobby and Marina.

The puppeteer, revealed in all his nasty, venal brutishness, was Tselmeg Yusupov.

The voice continued, quietly insistent. "Help us, Mr de Carteret. Help us avenge your friend's death. Soothslayer will contact you."

PART FIVE

RETRIBUTION

57

Nasta and I were in complete shock. We couldn't think straight, let alone cook, so, once we had begun to get ourselves back under a semblance of control, we went to a local restaurant, the Casa Rosada, to gather our thoughts.

"The bastard," I hissed, clenching and unclenching my fists.

"Those rebels are right; there is nothing he won't do to further his ambition." Nasta shook her head. "We are all pawns in his little game."

"The man's psychotic, and I led them to him."

"Don't blame yourself, Nick. You did what you thought was right." She held her hand out to me.

"I want to kill him." I slammed my fist down on the table and glared round the room. A couple of diners stared at me, but turned away when they saw the expression on my face.

I looked up at the ceiling and then across at Nasta, shaking my head. "Where is it all going to end?" I whispered. "And Bobby said he wished he'd never met me."

Nasta winced, and reached out to calm me. "You know Bobby didn't mean that. He adored you." She gently stroked my cheek. "Don't blame yourself. The man in the video said they were already doomed. Yusupov had decided to kill them; they couldn't escape." She looked at me pityingly.

I shook my head, torn between anger, sorrow and despair.

"I can see how desperately you want to punish Yusupov." Nasta took a gulp of her wine. "And yet, you are so inextricably drawn to him. He's your doppelganger, isn't he?" She flinched as she said it;

whether at the depth of her implied criticism, or at the eruption she expected might follow, I don't know.

Seeing that I struggled for words, she changed the subject. "Have you noticed his left hand? It's not quite right. I wonder what happened."

"Probably a childhood accident," I replied distractedly, still considering her accusation. "And he's not my doppelganger; he's my nemesis. I suppose I was drawn to him, and he to me in some strange way; I don't know why or how. But that's all finished. It's history," I vowed. "He killed my best and oldest friend…"

Nasta nodded gently, and we were silent, each buried in our own frenzied emotions.

"But you don't need to help the rebels. He's doing your work for you. He is alienating everyone around him. Just listen to the hate in those recorded voices that we heard. There are so many who want to destroy him. Let them do it for you, Nick. He is so dangerous, and he's got nuclear weapons, too." She looked at me fearfully. "Do as Marina said in her message to Bobby, and leave the bank. Let Yusupov destroy himself."

I lowered my head and tapped my forehead against the table a few times, as if to clear my confusion. I looked up after a few seconds and held her gaze.

She leant over and kissed my temple, which was now sweating profusely.

I placed my hands on hers, to reassure her, and said quietly, "Right now, after what he did, all I want to do is kill that bastard with my own bare hands." I made as if to spit on the floor.

Nasta was shaking her head fearfully. "But he will destroy you first. He has the power to do it."

I breathed in deeply, and as I did so, I felt a ripple of serenity wash over me. I drew her hands together, inside mine, and gazed up at the ceiling.

"It's almost as though Bobby's here with us."

We were both quiet, and I swear I could feel his presence.

"I suddenly feel strong, almost calm, and so completely sure." I stared into her eyes which were inches from mine. "You heard the rebels on that memory stick; they are ready to topple him at any moment. I am going to do everything in my power to help them do exactly that."

"They're dreaming," said Nasta, contradicting her previous words and shaking her head frantically. "It will take time and resources beyond their means. Be very careful, Nick. He is so evil, and so powerful. Look what happened to your friend… our friends."

"I promise you, Nasta, I will stay out of harm's way, for you and Chloe." I touched her cheek. "Somehow, I can feel it. I know I will be safe, but I have to do this."

She still looked scared, but she realised I was not for turning, and her fear was mixed, I think, with a hint of pride.

"I am going to do anything I can behind the scenes to help those rebels overthrow him. I know he is strong, and he may survive their first attempts." I saw her flinch, and realised that my grip on her hands had tightened. I relaxed them and gave her what I hoped was a confident smile.

"And what if he destroys them? What then?" she asked. "What if one of them reveals your role?"

"I will be fine. I feel it in my bones. I know that's not much comfort to you, but at the very least I am going to meet these people, for Bobby and Marina's sake. If I believe they can do it, I am going to help them bring Yusupov down."

Nasta could see my resolve, but she couldn't help herself.

"And if they can't?"

"Then I'll find another means, and I'll do it on my own."

She winced again, this time out of fear, not pain.

"Don't worry, I won't antagonise him, I will work with the bastard, flattering him and bloating his ego, weakening him, suffocating him from the inside, learning every day how to be better than him at what he does, so that soon I can challenge him, and face him as an equal."

Nasta was nodding now, and almost looked relieved to hear some method to what she had worried was becoming my incipient madness.

"But, either way, that bastard's going to know before he dies, that when he murdered Bobby, he signed his own death warrant."

I was suddenly clear, and my mind was made up. For the very first time in my life, I felt the conviction, the self-assurance, of a man who knows his purpose in life.

58

By the time we got back to the house, we were emotionally drained. It was late, and we prepared for bed, but the phone on Nasta's laptop started to ring.

She picked up her phone, but that itself was silent, with no apparent activity.

She opened the laptop, looking puzzled.

"Want some help?" I asked, knowing the signs. She was fairly tech-savvy, but if something didn't work, she was inclined to keep pressing the same button harder. Right on cue, she hit the 'Delete' key several times. "Seems like I've got a piece of dodgy-looking spam, making a call sound without any call. I'm trying to delete it, but it won't go away." She jabbed the delete button again.

I looked over her shoulder, and took the laptop from her, excitedly.

"It's from Soothslayer. That's who the rebels said would contact us. They're using your laptop, as mine's a bank one."

With only a hint of misgiving, I opened the message. It started to play an old Muddy Waters track which was one of Nasta's favourites. We looked at each other warily.

"God, they know everything about us," said Nasta.

"Could be coincidence," I replied, not believing my own words, and wondering uneasily how deep their knowledge went.

We were just beginning to enjoy the music when it was overlaid with an ugly electronically-synthesised voice.

"Good evening, Mr de Carteret. We are glad you enjoyed a quiet flight back, and your meal at the Casa Rosada."

We couldn't disguise the shock on our faces and Nasta looked scared. I found myself looking round nervously, listening for any sign of intruders.

"Do not be frightened. I am Soothslayer; your friend; Yusupov's worst enemy." The lack of pause or inflexion in the tinny, metronomic voice took all emotion from the message. It was unnerving.

"We need your help to destroy 'The Pig'. If you are willing to help us avenge your friends' deaths, then please open my next message, using your best friend's name, in capitals, as the password."

We were back to Muddy Waters, but without the pleasure.

Mesmerised, we watched the screen, as the message deleted itself. After a few seconds another appeared.

Nasta put out a hand. "You don't have to do this, Nick."

I nodded slowly. "I need to help them. That bastard's crossed his red line."

I followed their instructions, and we immediately found ourselves 'Sittin' on the Dock of the Bay' with Otis Redding, just as we had been on our first evening together.

Nasta opened her eyes wide. "How much exactly do they know about us?" She looked uncomfortably at me, but before I could reply, tin-tonsils welcomed us back.

"Thank you for your help. With your assistance, we can destroy him. On your forthcoming visit to Szchymkent next Thursday, you will have the afternoon free."

It was clear that he knew more than I did, which, while adding to my paranoia, did also bring about a grudging confidence in these people's abilities.

"Please leave both phones in your hotel room, having taken out the batteries first. Wear a wide-rimmed hat. Then, walk slowly along the north side of Yusupov Plaza, carrying a Marks & Spencer shopping bag. Fifteen minutes later, wait with your shopping bag on the south-east corner of the plaza. A taxi will stop there. He will tell you that Bobby sent him. He will take you to us."

Nasta reached out her hand to me nervously, but our self-professed friend waited for nobody.

"If you are willing, then please sign into the next message using your first dog's name in capitals. If you cannot do so, then sign off using your friend's name, as before. I hope you will help us, Nick. You will hasten his end."

We were back with Otis.

Nasta sighed deeply.

"You're going to go, aren't you?"

The next mail hit her spam folder and I opened it. I carefully typed in 'SCRAPPER'.

59

Soothslayer had been right. My Thursday afternoon was clear, in anticipation of the following morning's board meeting. I instructed my secretary to keep it so, and after a hectic morning I was glad not to have seen any sign of Yusupov. I had a quick lunch at my hotel and changed into jeans. If I was going to help bring down the chairman of my bank, it somehow didn't seem right to be wearing work clothes. I felt naked without a phone.

I stepped warily out into the Szchymkent spring, pulling my hat down over my eyes, and headed towards Yusupov Plaza. I had spent most of my early years avoiding people, mainly my siblings, but sometimes their street-gang buddies. I knew the tricks, and I wasn't going to take any chances. After a few minutes I ducked into a shop with a good view out, and waited. There was no one following. I carried on and, when I reached the plaza, I guiltily picked an M&S bag out of my jacket pocket and walked slowly along the north side.

I stopped when I reached the corner, with a feeling of anti-climax. Which could only be good, I told myself. I found a little café off the square and took fifteen minutes to drink my coffee.

My nerves were not playing ball, so I reminded myself that this was for Bobby. I walked to the south-east corner, and waited like a wallflower at a teenage dance.

It felt like hours, but was probably seconds, before one of the many battered taxis drew up. I stood there in two minds. Luckily the driver had more initiative than me. He rolled down his window and, looking round carefully, beckoned me. I marched hesitantly over to him.

"Bobby sent me," he said, nodding his head towards the back seat.

I got in and he set off slowly, checking all his mirrors.

After a couple of turns, he looked at me in the mirror and nodded. I smiled back and settled low into my seat.

The ride took an hour.

I know, because I was checking my watch about every two minutes.

We traversed the suburbs and headed towards the mountains. There wasn't much sign of habitation; we had left the tarmac way behind us.

We finally turned down a heavily pot-holed track. I had an uneasy feeling that we were being watched, and after a mile he pulled up at a run-down farmhouse.

"We here."

A small group were waiting outside the house, and their leader greeted me.

"Thank you so much for coming, Nick. Your help will be invaluable to us."

I recognised his strong, accented voice from the memory stick. He shook my hand firmly, and an engaging smile peeked out from the bushy depths of his straggly black full-face beard.

"I am Grigor." His eyes sparkled, and he introduced me rapidly to three others who all nodded animatedly. The men were almost clean-shaven, and any vestiges of facial hair seemed to be more fashionista than fundamentalist. It was the two women who frightened me.

He ushered me inside, and coffee was served at a basic wooden kitchen table.

They were all wearing varied descriptions of casual dress, denying any paramilitary, or indeed any other pretension.

"We have no political, religious or social affiliations." His accent did not remind me in any way of Yusupov. I supposed their president's locution, if not his morals, had been polished by his English schooling.

"We are just middle-class Kuikbakhs who love our country and refuse to see it raped and destroyed by Yusupov."

"Kill 'The Pig,'" the two girls intoned, their eyes flashing. The others nodded; two thumped the table.

"We have all lost money and loved ones." He nodded at the girls. "Inkar lost family members…"

"They killed parents, stole home and fuck me for good riddance," she almost whispered. "Medina too." She nodded at the other girl, who took her cue.

"They force my father give his business to them, but he fighting them back. They rape my mother and me for fun. But you know all this, I think?" She let her words tail off, raising her tone and leaving the question trailing.

"You work with 'The Pig'?" accused Inkar, and I could feel the mood changing.

"They killed Nick's best friend and his wife in cold blood," cut in Grigor. "He is only here to help us bring 'The Pig' to justice." I won't deny that I was happy for his intervention.

"Yusupov told me to invest a billion dollars for him," I began, failing to mention my delight at the time about that development.

"Stolen from us," spat Medina, and the others all nodded.

"I fully realise that now," I admitted, and I think they could see the truth in that.

"When he killed Bobby and Marina…" The words still made my voice catch. Raw emotion always speaks the truth, and they all nodded sympathetically.

"… whatever I had done before that, I swore an oath to avenge their deaths." I looked round, eyeballing each of them in turn. "That's why I'm here. Anything I can do to help your cause, you only have to ask." I don't think I had quite appreciated, until that moment, just how much I meant that.

"Death to Yusupov," I whispered.

"Death to 'The Pig,'" echoed Inkar and Medina.

"Justice for Kuikbakhistan," they all declared.

60

I believe I passed their test. I did wonder, fleetingly, what Inkar and Medina might have done if I hadn't, but I laid that thought quickly to rest.

My importance to their group was obvious. I was the closest they were going to get to Yusupov.

"His security forces are everywhere in and around Szchymkent," sighed Grigor. "Well-trained, fully-equipped, and vicious. Ask anybody."

"But do not ask anybody," advised Inkar, making a cutting motion across her neck.

"They have informers everywhere in the capital," agreed Grigor. "That is why we need your help, Nick." He placed his forearms on the table in front of him, his face close to mine. "We need to catch them off guard. That only happens when he has a sudden change of plan."

I could see what was coming.

"An urgent, unscheduled, last minute meeting out of town," I mused out loud.

"Exactly," replied Grigor.

"He's pretty organised," I said doubtfully. "Sticks to his agenda like clockwork. I can now see why." I waved my finger at them. They laughed.

"You are big at bank. You make meeting for him," prompted Inkar. I thought of laughing, but the look on her face convinced me not to.

"He doesn't take orders kindly," I shrugged, while I wracked my brains. There was an expectant silence. I could see that, for them, this was my moment; coughing-up time.

"There are some large clients which the Bank of Kuikbakhistan is trying to put into insolvency." I started to go through the list: "Kuikhkommertsbank; Ekivastuz Energy…"

Medina jumped to her feet, and I could see her anger. "My father's business." She looked at me accusingly.

"Ekivastuz Energy? Is your father still working there?" I asked.

She nodded and glared at me. "He the boss."

"They are obviously causing big problems for the bank. If you can get him to call Yusupov to an urgent meeting you could ambush him?" Terrorist activities weren't my forte, but it seemed feasible.

"Many roads that way," said Grigor. "They never go direct."

"If I am with him, you could track our movements on my bank cell phone and intercept us at a suitable point."

The smiles on their faces confirmed we had a plan they were happy with.

Medina too, although I wasn't sure if her happiness was brought on by the prospect of Yusupov's demise, or the possibility of mine.

A nasty thought struck me. "What is their surveillance like? Can they track my movements, and all those emails and messages to Anastasia's laptop?" I was suddenly nervous.

They all smiled knowingly, as if dealing with a stupid child.

"Their surveillance is good. But Soothslayer is better," Grigor assured me, smirking at the others. "He leaves no trace, and also jams their satellites and drones." I remembered how the emails had disappeared off Nasta's laptop. "My cell phones too?"

"Be calm, Soothslayer is the best. You obviously do not inhabit his world on the Dark Web." I decided to trust them, but promised myself to do some research on him.

I needn't have bothered.

"Isn't he up yet?" asked one of the fashionistas.

"I'll check," replied Medina with the closest to a smile I had seen from her. She opened a door into an adjoining room.

"*Boa tarde*," said a tall, elegant man, dressed for a tropical clime with crotch-tight slacks, his shirt open to his navel, two strings of pearls hanging from his neck, and a small bowler hat perched incongruously on the back of his head. He walked past Medina, giving her a lascivious hug and a kiss.

"Morning, Billy," said Inkar, going over and kissing him on both cheeks.

"Good morning, sweetie," he replied, giving her nose a pinch.

The two girls were like putty. The transformation was scary.

He turned to me, with a smile that was quite definitely lustful.

"And who have we here? *Que gostoso*," he said to the girls, and they giggled.

"He think you sexy," relayed Medina.

We shook hands. "Nick, this is Billy Sapito. Billy, meet Nick."

Billy took my hand and drew me into an awkward embrace.

He was so engaging that I couldn't take offence.

"Bit of a slut, though," he added, to laughter, including mine, and he pushed me away theatrically.

Billy was obviously a performer. I wasn't quite sure what his speciality might be, or indeed what the hell he was doing with this crowd. They seemed to have absolutely nothing in common.

Grigor saw my confusion, and took pity. "You are lucky. Soothslayer normally sleeps through until five." Billy pouted, looked at his watch and gasped, wiping the back of his hand across his face as if about to keel over.

I stared, my gaze alternating between Grigor, the two newly converted jezebels and Billy Sapito.

"Soothslayer?" I asked lamely. "This is Soothslayer?"

Billy put on a blistering show of pique.

"That's right, Mister Whizzkid Banker. While you're playing with yourself all night, I'm busy safeguarding your wife and children along with all the rest of the world, from nuclear-armed psychopaths like Yusupov."

He flounced out, slamming his door behind him.

I began to apologise, but they were all laughing. I think it was the surprise on my face.

"Don't worry, he'll be back," said Grigor. "He's different, isn't he?"

I nodded. "That's an understatement. Where is he from?"

"He is Kuikbakh," stated Medina proudly, with a sparkle in her eye.

"But he thinks he is Brazilian, and wants to be British," added Inkar, giggling like the schoolgirl she might have been in another world.

"He is confused," explained Grigor. "In every way. I guess that is why he is so good. He thinks differently from us. Kuikbakhistan is not a good place to be gay, and he fell foul of Yusupov's heavies. After a nasty few weeks, they forced him to work in their cyber warfare team, from a prison cell."

That brought a smile to all their faces. "He was so far ahead of them that, having changed all their protocols, he altered the security rotas so that one night all the prison guards were given the same shift off. Then he unlocked and jammed open all the electronic doors. The entire population of his high security jail escaped, and he booked himself a first-class government-sponsored flight to Rio de Janeiro. At their expense."

"Brilliant. He does look quite like a Carioca," I suggested. "Apart from the hat."

"Thank you, darling." Billy was back, strutting onto centre-stage, and patting my buttocks on the way past. "The hat is my British passport."

My expression told him I wasn't following him.

"All the gay boys down Posto Seis in Copacabana think I'm an English public schoolboy, and they know they're onto a good thing." He shrieked with laughter which he turned off suddenly, like a sluice gate.

"I only came back to this godforsaken place to help these lovely people get rid of 'The Pig'. I'll be off to London as soon as the 'fait' is 'accompli'.

"You need to be careful." He was looking at me, and he was suddenly completely focused. "Yusupov isn't sure whether to trust you after Bobby's death. He is preparing Inzhu Alani to take on your role at the bank. I am working hard to allay his fears, and also to plant seeds of doubt about her loyalty. But you should be very careful not to rile him just now."

"Surely he wouldn't dare get rid of both Bobby and me? What would the media say, or the UK government?"

"I don't see them making much of a fuss over Bobby, do you?" He raised his eyebrows enquiringly. "Just one less adversary to worry about, while he carries on shouting about terrorists and traitors."

His words rang true. I didn't find them reassuring.

"And don't trust that Alani girl, either," he added. "You don't think she fucked you because she was in love with you, do you?" He slapped his thigh theatrically, but without any laughter. "She just wants your job. While you're preening yourself for the cameras, she's planting bugs in your jacket, so they can keep tabs on you." That brought me up sharply. So, rather than me playing with Inzhu, as I had fondly imagined, in fact it had been entirely the other way round. I felt a bit foolish. What's more, Billy had obviously been watching.

He could see my confusion. "Don't worry. I nullified that little bug. But watch her closely."

The sparkle returned to his eyes; he turned theatrically on his heel and headed back to his room. "Time for business."

He paused in the doorway. "Oh, by the way, I loaded an app on your mobile. In case you get that neat little arse of yours into any trouble, you can contact me on it. It's a weather app. I know that's all you Brits ever talk about, so I thought it was appropriate."

He slammed the door again.

I reached for my phone, remembering as I did so that it was in my hotel.

"Don't worry, Billy will look after you," said Medina. They all nodded.

"Luckily he fancies you," put in Inkar, with a definite hint of jealousy. "So, he'll keep you very safe."

I tried hard to believe that, and to put his warning out of my mind.

"What do you plan to do with Yusupov when you capture him?" I asked, bringing us back on track.

"Kill him," chorused the girls, but Grigor held his hands up.

"No, we do not lower ourselves to his level." I could see the girls were not happy, but Grigor was obviously the boss for a reason.

"We take him to the mountains which is our homeland. The security forces would not dare attack us there. Then we put him on public trial." He looked at me proudly. "We have underground TV channel. When the people see what he has done, the whole country will join us."

Even Yusupov accepted that he had serious opposition across the country, and God knows, he had robbed his country blind, but I worried that they were confusing optimism with fantasy.

"What do you do if the country doesn't buy that?"

"It will," promised Grigor. "Trust me."

"But what if something goes wrong?" I persisted.

"Then there will be civil war," he replied.

"And we kill him," came the chorus.

My same taxi took me back to Yusupov Plaza and I walked to the hotel.

The day's events cascaded through my mind as I grazed slowly through my meal, and polished off the best part of a bottle of wine.

I probably checked out the other guests too often for the carefree traveller I was supposed to be.

61

After a turbulent night's sleep, I don't think I looked my best for the BOK board meeting the next morning.

I certainly didn't feel it, and was ready to plead a head-cold, if anybody asked. In truth, my nerves were scratching at my insides. The ebb and flow between Grigor's henchmen, and Yusupov's hoods, was testing my self-control to the limit. I began to understand what a spy went through every day. Of course, I could count on a bit of practice from my so-called family, with their street-gang buddies, and also from my days juggling Debs and Anastasia, so I wasn't a complete novice. It was just that the stakes were a whole lot higher now.

At least I wasn't arrested at reception.

I settled myself, and put on my best poker face. By the time I entered the boardroom I was completely under control.

All the board reiterated their condolences, and I could see that some of them meant it.

As usual, when important decisions were involved, the minutes had been drafted in advance. There was only one issue of substance: 'Appointment of new CEO'.

Bolat Karimov, the deputy chairman, was running the meeting. Yusupov would be coming later, although I assumed he had made his wishes clear.

"I would welcome your thoughts, Nick, on how we find a replacement for Bobby," prompted Karimov.

"The three executive directors have been excluded from this meeting, as they are the internal candidates for the role."

I had done some thinking on the subject and was absolutely clear in my mind. The choice was obvious. The only cloud was in Billy Sapito's warning to me.

"We could go to the market, and I expect we would find some very good international candidates, as the bank is generally held in high regard. However, the recruitment process would probably take six months or even more, depending on the notice period in their current role, and then an ex-patriate would need to settle into life in your country."

They were all nodding.

"Bobby found acclimatising easy, because he had met Marina."

I looked round to see if there were any reactions to my use of their names. I couldn't see any giveaways. "So, there would be an obvious advantage in taking an internal candidate. But only if there is a genuine contender for the role."

I looked around, and they were all nodding.

"Would you take the job, Nick?" asked Karimov. "Or at least, stand in on an interim basis?"

I had seen this coming and had discussed it with Anastasia.

"I am afraid not. As you know, my recovery from the stroke has been miraculously good. I barely even need my pills. However, the doctors have always told me that the chances of a recurrence would increase rapidly with further stress."

I looked at each of them.

"Both Anastasia and I are keen to avoid that, as it is likely to be terminal."

There was a round of sympathetic nodding from them.

I continued.

"Luckily I believe we have an excellent candidate at the bank: Inzhu Alani. She is a well-rounded banker, with good experience and knowledge of the bank's main product lines. She is well-connected in Kuikbakhistan, but has also worked in New York and London. She is a strong, tough leader, respected by her peers. We would be hard-pressed to find a better candidate, even if we carried out a full search."

I meant everything I said and, while the other two potential candidates were also good professionals, Inzhu was streets ahead of them. What's more, my sponsorship of her promotion should help to neutralise any suspicions she, or Yusupov might have. Thanks to Soothslayer, I was now onto her game. Keeping her close would be safest.

Also, she would be grateful for my support, and I might be able to use the physical aspects of our relationship to turn the tables on her. It riled me that she had been taking the piss out of me up till now.

A couple of the other non-execs aired their opinions, but my case was watertight, and we quickly put it to what turned out to be a unanimous vote in her favour.

They called her in, and Bolat gave her the news in their native tongue.

She thanked them profusely and reserved special gratitude for me, which was encouraging. I noticed that she wasn't phased at all by her promotion. I was now unsure whether that was a result of her closeness to Yusupov, or just an overriding confidence in her qualifications for the role.

The other directors were called in, and only one looked a bit disappointed, as though he might have been expecting the call. The others congratulated her with genuine enthusiasm, which boded well for her chances of pulling them all together.

A waiter came in with a tray of glasses, and we toasted the news with the local firewater.

"Our PR advisers will make the public announcements next week. Nick, you will inform your local management team?" asked Bolat.

"I will call them together tomorrow, as soon as I get back," I agreed, and I raised my glass to Inzhu, with a conspiratorial, if newly guarded, smile.

62

We worked hard bedding in Inzhu as our new CEO. She was good, but I kept all my antennae fully tuned for any hint of duplicity.

My relationship with Yusupov himself had always been schizophrenic, the allure and repulsion boiling away gently together under the surface.

So, in a funny way, little changed after Bobby's death.

I just took every step warily, as if treading on eggs stuffed with Semtex.

I soon got used to deputising for Inzhu when she was away. So when, six weeks into her regime, she took a longstanding holiday with her family, I spent four days in Szchymkent, holding the fort.

On the Tuesday morning we held an ExCo meeting. Yusupov was there but, in Inzhu's absence, I ran the meeting. It wasn't difficult as everything was going well. Ekivastuz Energy was, perhaps, the only blot on the horizon. Medina's father was indeed fighting back. He was a brave man. With a daughter like her, I wasn't surprised.

"Their fool of a CEO continues to defy me," stormed Yusupov.

"They are the twelfth largest company listed on the Szchymkent Stock Exchange," said our legal director. "And I should point out that, as I mentioned in my memorandum to the board, our interpretation of the covenants on their loan agreement is most certainly open to legal argument," he continued, punctilious as always, to the last full stop.

Yusupov had never been much of a one for full stops, and he roundly ignored him, ushering us all into lunch.

Towards the end of an excellent meal, Yusupov's PA entered

the dining room nervously. She excused herself, but said that the CEO of Ekivastuz Energy wanted to speak to Inzhu Alani. As she was not in, the man was insisting on speaking with the chairman. Yusupov was surprisingly accommodating with her, and she passed a phone to him.

Lunch and the ExCo meeting had obviously put him in a good mood, as his tone was almost cordial over the phone. I always admired his chameleon-like powers of adaptation.

"He wants to meet me at three this afternoon for the usual pointless circular arguments. I suppose my legal director will tell me that I must go." He sighed. There then followed a surprisingly forthright conversation. The legal director, who I was coming to admire more and more, managed to persuade his boss that having an informed legal opinion would not help his cause as the law was against him.

"In Inzhu's absence, you should take another senior board member." He looked at me.

"At least I will get the opportunity to look over the facilities that we are about to donate to Curzon," muttered Yusupov.

Realising that my chance had come, and feigning reluctance, I offered to accompany him.

"Are you up to speed with the case?" asked Legal doubtfully.

"We have very similar cases in London, and Inzhu took me through the files recently, so I can also make useful comparisons with the UK situations."

Legal nodded his head. "That could be useful."

"Excellent," said Yusupov, "I will pick you up at the hotel."

The die was cast.

At the hotel, I texted Grigor on my personal UK mobile, with timings and details, and we checked they were picking up the location of my bank phone.

My heart was pounding.

63

The bank Mercedes slunk to a halt outside the hotel, and I climbed in. One bodyguard filled the front passenger seat and the usual escort car behind us carried four more. That was light protection for Yusupov these days. It did cross my mind that Grigor would have to use some serious firepower, and I wondered fleetingly, how they were going to take him alive. I pushed the thought firmly back down.

We set off, and I ran through our dealings with Ekivastuz and their CEO/shareholder. Our chairman was surprisingly aware of the situation, considering how much he always appeared to delegate, but he wanted to know the details. Of course, he only had one objective in mind. He wasn't going to be arguing any of the finer points with them. Ekivastuz and their management had shown themselves to be astute and tough, and had defended their position effectively. Inzhu had needed to use all the force of the bank's political connections (including a particularly corrupt local judge who was an old friend of Yusupov's), and brute financial strength to bring them to heel. Yusupov was out for blood.

My monologue also served to camouflage the nerves which jangled louder with each kilometre that we drove away from the safety of Szchymkent, and towards the ambush which, I knew, awaited us. My fears were threefold: that Grigor's mission should not fail; that I, myself, should avoid harm during the encounter, and that, whatever the outcome, and above all else, Yusupov should never get wind of my treachery.

After about thirty minutes driving, we had pretty much covered all he needed to know. I took a look out of the darkened windows. We were entering a cutting with steep sides. It looked as good a place as any. I tried to look nonchalant, and checked my mobile.

"You look distracted today, Nick," said Yusupov. "Is everything alright at home?"

I could not look at him, and chose the mountains instead. "Such a beautiful country," I murmured, giving myself time to think. "Nasta is still distraught at Bobby and Marina's death." I turned slowly to watch his reaction, just in time to see the escort behind us disappear in a sheet of flame. Either a landmine or some form of anti-tank weapon. Our vehicle was thrown sideways but kept upright and Yusupov was thrown to one side, forcing me down into the footwell.

To his credit, our driver executed a perfect handbrake turn and gunned the engine, heading back the way we had come. Yusupov was catapulted back across the car to land on top of me.

I could see nothing further than Yusupov's overcoat which covered me, with his body adding another, weightier, layer. I was pinned down, but I could hear the bullets ripping into the car. I assumed that the security fleet was suitably armour-plated, but obviously Grigor had done his homework, and I felt the thud of two bullets striking the interior, whether hitting the body above me or part of the upholstery I could not tell. Yusupov was yelling in his native tongue; then he screamed in agony and struggled off me. He was holding his shoulder and swore quietly to himself, before gently subsiding against the side wall. I wriggled my torso onto the bench seat, still keeping my head down.

The noise of gunfire, which had reached a crescendo as we repassed the ambush point on our return journey, was just coming off its peak when the goon in the front seat gave a loud gurgle. The car lurched to one side and the driver swore, pushing the inert body off him to regain control of the speeding vehicle.

It was at the exact moment when I was beginning to think that we had achieved the best possible outcome: Yusupov dead; me unharmed, and safely returning to Szchymkent, when what must have been one of the last of Grigor's bullets struck my upper thigh, passing right through it and piercing the leather seat behind. It was excruciating and knocked the breath out of me. Yusupov and the bodyguard were out cold, and the driver was otherwise occupied. Holding a handkerchief to my thigh and groaning at every rut in the road, I peeked my head over the front seat to check our pilot was in working order.

"You ok?" I asked, not knowing if he understood English.

"Ok," he nodded. "We go hospital."

I could hear the fast-approaching sound of a helicopter.

"Army," he muttered. "How is president?"

The gunfire had stopped. I assumed Grigor needed to evade the army helicopters. In any event we were probably out of range.

I checked Yusupov's pulse. It was strong, although he was losing blood fast.

"Alive," I put a thumb up. "Bleeding."

He spoke briefly, hands-free.

"Hospital five miles," he promised me. "They waiting president."

With that, he put his foot down. Before long we could hear a cacophony of sirens. He picked his way through them without slowing and they fell in behind us. Frankly they were a bit late, but they say it's the thought that counts.

64

In less than five minutes, we tore into the beautifully landscaped grounds, past raised barriers and saluting soldiers, up to the A&E entrance of a large, modern hospital complex. It looked like every doctor and nurse in the hospital was waiting for us.

The large car park was almost empty. I got the feeling that the man on the Szchymkent omnibus didn't get to use this clinic much.

A cordon of tough-looking security hoods surrounded us. They were obviously on red alert.

Yusupov disappeared fast into the bowels of the building on a trolley.

A doctor checked the bodyguard's pulse, and issued rapid instructions to a couple of orderlies who dumped him unceremoniously onto another gurney and took him in another direction. I assumed to the morgue.

He pointed at me, still sitting inside, holding a handkerchief to my thigh. An orderly and a nurse came over, and lifted me carefully onto another trolley. They strapped me in, cut off my trousers and began to clean my wound. The pain was excruciating, and I duly yelled.

The doctor looked the driver over and, after a brief conversation, he was passed over to the hoods. He looked scared. I tried to tell them how he had saved our lives, but they didn't seem interested.

The medic turned to me. "Does it hurt?" he asked unnecessarily, in good English, feeling it gently.

I grimaced bravely.

"We will clean it up, give you some pain relief. You will be fine," he said with a pleasant smile.

"That driver was brilliant." I pointed at his receding shape, surrounded by goons.

"He can tell them that himself." He obviously didn't want to get involved and turned away. I can't say I blamed him.

One of the security guys took my trolley firmly from the orderly and started to push me through the cordon. I raised myself up, trying not to panic.

"I thought you said you were going to clean me up?" I half-shouted at the receding shape of the doctor.

He shrugged, his back to me.

"First you answer some questions," lisped a dark-haired girl, who can't have been more than thirty, pretty, with a leather jacket which barely concealed a tight sweater. She regarded me with hardened eyes. Her mouth and sweater smiled at me; the eyes held their counsel.

She was obviously the boss, as the ranks of goons parted immediately. They actually looked scared, and following her lead, pushed me into a small consultation room.

She shut the door, looked round the room, and came slowly over to my trolley.

"How is your wound?" she asked solicitously, tracing her finger up my inner thigh. "Grigor asked me to say thank you." Her jacket fell further open, the sweater threatening to unravel.

My god, I thought. *She must be one of Grigor's girls. His people are everywhere.*

She leant down and caressed her lips across mine. The sweater brushed my chest, and if it had not been for the hole in my leg, lust might well have overcome the relief that swamped my whole being.

As she straightened up, it wasn't much at all; perhaps nothing more than the simultaneous retraction of lips, fingers and sweater, and the cold concentration with which she suddenly searched my eyes, but I was immediately alert.

"Who is Grigor?" I stammered, dragging myself back into fear-induced focus.

"You know him, I think; Grigor Krakhtovich." It was not a question. Her smile returned, and she pressed down on me again. This time it felt more like a tarantula, weighing up its prey before devouring it.

She was not Grigor's girl, and we were not discussing mutual friends.

We were transacting life and death.

Mine.

I thanked the god, that I had never until now acknowledged, for the tough lessons I had learned in my early years. They had taught me how to lie for a living. And to trust no one. I hoped my lapse was recoverable. She was hard to read.

There was suddenly a loud scream from the room next door, and I recognised the driver's voice. I struggled against the straps, but couldn't move, and only with a supreme effort did I stop myself panicking.

Recognising that her ploy had failed, she changed tack. "Let us try another way," she lisped, and grasping a metal probe, attached by wires to a machine which I suddenly understood was not standard hospital issue, pushed it into my wound.

I screamed; the pain was mind-blowing.

"Sorry," she lied, examining me forensically, and wiping a speck of sputum off my cheek.

My heart was beating so fast I panicked it would pack up altogether. I thought I'd better start getting some control of this situation, before it became terminal.

"I am the head of the London office of the Bank of Kuikbakhistan," I shouted. "I am President Yusupov's right-hand man and his trusted confidant."

If I had thought that would impress her, I was sadly disappointed.

"I want to find out if that trust is well placed," she replied, spraying me again. "Your friend Bobby is dead." I could not stop the anger in my eyes. "Grigor killed him." I knew that was untrue, but made myself believe it, so my anger would remain.

She smiled, seeing me riled.

I overcame my fear, pushing it back down, and began to fight back. My eyes showed only surprise and pain.

"Who is this Grigor? Is he one of Tselmeg's men?" I gasped.

She studied me closely, giving nothing away.

Silence is golden, I reminded myself, staring back at her. She blinked first.

"You contacted him and led our president to him. You arranged the meeting with Danyar Maratov at Ekivastuz Energy and led the president into a trap."

I did not let the relief I felt show in my eyes. She knew nothing, and was just fishing. Whether that would help me, I wasn't sure.

I managed a confident glower.

"How is Tselmeg? I didn't arrange the meeting. Maratov called him and demanded a meeting. BOK's legal director insisted on me, as the senior banker available, accompanying him. Check your facts."

She didn't like that, and my thigh exploded again as she twisted her probe in my wound, enlarging and enraging it. I screamed and fought against the straps that held me. My back arched so that I feared my spine would crack.

I tried to think of Bobby, of Nasta and Chloe, of anything worth living for. The pain took over my entire being, as she played with me, digging and probing. I was searching for something to tell her, anything to stop the pain, except the truth.

Then, just as the pain took over completely, and even the truth and death seemed preferable, oblivion came to my rescue.

65

When I regained consciousness, I was in a hospital ward. I looked frantically round for instruments of torture, but everything seemed routinely clinical. A drip feed was attached to my arm, my thigh was bandaged up, and a monitor beside me told me my heart and pulse were normal.

A doctor came in, handed me a phone, and left, allowing me the privacy of a closed door.

"My god, I have been desperate. Are you alright?"

It was Anastasia. My relief was so complete I had to wipe away a tear. I was tempted to collapse and tell her everything. But I had fallen hook, line and sinker for Lispy-tits and her games, and was not going to incriminate myself now, if I had not already done so.

"I'm fine. I'm in good hands. This hospital is top class. The interrogation wasn't so friendly." I wasn't sure how much she had been told, but my childhood training kicked in again, and I repeated my story, in all its innocence.

"Of course you had nothing to do with it," she exclaimed, burnishing my story for any listening ears. "You had always been worried about those wretched rebels who murdered Bobby and Marina. Are you in pain? How long before you can fly home?"

It was tempting to think about flying back to safety, but I needed to stay in the present.

"I imagine I'll have to stay here a few days. When Tselmeg realises that the CEO of Ekivastuz set this ambush up, which is the only possible scenario I can think of, we will want to get the business into Curzon's hands pretty quickly. Inzhu Alani isn't here this week, and they'll need my expertise."

I was sure our conversation was being monitored, so I thought I'd remind them what I brought to their party.

"I expect I'll see you sometime in the middle of next week. I'll be fine." I was actually beginning to believe that.

"Is your cell phone still working? They rang me for this call, and your end looks like a landline."

"I imagine they're checking it out, and once they're satisfied it's clean, they'll return it." I was crossing my fingers that Soothslayer was as good a 'sanitiser' as Grigor and his team had assured me.

"Anyway, I'll keep you posted. Stay strong, and look after Chloe."

"I will," she promised, and I could feel her love and strength. I needed both.

As soon as she rang off, an orderly came in and took the phone. They had obviously been listening. Fine by me.

"When can I leave?" I asked, but he obviously spoke no English, and hurried out.

The doctor returned immediately. Looking at his notes, he smiled at me encouragingly. "You were lucky. The bullet passed right through your flesh, leaving a clean wound."

Until Lispy-tits got to it, I thought to myself.

"How is the president?" I asked.

"Recovering," was all he would say.

I thought I would show some concern. My feelings were genuine; schizophrenically so. I had skin in both games. If he survived, I wanted to keep his trust, so I could lead him to his final denouement. If not, I wanted the next plane out, before his underlings decided they didn't like me, and my shit really hit the fan.

"Is he going to be ok?" I asked with unfeigned concern.

He paused, and the faintest of smiles flashed across his eyes. That was the moment I knew I was going to get out alive.

"He is going to be fine. Thanks in part to you." That sounded positive, although I was at a loss to know why.

"He needed blood. Yours was a good match."

He turned for the door. As he was closing it behind him, he looked over his shoulder and nodded, almost respectfully.

"A very good match. Now relax, you need to rebuild your strength."

66

Yusupov knew that he had to get back in the saddle quickly. Running a country the way he did, and with the opposition he had managed to create out of nothing, he had no option.

Absence suggested weakness, or death.

Weak or dead autocrats didn't prosper.

Of the two, the dead ones were usually happier.

So, I was not surprised to see him being wheeled in to interrupt my physio session the next morning.

"I am so glad to see you are recovering quickly, Nick." He was all smiles, and did look genuinely pleased to see me. In other words, the usual paradox. He handed me my mobile. It seemed that Soothslayer had lived up to his reviews, and my secrets were safe. I smiled back.

The bodyguard herded the physio and two assistants out of the room, and stood by the door.

"That fool Maratov at Ekivastuz. It was him who set up the ambush, you know." He looked closely at me. "At first I thought you must be the traitor, Nick."

"I assumed that, from the way I was interrogated," I responded with genuine anger.

"My people were right not to take chances. They realised their mistake soon enough, but you did appear, at first, to be the weak link in our security. Someone tipped off those terrorists, Nick. They thought that your friend Bobby's untimely death…" His eyes continued to bore into me in that familiar manner of his that made you feel like a fly in a spider's web, "… might have unhinged you."

214

But this fly was beginning to learn a few tricks of his own. "You may think I am stupid, Tselmeg, but setting up an ambush in which I am likely to be one of the early casualties, would seem to be less a weak link in your security; more a highly principled suicide mission. My principles don't stretch that far."

He laughed, and shrugged.

"I am sorry about your injuries." He nodded at my leg. I think he was referring to my interrogation, rather than the wound itself. I don't think I had ever heard him apologise before.

"I hope you will wear it as a badge of honour, Nick. Just as I, myself, consider this suffering a necessary price for the development of Kuikbakhistan."

Thinking of my run-in with Lispy-tits reminded me of the screams I had heard in the next door room. "I hope your driver has been well treated. He saved your life."

"My people can take no chances, Nick. The terrorists are everywhere. I will make sure he is rewarded well, if he is innocent."

His face clouded over again. "As for that cockroach, Maratov, he will die a painful death."

I remembered his daughter, Medina, and figured her fanaticism would go ballistic, along with all the rest of the opposition, if her father suffered. Yusupov may have won this particular battle, but he was losing the war, even if he didn't know it. I kept the life-preserving mask of my poker face firmly in position.

"So, I need you to make sure that Curzon acquires Ekivastuz without any hitches, Nick. Inzhu will be back on Monday, but please take charge of that for me until she returns."

At his signal, an orderly came in and started to wheel him out.

Yusupov put his hand up and they halted.

"I should also thank you for your blood, Nick."

He looked at me with real warmth.

"I am sorry that you lost a little from your wound. However, it was an excellent match with mine, so they borrowed some extra. I hope you don't mind." He seemed pleased, and beamed at me.

If that's what it took, I thought, *then what's a little blood between friends?*

They wheeled him out.

67

I was discharged later that day. Yusupov needed me to deal with Ekivastuz Energy. He checked himself out before that. Bandages look good on TV.

He insisted that I went out to Ekivastuz Head Office immediately on my return to the bank. For the trip out there, I had an even bigger security escort than last time.

Of course, Yusupov had instigated a massive clampdown, with soldiers and mercenaries (they all looked like hoods to me) on every corner. Grigor and his boys would be keeping a low profile, other than in their heartlands, but we weren't taking chances.

I met with the senior managers at the company. Not Danyar Maratov. I suspected he was having a session with Lispy-tits and her crew. I didn't envy him. Or her, when Medina got hold of her, which I suspected she eventually would.

Maratov's team obviously held him in high regard.

"Do you have any news of Mr Maratov, our CEO?" asked the chairman when, immediately on my arrival, we sat down round the boardroom table. "He is both my son, our leader and a very dear friend. We understand that you have the president's ear."

That made me a little nervous and I rapidly disabused them of the notion that I could help them. I think they got the message, although they looked at me quizzically, as though things weren't quite adding up for them.

The CFO broke the awkward silence. "I have to say your bank has been extremely harsh with us, Mr de Carteret."

There was a pregnant silence, and I could feel from the looks

I was receiving that, while they dared not criticise their president, they were no fans of his, and they were looking forward to his downfall. I was beginning to understand how thin was the skin of his popularity, outside his own little bubble in Szchymkent.

The chairman rose to his feet. "Mr de Carteret, we have not met before, so let me tell you a few home truths from an old man who has not much time left on this earth."

He took off his glasses, and placed both palms flat on the table. He leant towards me, transfixing me with clear blue eyes.

"I have been in business around the world for many years, sir, and my family founded this company over one hundred years ago. I have seen a gradual decline in moral standards, internationally, over the years but especially from the ruling class in this wonderful country of ours. Be that as it may, I have never, ever, in the years that have been given to me, witnessed such sinful, dishonest and corrupt treatment as that inflicted on Ekivastuz Energy by your bank over the past few months. We have heard of your own shameful reputation in London, Mr de Carteret, but I can see, deep down, a thread of humanity lingering somewhere there. And indeed, your behaviour pales into paltry insignificance when compared to the behaviour of Mr Yusupov, both in his capacity as chairman of your bank, but more importantly, as president of this country. The only thread that runs through his body is one of dark, satanic evil."

The old man slumped into his chair, exhausted by the emotions which had cascaded out. The other directors looked fearful, but presented a united front.

The CFO looked at me with a mixture of anger and concern. "You must excuse him, Mr de Carteret. Danyar, his son, is in the hands of the secret police, and is no doubt suffering the atrocities to which we have become all too accustomed." He looked at the others before continuing. "We understand you know Grigor Krakhtovich."

It was the statement I had been dreading.

There was silence. They were all staring at me.

"We also understand that you know how your friend Bobby Jones and his pregnant wife died."

That really stunned me. I was speechless.

He smiled. Of course, he was holding all the cards in this particular situation. "Your secret is safe with us, Mr de Carteret," he said softly.

That came as no small relief. I was playing with fire, and I was beginning to understand exactly how hot it was burning.

He looked at me, as if weighing something up.

"So, let me take you into our confidence as well, Mr de Carteret. Strictly between us, and I trust this will go no further, we are about to change our banking arrangements."

I was coming to admire these people, even if they were holding a few too many aces. However, I thought I should reel them in a little.

"I am afraid that, as soon as we get our insolvency order, that option will not be available," I reminded them.

He smiled. "We will, very shortly, be signing up for sufficient facilities from one of your international competitors, to pay off all the outstanding liabilities to your bank."

"Strictly between us," I threw his warning back at him, "you will need to move fast."

He remained unphased. "We will be out of your bank's clutches by close of business tomorrow. Will that be fast enough?"

By now, the chairman had recovered his composure. "We can help you to avenge your friend's death, Mr de Carteret. Help if you can. Do not press your insolvency order until the weekend; help us keep our business out of Yusupov's hands. We know you are starting to work against him. Imprison him in his little bubble of sycophants who fear to tell him the truth. Continue to flatter him, prevent him from understanding the powers that work against him; pull together your friends in the West, your business associates, and bring him down; help us survive, and we will together make him dig his own deep grave."

His eyes penetrated my very soul.

"Help us if you can," he pleaded. "For Bobby's sake, if nothing else. Your friend was a good and honourable man."

68

My return trip into the city centre passed without incident, apart from the turmoil in my own mind. I went straight to my hotel to ring Nasta, even though it was late for her. I couldn't risk telling her anything, but I needed to hear her voice. We chatted about nothing very much and it gave me strength. She felt the same.

"I'll be back tomorrow evening," I promised. I could feel all the questions that she was dying to ask and knew she couldn't.

"Look after yourself," she whispered. "I love you." And, with that she was gone, knowing she could not trust herself any longer on our very public hotel connection.

I slept surprisingly well.

I was woken early by my secretary in London. She apologised, but had stayed up to make the call, as she had a number of crises of varying magnitude. I went through them all with her, and so was late down to breakfast.

After several discussions with my UK team to put out the fires in London, I went into our head office, three blocks from my hotel, at about midday.

There were, inevitably, messages from Yusupov. First, the normal ranting about the UK government's position on his human rights transgressions. He wanted me to raise it with Petra Marinelli immediately on my return. He also wanted an update on Ekivastuz. The Kuikbakh courts were not renowned for their efficiency, so I felt that, if I let things hang until mid-afternoon, then even with the president breathing down his neck, Yusupov's puppet judge would not be able to process the insolvency order before the weekend.

That was all old Mr Maratov had needed, and I was going to come through for him.

I waited until well after lunch before phoning the lawyers. I told them to expedite the process, knowing full well that we were too late; the courts would be closing soon.

Then, I rang Yusupov. I explained that I had been tied up for the morning, but that I had chased the insolvency order urgently.

He seemed relaxed. Of course, the judge on the case was his old friend who was utterly impartial. Impartial, that is, as to whether he followed the law, or his president's whims. What Yusupov didn't know, as I did, was that by Monday, Ekivastuz would not be a client of BOK anymore, and by then not even his crony judge could help.

I also promised to talk to Petra Marinelli about her stance on human rights.

"If they cannot show a little more understanding to one of their main benefactors, tell them I will require repayment of all the finance I have showered on them at the upcoming break clause."

I thought about challenging him, but somehow that seemed more Bobby's role. I had enough conflicts going on. It wouldn't make a blind bit of difference anyway.

"I'll raise it with her next week," I conceded.

A bank driver deposited me at the hotel. I would normally have walked to clear my head but, even with crutches, my leg hurt. I packed my things, signed the bill and headed to the airport.

I think it was a good flight. I couldn't be sure, as I was asleep before take-off, and had to be woken for landing.

69

Nasta insisted on meeting me at the airport with a wheelchair. She gave me a closer examination than any of the medical team in Kuikbakhistan, followed by a long embrace.

"I wondered if I was ever going to see you again." Tears started to flow, and she looked up at me. "And do you know what was the hardest part to swallow?"

"Yusupov?" I ventured.

She nodded. "The thought of having him crawl up to me with his creepy 'heartfelt condolences', while we would both know full well that he had murdered not only Bobby and Marina," her face creased up, "but you as well. What on earth will our lives be like from now on, Nick?"

I tried to calm her. "We are totally safe here. I will tell you about everything going on out there, but you have told me many times, and you were absolutely right; he is doing my work for me. Believe me, I am getting his measure, but he has so many enemies, and they hate him with such a loathing, that he cannot last long. He rules only by fear. I will win my own personal struggle with him in time, and in so doing, bury my own demons, but there are decent people out there across the spectrum in Kuikbakhistan, praying for his demise. It will not be long."

She clung to me, and calmed down slowly. In truth, I was probably exaggerating. With his latest crackdown I guessed he had the place mostly back under control, at least for now.

Hard as I tried to persuade her, Nasta wouldn't let me walk through the terminal. My leg was sore, so I didn't complain, and subsided into the wheelchair. In the car park, she almost lifted me physically into the car.

As soon as the car started rolling, the questions started.

I spent the forty minutes, as she wound her way through heavy Saturday evening traffic, recounting every detail of my eventful visit. It also helped me to put things into perspective.

We grilled two rib-eye steaks and, with the help of a bottle of Chilean Merlot, began to relax.

I think I persuaded her that we were safely out of Yusupov's clutches in London, and perhaps more importantly, that having fully recovered his trust, I was going to give him and his heavies no possible further excuse to harm us.

She seemed happier.

I'm not sure I wholly convinced myself.

"I have to admit, that even with a bullet hole in your leg, you seem somehow more at ease with yourself than I have seen before." She took my hand. "You finally seem to know where you fit in the world."

"You're right. Perhaps that's one good thing to come out of Bobby's death."

"Do you think Grigor can really bring him down?" Nasta was no fool and she knew what the rebels were up against.

"I think Yusupov has probably put them back a bit with his latest clampdown, so he's won that battle. But, believe me, they will win the war."

Nasta smiled at me, but this time she didn't challenge me, and instead filled me in on all her news.

As I lay awake that night, tossing and turning, I tried to evaluate and compare all the available alternatives. I eventually came to the conclusion that I was going to have to play my long game with Yusupov. Grigor would rebuild the opposition in time, but he was not currently in a position to provide a credible challenge.

That was my job now.

I also realised that, with Anastasia's help, I was beginning to learn how to be happy in my own skin.

Yusupov himself, I suspected, was beginning to find his skin rather claustrophobic.

He was hated by a large minority in his own country, by most of his neighbours, and by all the international press. He really was running out of friends.

What's more, he was not, and never had been, an appropriate partner for the authorities in the UK. His human rights abuses were vicious, innumerable, and escalating, and that was just counting the ones that came to the light of day.

But, as I knew all too well, greed always wins. The terms he had offered on all the UK infrastructure finance were just too good to pass up, and the voracity of all the players, myself included, had done the rest.

So, we just carried on our little game of Kuikbakh roulette, with the UK government complaining about all Yusupov's perceived human rights transgressions, him ranting about their duplicity, and me playing piggie in the middle, trying to keep all the toys on the track, while I worked out how to bring him down.

It was a full-time job, and I still had one of those at the bank.

70

They say there is no rest for the wicked in this world. So, I knew where I stood on the cosmic temperature gauge when, on my return to the office and hoping for some normality, I was hit by a maelstrom of problems.

That first day flew by, and it must have been ten thirty before I got up from my desk to leave. Snapper pulled himself up and, hobbling on his stiff back legs, beat me to the lifts.

I pressed the 'Ground floor' button on the space-age pod, which had been put in, as part of the latest refurbishment for Yusupov's 'Bakhtu Basics' business in the basement. Unusually, the car took a little time to arrive. I must admit, I didn't like the pre-programmed system much. I often found myself getting in without concentrating, only to find that there were no control buttons in the lift car, which then took me to every floor I didn't want to go to.

The refurbishment work had gone without hitch. It seemed to be state-of-the-art stuff. I wasn't complaining, although I thought that for a building of our size to have six elevator cars in two opposing banks of three, including two 'freight-size' cars, all with remote control, was a bit over the top. We also used their big sound- and bug-proofed room in the basement for our board meetings, which worked well. Apart from that, the bank and Yusupov's import business went about their separate ways.

The lift door opened silently behind me, and if it had not been for some animated growling from Snapper, I might not have even noticed.

As I turned and walked towards the open doors, I saw it was

full. Snapper was barking furiously by now, and I recognised one of our security guys, who was looking desperate. There were four thugs behind him, all trying to block my view of what looked remarkably like a body-bag, with an obviously live, and clearly unhappy, body in it. Two of them put their hand out, in that menacing way that officious security men often do, and one actually pointed a pistol at Snapper. Their message was clear. They didn't want us joining them.

"Problems, Jonny?" I asked, picking up Snapper and trying to sound nonchalant.

"I am really sorry, Mr de Carteret. These gentlemen are trying to get to the basement. These new lifts…" He continued to look frantically for a control button.

"This one will take you to the ground floor. Get out there and press 'basement' on the central pod in the lobby there. The next elevator that arrives will take you down there.

"Do these guys have proper clearance, Jonny?" I knew the answer, but thought I would ask anyway.

"Mr Yusupov…" was all Jonny managed to stammer, before the doors closed on him. Now none of his fellow occupants looked happy.

71

It was all over the early news bulletins in the morning. 'Ambassador from Kuikbakhistan kidnapped by extremist rebels. President Yusupov 'disappointed' at lax UK security. Threatens to withdraw diplomatic staff'.

"The wily old bastard," I muttered.

"I wonder if those are the same 'extremist rebels' who were supposed to have killed Bobby," said Nasta bitterly. I had told her of my night-time encounter with the body-bag, at the bank.

We watched the rolling news programmes as we got ready for the day.

"You need to be careful, Nick. He knows you saw those thugs last night." Anastasia looked concerned. "You should go to the authorities and tell them what you saw. Get official protection for us. Yusupov won't dare cross the UK government so openly."

I only had two problems with that approach. First, there was more likelihood of a sparrow blowing down the Taj Mahal with an early morning fart than the UK security services protecting me from Yusupov; and second, I was interested to see how I might turn this to my advantage, or rather Bobby's, for I measured everything to do with Yusupov now, in terms of how much closer it got me to avenging my friend's death.

Anastasia saw the look on my face, and fear clouded hers.

"Be very careful, Nick. The man's psychotic, as Bobby found to his cost; he's also clever, and powerful. Please watch out for his hoods. If they can snatch his ambassador, I don't suppose they'd have much problem finding you."

Her words rang disturbingly true.

"Don't worry, I will. But I'm not going to pass up an opportunity like this to turn the screws on him."

She hesitated, in that way I was coming to know well, and which meant she had something else to tell me.

"What is it?" I asked, just winning the battle not to look at my watch or answer my mobile, which was vibrating in my pocket. I had a busy day at the bank, even without Yusupov.

"I have a lead which I think is going to find your mother."

With all that was going on in my life, that was exactly the last thing I had been expecting to hear. My mouth dropped open, and my heart started thumping, as a range of emotions stampeded around my head.

"Where?" was all I could think to ask.

"I don't know yet, but I'm on it. Are you ready for that, Nick?"

I didn't know the answer to that and fell to temptation, picking the phone out of my pocket and seeing various urgent messages from my secretary. My day was going crazy.

"Nasta, I have to go. I'll think about it."

We both knew I was prevaricating, so she persisted.

"I think it's time you met your mother, Nick. Actually, I think it's way past time. I'm going to find her."

I literally ran out of the door.

72

If I had expected to find any sanctuary in my office, I was to be disappointed.

The place was mayhem. Paparazzi were all over the pavement outside; we had security guys all over reception frisking every visitor, and a scanning machine had miraculously appeared, and was being used to examine their hand luggage. Yusupov was obviously playing up the failings of UK security as hard as he could.

Upstairs, my new secretary of a couple of weeks was clearly struggling to keep her head above water.

"Mr de Carteret, I have been leaving messages on your mobile since I got in. Mr Yusupov and Miss Alani need to talk with you urgently, and Mr Gough is in meeting room three. He has been asking for you."

"Put me through to Tselmeg Yusupov first, please, Anna. Please use the secure video feed," I said. "Tell James Gough I will be there as soon as possible, and Miss Alani that I will call her when I can."

I wanted to get straight with Yusupov first. As always, he was the key to everything.

"Good morning, Nick," he said in a neutral tone, although voice and video were slightly out of sync, which I always found unnerving.

"We seem to have a lot of security in reception suddenly," I probed, unsure exactly how much he knew about my coincidental involvement, and keen to find out.

"Do you blame me, Nick, when your country is unable to protect my diplomatic staff?" he smiled. "Both the bank and Bakhtu Basics are extremely sensitive operations. I cannot afford either key personnel, or valuable information, falling into the wrong hands. Call it basic insurance."

I couldn't read him, so decided to push a bit.

"Was it the same rebel group which killed Bobby and Marina, who took your ambassador, Tselmeg?" I asked, anger flaring up suddenly, my lack of control alarming me more than him. "How did they get into the UK?"

He didn't blink.

"Let's not play games, Nick. We both know you saw the extraction operation last night. That is a pity for both of us. Nevertheless, life goes on, and I admit I have come to admire some of your character traits that others may not find so attractive; your greed, for instance."

At least he wasn't pulling any punches. While an image of pots calling kettles black flashed across my mind, I controlled myself. I stayed silent and waited for his offer. "We have two simple choices, Nick."

I stared him down, not offering anything.

"The first is the one which will make everyone happy."

He paused, glowering right through me.

"And rich. It involves you signing a non-disclosure agreement covering everything that you transact, become aware of, or are in any way involved with, on the bank's business, or on its premises, anywhere in the world. James Gough is waiting with the document for you to sign."

He paused. "Mr Gough also has a document doubling your carried interest in all Curzon's investments. He has been instructed to hand that to you, once you have signed the non-disclosure agreement. Does that sound fair, Nick?"

"I will need to review the document," I said, rather pedantically.

He didn't much like that, and I could see he was riled. I was learning how to play him, but I had to be careful.

"If by any chance your 'review'…" He spat my choice of words back at me.

"… leads you to believe that your conscience will not allow you to sign it, then we will have to activate the second of our simple choices."

I felt it was time to throw him some slack, so I muttered, "I am sure that won't be necessary, Tselmeg."

He glared at me, as if annoyed at the interruption.

"As you can imagine, Mr Gough's document does not spell out the exact penalties which will be applied to you and your family in the event that you sign it and then proceed to break our agreement," he continued coldly, hesitating momentarily.

"I believe we know each other well enough by now, to be able to leave such unpleasantness unsaid, and unwritten. Suffice it to say, that those same penalties will be exacted immediately, if you do not sign the documents. You have fifteen minutes to review them with James Gough. I will ring you back at that time."

The line went dead.

I knew I was going to sign, but felt I had better actually scan the documents. I remembered Billy Sapito's warning. Bobby's death had passed the world by without making waves; mine would follow without so much as a ripple. Yusupov would make sure of that.

I needed to stay alive for both our sakes.

James Gough was waiting for me, and I could see he was not happy. He had obviously been woken early, probably by a direct call from Yusupov.

He looked around meaningfully, at the ceiling and light fittings, obviously wanting to know if the room was bugged.

I waved him on airily, although I thought it probably was.

He lowered his voice, as if that would protect him. "Before we go on, my firm has decided that working with BOK and Mr Yusupov is no longer viable for us, Nick. My head office in New York has decided not to accept any new work from your organization, and to hand over to your nominated successor."

He looked at me, with his eyebrows raised.

"We'd better use Slatkin and Ball," I replied immediately,

thinking of a top lawyer who could be our client service partner there.

James shook his head sadly. "I am afraid that your sponsor..." he was referring to Yusupov and I could see the distaste on his face, "... has chosen Featherstone's."

I liked James Gough, and his firm was bloody good. Losing them was a blow; having Featherstone's, one of the big magic circle firms with international reach to replace them, would not make that blow any softer. 'Bloodthirsty', was the best description for them. Both for the fees they charged, and the antagonistic way they did business. I could see how they would appeal to Yusupov.

James saw the look on my face. "I'm afraid his decision is final on this one, Nick," he said.

We stared at each other. "You are dining with the devil, Nick," he said quietly. "Be very wary of the dessert..."

He sighed resignedly. "... and indeed, the digestif, if it comes to that. However, we will complete all work in hand."

He drew a document out of his briefcase.

"Your non-disclosure agreement is straightforward, Nick, with the normal legal redress for any leakage."

He looked at me.

"Does Yusupov ever abide by these kinds of agreement?"

I ignored the question, looked quickly through it, and signed at the bottom.

He then held out the contract to increase my Curzon carried interest.

I reached for it, but he held it back, a look of revulsion on his face.

"What the hell did you agree to do to get a deal like this, Nick?" he asked, wincing. "Sell him your soul? I hope to God, you know what you are doing."

My heart was beating rapidly, but I was damned if I was going to let him know that.

73

Unusually, that evening, Nasta and I had a quiet dinner together, followed by an early night.

I woke suddenly; I could tell something was wrong.

Nasta was already up, and went to answer the door. "It must be a late delivery," she muttered distractedly.

I tried to stop her, but she was already there.

As she turned the lock, the door burst open and three men in army fatigues rushed past her, crashing her to the ground.

Yusupov followed them in.

"I trusted you, Nick, like a brother, and you have betrayed me."

He gestured at Nasta, and the cowering Chloe. The hoods cuffed them and pushed them down roughly onto upright chairs.

"Don't you dare touch me," hissed Nasta at one of them. He slapped her hard across the face.

"Your days of ordering people around are over," said Yusupov coldly.

He turned to me. "Our friend Grigor Krakhtovich has been very helpful." He flashed a reptilian smile.

"Who is Grigor Krakhtovich?" I bluffed.

He sneered, and shook his head. "Your good friend, Grigor Krakhtovich."

He grabbed Nasta's hair and yanked it down behind her. "After all I have done for you, Nick, you repay me with such treachery."

His eyes simmered. "My interrogation team were right. I should have let them have their way with you." I saw with horror a knife in his right hand. "Now, it is your family's turn to suffer."

My brain was spinning, and I was finding rational thought hard to come by. All I could think of was to double down on my imaginary innocence.

"I have never heard of the man. Who is he?" I was panicking. "If you interrogated a rebel, then I am sure he would have told you whatever you wanted under torture."

He wasn't even listening. "This is what happens to traitors in my country."

He raised the knife theatrically, then slashed it down and across Nasta's neck.

Her blood gushed. She gave a little snore, and her head fell to one side. I tried to rush at him, but my feet would not move. One of the hoods grabbed me and felled me with the butt of his gun.

As I began to lose consciousness, I heard Chloe shrieking, and gave one last mighty yell of rage.

One of the hoods grabbed my shoulders and started shaking me. "Nick, Nick, wake up." It was Nasta. "You're frightening Chloe." Our daughter was beside the bed, crying piteously.

"She already had one nightmare this evening. That's why she came in here screaming. You have to calm down."

"Sorry," I said, trying to regain my equilibrium. "Sorry, Chloe. Did you have a nightmare, baby?" I hugged her and, after an initial hesitation, she responded.

"Daddy. You're sweating," she whispered, as if trying loyally to keep it from her mother, and just between us. She pulled away gently.

I looked at Nasta, and was about to tell her about my own hellish vision, but she put her hand up gently, like a traffic cop.

"Tell me later. Let me get her back into bed first."

My heart was pounding.

* * *

It took some time for Chloe to rejoin her nightmares; and for me to emerge from mine.

When we had both succeeded, I got back into bed. Nasta eventually joined me.

She turned to me with concern. "What was all that about?"

I didn't want to ruin her night. So, I let out a gentle snore.

74

I had always known that Yusupov would weaponise his new-found status as a major provider of infrastructure to the UK. But I had not envisaged quite how quickly he would escalate the initial skirmishes into all-out nuclear conflict.

Within twenty-four hours of my signing those dirty documents, he swept unannounced into my office.

"I am here to see the Foreign Secretary about the abduction."

I nodded warily, still digesting all the swirling counter-currents of the past few days. My nightmare had made me see danger at every turn. Each interaction with Yusupov was now, for me, a battlefield of subterfuge.

I knew I could not hope for a rapid solution from Grigor's rebels. He had his own battles to fight, as Soothslayer periodically confirmed. They were a continual and slowly growing thorn in Yusupov's side, but they weren't going to be the quick fix I had hoped for. I was going to have to find other, swifter ways to bring him down myself.

As if ignoring my presence, he started to rant about the perceived injustices meted out to him by my government, and by extension, myself.

"After all the financial assistance I have made available, still your country has the nerve to complain about human rights abuses against those who oppose me."

He calmed down a bit, beckoning me as he headed for the door. "I told them you would accompany me, Nick; I think you will enjoy it, and I would welcome your views, especially from your privileged viewpoint. I understand your friend Petra Marinelli will be there for the Treasury."

I fully realised that this invitation was not made with any thought for my enjoyment. He knew my connection with Petra, and hoped that I could be useful.

I warned my secretary to cancel two meetings, and followed him to the bank car.

During the brief trip he swung between injured innocence and venomous retribution. I steered him gently towards the latter.

"You know Nick, Petra," oozed Yusupov, when we arrived.

"Of course I do. Lovely to see you again, Nick. How is Anastasia?" Petra Marinelli hadn't got to number two in the Treasury without learning how to handle a stressful situation by burying it in a quagmire of urbane protocol.

But she was only riding shotgun today.

The meeting was with the Foreign Secretary. A diplomatic attempt to stop all the recent, rather undiplomatic exchanges escalating into a major incident.

The latest of Yusupov's wide range of infrastructure projects was a recently-commissioned nuclear plant at Mersea Island in Essex, so Petra had been sent to keep an eye on things on behalf of her boss at the Treasury.

We were ushered into a small private dining room by two aides.

"Welcome, President Yusupov," smiled George Watkins, Bt, a tall, academic-looking man of impeccable breeding but, to my mind, dubious backbone. I was hoping that at least one of his forbears had been ennobled for something suitably dishonest, cruel or immoral, and that their DNA was still in his genes. Otherwise, he was going to be mincemeat. Looking at him, I wasn't confident.

"Thank you, Foreign Secretary," responded Yusupov. "You know Nick de Carteret, who runs my bank for me?"

"Only by reputation," responded the minister with the faintest of disdainful smiles.

"I hear that modern banking takes many forms, Mr de Carteret," he smiled. "And your bank is adept at all of them."

That was a double-edged compliment, if ever I heard one. *Perhaps he does have what it takes*, I thought to myself.

We all shook hands.

Yusupov was champing at the bit and could hardly hold himself back.

As the door closed behind the coffee-waiter, he barrelled in. "Before we get to the matter in hand, I would remind you that Kuikbakhistan has become one of your major energy suppliers, Foreign Secretary. And also, one of the major sources of funding for your new infrastructure projects."

He looked at Petra, who smiled. "We are extremely grateful, President Yusupov."

He ignored her, addressing the Foreign Secretary. "As you continue to lay these entirely unfounded accusations of human rights abuses at my door while, at the same time, being unable to offer my own citizens basic security, you force me to take retaliatory action."

He thumped the table.

"Your astounding security failings have allowed those same terrorists, who you accuse me of abusing in my country…" he looked round in wide-eyed innocence, "… free movement in yours, so you cannot even offer my own diplomats protection from kidnap."

He paused and continued quietly. "I think, perhaps, that your government should stop trying to lecture my country on how to behave and take some lessons from us in basic security measures."

As intended, he had their full attention.

"I am going to expel your ambassador," he stated grimly, punctuating the comment by slurping his coffee.

He stared round the small gathering, of whom only I was accustomed to his brand of balls-out diplomacy. The others looked flummoxed, which of course was his exact intention.

While I had come to detest the man, I also couldn't help but admire him. With a few pithy sentences he had put the UK's Foreign Secretary, two senior diplomats, and the Treasury number two, summarily on their back feet.

Actually, more like flat on their arses.

I caught his eye and could see he was enjoying himself.

Petra glanced at me, but managed to look unfazed.

Once George Watkins had got over his initial shock, which he just failed to mask, he quickly confirmed to me that at least some of his noble gene pool had been built on good solid skulduggery.

"I am sorry you feel like that, Mr President. You will understand that my government begs to differ." He raised his eyebrows gently at his coffee cup, which Yusupov had hijacked and was swirling round in his hand, as if judging its pedigree. In these games of political chess, I was never entirely sure who was for real, and who was just making a point.

He continued, as Yusupov handed him back his cup, having taken a swig.

"My country's position on human rights is very clear. Every citizen has the right to a fair trial and, tempting as it sometimes is…" he smiled patronisingly, "…we stopped locking people up and torturing them on a whim, at the time of Magna Carta, in 1215."

He placed the stolen cup firmly on the tray and took a replacement.

"We expect our allies to do the same." He swallowed elegantly.

Yusupov looked to the heavens in exasperation. He didn't like being patronised.

"We exist in very different environments, Foreign Secretary," he responded, and we all knew what was coming.

"If your ambassador to my country were to be abducted under the noses of my security forces, I would find him and return him to you, and the only human rights we would be considering would be those of your countryman."

There was silence. I felt he had a point.

"Apparently in your country, when the same thing occurs, all your efforts are directed at comforting your goddamned human rights lobby, while my ambassador is left to the mercies of those same terrorists who your lobbyists are campaigning to protect."

He slammed his fist down again. I could almost believe he was losing it, but that steely glare never altered through the squalls of his simulated emotions.

Watkins began to bluster slightly. "We are putting all our resources into the search for your ambassador, Mr President. I can assure you of that. If he is still alive, we will find him."

Yusupov jumped to his feet. "If he is still alive? What exactly do you mean by that? Do you mean you have lost all track of him?"

If I hadn't seen evidence, with my own eyeballs, that the poor bloody diplomat had actually been abducted by his own people, I would have fallen for Yusupov's ruse. Even knowing what I did, I began to question my own memory.

"We are following a number of avenues," Watkins answered enigmatically, and I saw, with some relief, that his ancestors were back in charge.

"One of which suggests that fragments of the container, in which he was placed at the embassy, were found at the entrance to your own Bank of Kuikbakhistan. There is a fully authorised search of the premises going on at this very moment. Would you, or Mr de Carteret, like to comment on that at all, Mr President?"

Yusupov's eyelids narrowed in that mannerism I knew so well when he was pissed off. He turned to me.

"Do you know anything that could throw any light on this ridiculous accusation, Nick?"

"It's complete news to me," I replied. Under the circumstances, I could hardly say anything else. I just hoped they had covered their tracks properly.

Yusupov rose slowly to his feet. He was the personification of composure.

"I am sure you are aware that the ground floor and basement in that building also host our official consular offices. As such, any intrusion into that space by your security services would constitute an act of war, under the Vienna Convention. I hope you will be extremely careful to avoid that eventuality. Remember…" he glared at them "…Kuikbakhistan has nuclear weapons." He bowed to the assembled company, rose and headed for the door.

His hand on the handle, he turned and addressed Petra, who had been almost entirely silent.

"Mrs Marinelli, please inform your colleagues that, unless this stupid misunderstanding can be resolved, and in accordance with the terms of all our infrastructure financing facilities with you, we will be requesting repayment at the time of the next break clause."

Petra looked horrified. The break clauses had only been included, at the insistence of her department, to allow them a get-out in the eventuality that Kuikbakh behaviour towards its neighbours, and especially China, escalated into war. That issue had so far been a complete damp squib. Unlike Yusupov's threatened foreclosure. That would require refinancing a few hundred billion of infrastructure loans; in one month's time.

75

There was a flurry of diplomatic activity after that meeting.

It transpired that the 'consular' status of the BOK building had not been made official.

Well, strictly speaking it had, under Kuikbakh law, as a presidential decree was produced to that effect, dated (or more probably pre-dated) a few days before.

Yusupov's people stuck by this document and argued their case forcefully, but it was too late. The decree had not been registered with the British authorities, and anyway the security services had done their search.

They hadn't found much, other than a few suspicious emails in Kuikbakh referring to delivery of 'the bundle'. Yusupov's boys had cleaned up well.

So, it was pretty much a Mexican stand-off. Or at least a Kuikbakh one.

Yusupov kept beating the shit out of anyone who disagreed with him in his country, and threatening to break diplomatic relations with us; the UK kept complaining, to little effect; and BOK made noises about asking for repayment of its infrastructure finance which it didn't really want back anyway. The loans, after all, provided a useful stick with which to beat the Brits when they complained too much.

What was more important was that Yusupov was stretching himself on too many fronts. He was printing money, through a quantitative easing programme, like it was going out of fashion (it was becoming clear that the country's oil reserves were not as infinite as he liked to make out); he continued to pick fights with the Chinese, and his other neighbours, over rights to minerals and oil near their borders, and with the British in response to their human rights protests. In his own country, he had managed to conjure up an opposition out of thin air by his blatant confusion of the State's and his own property, and by his mistreatment of anyone who dared to complain. My worries for Grigor and his gang were slowly confirmed. The authorities had indeed screwed down tightly after the ambush, and the rebels were largely confined to their heartlands in the mountains. They would come again.

I was sure he was setting himself up for a fall.

But I never forgot what he had said all that time ago to Bobby and me. 'Those who benefit from my largesse always pay me back with interest. If they expect to survive.'

We had both believed every word he had uttered then, and I played them back to myself more frequently these days, especially now Bobby was gone.

I wondered if I should warn Petra Marinelli.

The UK government probably didn't need any advice from me on how to look after itself. I just kept asking myself what measures he was going to take to get his 'largesse' back from them and, even more important, how I was going to make sure that if things went wrong, I would survive, along with my growing family.

PART SIX

FRIENDS REUNITED

76

The next morning, Nasta needed Jimmy to drive her, so I took a cab to the bank.

Jimmy had a soft spot for her, and I would tease him that he enjoyed driving her around more than me.

"Bloody right, boss," he'd say with his infectious grin. "She's so much better looking than you." I would laugh at that, and shake my head. We both knew where his loyalties lay, and I trusted him with my life.

My cab reached the office in good time. I paid the cabbie and opened the door without looking, almost knocking down a woman who was striding out on the edge of the pavement.

"Mind where you put that fucking door," said a familiar voice, which I recognised immediately.

"Is that any way to talk to an old friend, Angie, honey?" I said, picking up a parcel she had dropped.

"Nick de Carteret," she laughed, turning round to face me. "Always trying to get somewhere too fast. How are you, Nick?"

Angie took the parcel, which had been the only actual casualty, and gave me a hug.

"Long time no see, stranger."

I got a wave of genuine pleasure from seeing her.

"Time for a coffee?" I asked.

"Love one," she nodded. "There's a great little Italian place just round the back." She pointed, and I followed her into quite a simple, old-fashioned café, with round wooden tables.

"My office is just across the street." She pointed at a small building, with a large sign, announcing 'Enigma Analytics'.

"EA. It's mine," she said, proudly. "I started it with the cash I made at the bank."

"That's brilliant," I said, genuinely meaning it. We ordered two coffees.

She started to ask about me. "How's Anastasia?"

"She's good, and Chloe, but Bobby's dead."

She held her hand over her mouth. "Oh my god!" she murmured and then, putting her hand on my arm, "I'm so sorry, Nick. He was your oldest friend. There was nothing in the news. What happened?"

"He pissed off Yusupov one too many times." I couldn't stop myself looking round warily.

She shook her head, pensively. "I bet you wanted to kill the little bastard."

I thought it best to change the subject.

"Tell me about Enigma."

And so, after a few further condolences, she did.

"You remember that guy in wealth management at Davenport's, who I was dating?"

"You mean the one who told you about all the deals his clients were doing, so we could pre-trade them?" We laughed. "Yeah, I remember him. Marcus, wasn't it?"

"Yeah, that's him."

I was embarrassed to feel a little twinge of jealousy; which was pretty selfish, as I had dumped Angie unceremoniously.

But she looked good; and happy. I told her that.

A smile stole across her face. "I just feel stronger in myself, with Marcus. I don't need to keep flaunting myself like I used to." She cupped her breasts and pushed them up, giving me that same come-hither look that had got my juices going outside Elbows' office that first day at Davenport's.

"Well anyway, one of Marcus's Arab clients had an IT business. Sorting out the family group's quite considerable system needs, and analysing their competitors' business stats, to use against them.

They were also hot on fraud and security, and they occasionally strayed over the line and did a bit of malware insertion into their major rivals. They had some good young guys and girls working for them, mainly in the Gulf. Didn't treat them too well, so staff turnover was high."

"Sounds like a potentially good business," I nodded.

"It would have been, if the family ever thought of paying for the pleasure. In general, they didn't. They had some proper clients also, but the Emir wanted to sell the business, so someone else could take responsibility for collecting debts off his relations."

I could see what was coming. I had always backed Angie, and felt she could have been successful in a lot of things.

She sipped her coffee and continued.

"Well, I did a few sums on my spreadsheet…"

She laughed, without rancour. "You remember how good I was with spreadsheets, Nick?"

"Uh, huh," I laughed, feeling vaguely uncomfortable.

"Well, Marcus and I acquired EA together." She smiled. "We built it up fast. He understands finance, and I know my way around the whole tech world. I'm no super-nerd, but we've got some of the best of those on our books, now that we pay them properly and treat all our people like human beings. I totally understand what the latest technology can do, and I know how to explain it to my clients in words of one syllable. It all works pretty well. We have offices in London, New York and Moscow, as well as our main operations centre in Abu Dhabi."

I continued to look impressed, as indeed I was.

"We work for your friend, Mr Yusupov, quite a bit, on his UK infrastructure plants," she continued, with a self-conscious smile. "Pays well. We maintain all his systems, keep them optimised, up to date and infection-free.

Works well for both of us."

Her pensive look returned. "I'm going to be doubly wary of him now, though."

"Just go with his flow and don't challenge him too much," I advised. "I bet he pays well."

She laughed. "That's one bonus, for sure. On time, and no questions asked. We get a premium for any special work."

"What kind of thing?" I asked, interested to know how much she knew of Yusupov's devious schemes.

"We occasionally plant a few viruses in his competitors' systems." She grinned. "Nothing too illegal, so far. It's a case of 'ask me no questions, and I'll tell you no lies'. We both like it like that."

She looked at me with a hint of amusement. "That's how you play it with him, Nick, isn't it?"

I looked at my phone to see the inevitable message from my PA. "I have to go, Angie. Wonderful to catch up and I'm so glad it worked out with Marcus." I meant it.

She laughed. "You actually did me a favour, believe it or not. Black guys are so much easier to deal with." We both laughed at that. "And I can see you're starting to move on from your past, aren't you, Nick? That's great."

I held her shoulders.

"And you're doing amazingly, Angie. I'm really happy to have found you again."

She smiled, and kissed me on the cheek.

"You must meet Marcus. You'll like him."

She looked at me in that intense way which made her pupils dilate. It always used to turn me on. "Life's good." She chuckled. "But you and I used to rock'n'roll together, didn't we, Nick? Oh boy, did we ever rock'n'roll."

"Those are some hellish good memories," I agreed.

We both laughed, like old lovers should.

77

The next BOK board meeting took place later that week.

The bank was doing extremely well. Curzon Asset Management was doing even better. Harbour Oil and Greensleeves Engineering were moving rapidly up the FTSE, and with a slightly more secretive, and extremely litigious approach by their new owners, there wasn't much dissent or protest to get in their way.

The only contentious point on the agenda was Yusupov's continued insistence that we request repayment of all infrastructure finance from the UK government, at the upcoming break clause.

"Do we really want repayment?" Inzhu queried. "It's a very safe, blue-chip asset for the bank, and it keeps the government firmly obligated to us."

"Not sufficiently obligated to stop them continually moaning about our supposed human rights failings," he retorted. I could see this, for him, was more a matter of principle than business.

BOK usually followed its chairman's whims, and after a brief discussion, the motion was passed, and she was charged with instructing Featherstone's.

I agreed with Inzhu. The loans suited the bank well, but I didn't press the point.

I was continually studying every facet of Yusupov's character, watching his every move, searching for any weakness; and doing whatever I could to bring him into conflict with all his many and varied counter-parties. Insisting on repayment by the UK government would be doing that job for me and turning them into yet another enemy.

I knew I was walking a tightrope, and that one false move could be fatal.

But at the same time, I was coming to grips with my own demons, and beginning to realise that some people did actually respect me for my achievements. I had Nasta to thank for that.

As a result, I was starting to think a little about people other than my own Fairy Godmother, as Bobby had suggested I should, all those years ago. I even put some small amounts into a couple of local charities that Bobby and Marina had supported. They didn't register as rounding errors on my personal balance sheet, but they did make me feel incredibly good about myself.

In fact, those little donations were the best bang I got for my buck, since Cindy Cavendish let me put my hands down her knickers at nursery school, as a reward for giving her my sister's Barbie.

So, I went rather easier on the young bloods coming through the bank, and began helping them, rather than grinding their noses in shit and spitting them out at the end of each deal, well trained, but emaciated and emotionally broken husks.

As for sex, I'm not saying I had turned into Mahatma Gandhi overnight, but I just didn't feel the need to pick every fucking flower in the garden, whenever I took the dog for a walk.

78

Yusupov, on the other hand, was reaping what he'd sowed.

The Kuikbakh economy was booming, so there was plenty of wealth being created. But his people were finally waking up to the fact that their president was snaffling most of it for himself, while the neighbouring states were getting stroppy with his never-ending attempts to grab their resources.

He kept his people in line with some reverse income tax, a network of paid informers, and some vicious secret police; his neighbours, with a set of missile-based nuclear warheads, and a small army, composed almost entirely of highly paid mercenary special forces. Grigor and his bunch got the full brunt of both.

However, his quantitative easing programme was beginning to stoke up inflation, and the bond markets (of which he was becoming a voracious client) had already spooked once, when some figures leaked out, suggesting that the country's oil reserves were running dry.

I had dinner with him the night before our board meeting, as we usually did. He always wanted my reading of the political and financial temperature in the UK, as well as any gossip about what people thought of everything Kuikbakh. He still almost trusted me. That made me a member of a virtually extinct species; probably an endangered one, after his oil reserve figures had inadvertently gone public.

"Can you please tell me, Nick, why…" he shook his head angrily, "… when I have financed most of the new infrastructure in your country, I get no gratitude; just condemnation for our purported human rights violations?"

I knew the warning signs. He was like a pressure cooker; as the temperature rose, and the steam built up, the threat of an explosion grew exponentially.

On these occasions, I functioned as his escape valve, calming and reassuring him. I made sure I told him what he wanted to hear, partly, I admit, because he didn't take kindly to anything else, and any messenger bearing bad news usually took the bullet; mainly, however, to inflate the bubble of optimism that his own circle of sycophants was continually raising.

I chose my words carefully. "As you are aware, the human rights lobby is too strong for our own good in Europe." He smiled and nodded. "You have become something of a target for them recently, what with the way your police dealt with the recent student riots…" he sighed, "… and those rebels, who abducted your UK ambassador."

We looked knowingly at each other, both remembering the price he had paid for my silence.

"I try to explain to Petra and my other contacts that your country is different from ours, and that it requires a different approach to human rights. They will get the message in time," I lied. "Just try not to rub their noses in it."

It was what he hoped to hear.

"What my people yearn for is a strong leader, who will keep them safe and let them prosper. That is my role. Do you think I am succeeding in that, Nick?"

He felt he was on safe ground there, although I was reassured to see his need for approbation; a need which revealed weakness.

"You've certainly built a lot of infrastructure, and everyone likes the reverse income tax, while all the economists these days say these infrastructure bonds are risk-free for a country with its own currency."

I didn't mention his quantitative easing programme, or the enormous debt that resulted from it, already bigger than GDP; nor that one day his cost of finance would go up and cripple him.

I also didn't raise the fact of his diminishing oil reserves. If he ever mentioned them, I just agreed it was all fake news.

"Overall, the country seems to be booming and, as long as you keep standing up to your neighbours, your people will be secure."

We both smiled at that as, for him, his border disputes were mere school-playground squabbles.

"They do not dare challenge me with the nuclear weapons and forces I command." He puffed out his chest. "But you liberals in Europe…" He raised his eyebrows and breathed out deeply, shaking his head again.

"I cannot afford liberals, Nick. And frankly, your government cannot either. Otherwise, they would have been able to finance that infrastructure themselves."

We cradled our glasses, each deep in his own private thoughts. After a long silence, he began to speak quietly, almost shyly, as if raising an old taboo.

"I had no mother, Nick, rather like you."

"I had a mother," I corrected him. "I just wish I didn't."

"Have you ever tried to find her?"

The question caught me unawares, and I stared at him uneasily.

My discomfort banished his own reticence, and he patted my shoulder. "I can see not. Perhaps you should." His tone confused me. It implied a question but also, as always, an underlying command.

Now he was looking at me as though he were a child with a Christmas secret, who was suddenly bursting to unwrap it.

"Do you remember the clinic in Szchymkent?" he asked.

My mind flashed back, immediately recalling the respectful look on the doctor's face. The image had kept recurring, even as I had constantly pushed it back down.

"Those blood tests…"

He nodded. "Blood, stem cells, DNA. They all point the same way, Nick; we are brothers."

"That couldn't be…" I stammered.

"It could be, Nick. In fact, according to those tests, it definitely is."

Any mention of family had always brought beads of sweat to my brow, but the thought that Tselmeg Yusupov, killer of my best friend, could also be a blood relation of any kind, let alone my brother, confused me and filled me with revulsion.

I did what I had always done when a conversation got too personal: I closed it down.

"I am English, Tselmeg," I said haughtily. "You may have gone to school here, but you are from Kuikbakhistan."

To his credit, he swallowed my scornful put-down without flinching, and responded in kind.

"Your mother was a whore, Nick. Now it appears that mine was, too. We are brothers."

I could hardly be offended, but the truth stung. I remained silent.

"I have always felt a connection with you, Nick. I chose you to work with me on purely professional grounds, but I was always drawn to you, never knowing why."

I started to interject with something disparaging, but he held up both hands, as if conceding. "We may have had our differences, Nick, but you too, have felt the strange tie that draws us closer. Deny it if you will. You rail against it, even despise me at times..." He was watching me closely. "... like a younger brother."

Deep in my heart, I could feel the baleful ring of truth.

I was lost for words, which left the floor to him.

He ordered more drinks, before taking up his story again. The alcohol loosened his tongue, and it all spilled out.

"Like you, I have been confused for some time. One minute you make me proud, the next I can barely stand the sight of you. Just like brothers."

"I hated my brothers," I said.

He could see I meant it, but shrugged his shoulders, as if passing the buck to some greater power, smiling as he continued.

"Then, in hospital those same extremes were amplified beyond all reason. One second I held you responsible for the ambush…" He held up his hand again, as if seeking absolution for my treatment. "… the next minute your blood was saving my life. When those tests came back, it was all suddenly clear."

"I just don't see how that could have happened," I reasoned. "You were raised in Szchymkent; I in London."

"I have thought about it every day, since. Although I can't say those results turned my life upside down, as they seem to have done to yours." He laughed again at my confusion, but this time with kindness. "Just remember, Nick, we are still the same people that we always were."

He continued. "My father told me my mother had died in childbirth. I have since found out that was not true. All I know is that he spent some time in our embassy in London. He died when I was young." His eyes flashed with pain and real anger.

Nasta's words came back to me. "Anastasia thinks she is close to locating my mother," I said. "She asked if I was ready to meet her."

"And are you ready, Nick?"

I nodded. It was the best I could manage.

"Are you, Tselmeg?" I countered, finding my voice with difficulty.

Yusupov's face hardened, and there was another long pause before he spoke again.

"My father supported the old king." He sighed. "My stepmother, who supported Armenov's revolution, had him killed. I was five when the police came for him. I tried to stop them, but they broke my hand with a rifle butt."

He showed me the scars of a badly healed break.

"I had always assumed it was a playground accident," I replied. "Some playground."

He smiled. "I loved my dad, as only a young boy can. Your mother rejected him, Nick. In so doing, she rejected me. All she wanted from him was money. She sold me to him. So, while you and I are brothers, she can never be my mother."

He looked at me with that penetrating stare of his which was impossible to read, shaking his head slowly. "You go and meet your mother, Nick, if she is still alive. I think you should. But I am not ready now, and never will be, to meet the whore who passed me like a parcel at a party game, to that vile woman who became my stepmother."

"Why so much hate for your stepmother, Tselmeg?" I asked quietly.

He paused, and took another swig. I had barely seen him drink before. It seemed to loosen his tongue. That was probably why he rarely did so.

"She raised me and my four stepbrothers. I was the youngest, so I got all the dirty jobs." He looked at me angrily. "And the beatings." I recognised, and could suddenly appreciate the hurt, the source of all his ambition, his obsessive lust for power.

Like mine.

"And that even included servicing the drunken bum she took for her next husband." Anger swept across his eyes and his whole face. I had seen it many times before, and its feral power never failed to frighten me. "And his drinking buddies."

He breathed in deeply.

"Do you know what it's like, at the age of ten, to be raped by a bunch of drunks, with your stepfather watching, Nick?"

"Yes," I replied.

That stopped him in his tracks.

"You do?" he asked sceptically.

"My stepfather tried to rape me," I said quietly, surprising myself at how those words I had never previously uttered, describing scenes my mind had kept firmly locked away, flowed freely, while my world still stayed upright.

We looked at each other warily.

He nodded. "I say again, Nick. I have always felt a connection with you; from the first day we met. I just couldn't know quite how close it actually was, how similar our demons."

We smiled, and the bond between us seemed to tighten; but somehow, at the same time, to throttle and constrict.

"I never saw that stepfather again," I said. "My mother kicked him out."

My words were giving birth to memories I had, until now, managed to repress. It was almost a relief, when he cut them off.

"I killed mine," he whispered. "Slowly and painfully."

"Jesus," I whispered. "You were ten years old?"

He nodded, and his eyes narrowed. I could see the hurt and anger, welling up from inside his soul, spilling out into the world, dressed in the guise of revulsion and bitterness.

He controlled it well, reaching out and putting his hand on my shoulder. We stared unsurely at each other.

Two damaged souls, now brothers. Torn apart at birth, and thrown back together, like flotsam on a high spring tide.

"I suggest you keep this to yourself, Nick. It would be best for both of us. You are my brother…"

He narrowed his eyes, his bitterness returning.

"… but I can never admit that woman as my mother."

"I will tell nobody other than Anastasia," I said. "I tell her everything."

He looked at me with a doubtful smile and raised his eyebrows. Then he started to nod.

"I am glad for you, Nick. Not so long ago I feel you were not always so candid with her."

I tilted my head, acknowledging the truth of his point.

He watched me closely, his rattlesnake eyelids almost closed.

"Above all else, do not tell that whore, that the son she sold like a cheap toy survived and is alive."

We sat there, each engrossed in his own thoughts. I don't know for how long.

Finally, he raised his glass. I mirrored his action, slowly and deliberately. Putting some of the past behind us, we drank to the future.

"That our paths may always be aligned," toasted Yusupov. "Always aligned," he repeated himself, as if by so doing he would make it true.

I held his gaze.

I didn't blink.

* * *

"That is unbelievable." Nasta had waited up for me. She never knew what to expect after I met with Yusupov, so usually stayed awake. "Although I suppose it does explain some of the conflicts and paradoxes between you two."

She smiled at me and kissed my cheek.

"Having said that, if you do both share a mother, I would love to meet the woman who bore you both."

She stared in my eyes and hugged me. "But your fathers must have been totally different. Yusupov killed Bobby. You could never do that."

"Perhaps it does explain my empathy with him; why I seem to understand his point of view, even take his side, when we deal with Petra and her gang," I mused, as much to myself as to anyone.

Anastasia nodded.

"Nick, I am going to find your mother, and then she can tell you what happened herself. But does this change the way you deal with Yusupov in any way?"

Nasta had that knack of asking those searching questions which always went to the very heart of any problem.

"No," I whispered. I clenched my fists and breathed in deeply. "Tselmeg Yusupov killed Bobby. He is going to pay for that. Being my brother only makes it worse."

79

The next morning, Petra Marinelli left an urgent message for me. When I rang her back, she was in some state. Yusupov had been as good as his word, and BOK was duly requesting repayment of all the UK infrastructure finance.

"Is he bluffing, Nick?" she asked. "For Christ's sake, he can't just withdraw his credit on a whim."

"You agreed that break clause, Petra," I reminded her. "From what I remember, you felt that it would be appropriate, in case he embarrassed you by pissing off the Chinese. I would call that being hoist with your own petard." I admit that I was rather enjoying her discomfort.

"Can you reason with him, Nick?" she pleaded. "This is really quite a major issue."

"While not always reasonable by any means, Yusupov certainly responds to reason," I advised. "Go easy on the human rights nonsense. It's the only way you're going to keep that finance. As he said to me earlier this week, his country isn't like ours."

I thought I would make the point to her that I was close to her tormentor. I wasn't going to let on about any of the tensions in my own relationship with him.

"Kuikbakhistan needs a strong leader who can keep them fed, watered and safe. It's quite simple, and that's exactly what he's doing. His people mostly like it, even if you don't. Cut the liberal crap, Petra, and you will find you can get on really well with him."

There was silence, and I thought she had disconnected, but she let out a sigh. I could feel her anxiety.

"Thanks, Nick. I will talk with George."

"Tell the Foreign Secretary that modern diplomacy takes many forms," I told her, echoing the aspersions he had cast at my own loose approach to banking regulation. "And the Foreign Office needs to be adept at all of them. In plain language, that means that if you want to keep your finance, then get off his fucking case."

"I will tell him."

I don't know if it was testament to George Watkins' pragmatism, or Petra Marinelli's powers of persuasion, but suddenly there wasn't another squeak about human rights; which showed me all that nonsense had been coming from the FO, and also that Petra was a force to be reckoned with when she had to defend her position.

Yusupov swallowed his pride, and let the break clause expire.

So, I felt let down when, in less than two months after that event, Watkins called in the new Kuikbakh ambassador, and hauled him over the coals for the same set of transgressions which they had so recently decided to overlook.

Yusupov was fuming, and again threatened Armageddon. With my particular knowledge of his emotional drivers, I should have realised that George Watkins' volte-face reminded Tselmeg Yusupov of his stepfather. Yusupov had now been screwed by both of them.

The last time that happened, it hadn't ended well.

PART SEVEN
DIPLOMATIC FISSION

80

"I wanted to let you know who the new ambassador to Kuikbakhistan is going to be, Nick. I think I have managed quite a coup." Petra Marinelli had summoned me for an update on Kuikbakhistan.

The British ambassador's term had just expired, and his replacement was currently being selected.

"I persuaded George to send a real heavyweight." Petra Marinelli paused for effect. "Someone already known to President Yusupov."

Petra was, as usual, acting as clandestine liaison between the Foreign Office and Yusupov, using me as her sounding board.

I put down my coffee. This sounded hopeful.

"It has not been an easy choice, Nick, as I am sure you will understand. On the one hand, their president has been extremely helpful to us financially." She gave a tick-box smile. "As against that, their human rights record is, shall we say, less than we would hope for in a country with which we maintain such strong commercial ties."

Diplomatic jargon never ceased to frustrate me. I always wondered why they couldn't just come out and say what they meant.

"You mean you want to take their money, while maintaining your moral superiority, Petra. Is that what you are trying to say?"

After a slight hesitation she smiled and nodded. "You always put things so succinctly, Nick. That is why I sometimes…" she emphasised the word, "like doing business with you."

She sipped at her coffee diplomatically. I was not sure if she actually swallowed it.

"If you have any sense, you will send a very seasoned diplomat, who is a good linguist, and whose wife will become a stalwart of the social scene there. They are strong on entertainment, especially in their long, diabolical winters."

I detected a hesitation. "George Watkins has selected probably one of our brightest and best diplomats for the role, which I hope President Yusupov will take in the positive vein in which it is intended. He also speaks a number of languages, including Russian."

"What's the catch, Petra?" I asked, resignedly.

"Matthew Abbott isn't married," she replied.

"Isn't currently, or has no interest?" I asked, as diplomatically as I knew how.

"He's a bachelor." She hurried on, trying to ignore my facial expression.

"Matthew is the height of respectability. Second son of an earl, with impeccable connections and a razor-sharp intellect. He was our man in Japan and was a great success there."

"For Christ's sake, Petra, is he gay?" I held up my hands. "I don't give a shit which way he swings. Each to his own. But do you have any idea how inappropriate that could be in Kuikbakhistan?"

"I am assured Matthew is asexual. There is absolutely no record of any activity of any sort in that department." She smiled triumphantly, and I could see she was saving her best for last. "He was at school with Yusupov."

"That's great, Petra, as long as they both enjoyed their time there. But there is no such thing as asexual. Whatever appetites he has, they may be well hidden, and the British establishment may have closed ranks in behind him; but I can absolutely assure you that he does, has had, or wants to have sex with somebody or something."

Petra put both hands up in a valiant effort to stop the flow of this conversation.

But I wasn't going to let her off the hook.

"And for your ears only, you should know that Yusupov was raped by his stepfather and friends when he was a young boy."

Now she looked shocked.

"He killed him, as he explained to me in some detail." I exaggerated, to make my point. "Slowly, and excruciatingly painfully. Yusupov was ten years old at the time."

There was a long silence, and to her credit she stared right back at me.

Very quietly she said, "Thank you, Nick. I will talk to George."

* * *

I wasn't surprised that George Watkins would not be moved in his choice of ambassador. Nor, that he handed me the task of breaking the news to the powers that be in Kuikbakhistan.

Yusupov took it well. "I remember Matthew from school. I see he has become one of your top people, Nick," he said, sounding pleased.

Petra had done her research, and not a whiff had been unearthed of any sexual activity at all, throughout Matthew Abbott's entire career. From Yusupov's reaction, I could only assume that extended back to his schooldays. I breathed a sigh of relief.

"I look forward to welcoming Matthew to Kuikbakhistan," he continued. "When does he arrive?"

"He is scheduled to present his credentials to you on the first of September."

"Excellent," crowed Yusupov. He was obviously judging this to be a statement of friendly intent by the UK Foreign Office. I had to hand it to George Watkins.

* * *

Matthew Abbott's entry into Szchymkent society was the success that George Watkins had hoped for. The embassy hosted a cocktail party for all the diplomatic and business high-fliers. Nasta and I were there.

His Russian was excellent, and most of the elder Kuikbakhs spoke it, from their time as part of the USSR. He was smart, witty, well-informed; in short, the perfect diplomat. He and Yusupov struck up quite a friendship, based on their shared old-boy network and memories. They had been exact contemporaries.

He would have been a good banker, I thought. Nasta and I scrutinised him minutely, for any hint of weakness.

"I don't know what he is, but he sure as hell isn't hetero," declared Nasta in our hotel room, afterwards. "I love him. Unbelievably charming. But there is no spark there at all. Zilch. Nada."

She sounded disappointed. She was not accustomed to people failing to find her attractive.

"Did he go for you?" she asked with a smile.

"I couldn't tell," I replied honestly. "But I enjoyed his company, and found him amusing, urbane and intelligent."

"The entire machinery of UK government has examined and passed him. So, he has my vote," she argued.

"I just don't think he's the right person for this posting, but I won't argue with you," I conceded, holding up both hands with fingers firmly crossed.

81

I always like to be in early at the office. To stay ahead of the pack, you need to keep abreast of everything that goes on. While I wasn't looking over my shoulder anymore (my demons were taking what I hoped would be at least an extended sabbatical), I found habits hard to break, and so I continued my early-doors routine.

The only danger with this strategy is that when shit happens, you land up with your thumb in the dyke, so to speak.

One Thursday morning, my phone rang as soon as I got to my desk. It was George Watkins himself, on my direct line.

"I've sent a car for you. It should be outside your door. It would be unwise to discuss this on the telephone."

He rang off, and almost immediately, reception rang up to tell me that my car was waiting.

Obviously, some serious sewage had floated to the surface at the FO.

I needed to find out, so I rang Yusupov from the car.

"What has happened, Tselmeg?" I asked. "George Watkins has called me round urgently, and says he has to talk with me, but only face to face."

Yusupov spoke so quietly, I could barely hear him. That got my alarm bells ringing loudly.

"Your ambassador has disappointed us badly, and I have sent for him," he almost whispered.

"Christ…" was all I had time to say.

"I would never normally trust an older, unmarried bachelor, Nick."

I had a nasty feeling I knew what was coming.

"But I have always had deep respect for everything British, and he did after all, go to school with me." I was straining to hear him now.

"What is more, I trusted your judgement, Nick." That put me firmly on the hook.

"However…" he paused, and I hoped he was getting himself under control.

I was wrong.

"… it is the last time I will ever accept your judgement, or my old school or even British citizenship, as an indicator of good character." Now he was almost screaming.

I feared the worst, but thought better than to interrupt him. He paused, sounding calmer.

"You know me as well as anyone, Nick. So, what do you think my particular bête noire might be?"

"Paedophilia," I thought to myself, not realising I had actually voiced it out loud.

"Exactly," he whispered again.

"Tselmeg, for God's sake don't do anything rash. He will be brought to justice in the UK, I promise. You must trust us to do that. If you take things into your own hands, it will produce the biggest diplomatic scandal of all time."

I was imagining what Yusupov had done to his own stepfather. Extrapolating that treatment to the UK ambassador, in a Kuikbakh jail, would not make for good headlines. I wasn't so much thinking of Yusupov; the more fights he picked, the sooner I would be able to bring him down. I was just horrified at the thought of what he might do to the charming old ambassador, who Nasta and I had liked so much.

"Tselmeg, where is he now? I implore you to calm down, and follow the normal diplomatic channels," I begged.

"Do you know, Nick, that he procured himself a ten-year-old boy from the city slums, took him to a cheap hotel, and abused him.

How he found the poor child I have no idea, but I will establish that, and the culprits will be punished. And please tell your Foreign Secretary that I hold him personally responsible for any harm which comes to your nauseating ambassador."

I thought he would put the phone down, but he wasn't finished.

"And as for you, Nick." He paused, and I was at a loss to fill the silence. "I can only assume, in spite of all I have done for you, and the way I have opened my heart to you, as I have to nobody else alive, that you were involved in the selection of this ambassador to my country. I assume you knew full well his vile tendencies, and my inevitable reaction to them."

"Tselmeg, I can guarantee you, I was assured of his impeccable morals, and even so, I suggested strongly to our Foreign Secretary that Matthew Abbott was not a suitable candidate. I would never do that to you."

"I have been betrayed," he muttered. "By your government, and by you, my own brother. I cannot forgive you for that, Nick. You are exhausting my patience."

"Tselmeg, I am just going in to meet George Watkins. Please, bear with us, and don't do anything rash."

The connection went dead.

82

George Watkins was waiting for me, with a small crowd of henchmen.

"Matthew Abbott has fallen foul of the Kuikbakh authorities."

From the look on George's face, he was hunting for someone to take the rap for this. As our eyes met, I realised; he was looking at him.

My thumb was plainly the only piece of the dyke which was still holding, and it was time for a bit of self-preservation.

"I did advise you very plainly, Minister, that Matthew was the wrong candidate for this posting. The only important thing now is to extract him without further damage to our relations with Kuikbakhistan; or to Matthew."

"We are all ears, Nick," he replied, gesturing at the half dozen senior diplomatic and security high-rankers, who were present. I saw Petra Marinelli at the back, looking uneasy.

"I have just spoken to Yusupov, and he has 'sent for' Matthew, whatever that means," I informed him. "Yusupov is seething," I continued, in case he hadn't got my gist. "Have you called in the stand-in Kuikbakh ambassador?"

"Of course. He is on his way, and we are trying to get through to our embassy on the secure line."

"Did Petra tell you that Yusupov's stepfather sexually abused him?" I asked, as bluntly as I could.

Watkins and Petra looked uneasily at each other. She obviously had.

"Did she also tell you that Yusupov, who was ten at the time, then proceeded to kill the man in an extremely vicious manner?"

"Matthew Abbott was without any doubt the ideal person for this role, Nick," he smarmed.

"Well, try telling him that, when Yusupov is separating him from his testicles, without anaesthetic," I responded quietly.

They all looked shocked.

"Because I suspect that is what he is intending to do, as soon as he gets hold of him. And thanks, Minister, for completely ignoring my advice on this."

I was losing my cool, and started to shout.

"As a result, Yusupov, who had only recently confided in me about the traumas of his early life, now believes I was somehow responsible for choosing the exact ambassador who most resembled his nemesis."

A video link crackled into life.

The embassy spook out in Kuikbakhistan was manning it. He looked strained.

"What's the situation out there?" asked a wiry little man beside me, who I hadn't noticed, but now recognised as the head of MI6.

The spook looked over his shoulder as he saw Matthew Abbott, who quickly joined him. Matthew was looking very un-ambassadorial, obviously hungover, and thoroughly dishevelled.

"I am so sorry, George," he said, and I had to admire him for his openness. "I screwed up. You have my immediate resignation."

That eased the tension, and allowed us to get on with things.

"Thank you, Matthew, but that is somewhat secondary. We believe the Kuikbakh security services may be coming to detain you, at this very moment."

"Here in the embassy?" he asked, his eyes widening fearfully, as he began to understand what he had undoubtedly been told; that diplomatic niceties were not always Yusupov's top priority.

MI6 tapped Watkins on the shoulder and whispered in his ear. Watkins nodded, and made way for him.

"Matthew, I need you to listen very carefully," he said. "Adrian and his team are going to extract you." The embassy spook came back into view, looking completely in his element now, and consulting his smartphone.

"Are you good to go, Adrian?" asked MI6. The spook nodded.

"Vehicle fully manned and waiting for us. 'Operation Corkscrew', with helicopter RV just inside the border and backup team, all ready and waiting."

MI6 looked at Watkins and raised his eyebrows questioningly.

Watkins nodded, almost imperceptibly. I got the impression he was still hoping to avoid any of this shit sticking to him.

"Operation Corkscrew is authorised. Good luck."

We could see Matthew Abbott being manhandled towards the door, looking back over his shoulder with alarm.

"You need to talk with Yusupov, George," I told Watkins. He looked momentarily fearful but, to give him his due, he manned up quickly enough.

"I want you to stay with me, Nick. You know him better than anybody."

"I am afraid that may actually count against me, now," I retorted, wanting to add 'Thanks to you, arsehole', but restraining myself in the interests of diplomacy.

"We have to give them a start. Keep stalling him, as much as you can. I will prompt you if we need to change tack, because if he gets a whiff of what you are doing, all hell will break loose."

I felt it was my job to coach the Foreign Secretary, as I was the only one who had any idea how to deal with Eurasian psychopaths.

The integrity of Matthew Abbott's testicles depended on it, and with them, the whole gamut of Anglo-Kuikbakh diplomatic relations.

83

"Good morning, Mr President," intoned Watkins, a shade obsequiously.

"Your ambassador is a paedophile," stated Yusupov, ignoring the greeting. "And as Nick tells me he has already informed you," he looked questioningly at each of us, "I regard paedophiles as scum, who deserve to be eradicated."

"I can only apologise on behalf of Her Majesty's Government, if this alleged incident turns out to be true," replied the Foreign Secretary, sticking to the diplomatic script.

Yusupov didn't like scripts, especially diplomatic ones.

"The incident happened, Foreign Secretary. I can assure you of that. I have the poor wretched boy in my care. As you would imagine, he is very distressed. Depending on your response to this revolting incident, I will be inviting the world media to interview him."

George Watkins was a diplomat and a wily negotiator, but his face gave him away.

Blind panic.

"Can we see him?" he asked, trying to give himself time, in the hope that his ambassador could be spirited away before Yusupov got to him, and that the boy would just vanish.

"That will not be possible I am afraid, but you can rest assured he is in good hands. Unlike last night," he almost spat.

Watkins was nothing, if not persistent.

"Matthew has resigned as ambassador. I can assure you, he will face the full force of the British legal system when he returns here.

We will need to get the boy's statement. Mr President, you cannot put the poor child through the added trauma of being interviewed by the press."

"After what your ambassador put him through, I am surprised you have the gall to infer that anything could be worse."

The thought did cross my mind that the whole incident could have been a set-up. I definitely wouldn't have put it past Yusupov. I never underestimated him and I certainly wasn't going to start now.

"Until this happened, I would have been inclined to defer to your sense of British fair play, and allow you to deal with your own people, in your own way," murmured Yusupov.

That, to me, familiar wave of anger swept across his face.

"But I now realise that old school friends do not necessarily keep to their old school's moral codes; old friends…" he scowled at me, "betray intimate confidences without scruple…"

I interrupted, not wanting to let him get away with that repeated accusation.

"Tselmeg, I absolutely did not betray your confidence. You and I exchanged some very personal history the other day. I appreciated your honesty, and I hope you felt the same way. I subsequently told the Foreign Secretary, very clearly, that Matthew Abbott was the wrong choice for ambassador, even though we had absolutely no intimation at that time that he had any paedophile tendencies."

Yusupov looked at me as if I had just crawled out of a piece of cheese.

"If you had taken what I told you seriously, you would have sent an ambassador to my country with a loving wife and family, knowing full well that we take our diplomatic entertainment very seriously, not least in the winter. Not an unmarried paedophile."

"I can only repeat again what I said before, Tselmeg. I made that exact point to the Minister…" I eyeballed George Watkins, "… but I was over-ruled."

I didn't want to expose to Yusupov my lowly place on the British diplomatic totem-pole, but at the same time, I didn't want to take the wrap all myself. George looked away self-consciously.

Yusupov ignored me and raised his voice. "Instead, you all conspired together with your intricate networks of schools and diplomatic associations, to send out someone who, within months of arriving, has abused not only our hospitality, but the very core of our Kuikbakh self-esteem – our youth."

There was little we could say from our end. Neither did Yusupov give us the opportunity to do so.

He started ominously quietly again. "If you think that I am now going to put my faith in your legal and diplomatic system, to right the wrongs that your ambassador has committed, then you are sadly misguided."

His rage was there for all to see by now, and the words gushed out, leaving no room for misinterpretation. "I will deal with Matthew Abbott. He will face Kuikbakh justice in this matter. He has defiled our Kuikbakh youth and innocence."

"I beg you to reconsider, Mr President," whined Watkins. "I implore you not to violate the sanctity of our diplomatic immunity."

I looked at George Watkins, to see if he was trying to wind up his adversary. His choice of words seemed to point to that, but I saw that his expression was guileless. Or should I say, clueless. He was out of his depth. To be fair to him, most people would be when dealing with Tselmeg Yusupov.

Yusupov duly exploded.

"The sanctity of your diplomatic immunity…" he yelled, the veins in his neck bulging.

"What about the sanctity of that young Kuikbakh boy? What do you care about that, with all your begging and imploring?" he sneered.

"My people are on their way to your embassy, and I suggest you allow them free entry, so that this crime against my country can be dealt with under Kuikbakh laws and customs."

The Kuikbakh legal system was fairly robust, but I didn't like the mention of Kuikbakh customs. They were likely to be vengeful and vicious. Just like the man on our screen.

"Otherwise, your fatuous immunity will be extinguished, along with all diplomatic ties between our two countries."

He glared out from the screen. "Those ties will be strained in any event, I imagine, when the poor boy is interviewed on global TV. I am giving an exclusive to the Russian state news channel. They are on their way here.

"Make your choice, Foreign Secretary. Either you deliver your ambassador to me now, or the interview goes ahead, and the English public-school proclivity for deviant sexual behaviour will be the talking point of the world." He spat the words out and was gone.

First making sure the equipment was turned off, George Watkins looked round, in shock.

It seemed I was the only one who wasn't fazed by Yusupov's histrionics.

"I think it could have been a honeytrap," I ventured.

Watkins liked that, and opened his mouth.

"But we can never prove it, and certainly not in the timescale available," I added, watching him deflate abruptly.

"We need to make sure Abbott is getting out of there," MI6 advised, tapping his watch.

"We can't let that boy on the news," insisted a girl, who I recognised as one of the PM's spin doctors.

"We also can't let the ambassador face a Kuikbakh interrogation," replied Watkins, showing a level of humanity I had not thought he possessed. Or was he just playing diplomatic games? I couldn't tell.

Everyone except MI6 seemed to be wading through knee-deep puddles of shit, for all the decision-making urgency they were displaying.

It seemed only too obvious to me, that the first priority was to get Abbott out of danger. Then we could negotiate from a position of, if not strength, then at least not from one of splayed-leg vulnerability.

MI6 took things into his own hands, and I admired him for it. He called the embassy, and was quickly put through.

They confirmed that the ambassador had left.

They didn't mention the manner of his leaving, with a heavily armed escort.

That would have been undiplomatic.

84

British special forces are second to none.

I wasn't at all surprised to hear that Ambassador Abbott had been extracted successfully. They had driven him to the border in a 'clean' car, which they had dumped and burnt. A stealth helicopter had picked him up at the agreed RV and taken him, almost at the extent of its range, to an aircraft carrier, which was fortuitously in the area, on exercise.

"Piece of cake," said MI6 to the PM.

George Watkins had asked me to be present at the PM's security briefing, as he felt my knowledge of Yusupov was critical.

The whole situation had escalated exactly as Yusupov would have wanted.

Russian TV had interviewed the president himself, who had given a bravura performance of outrage and injured innocence, peppering his diatribe with allusions to 'my former friends in the UK'. The fact that the ambassador had been spirited out from under his nose was particularly irritating to him, and he ranted about 'proper diplomatic protocols, which were invented by the British, but which they now see fit to contravene, with the sole objective of enabling their disgusting pervert of an ambassador to evade Kuikbakh justice'

He skipped pretty quickly over the fact that he had actually been intending to assault the British Embassy, disregarding all those 'proper diplomatic protocols' himself.

Then the Russians talked to the boy himself. It was clever. They dredged up some family video of him talking happily about a holiday he had enjoyed. Then they cut to the institution where he was obviously being held, but kept him behind a screen, while he answered their questions morosely and in tear-spattered monosyllables.

The impression given was of Kuikbakhistan, a small family-oriented country, looking after its own innocent youth in the face of foreign aggression and malevolence. The message came over loud and clear.

"Nick, you feel this may have been a honeytrap?" asked the PM.

"It has some of the hallmarks," I replied.

I could see their minds fast-forwarding through the possibilities such an option could introduce.

I hated to disappoint them. "However, on reflection I think it probably wasn't. I just don't see what advantage Yusupov would gain from it. He never does anything if he's not going to benefit from it. In any event, we can never prove it."

They looked disappointed.

"His benefit, surely, is to hold the UK to ransom, to see what he can get out of it," said George Watkins emphatically, showing real feeling.

"But he actually likes the UK, and wants to do business with us," I retorted. "Or did. He feels a loyalty to us, as his alma mater. He was genuinely delighted to have an old school friend as our ambassador there. God knows, he has made enough enemies on his borders, and even in his own country, not to want to make one out of us as well; especially when he has invested so much with us, in both diplomatic and financial terms."

They looked thoughtful.

"As I explained to the Foreign Secretary, when he asked my advice on selecting an ambassador, Yusupov was abused by his stepfather, so Abbott's behaviour is pretty much at the top of his list of unacceptable activities." I looked at Watkins who, as usual, failed to rise to the challenge and looked away.

I drove home my point. "I also explained, as Yusupov reiterated when we spoke to him earlier, that diplomatic life in Kuikbakhistan revolves around lavish family-based hospitality. They don't like homosexuals, so an older bachelor who has never been married, was not an ideal choice."

"But Ambassador Abbott went to school with the president, didn't he?" asked the PM. "That sounds like an excellent connection."

"They were getting on extremely well, Prime Minister, which was exactly my intention," oozed Watkins. The way he was trying to sidle out of all responsibility for this disaster was beginning to piss me off. I wasn't particularly interested in gaining any Brownie points myself, but I was fucked if I was going to let him get off the hook.

"I had an intimate conversation with Yusupov recently, where we took it in turns to recount our experiences of being sexually abused in our youth. It strengthened the bond between us, as you can imagine." I did not find that an easy confession. They looked uncomfortably at each other, as if I had admitted that I was contaminated by some infectious disease.

"Having had that conversation with him, I can assure you that he finds this kind of behaviour so utterly deplorable that he could never bring himself to envisage, let alone accept, its enactment, in any shape or form on Kuikbakh soil."

Watkins still looked unimpressed.

"And all those fond memories and old school connections drawing Yusupov closer to the UK have now disappeared out the window, like a milkman caught with his bottle up the wrong nightie."

They didn't appear to appreciate the image I was trying to conjure up. Fuck them, it was the establishment which had screwed up, and they had better learn to admit it.

"Now we've repatriated Abbott, you can say goodbye to cordial relations with them or any more oil, and watch out you don't break any of the covenants on the finance he provided, or he will want full repayment." I was getting their attention, now that I was talking hard cash.

"In fact, I would be very much on guard that he doesn't try and pull some terrorist stunt, like spiriting his own ambassador out of the country and blaming it on you." I looked round, interested to see whether a reminder of Yusupov's previous coup would elicit any reaction.

MI6 looked embarrassed. At least someone had the decency.

"Or pulling some nasty stunt in the UK, and blaming it on terrorists. Because, believe me, I know the guy well, and he will be out for revenge now."

"I think our security will be up to that, Nick," chortled the PM, looking smugly at MI6.

The security chief raised an eyebrow, and nodded almost imperceptibly.

"We have to hope so, PM," he murmured realistically.

I decided I liked the guy.

85

Yusupov kept exactly to the first act of my script. He withdrew his ambassador, and left a skeleton staff with a low-level team, whose bearing was more pugilistic than diplomatic.

I was in considerable demand with the powers that be, as I still maintained some dialogue with the rogue president, although it mostly consisted of protests about my compatriots, and sometimes about me. If they had known of the full extent of my blood connection with him, I suspect I might have lost their trust. I had already lost much of his.

I was still working hard at the bank, although more as a rainmaker now. I won the business though my connections, while others did the grunt work. The London branch was expanding rapidly, shrugging off the diplomatic impasse as if it had nothing to do with BOK. The main development I did notice was that the number of 'pre-packs' increased, partly due to a tightening in the economy, but also without doubt, as part of an unstated policy to increase Curzon AM's portfolio of UK assets.

It was Yusupov's way of getting his own back.

I could understand that. I would have done the same myself.

"I still feel a strange sympathy with him," I explained to Nasta one evening. "I just can't seem to get rid of it."

"Blood is strong, Nick. He is your brother," Nasta reminded me.

I nodded thoughtfully. "Agreed, but he's also got to a position of tremendous power and wealth, entirely due to his own efforts, driven by his past, using his talents ruthlessly and single-mindedly, to the very best of his ability. I admire that."

"Just like you, Nick," she nodded. "You are really quite similar. You just don't have his nasty murderous traits."

"I suppose you're right. I am also beginning to understand myself, little by little, and him too. Both of us know exactly what it's like to be forever running, but never knowing why, or from what. Perhaps that is our common inheritance." I blinked, a picture of my other siblings suddenly taking me by surprise, as it often did. "After all we have been through, I certainly empathise more with him than with George Watkins and those tossers at the Foreign Office."

"But he's also the yardstick by which you measure yourself."

I nodded. "I have to surpass him, outdo him, in everything. I need that for myself. To bury my demons." I stared out of the window, my fists clenched. "And I'm going to make him pay for what he did to Bobby."

"Just have patience," insisted Nasta. "We can see him making so many enemies and in the end that will be his downfall." She hugged me. "Just let him self-destruct. Don't risk everything." She smiled at me. "You're so much better than him, you just can't quite see that yet."

I had to admit that her faith in me felt good.

"And when that vile man has finally met his end, Bobby and Marina will be avenged, and you'll be able to live your life untrammelled by the nightmares from your past. I, for one, can't wait for that happy day."

I gave her a kiss. I had come to rely on Nasta. I found that she was usually right, and I listened to her advice more and more.

86

So, I suppose I shouldn't have been surprised that by the time I awoke the next morning, Yusupov had given added credence to her theory about making too many enemies.

The news was full of it. A female English doctor called Sophie Maddox, working in Kuikbakhistan, had been arrested on charges of spying, and aiding terrorists.

Yusupov's foreign minister was on the Russian news programme, relayed on an early BBC bulletin, ranting about 'foreign backing for the enemies of Kuikbakhistan'.

They gave what remained of our embassy staff twenty-four hours to leave the country.

A UK Foreign Office spokesman was on next, claiming that the woman had simply been giving medical support in poor areas for a charity, and had absolutely no connection of any sort with either terrorists, rebels, or the UK government.

Nasta looked at me with a triumphant 'I told you so' look on her face.

"Ok, you were right," I laughed, happy to admit it.

Jimmy was waiting for me, and the traffic was light at that hour. A call from Yusupov was waiting for me as I got to my desk. I took it on the secure phone. I thought it quite likely that Watkins was keeping tabs on me.

After the normal rant about the 'ungrateful and traitorous' UK authorities, I managed to get a word in. "What's the story with this British doctor? Is she really a spy? Isn't she just a doctor, working for charity?"

He sighed.

"She was treating rebel forces, who had been wounded in yesterday's attack on a rural police station. Anyone who supports terrorists in our country is an enemy of my people. Your government refuses to condemn her, and I now understand there is a whole network of foreign so-called charity and aid workers who are actually helping these criminals, not only with medicines, but also with communications and supplies. They are also procuring sex from the poor wretches they are supposed to be helping. I will not accept this. I am searching for culprits of this depraved practice, as we speak."

"Do you really need to excommunicate our entire diplomatic team? I know Watkins gets up your nose, as he does mine, but wouldn't it be better to see what diplomatic leverage this can give you?"

"She has confessed already," he stated bluntly.

"You've not handed her over to your security services, have you?"

"Of course, I have," he replied angrily. "Do you think she would voluntarily answer our questions over a cup of tea? Not even you could be so naïve."

He lowered his voice, and there was a note of satisfaction to it. "She has been very helpful, Nick. She has implicated others, and made us aware of their supply chains, for both weapons and new recruits. She has also fingered the perverts working for these so-called charities. We are acting on this information."

"Tselmeg, if you have tortured a British citizen, there will be hell to pay." I tried not to sound too happy about that. "Just put any other aid workers you suspect on the first plane out. Taking your revenge on them will put the whole world against you." I knew that he would not take any notice of my advice, but I gave it anyway.

"Her guilt is plain for all to see, Nick. All will become clear to you, too, when you watch the news today. As for the others, we will be rounding them up shortly."

I could see he was past taking any counsel from me on this

one, so I gave him one piece more, for appearances sake. "That's a dangerous game to play, Tselmeg."

He seemed not to hear. "It will also come out under due process in a court of law, as will the complicity of your own, and other, governments. We will take into account her cooperation when sentencing her. The normal penalty for her crimes in Kuikbakhistan is death by firing squad."

87

"She's admitted everything, and implicated various other aid agencies working in Kuikbakhistan," I informed them when I returned to the Foreign Office, an hour later.

"Under torture, I assume," muttered George Watkins, angrily.

"He tells me they are airing her confession on the news channels. Perhaps we should watch, and make up our own minds," I replied. Watkins looked at me, in that lopsided way of his, which I was beginning to find so unappealing.

An aide flipped through the channels on a large screen, which lowered on the opposite wall, until he caught 'Kuikbakhistan' in large headlines on the Al Jazeera news channel. Sure enough, the newsreader introduced the story, and there was Miss Maddox, looking dishevelled and tearful. Whether tortured, terrified, or just remorseful, it was hard to tell.

Watkins opted for tortured and terrified. I couldn't blame him. I had, after all, heard Yusupov virtually admit it. How guilty she was of the charges brought against her, I couldn't tell.

One thing I was sure about. The world was going to unite in her defence, against this renegade president, and no amount of process in a Szchymkent court was going to change their minds.

Just as Nasta had predicted, my nemesis was finally managing to unite most of the western world against him.

The Foreign Secretary bought me back to the present.

"I have called whatever passes for their ambassador these days, and have cleared it with the PM. We are going to dispatch any last vestiges of diplomatic relations with the miserable man, and his country."

I didn't bother to point out that the Anglo-Kuikbakh diplomatic stable was already pretty empty, most of the horses having long-since bolted. I simply asked, "How do we get her back?"

"We will put every possible pressure on him," he smiled artfully. "We are supporting what passes for an opposition to him, in their attempts to have him impeached or overthrown."

"You need to get your security boys to come to an agreement with those rebels," I suggested. "It's only brute force that is going to get him out of power, and with our help, they could become a force to be reckoned with."

Watkins turned to me, but he wasn't listening. "And I hope we can rely on you, Nick, to use your personal ties…" a look of profound distaste crossed his face, "… to help us in that endeavour?" He finished the sentence with raised tone and eyebrows, both gestures subtly questioning my loyalty to his cause.

Little did he know that, while our sympathies diverged, our causes were completely aligned. We both wanted rid of Yusupov.

Things moved quickly after that.

Any remaining diplomatic ties with Kuikbakhistan were quickly severed, and all necessary communications were fed through US channels. I think we kept a few spooks in their local delegation out there.

BOK became Yusupov's unofficial consulate and, purely through force of circumstance, I became the conduit for any diplomatic traffic, at least between him and George Watkins.

While I had never recovered the Kuikbahk's complete trust after Abbott's behaviour, I was still his primary liaison with the Western powers-that-be. That suited me in every way.

88

As I opened my front door, Nasta was standing in the hallway, looking triumphant.

"I found your mother," she declared. "She wants to see you."

My mouth dropped open, and my heart started thumping.

"Where?" was all I could think to ask.

"She's in a home in the East End. It's not too bad, although the staff aren't great."

"Oh my god," I whispered, instinctively heading for the drinks-cabinet, and helping myself. Just the mention of my mother as a possible reality brought all my childhood contradictions flooding back.

Nasta followed me. I poured her a gin and ginger ale and passed it to her.

"She loves you, Nick. She has been off the game and clean from drugs for years and has followed your every move. But she didn't want to shame you by getting back in touch. She changed her name. She's getting old, Nick, and she wants to see you, before it's too late. She has some things from your father."

Holy shit, this was all getting too complicated.

I held my head in my hands. "I can't do it, Nasta. It's been too long." All the old feelings of fear, shame and inadequacy which I had struggled so hard to bury, came hurtling back, threatening to drown me.

Nasta prised my hands gently off my head. "Perhaps she can tell you about Yusupov."

That did little to relieve my anxiety.

We sat there in silence, sipping our drinks.

After a bit, she murmured, "You don't have to be ashamed of where you came from, anymore, Nick. You should be doubly proud of how far you have come."

I shook my head slowly, as if in pain. "You can have no idea of exactly how bad it was…" I stared at her. "…is. People look at me, and I can see them sizing me up, somehow knowing that I came from the gutter."

"But that is only your perspective; it actually makes them respect you all the more," she pleaded, shaking my right hand in both of hers.

"Some of them," I whispered angrily. "But most of those supercilious bastards just look at me and write me off, as someone whose mother really was a whore. That's how much they respect me. Until I rub their faces in the dirt."

I clenched and unclenched my fists. I held her face between my two hands.

"That's why I will always have to prove myself, Nasta. However successful I am, it is never enough, and I will always have to go further."

Nasta was shaking her head and saying, "No, no, you have it all wrong."

"You just don't know what it's like," I repeated. "I know I'm a fool not to be happy with all I've got, especially after all you and Chloe have given me."

I kissed her forehead.

"But for me, fulfilment still just keeps tantalisingly out of range. I dream almost every night that my mother taunts me, as she lies in bed with a couple of bearded down-and-outs, shaking their beer cans at me. 'Loser,' she says, as though she is on the right path, and I am going downhill. My sisters all come in and echo the refrain. 'Loser, loser, fucking loser,' they all chorus, dancing round her bed. And Bobby is there, peering out naked from behind the door, ogling my mother."

I could feel myself beginning to sweat.

"And do you know what the worst thing about that nightmare is?"

Anastasia looked at me with compassion. Or was it pity? She shook her head.

"Everyone from my present life is watching the scene, as if through double mirrors. Watching my own family taunting me. And they are all laughing. Laughing at me."

I drew away from her.

"That's why I wake up sweating every night."

She sat herself on my knee. She could see my pain.

"That's why you keep driving yourself on," she half-told, half-asked me. "You feel you need to prove yourself to your family, because you think they didn't love you; and to your colleagues, because somehow you think they know the truth."

She looked deep into my eyes. "Is that everything, Nick?"

I nodded, although I was indeed grasping for something even deeper, which nagged and tugged, but would not come free.

"I feel them all chasing me down, pursuing me. So, I keep on going. I don't know why, and I don't know where. I just keep running, to stay ahead of those demons, who are so real, all spitting venom at me, baying for my blood."

After a long silence she whispered, "So, this obsession with success is just to get your own back on your family. To prove to your mother who rejected you that you don't need her. That's why you're scared to meet her, in case you find you really do."

"No way," I protested. I had never thought like that before, but the way she put the words together, it somehow didn't feel as wrong as I made out.

"Your dinner's ready. Let's eat." She ushered me into the kitchen.

In retrospect I can see how cleverly she manipulated me that evening. We talked, I drank, we made love.

By the time I slept, she had almost persuaded me to meet the mother I never had.

The mother of my brother.

89

The morning's business flew by in a flurry of activity.

Every aspect of our business was rocketing.

So was the public relations team. They had their work cut out, mainly countering outbreaks of bad press from unhappy clients, whose businesses had been 'whipped out from under their feet', as they complained to the press.

Harbour and Greensleeves shareholders were merely the largest, if currently the most vociferous, of these groups.

The other poor bastards realised there was little they could do, as the letter, if not the spirit, of the law had been adhered to rigidly. So, after a flurry of angry legal exchanges and press interest, the heat died down, and the public interest with it.

The PR team comprised a motley blend of pretty girls with agile brains, interspersed with seedy-looking hoods who ran shotgun for them if things turned nasty.

"Anna, can you get me a sandwich?" I shouted through the door, as the calls and emails piled up.

Anna came in.

"Remember that Mrs de Carteret is picking you up at two, to go and visit your mother. That's in five minutes."

"Holy fuck, I had completely forgotten," I exclaimed, feeling a rush of anxiety, as my conversation with Anastasia flooded back, out of some watertight compartment in my brain where I had stuffed it. Anna blushed.

"What's in my diary for this afternoon?" I asked, hoping I would be able to excuse myself.

"Have you forgotten, Mr de Carteret? She told me to keep the afternoon completely free for you."

"Why the hell didn't you remind me, Anna?" I shouted, realising how unfair that was, as I saw her face crease up, narrowly avoiding tears.

"I'm sorry, it's not your fault, Anna. How the fuck didn't I remember that?" I asked nobody in particular.

Anna pulled herself together. "You are going to see your mother, Mr de Carteret," she explained, in a gentle tone which reminded me of those counsellors who had occasionally been sent to my childhood home, before I gave up and left. "Your wife did explain that you would find this difficult, and that you might come up with any excuse not to go." She held my coat out for me.

Her outstretched arms blocking the doorway left me with no other cards to play, so I turned reluctantly, called Snapper, and slipped my hands into the sleeves. There was nothing for it. I was going to have to go and meet my mother.

I was fucking terrified.

90

The care home was disgusting. There was a smell of antiseptic, which barely managed to conceal an undeniable whiff of urine.

The receptionist was glued to her computer, and when Anastasia announced, "We are here to see Mrs Tilly Bloomfield," she didn't react.

I half-turned for the door, but Nasta grabbed me.

"You see, she's not here," I whispered lamely.

Then, I thought a little. "Who the fuck is Mrs Bloomfield?"

"She changed her name," said Anastasia quietly, squeezing my hand.

"Room twenty-seven," muttered the receptionist, without looking up.

Nasta took me firmly by the arm, and guided me down the passage. One door was open; the occupant was slumped in her chair, drooling so badly that the front of her nightdress was soaked, as was the floor at her feet. She had pissed herself. She was snoring loudly. Someone I took to be a nurse wandered past, raising his head briefly from his mobile and checking her room.

"You've wet yourself, Nelly," he said disapprovingly, shaking his head and moving on, without any offer of assistance.

An old man in a wheelchair caught sight of us and rolled himself in our direction, gesticulating.

"Coach, Coach, Albert got a hole-in-one on the seventeenth…"

But before he reached us, a look of horror flashed across his face, and he held up his arms to cover his face. He was shaking and suddenly petrified.

"Oh, you're not the coach; I'm sorry. Don't come in here, we're not ready yet. Please don't hit me." He crouched down in his wheelchair and was quiet.

There was a yell from behind a counter down the corridor. "Shut up, you old goat, or you'll be missing your supper."

I looked around, but nobody came.

Nasta saw the horror on my face and took my hand.

"They're all mad in here," I murmured. "My mother can't be in here."

"You're going to be nicely surprised," she soothed.

She held my hand tightly and thrust me gently down the passage, until we reached a door with the number twenty-seven hanging awkwardly, one screw missing.

She knocked. I turned to leave, but my brain wasn't working well and I almost tripped. Nasta supported me.

"Are you ok?" she asked. "Do you need a pill?"

I shook my head and breathed deeply.

"No, I'm fine." Actually, I was shaking, but it wasn't my neurology that was the problem. It was the terror of confronting my past.

"Let's do it," said Nasta, and she knocked on the door.

A quiet voice said, "Come in," and we did.

91

I obviously didn't recognise her. She was a different person.

But she knew me. There were tears coursing down her cheeks.

The ravages of a hard life had done her few favours, but she still looked good for the drug-addled prostitute I had known all those years ago. She sat in a reclining chair, her frail little body dressed simply, with well-styled, short grey hair.

I stood there, and we stared at each other, both waiting for the other to blink. Snapper broke the ice, just managing to jump up on her lap and lick a proffered hand as if he had known her all his life.

That brought it all out in a babbling flood. Words and tears together.

"I'm sorry, Nicky. I wasn't the mother you deserved," she croaked, in that deep, rasping voice that demanded attention and utterly belied the femininity of the body from which it emanated. More than anything, the voice brought back memories of another life; another, unhappier time.

"I did my best, but I didn't have much of a start in life either, so I should have known better for my own children. But I was young and easily influenced." She shook her head sadly.

"Your father wasn't a bad man, Nick. He was already my second. He got me off the drugs for a while." She shook her head, before hurrying on. "But, I must have driven him crazy, the way I was carrying on. He eventually gave up and left. I don't blame him. I would have done the same in his shoes."

She looked relieved to have got it off her chest, and mouthed 'Sorry'.

I couldn't move, so she continued, her sadness returning.

"I threw it all away and moved on to the next one. When he was killed, I was desperate and married your stepfather, the bastard."

Nasta looked at her with a pitiful smile.

"I was a looker then, you know," she murmured. She started to preen herself nostalgically, but stopped short, turning her attention back to me.

"Like you, Nicky." She looked me up and down proudly. "You always had the looks." The words came out quietly, and the love was there, plain for all to see, as she nodded her head in my direction. "Those eyes of yours, just like your father's."

Part of me started to soften and I could feel my confused emotions simmering. Hers were out in the open, the words tumbling forth as if from a breached dam.

"That's when it all started to go wrong," she mumbled. "I just didn't know what to do, how to feed you all, so I went back on the game." I thought, for a minute, she was going to cry again. "The other girls were all on drugs, the stupid bitches. I tried to keep to the soft ones, just some uppers to stay awake…" she excused herself to me, "… and then a little weed and coke. But, I'd been there before, and I just couldn't stop."

I could feel myself tense up at the memory of her drugs. She could feel it too, and she straightened herself.

"Hell, it almost killed me, the heroin. Some would say it bloody should have done," she laughed sadly.

"That's when you left me, Nicky." She breathed in deeply. "I knew you were a winner, to walk out on us at your age, after the way we treated you. You and that friend of yours, Bobby."

Bobby with my mother was a memory too far for me, and it brought conflicting waves of anger and sadness. I think it was luckily outside the ambit of her own recollection, but she saw my expression, and held up her arms, apologetically, all too appropriately exposing the old scars from her addiction.

"I didn't blame you, Nicky." The tears were pouring now in

rivulets down what looked like laughter lines on her face, although I knew better.

"To be honest, I would have topped myself if I could." She mimed cutting her wrists. "I tried it once, after you were gone, but I didn't have the nerve."

The picture she painted induced conflicting feelings: bitter resentment for what she had put me through; admiration for the way she had turned her life around; but all overlaid with uncharacteristic pity for the wretch I had left all that time ago, sinking in her own sea of despair. I could feel a tear of my own, and wiped it away, angrily. Nasta squeezed my hand, but I couldn't look at her.

"I've followed your progress all this time, in the newspapers." She reached down and opened an old scrapbook with cuttings, gently fondling the pages as she turned them.

She looked suddenly anxious. "But don't you worry, I never let on that the person in the news all those times was the son of this old fool. I didn't want to bother you and ruin your life a second time."

"Is that why you changed your name?" I asked, the words catching in my throat.

She nodded and heaved a huge sigh.

"When your stepfather left…" She collapsed her head momentarily onto her chest, and then the anger welled up like a flash flood. "… the bastard," she whispered. A look of hate filled that lived-in face. She was shaking her head.

"What he tried to do to you, my little Nicky…" She looked aside and heaved three huge sobs, before looking back at me.

"I am so sorry, my love. I kicked him out as soon as I found out, the drunken shit. And you were so brave."

I was losing control of the emotions which were swirling around inside my head, and indeed invading my entire being. I felt once more, the extraordinary pain of that little unloved child. Try as I would, I could not stop myself; I began to cry.

I went over to her. She started to get up, but I sat down beside her. We sat there, sniffling.

Nasta just stood there watching us, her tears pouring down too, before coming over to join us.

I have no idea how long I sat there, but it was the perhaps most cathartic experience of my life.

"I am so sorry," she kept repeating in that strange, somehow comforting croak of hers, shaking her head.

"He tried to abuse me, didn't he?" I whispered, the words seemingly finding their own life and, in so doing, bringing back that awful scene in all its ghastliness.

All she could do was nod, wincing as if the pain was hers alone, and taking my hand.

"The bastard," she cried, eventually.

"The bastard," I echoed.

"I almost killed him when I found out. But you saw him off, Nicky. You were strong," she muttered.

Somehow the memory that we, and we alone, shared, of a half-clothed drunk, unconscious on that bedroom floor, brought us careening back together.

The bleeding welt on his head and the cringing, terrified boy, his back to the wall, still gripping a bloodstained baseball bat, all testified to the struggle that had played out in that sparse little room. The barely-conscious mother, looking on through blood-soaked eyes, but dragging herself together and first attacking, and then lugging the inert body out into the street, somehow completed the scene; a distant, forgotten horror that she had dredged up out of the deeply shuttered recesses of my memory.

We sat there hand in hand, drowning together in a sea of dire memories. As compassion began to overcome all other emotions, I could feel a burden begin to lift.

After a while she shrugged and whispered, "Your siblings are all dead."

I felt a little ashamed, but could not suppress my relief.

"They deserved no better, the fools." She was shaking her head, and breathing deeply.

A wistful look flashed across her face.

"Apart from one they took from me. I never found out what happened to him."

Nasta raised one eyebrow at me, but I was determined that Yusupov should not gatecrash this reunion.

Mother seemed to agree, and stroked my cheek.

"I tried to stop their bullying, Nicky. I did try. I really did." Her repetition was bleakly remorseful, and she fondled my hair. "I loved you so much."

Those few simple words, unembellished, but full of forlorn tenderness, started to put me in distant sight of the validation that I had been seeking for so long.

"They followed your stepfather," she sighed. "Can't say I blame them, the way I was carrying on." She laughed, again making herself the butt of her own black humour.

"That prick always managed to take the wrong side, in whatever battle was going on, and they all joined him. I tried to dissuade them." She shook her head again, smiling. "But my credibility was in short supply."

I began to realise that, in spite of the self-deprecation, my mother had found peace with herself.

A little nagging voice whispered that she owed me a share of that serenity.

"Your stepbrother George was pimping his own sisters. They tried to get me too, but once you left, I found my path. Do you remember George? He used to beat you up most days. He was the first to follow in his father's footsteps."

I blenched, and my arm instinctively covered my face, the memory ambushing me suddenly, rather like George used to do.

She fondled my hair. "I tried to protect you when you were small. He was such a bully. Just like his dad. You learned to see him off though, once you grew a bit. You were a good fighter, you were."

She fumbled in her bag and produced an old dog-eared photo. She handed it to me reverently.

I looked at it with trepidation. There was a man, apparently handsome, although barely discernible through the scuff marks on the old print, smiling and holding a tiny newborn. Mother was in bed in the background. She looked so happy.

Words seemed inappropriate, and silence overcame us all.

"I threw it all away," she sighed, with a shake of her head, stroking Snapper gently. "But that's you, and he's your dad."

I could see how much that little relic meant to her, and I inspected it carefully, mentally photographing my father's likeness.

With a monumental effort of will, and a strange feeling of bereavement, I passed it back to her.

"You keep it, I'll take copies later."

"Thank you," she murmured, kissing the photo and holding it to her chest. "That was the happiest moment of my life, you know."

She looked at me and took my hand again.

"Until now.

"I threw it all away," she repeated. "But you saved me, Nick, even if you never knew it. You were my salvation, even though your dad was gone within months of that photo."

My early life was coming back to me slowly, in all its horror, but sitting there, hand in hand with the mother I had tried so hard to disown, and Nasta who had suffered the results of that traumatic childhood, I could somehow begin to process and digest it all.

"We're going to get you out of here, Mother," I said firmly.

"I'm peaches here," she insisted, using a term I had not heard since it last passed her lips, in that other world.

"I can get to work easily from here. I love my work." There was pride in her voice.

Nasta and I looked at each other in surprise.

"I'm no burden to anyone here. I run the 'Pudding Bowl' down the road. It's a hairdressing salon. A good one. The name's meant as a joke," she added hastily, obviously wanting our approval.

"We have three branches now, all round these parts. I want to expand."

"You should let us do yours, dear," she smiled at Nasta.

"I will, Tilly. I definitely will," replied Nasta politely, if without conviction.

92

I wanted to get my mother out of the home then and there, but she wouldn't budge. She claimed she liked it there. She was a stubborn old cow. That's what she told me, and she was right.

"I've been here over twenty-five years, now. When I first arrived, I was in a bad way, and it was the only place that would take me. It was my haven from hell. Now, it's just become my home."

However, she did agree to let me buy her a small house, slightly closer to her work, and that weekend we took her to see some possible candidates.

At her insistence, we met at the 'Pudding Bowl', just as it closed, and I must admit I was interested to see it, although Nasta was not keen to sample their wares.

"Good morning, Mr and Mrs de Carteret," said the polite young receptionist, without prompting. "Mrs Bloomfield is expecting you. Would you like a coffee while you wait? She won't be long."

Nasta and I looked at each other with wide eyes, and our two strong, freshly brewed coffees arrived almost immediately. A succession of well-groomed and coiffured people, of all types and ages, wandered in and out of the salon.

"She runs a good business," I said, looking round approvingly.

Nasta nodded. "Perhaps I will give them a go myself," she pondered, as a handsome man with 'I love Jamaica' on his T-shirt shimmied past her, giving out some shameless eye contact. She grinned at me and, excusing herself, went looking for the girls' room.

There was a buzz of activity at the other end, and a soap actress who I thought I recognised, got up and gave what was obviously a large tip to her stylist, who immediately asked for her autograph.

She smiled at me as she came towards the exit, and that jolted my memory. I had seen one of the episodes, and it had definitely been more sex than storyline. She was from somewhere in Eastern Europe; Sashenka Stiepel. The girl was gorgeous, with beautiful dark skin and flashing, intense oval eyes, which seemed almost black.

"Hi," she grinned, fixing me with those mesmerising eyes. I tried desperately not to be mesmerised.

"You're Tilly's son, Nick, aren't you?"

It was the first time I had been called that, and the experience was, on balance, a positive one.

"Call me," she suggested, addressing her smartphone. My own mobile buzzed demandingly, and I acknowledged the connection.

Anastasia had returned, and was looking at me watchfully, her eyebrows raised.

"Hello, I'm Nick's wife," she challenged, offering her hand.

"You're a lucky girl, then," grinned Sashenka, completely unphased, and shaking it peremptorily. She gathered up her belongings and swept out.

Suddenly we heard a couple of loud expletives coming from a backroom. Mother's voice was unmistakeable. The receptionist looked nervously around. Then silence reigned.

In two minutes, Mother was with us. It was plain for all to see, from the deference with which both staff and customers treated her, that whatever the ignominy of her past, she had used it as her motivation to seek and find accomplishment, and thus fulfilment. I knew where she was coming from. I was on that path myself.

"Sorry to keep you. Just had a little difficulty with one of our new girls. She's been late her first two Saturdays, and ignored our dress code. They all know that's not acceptable."

At that moment a young girl, who can't have been more than sixteen, came out, snivelling quietly to herself. When she saw my mother, she backed against the wall. She looked terrified.

Mother looked at the sorry sight, and I could see immediately the soft centre behind the hard, world-weary exterior.

She looked at the girl and nodded imperceptibly.

"I'll give you one last chance, Talulah. I won't hold this against you if I can believe you really mean to try your hardest."

Talulah was overjoyed. "Thank you, Mrs Bloomfield, thank you so much. I promise I will do everything you need me to. You know what my bro's like. I just let things get out of control last night. I am so sorry. It won't ever happen again." She plainly meant every word.

Mother smiled at her. "You tell Nelson from me, he can have a job sweeping the floors and cleaning up, whenever he can get his lazy arse down here by seven in the morning," she smiled.

"I'll tell him, I will," promised Talulah, looking proud at the news she was going to deliver. "I'll get him down here, I promise."

"And you make sure you pass your exams this term, otherwise you'll be washing folks' hair for the rest of your life," warned Mother with a severity only belied by the smile on her face.

As we got into the car, she turned to us.

"She's not a bad girl, really. Those parents of hers, they just don't know how to bring a child up properly."

She looked at me with a self-conscious shrug. "Takes one to know one." She gave one of her rasping laughs, but her embarrassment was obvious.

"You should get a doctor to look at that throat of yours, Mother," I suggested, wanting to ease her discomfort, but at the same time wondering what could possibly be lodged in her gullet, to produce such a horrible sound.

"I think that's a job for an exorcist, dear, not a doctor," she laughed.

She looked at Anastasia. "Be careful of that Stiepel woman, dear," she smiled at her, pinching my cheek hard and flashing a disapproving look in my direction. "She's an absolute tart." She looked round, checking that nobody had heard her lowered voice.

Nasta smiled, patting my other cheek.

"We will, Tilly. Thank you. Won't we, Nick?" They both smiled at me.

I got the message loud and clear. While I was enjoying seeing the bond build between my mother and my lover, I got the definite feeling that I was entering a new phase; one where that alliance was going to have an ever-stronger influence on my life's direction, while my own free will, and in particular my libido, was beginning to take a very sedentary back seat.

The prospect was not wholly unappealing.

93

It transpired that Mother was not very fussy about the kind of house she wanted.

"A couple of bedrooms would be peaches, so you two can come and stay sometimes. Apart from that, a nice little living room and a small lawn is all I need, in walking distance from the Pudding Bowl."

The five houses we saw more than fitted that bill, and I went to see all of them with her. Nasta came with us, Chloe's timetable permitting.

I arrived on my own to the first viewing. I had picked up the keys and was looking round. It was well-proportioned and there was plenty of daylight. As I came back downstairs, something was blocking it out. The entire downstairs passageway was filled by an absolute giant. He could barely squeeze his huge, muscular frame into the available space.

For a moment, I feared the worst, but decided to brazen it out.

"Can I help?" I asked, as innocently as I could, trying to look past him towards the front door and picturing the layout behind me, for a possible escape.

A broad smile spread across his face, and he held out a giant hand.

"Nosey Johnson, Nick. Nosey by name, and nosey by nature."

I could now see Mother behind him, together with another nasty-looking character. Slightly smaller but, if possible, even more threatening.

"His dick's as big as his nose, and he keeps putting it in other people's business," laughed the accomplice. "That's the only reason he's called Nosey, and don't let him tell you otherwise." They both howled with laughter.

I kissed Mother on her cheek and shook their hands.

"I'm Swami Baxter." The second goon almost broke my hand, and fixed me with a penetrating glower. He was obviously the leader.

I appeared to pass the test, for he relaxed his grip, and his face broke into an infectious grin.

"Just checking your Mum's in good hands."

There was movement behind them, and I could make out a scrawny little chap, with a shifty look and an enormous head of dark hair, culminating in a violent quiff, like a rocker from the sixties.

I held out my hand to him, and he grasped it limply.

"You did some great deals at BOK, Nick," he nodded. "Some of those pre-packs were bloody brilliant." He finally managed a smile, but left it to the others to introduce him.

"Baldy Carruthers, at your service," intoned Nosey. "He's the brains behind our show, God help us." They all three roared with laughter. "And if you're confused, it's a wig." Baldy didn't look too amused, and held his head nervously.

"I'm so sorry about these three," Mother smiled without appearing to be. "They insisted on dropping me off. Said they wanted to make sure you were treating me right."

"Thanks, boys, and look after yourselves," said Mother, reaching up and kissing each of them.

"You look after yourself, Tilly," replied Swami, turning to me.

"We'd do anything for your mother, Nick." He handed me a business card.

"Now you're part of the family, that goes for you too. And I mean, anything."

The way they looked at me, I didn't doubt them.

"Just call, and we'll be there."

They let themselves out carefully, just about managing to do so without breaking anything.

As the door closed, Mother started to look around approvingly.

"Who the hell were those three?" I asked, when I was sure the door was completely shut.

"Just some old, and very dear friends," she replied.

"They look like thugs," I remarked.

"They're definitely thugs," she laughed. "But wonderful thugs, if you're on their side. They were in the SAS, I believe. But they found it boring, so they went into business themselves."

She put her hand up to stop the conversation. "I don't ask questions. We prefer it like that, and they've saved my bacon a few times."

She looked round the hallway, beginning to appraise the little house, but some memory obviously dragged her back to Swami.

"There was one particularly nasty man from a foreign embassy." She looked angry.

"I needed money." She shrugged, and shook her head apologetically. "For the drugs. That was my low point." Memories obviously overwhelmed her for a few seconds, but then she continued quietly.

"He was vicious. Swami sent him packing back to wherever he came from. He took my baby with him."

She sighed.

"Do you know the sad thing, Nick?" she whispered. "I never warmed to that little baby, like a mother should."

In the short time I had known her as an adult, I had only seen fortitude; now she seemed forlorn, lost.

"I wouldn't have let him go, though. The bastard forced me." She frowned. "He never slept a wink, that little boy, and what a temper, even at that young age."

"Where was his father from?" I asked, thinking I already knew the answer.

She shook her head. "Not sure. Somewhere abroad, out far east?"

And, with that, she changed the subject, pulling herself back to the present, and resuming her appraisal of the property. "This is peaches," she murmured.

I decided not to ruin her happiness. Yusupov could wait.

We saw the other four places in quick succession and, after some discussion, and complaints from her that it was too expensive and much more than she needed, we chose one.

Contracts were exchanged within a fortnight, and after three or four shopping trips to find some basic furniture and all the accoutrements, she moved in.

Her gratitude and pride were off the Richter scale.

I had never dreamed that I could feel so good about myself.

But life can play funny tricks.

I was actually on my way back from the lunch celebrating Mother's new home, when my phone rang.

"I have some information for you. Meet me tonight at Nicosia's; I have booked a table at eight."

Sashenka Stiepel had never lacked confidence. I liked that in a woman. But I was damned if I was going to go against my mother's very clear counsel, so soon after she had delivered it.

"I am afraid I can't do that, Sashenka," I lied.

There was a pause. "You don't want to miss this, Nick," she breathed. "It's about your mother."

That stopped me in my tracks. "Don't play games with me, Sashenka," I advised her. "You can tell me over the phone."

"I don't think you'd want me to do that," she stonewalled. "Your phone's pretty public. I'll see you at Nicosia's at eight. I'm staying there. Table in my name."

And with that she put the phone down.

I could still almost feel the mark where Mother had pinched my cheek, and I convinced myself that I had turned over a new leaf, as far as girls like Miss Stiepel were concerned. But I had to admit, she did move in rarefied circles. Any shit she had unearthed about Mother would be worth hearing.

At the same time, those eyes were very tempting.

I pulled myself together. I had no intention of letting myself be tempted. Jimmy and Snapper would look after me.

94

Jimmy dropped me at eight, on the dot. Snapper was curled up in his basket, on the back seat.

"Pick you up at ten thirty, you said, boss?" he confirmed. I could feel his lack of conviction. "That's a bit early for you, isn't it?"

I patted him on the shoulder. "There are only two women in my life now, Jimmy."

He nodded. Jimmy had never approved of my louche behaviour, but his loyalty to me overrode everything else.

"I'm glad, boss. Family man, now," he smiled. "Congratulations." He parked neatly, and I got out.

Sashenka was ready for me. Dolled to the nines, but she was a soap star, and that sort of comes with the territory. I'm not sure the same could be said of the full-frontal kiss she planted smack on my lips.

"Hi," she smiled, totally aware of the effect she was already producing.

She ordered drinks for us.

I looked warily around. "You have some hot information for me," I said, trying to remain businesslike.

"Cheers," she replied, chinking her glass against mine, downing her large, neat vodka and motioning for me to follow suit.

"Your mother's business is under threat," she whispered, her face so close to mine, I could feel her breath.

"How so?" I replied, pulling back, my pulse quickening. I did not want any of her type of friends causing problems for Mother. They would play hardball.

She shrugged. "Usual thing. They think her business model is a good one. Too good. She is taking their business. They don't like that."

"Who are they?" I asked, not really wanting to know.

She reeled off a couple of names I recognised only too well. Part of her set; a very nasty part. Mostly Russian.

"How do we stop them?" I continued probing.

"I know them very well," she murmured, stroking a long finger down my nose. "I am sure there is a way we can stop them." She emphasised the 'we'.

I was not used to being seduced; that had always been my job. I dug my heels in.

"I am not going to sleep with you, Sashenka," I stated quietly, pushing her away. "I am with Anastasia, now."

I am not sure who was more surprised to hear those words pass my lips, she, or I.

"That is great that you have decided to settle down, Nick. I am so happy for you both."

She ordered another round of drinks and, as if in immediate denial of her 'happiness' she sidled closer and stroked my thigh.

I tried edging away, but she was adhesive.

* * *

I could hear my phone ringing and blundered round the strange room, following the flashing light.

"Time to go home, boss. It's two o clock and I need to get you back to Miss Anastasia." Jimmy sounded disappointed. He had taken to calling Nasta 'Miss', and often made plain his wish for me to make that a 'Mrs'.

"Shit, Jimmy. I'm coming now. Are you outside?"

"Still here," he agreed.

"Give me two minutes."

Sashenka was sitting up in bed, looking entirely happy with life.

"You are leaving so soon?" she pouted.

I took her shoulders and stared into those intense eyes.

"I'm a family man now, Sashenka. I don't know what happened tonight, but what's done is done."

"Do I take that as a compliment, then?" she smiled. "The upright family man, Nick de Carteret, trying desperately to show his devotion to his fiancée and mother, deflowered against his will by an 'absolute tart'?"

That brought me upright. She had repeated the exact term that Mother had used as she got into my car at the Pudding Bowl. My phone was, as Sashenka had suggested, obviously now 'pretty public'.

I shook her shoulders warily.

"We have a deal, Sashenka. We will stop these friends of yours, who you know so well, doing anything to harm my mother's business."

I tightened my grasp.

"Don't we?"

Suddenly she was the playful little girl again, and she screwed up her nose and shook my hand, kissing my cheek.

"Ok, Nicky, my darling. We have a deal. I had a lovely time. I will talk with my people."

I thought about reiterating that there would be no further lovely times, but I was tired and decided to leave it. She probably wouldn't have believed me anyway.

Once outside, I pulled myself wearily into the back of the Roller and lay back. I reached out to pat Snapper, but he growled, his teeth bared in a manner reserved for those on his blacklist.

Jimmy started the engine, and pulled off.

While Jimmy drove in silence, I examined myself.

I did not particularly like what I found: weakness.

The speed with which I had failed this latest test made both of us feel bad; Snapper too, apparently.

But more important than that, in the business world that Sashenka Stiepel inhabited, as also Tselmeg Yusupov, such weakness could quickly lead to disaster. I could hardly support a family from underneath the concrete foundations of a local motorway.

I was going to have to get myself under control. For Mother's and Anastasia's sake, certainly, but also for my own. For the first time in my life, I felt dirty; and foolish.

Jimmy pulled up to the house. I thanked him sincerely. He nodded and smiled, looking at me sadly. Snapper followed me, at a distance.

I was uncommonly relieved to find Nasta sleeping soundly.

95

Anastasia would obviously have found out; Sashenka would have seen to that. So, I fronted up to her, and apologised first thing in the morning. She was pissed, but I meant it, and I was determined not to repeat it. I think she could see that.

The next day, I had my office, and all my electronic equipment, de-bugged. I felt a bit naïve that I hadn't done it more recently. I recognised the signs; I was getting over-confident.

My premonition, that Sashenka Stiepel would play hardball, was also confirmed immediately.

Mother called me two days later. She was seething.

"How could you play games with that little bitch, Nick?" she asked coldly. "With that lovely Anastasia and Chloe waiting at home for you? Have you no shame at all? I warned you, but you just went straight ahead and bedded the little tart. How could you?"

That got me a little angry. So, I decided to get it all off my chest. Truth to tell, I was feeling a little guilty, for all the reasons Mother had mentioned.

"That's pretty rich coming from the mother I never had," I started, and I could hear her intake of breath. "Has it ever crossed your mind, that the reason I find it so difficult to treat women decently is, in large part, due to the role models in my own family?" I knew I was going overboard, but I needed to say it. "Not the least that prostitute who lived with us, when I was young."

She paused to take that in, and I could feel the hurt, although she tried to hide it. "Do you know how we found out?" she challenged, anger blotting out her distress.

She didn't wait for me to hazard a guess.

"That little bitch was in today, and she showed poor Talulah a rather unflattering picture, which she referred to as 'Son of Pudding Bowl'. When I say unflattering, I actually mean plain disgusting, which of course is exactly that girl's style. In case you were too engrossed to notice, she took a selfie of herself, smiling like a monkey, flat on her back, with just enough of your face and more than enough of everything else, to be absolutely clear what she was doing, and who with."

That momentarily silenced us both, but she was the first to recover.

"That poor Talulah didn't know what to think. It was only because I saw her looking so distressed, that I found out what had happened. Of course, when I confronted that tart, she just denied it and said Talulah was lying. Life's tough enough for that girl, what with those parents of hers, without getting mixed up in this kind of sordid intrigue. Luckily, she's loyal, and she won't tell anyone, but I can't say the same for that cow."

I briefly considered calling Talulah's accuracy into question, but thought better of it. I didn't want to cause any more ructions for the Pudding Bowl, and it wasn't as if I didn't know the truth of the matter, even if I hadn't noticed any selfies being taken.

"How could you, Nick?" continued Mother. "I know I was a lousy mother and, believe me, I pray every day that I can somehow make it up to you. I love you, and so does Anastasia, as does Chloe. Just get that into your thick skull, and stop behaving like a Neanderthal, or as you say, like that prostitute who lived with you."

I could hear a catch in her voice, and it tore at my heartstrings. But life had made her tough, and she immediately pulled herself together.

"There's one other thing I should tell you," she spoke slowly, as if trying to avoid faltering. "As you know, I am looking to open two more branches."

"I remember well," I confirmed, attempting to reassemble our relationship.

"Well, every time I settle on a new site, I find myself outbid by some chain called 'Crewcut'. They have a couple of rather expensive, and not very good, salons in the City. My accountant looked them up at Companies House, and the owners seem to be Russians. Do you know anything about them, Nick?"

Warning bells were ringing loud and clear, not the least after Sashenka's comments last night, but I didn't want to alarm her unduly.

"I'll see what I can find out," I promised. I thought it better not to mention that these Russians were the pretext on which Sashenka had got me into her bed. "And I'm sorry for what I said before. Having you back in my life is the best medicine I could wish for."

We were both almost in tears.

"Thank you, Nicky," she whispered. "You have no idea how much that means to me, to hear you say that."

There was a long silence, and I thought I knew what she wanted to say. So, I beat her to it.

"I'm sorry, Mother. I'm trying to swap that Neanderthal for the son you never had. I'm going to marry Anastasia."

* * *

True to my word, Nasta and I were married, in a simple registry office ceremony, two weeks later. Mother was there. Jimmy put white ribbons on the Roller. Chloe was our bridesmaid. Snapper wasn't sure about his bow with flashing lights.

Suddenly, I had a family.

PART EIGHT

FAMILY PLANNING

96

"I hear you run a group of hairdressing salons, Mrs Bloomfield. My people tell me it's a good one."

I knew Yusupov was on an unofficial visit to the UK, but had not expected to see him at the bank. Mother had dropped by to leave me a spare set of keys to her new house.

And so, whether by fortune or design, the two conflicting influences in my life were thrown together.

Yusupov, of course, knew who she was. But he did not allow a flicker of recognition; just cold indifference.

"Mother, this is Tselmeg Yusupov. Tselmeg, meet my mother."

Mother shook the proffered hand warily.

"It's just a little venture to keep me occupied. Something to help the local community," she parried, fixing him with a disapproving look. "And you, I imagine, are that Asian gentleman that Nick tells me about, who seems to have lots of money to throw around," she continued quietly. "He has mentioned your name to me; something Russian-sounding…"

"Tselmeg Yusupov." I could see he was riled.

Mother was not put off. "I seem to have some competition from your part of the world, Mr Yusupov. They are called Crewcut." She looked at him for a few moments.

He shrugged offhandedly.

An awkward silence ensued, which I felt compelled to break.

"The Pudding Bowl gets young, troubled people off the streets and into a useful occupation."

"Probably to relieve her guilt for the way she brought up

her own family. You should get our bank to help her expand the business."

I smiled, but only to camouflage my anger. "She has all the finance she needs, thank you, without any help from Curzon Asset Management."

Mother watched us thoughtfully.

As she prepared to leave, Yusupov turned to her frostily.

"A pleasure to meet you, Mrs Bloomfield. Welcome back into your son's life." He took her hand, and she accepted it reluctantly.

Yusupov normally knew how to defuse a situation, even when he had packed the explosives himself. It hadn't worked with Mother.

He didn't seem to care and turned to me. "Family is important, Nick. Now you have finally got one…" he motioned at Mother, nodding also at a newly-positioned photo of Anastasia and Chloe on my desk, "… I am glad you intend to look after it. That is very much the Kuikbakh way."

He gave me a wry smile, and patted my shoulder.

With a final glare in his direction, Mother excused herself. Blowing me a kiss, she closed the door.

As it shut, Yusupov eyed me guardedly.

"She is a strong woman, your mother. Be careful. I do not think she will be good for your dreams or aspirations."

97

The press began to pick up on the Pudding Bowl story, and they ran a few small articles. Mother even got an interview in one of the fashion weeklies.

My relationship with Nasta got even better. Probably, because she wasn't having to share me so generously as before.

We were getting ready one morning, when the phone beside the bed rang.

I was on the way out, but grabbed it.

"Nicky, I have the press all over the place," whispered Mother.

"Is that good or bad?"

"Very bad. Your friend, Sashenka Stiepel, is claiming that one of my girls managed to spill boiling water over her last night, before she was due on TV, and she's threatening to sue us. It's all nonsense; she asked Talulah for a hot coffee, and when it arrived, she purposely jumped to her feet, knocking the poor girl's hand."

"That bitch," I hissed with feeling. "I will deal with her, Mother. But, right now, I have to go. Can I call you back?" I asked, running for the door.

"I'll handle it, and I'll only call if I need you. I just wanted to know you were around," she assured me.

"You know I am."

Jimmy was waiting and we had a clear run to the office.

As soon as I got there, I called Sashenka.

"What about a coffee?" I asked, in as neutral a tone as I could muster.

"How lovely to hear from you, Nick," she gushed. "I was so hoping you would ring. I so enjoyed the last time."

"It seems you shared that enjoyment with Talulah, at the Pudding Bowl," I replied caustically.

"Are you angry with me?" she cooed, without any hesitation, putting on her little-girl act. "How can I make it up to you, darling?"

"Let's grab that coffee," I replied.

"What about dinner?" she offered.

"Coffee," I insisted.

"Let's settle for lunch at Nicosia's," she countered. "I'll see you at twelve. It's on me."

A little later, as I was hailing a taxi on my way to lunch, I called James Gough.

They put me straight through.

"Is your firm still acting for Yusupov, or any of his businesses?" I asked.

"Why do you ask?" he answered warily.

"Because I was hoping you could act for a business belonging to my mother. You may well land up acting against him or his associates as the counter-party, so if you still have any connections with him…" I let the sentence tail off.

"I mentioned to you that my New York head office had instructed us to make a complete break with him. It made it a lot easier for me personally, being able to blame it on the Americans, when I broke the news to him," he said quietly, but in that firm, correct manner of his.

"Yusupov was furious for a bit," he continued. "Then, he suddenly just switched off the emotion, thanked me for my efforts, and insisted that some of his security people come round to our offices to 'review our data security', as he put it." He laughed emptily. "He did give us an indemnity, but the nasty crew he sent round removed, or destroyed, every piece of data, either digital or physical, that we held which had anything to do with him, his business affairs, or the bank.

"What about you, Nick? From the extraordinary terms in the agreement I drew up for you to sign recently, I assume you still are on his payroll?"

"I still am, but I am trying to extricate myself from everything."

"Good luck with that," he murmured. "You're in with a bad crowd, there."

He paused before continuing, "I'm not sure why, Nick, but I've always liked you."

"Thanks," I muttered. Those kinds of comments were beginning to mean more to me than they used to. "Can you represent Mrs Bloomfield and her business, the Pudding Bowl, James?"

There was a long pause. "Mrs Bloomfield is your mother, Nick?" He queried in a tone that lacked any vestige of credence.

"It's a long story," I countered. "For another time, I'm afraid."

"I look forward to that conversation with great interest. I came across Mrs Bloomfield…" he hesitated, "… your mother, only recently and my firm would be only too happy to act again for the Pudding Bowl. She's a fine lady."

"Act again?" I asked with surprise. "You have acted for them before?"

"We dealt with them on a small matter of copyright, recently. We were impressed at all levels. Featherstone's were acting for some shady outfit which was trying to extort some cash from them. Nasty bunch called Crewcut, but with your mother's help and her team, we dealt with them." He smiled, unable to hide his satisfaction

"What is the precise issue this time?" he asked.

"Yusupov," I retorted. "In various guises, one of them being Crewcut, I believe," and I ran through the range of problems my mother was facing.

"Of course, it may be nothing to do with him," he suggested. I could tell from his tone, that he didn't really believe that either.

"And the Angel Gabriel might be pimping down the Old Kent Road," I retorted.

"Who can best fill us in on the details?" he asked.

"Mother will do that."

"I'll get one of our associates to go round and do the groundwork. That way, we can keep the costs down for her."

"James, I want your very best people on this, from start to finish," I insisted. "Send all the bills to me. I want to ram this one down Yusupov's throat. It's time he got his comeuppance."

James Gough was quiet for a moment.

"Be very careful, Nick," he said quietly. "He's ruthless, and he doesn't play by the rules. You, of all people, should know that."

"I know the way he plays his little games, James. I understand the way he thinks. I am close to him, and actually have some warped respect for him. I aim to keep one step ahead."

"I'd try and keep a little further ahead than that, if I were you, Nick. How about a few miles, with a couple of friendly militia groups between you?"

"Thanks James. I appreciate your concern," I replied honestly.

There was a brief pause, and then he said quietly, "I'll take this case myself, Nick."

"I would be extremely grateful if you would, James. Thank you."

"Can't have your mother crossing swords on her own with that reptile," he murmured.

98

Sashenka was looking as resplendent as ever. She had that animal attraction, where every diner's attention seemed to be focused on her. She smiled joyfully and rose to kiss me. I managed to redirect her lips to my cheek, and she pouted.

The girl was a born actress.

I held her chin and moved the shoulder of her dress, so I could see the small plaster covering her, supposedly burnt, shoulder. She flinched. I was tempted to rip it off, but could just imagine the fuss she would make, so decided on a little caution.

I gestured to her chair, and sat down myself.

"Doesn't look too bad," I said, nodding at her wound. "How did it happen?"

I thought she was going to cry for a second, but she saw the look in my eye and decided not to.

"That stupid girl, Talulah, at your mother's place, spilt boiling water on me, just when I was preparing to go to work."

"I heard you did it to yourself," I said quietly. "To get the Pudding Bowl into trouble."

She looked at me sharply and there was a microsecond of delay, where I could see her brain whirring, before she burst into histrionics. She jumped to her feet and (remembering to hold her burnt shoulder) cried, "How could you think I would do something like that, Nick," aiming a slap at my face.

I caught her hand and hissed, "Sit down."

She did so, partly due to the vicious way I twisted her wrist. All the diners in our vicinity were watching. I gave them a death-stare, and most of them quickly returned to their food.

Still holding her wrist and wrenching it sharply, I challenged her.

"Tell me what the fuck is going on, Sashenka. Why are your friends suddenly throwing everything at the Pudding Bowl?" I twisted a little further, and she grimaced.

"Let go of my arm and I will tell you what I know," she promised. I did so, holding her gaze.

"I don't know," she started, and I grabbed her again.

"No, let me explain," she actually pleaded. "Listen, Nick, I am only doing this because I like you. I am frightened." She looked around nervously. "My friends were playing little games with your mother. Nothing serious. Outbidding her on sites she wanted, poaching her clients, that kind of thing."

She paused, and frowned.

"But this is completely different. Two of them were beaten up badly, and one has disappeared."

"You mean, it's not your guys who we're dealing with anymore?" I asked angrily, convinced that she was trying to pass the buck.

She could see my expression, and held her hands up. "I swear to you, it's not them anymore. Some real badass has moved in on this. I don't understand why, as this is all pretty small beer. My friends were already right at the bottom end of their interest level."

We eyed each other in a kind of stalemate, and I was wondering whether to believe her, until I realised she was badly scared. Her previous acting skills suddenly went up in my estimation. "They contacted my production company, which is a big international concern." She looked around nervously again. "My manager handed me a sealed envelope. Told me that, if I didn't comply, and he nodded at the envelope he had just passed me, my contract would be cancelled with immediate effect. I had never seen him act like that before."

"What did the letter tell you to do?" I asked, intrigued.

She pointed at her injured shoulder. "Scald myself, blame the salon, and make a fuss."

Now, she looked genuinely alarmed. "I am doing exactly what they tell me, Nick. It has been made very clear what the consequences will be if I don't."

"Did anyone mention any names of the creeps behind this?" I asked, almost feeling sorry for her.

She thought about that for a bit, but shook her head.

"Does the name Tselmeg Yusupov mean anything to you?" I asked, watching her expression carefully.

There was not a hint of recognition. Even with her talent, I would have been able to tell.

99

The frequency of my interaction with Yusupov had fallen off a cliff. At first, I worried that he had discovered my connection with the rebels, and was plotting my demise.

But, in that case, I reasoned, I would be juggling halos by now.

Nasta pointed out that he was fully occupied keeping the various strands of local dissent in Kuikbakhistan from bubbling up out of control. While the official opposition in the country didn't have much of a say in things (anybody who spoke out too loudly had an uncanny knack of disappearing), Grigor's rebel forces were beginning to recover some of the ground they had lost after the most recent clampdown, and the financial markets were becoming increasingly nervous.

But we soon realised that his cooling had actually coincided precisely with Mother's appearance on the scene. I hadn't seen him since he ran into her at the bank. That encounter had obviously rekindled strong emotions, and had put us firmly in opposite camps, with Mother in the middle.

So, it was with mixed emotions that I received his summons to dinner at an excellent Chinese restaurant in Mayfair. His paranoid security team had taken the entire place over and swept it thoroughly for bugs. I had to surrender my mobile and was subjected to an unusually intrusive body search.

We sat in splendid isolation, with only the wide-shouldered backs of his henchmen, and the nervously fawning attention of the staff and waiters, for company.

I was, somehow, relieved to hear again his familiar diatribe.

"I fail to understand your government's position on this wretched woman," he griped, referring to Sophie Maddox.

Her trial was coming up the following week, and the international press was filled with comment and opinion, which had to substitute for the lack of any factual news coming out of Kuikbakhistan. He waved the front page of a broadsheet, quoting her local MP who excoriated him personally for 'kidnapping her and holding the UK to ransom'.

I gave him a wry smile. "I am afraid they are working on a case for your crimes against humanity."

There was a time when that would have produced an eruption, but Yusupov, like me, was growing up. He sighed stoically, and shook his head.

"I will be requiring immediate repayment of all the infrastructure finance, of course," he said quietly.

He had never stopped moaning about the way the UK government had double-crossed him previously on the break clauses in those contracts. I sympathised with him, but as he would be the first to claim, moaning gets you nowhere.

I told him and, to his credit, he laughed. "Never mistake me for a moaner, as you put it, Nick.

"You remember those clauses that I included in all the loan agreements? Immediate repayment if the UK were to engage in any activities deemed detrimental to the security of Kuikbakhistan?"

I remembered clearly and had counselled Petra against accepting them.

"Helping my enemies unlawfully to impeach their president is obviously the latest in a long line of breaches of those terms."

"I will run that one past the Foreign Office," I said, recalling only too well the Foreign Secretary's boast of his support for Yusupov's opposition.

"Inzhu Alani is on her way to London with instructions to obtain repayment of all the loans. If you feel you are unable to support her in that then I will expect your resignation."

"Let me think about that," I replied, realising that things were coming rapidly to a head, and that my senior position in a Kuikbakh bank in the UK was becoming less tenable every day.

"She is quite direct, Nick, and she has my clear instructions on this matter. She will be here tomorrow."

After a pause he said quietly, "You do realise that the UK stands to lose far more than me or my country over this sordid affair. Trust me, I will make them pay for their duplicity."

I had become used to these threats, but there was something in the way he spoke which made me take special note.

"Can't you just let it go, Tselmeg? Get the bloody woman to sign a confession; then show some magnanimity and let her go. It would be so much easier for you. You would keep diplomatic relations with the UK, as well as our support."

My words were falling on deaf ears, as I suspected they would.

"I think the time for that is past, Nick. Your government has decided that I am a pariah and, whatever I do, they will cast me in that role. So, if they want a fight, then they can have one. I assure you they will regret their actions."

I realised at that moment that if Yusupov was going to go down, he was going to do so with all guns firing. That of course was his style.

He eyed me coldly.

"How is your mother?"

There was little I could say. I, too, had felt the animosity between them. "She didn't even recognise me as her own child, but I could feel her contempt. It was as though she was rejecting me all over again."

His bitterness suddenly seemed to sour the whole room.

"Never under-estimate me, Nick, as your government appears to do."

He half-closed his eyes in that, by now, familiar warning sign.

"I feel us drawing apart, Nick. And if you decide not to support me, you will not be welcome, either at the bank, or at any of our premises. You will be treated as a trespasser if you enter any of my facilities."

I returned his gaze, not sure I was following him.

"I see you have taken up with your old friend Angie and her Enigma Analytics business."

I bridled at the suggestion that I had 'taken up' again with Angie, and said so.

He scoffed. "No, Nick, not like that. I hear you are a reformed character, now. But you met with her, and EA is heavily involved with my infrastructure projects here."

"She told me," I replied, trying desperately to hide the shock on my face. He seemed to know my every move and he had obviously breached either Angie's security, or mine.

"Many of them are very high-security premises and are not open to the public."

His eyelids almost closed, somehow focusing the intensity of his glare.

"If you are about to become a part of that public, Nick, then I repeat my warning; keep out of my facilities."

He got up from the table and gazed down at me.

"And don't let your erstwhile fuckbuddy persuade you otherwise."

PART NINE

HOSTAGE TO MISFORTUNE

100

I spent the next morning setting a pretty psychotic cat among the Treasury and Foreign Office pigeons.

There was an element of panic, when they realised that Yusupov's repayment clauses did exist, followed by some intense legal consultation to fathom out what to do about it.

The resulting advice was, unsurprisingly to me at least, clear-cut. Politics always trumps the law. The UK was not going to repay any finance. It was deemed that illegal acts, against international law and British nationals in Kuikbakhistan, invalidated the repayment clauses.

They called in the Kuikbakh representative, a thick-set bull of a man with little apparent intellect and extremely limited English. They told me he understood the message.

* * *

My CEO had summoned me for a late afternoon meeting, and she was waiting for me in the boardroom. She was, as Yusupov had suggested, nothing if not direct.

"Mr Yusupov tells me that you are not willing to help us obtain repayment of our infrastructure finance loans from your country. Is that right, Nick?"

I had never confirmed that to Yusupov, but I guess he had seen the look on my face last night.

'So, I am afraid I am going to have to fire you," she continued, without waiting for my reply, brandishing what was obviously my settlement contract.

I had become so used to mixing business with pleasure whenever I met with Inzhu that I made a pass at her, even though I didn't really mean it. I was actually past pulling that shit.

Inzhu had obviously been expecting it but the hard-arsed lust that had epitomised our previous encounters had been replaced by hard-headed business. She took my hand and guided it to the document.

Soothslayer had been right. Now that she had hit the top rung, she didn't need stepping stones anymore. I felt a bit foolish, as any self-respecting stepping stone would. At least I made sure that no bugs passed between us, like the last time.

After a quick scan, I signed on the dotted line.

"Thank you for all your support, Nick, both to myself and the bank," she said.

"The pleasure was entirely mine, Inzhu," I replied, smiling, and was glad to see the furtive trace of a smirk on her face.

She proffered her hand and, once I had taken it, she kissed my cheek lightly.

101

First thing the next morning, I called Jimmy, and he drove me in to help clear my office. I felt I'd better make the break quick and clean.

"End of an era, boss," he said sadly, as he ushered Snapper and me out of the car and into the building, shaking his head mournfully. "It's their loss, though."

"Morning, darling," he greeted the receptionist.

"Hello, Wheels, my love," she replied cheerfully.

I had never got more than a rather prim 'Good morning, Mr de Carteret' out of her.

Even that wasn't forthcoming today. I was already yesterday's news.

Another secretary walked past and blew him a kiss. If I had been worried about losing touch with all the goings-on and gossip at the bank, and indeed at Bakhtu Basics in the basement, I needn't have worried. Jimmy obviously had everything well covered.

I said a few goodbyes, and Jimmy helped me sort out my things, packing those few items I needed into boxes, which we then carried to the car.

I was just beginning to wonder how to fill the rest of the day, when my phone rang. It was Angie. "Do you have time for a coffee, Nick?"

I had barely come to terms with my unemployment, and the thought of a friendly half hour with Angie sounded great.

"Of course. You free now? What's on your mind?" I asked.

"I'll tell you when I see you," she replied, but I thought I noticed a slight tension in her voice.

"I've just been fired so I have plenty of time, as of now."

"What on earth brought that about?" she asked, her voice lowered.

"Bit of a disagreement with the bank about calling in all the infrastructure finance, although I think we all agreed it's for the best." I didn't want to go into any detail over the phone, especially after my recent warnings from Yusupov.

There was a long pause.

"That makes me doubly worried," she whispered. "How quickly can you get here?"

"I've got time right now if you're free. I can be there in ten minutes," I promised, looking at Jimmy, and raising my eyebrows questioningly. He nodded.

"Mine's an Americano." I placed my order.

"It'll be waiting for you."

102

I was sitting opposite her in less than fifteen minutes. My coffee was still hot.

Angie launched straight in, without prompting.

"I'm doing a lot of the systems work on Tselmeg Yusupov's UK infrastructure projects. He's a major client of ours now."

I looked round the room and at the light fittings. "This place clean?" I asked.

"I had it checked when we started working with him," she said.

I opened my mouth, but she was ahead of me. "And we sweep it every day. It's clean, Nick. Believe me, I went in with my eyes open when I started to deal with Yusupov. What I am beginning to suspect now, makes me doubly careful."

I held up my hand to stop her, and carefully placed my smartphone on the table, gesturing for her to do the same. I then ushered her gently towards the door, but not before she had passed mine to a colleague, pointing at the phone and her ear.

Once outside, I explained my conversation with Yusupov two days previously, and my conclusion that either her systems or mine had been breached.

"I had mine de-bugged at the bank," I said.

Angie smiled and gave me one of those looks that real professionals reserve for over-confident amateurs.

We found a random café which she had never used before.

"There is no way that he's accessed EA," she asserted. "My guys will check your phone in a few minutes."

She nodded slowly and took a deep breath.

"We've had a serious malware attack."

"Where did it come from?" I asked.

"We think it's Yusupov's own people," she replied, without blinking.

"They're hacking their own systems?"

"Hear me out," she responded, and the troubled look on her face immediately spiked my own anxiety. "Frankly, it surprised me that our government allowed him and the Chinese to build the plant and put in all the control systems."

I nodded. "It's a bit like letting the fox into the chicken run. It could give him tremendous scope to infiltrate our security."

"It could be worse than that," said Angie tersely.

"How do you mean?"

"Are we in Yusupov's bad books?"

I shrugged. "Yes, he's pissed off on various counts, what with the ambassador fuckup and the Treasury then double-crossing him on his finance break clauses, but he spends most of his time being pissed off with the UK. I have to say, I don't blame him some of the time."

"Do you think he would do something really cataclysmic?"

"Who the hell knows how that man's mind works?" I retorted.

She looked concerned. "If you don't know, Nick, then nobody does."

"He did make a couple of veiled threats the other night. They worried me at the time."

She watched me carefully. "Do you think, for instance, he might try to annihilate a large part of the UK population?"

That made me sit up straight, and brought Yusupov's warnings hurtling back to me.

"He definitely has psychopathic tendencies, and he does like parading his nuclear missiles but, for Christ's sake, why are you asking? Do you think he's going to nuke us?"

She made no attempt to reassure me.

"Not how you think. Last week, one of the new state-of-the-art blast furnaces bloody nearly exploded."

"I never saw anything about that," I found myself whispering.

"It's being kept quiet. Everyone's covering their arses, frankly, and trying to explain it away as just a random email phishing attack, which could have let in a virus."

"Was it?"

"Yes, and no," she retorted. "On the face of it, yes. Some idiot in IT was sending and receiving personal emails, and he let the virus in under cover of an offer for services of a personal nature." She raised her eyebrows at me. "He used a memory stick, first on his laptop, and then the same one to access the operating system. Men!" She shook her head.

"All the operating temperatures and schedules suddenly took on a very perverse life of their own. If it hadn't been for some pretty quick thinking by the duty crew, it could have been a lot worse."

She continued, shaking her head. "I can't believe how people can be so stupid. Some offer of pornography from a remote country. Wouldn't your alarm bells be ringing, Nick?"

"They would," I agreed, thinking to myself that I would probably have done exactly the same thing, if the subject matter had been sufficiently enticing. "But are we sure it was this virus which damaged the plant?"

"That's what really concerns me," she replied. "I think it's what we were meant to believe. Anyway, we issued all the normal warnings to staff not to open strange emails, we banned the use of memory sticks, changed passwords, tightened up operating protocols, and cleaned up what, on the surface, appeared to be a routine infection."

She paused. "Or so we thought."

I knew Angie well enough not to interrupt. She always cut to the chase.

"But there is something strange going on, Nick." She looked at me with that very direct intensity which had always turned me on in our other life together. In the current circumstances, it only served to alarm me.

"Somehow, it triggered a system update, which my guys can't

completely fathom, and which we can't work out how to interrupt. What's more, it disabled the emergency diagnostics system by overwriting it with fake data. As far as we can see, all Yusupov's UK projects are now undergoing a similar update, entirely off their own bat. It's as though there's an embedded sleeper programme in the operating system, which has been activated by the virus, and is now slowly coming to life."

"What are the effects? Anything dangerous?"

"Just the blast furnace so far," she replied, without conviction. "But there are worrying trends in several plants." She looked at me, and for the first time I could remember, there was fear in her eyes.

"Including the Mersea Island nuclear plant."

Silence reigned, as we both digested this news.

Eventually I asked, "Can you get to the bottom of it?"

"We've been working flat out, but my guys are struggling. The bug which caused the problem at the blast furnace was a really vicious one which we've never seen before, a zero-day exploit."

"What the hell's that?" I asked, not wanting her to lose me completely.

"You remember the Stuxnet virus, which damaged Iran's nuclear facilities?"

It was my turn to nod.

"That was a zero-day exploit. It found systems defects that nobody was aware of. Think of it like a game of chess. In chess, there are thousands of moves which have been tried before, and for which there are standard counter-measures. But when you confront a really intricate new move you've never seen before, what can you do?"

She looked at me anxiously.

"We're working on it as fast as we can, trying to come up with a patch. But it seems the core of the virus self-destructed after doing its work on the blast furnace, so we initially didn't even realise the extent of the damage. We cleaned up everything we found, but the really nasty bits had done their work and disappeared without trace."

I gestured to the door and paid the bill. We walked out into the air, which was somehow a relief.

"So, you're saying one of Yusupov's people has introduced a really clever bit of malware, which has activated systems changes, and you have no patches to counter it and no idea what damage it is actually doing, as it self-destructed before you could get to it?" I put a hand on her shoulder, as I didn't want her to think I wasn't on her side.

She blew out her cheeks. "That's about the sum of it. My guys believe that was the problem with the blast furnace. They are working flat out on a patch."

"How long will it take?" I queried, worried that I already knew the answer.

Angie looked at me and was silent for a few seconds.

"It could take months," she finally admitted, with a shrug. "Perhaps even more."

"And if I know Yusupov, we may not have that time," I surmised.

"That's exactly why I asked if you think he would try to annihilate us, Nick," she whispered.

We stared uneasily at each other as we entered her offices, and I don't know which of us now looked the more concerned.

The receptionist handed me my phone with a pained look.

"You need to look after that a bit better, Nick," warned Angie. "Now you're out of the bank, let us do that for you. Don't want you making things easy for him, do we?"

103

I paid all the fines and back-taxes for the Pudding Bowl, and James Gough dealt with the legal aspects. I think he liked socking it to Featherstone's. Lawyers are like that.

I didn't see much of Yusupov. Of course, I wasn't working for him anymore, but I somehow missed our dinners together. I was keen to probe him about Angie's malware problems, although I knew he would batten down all his hatches about that. I also wanted to challenge him about Crewcut and Sashenka Stiepel, but as things had quietened down, I felt it better not to stir up any of those old vipers' nests either.

Sashenka was phoning me continuously and sent a few extremely suggestive texts. In my previous life, I would have been onto her like a rabbit, but things were different now. I blanked her repeatedly, and the more desperate she became, the less attractive I found it. I actually began to feel sorry for her. Like me, she was driven, although I was beginning to wonder if, in her case, someone was doing the driving.

So, it wasn't a complete shock when I saw the headline: 'Soap star falls off party boat; drowns in Thames.' Unsurprisingly, there was a glamorous photo. She had a sad look in her eyes that I had not noticed before.

The story went through some of her more notable roles and exploits, and surmised that she had been high on a cocktail of booze and drugs. I was sure she never took drugs. "Alcohol, and lots of sex, Nick," she had explained to me in her brazen way. "But no drugs." She puckered up her face. "They steal your soul."

She had obviously run foul of Yusupov and his cronies at Crewcut, even if she hadn't known he was behind it all. He must have been using her to turn me against my new-found family, in his attempts to 'keep our paths aligned'. He obviously thought Sashenka had been as good a way as any along that path. While I was proud of my new-found virtue, I had to assume it had signed her death warrant. I felt bad.

When I told Anastasia, she was horrified. "Poor, wretched girl," she murmured, shaking her head with genuine sadness. I had thought she might be pleased to get a rival out of the way. That would probably have been my own reaction. Her compassion made me think about myself a bit more; the thoughts weren't wholly positive.

"Is Yusupov behind that, Nick?" she asked. When I nodded, I could actually see her jaw set firm. "We must go to Sashenka's memorial together. We must show him that your paths are diverging."

She watched me carefully and asked quietly, "They are diverging, aren't they, Nick?"

I could feel her strength, willing me to change.

I nodded. "Our paths are no longer aligned," I intoned, as if reciting an incantation against evil spirits.

Anastasia nodded approvingly, and kissed my cheek.

It's funny sometimes, that you only know whether a decision is the right one when you've actually made it.

As I intoned those few words, I thought of Bobby. I realised that the time really had come for me to get out from under Tselmeg Yusupov's shadow, finish with him finally, and live my own life, with my wife, my children, and some well-chosen friends.

I felt excited, in a way I could never have foreseen. Ashamed that I had been such an arsehole all my life to date; but energised by the possibilities that lay ahead.

I felt a warm breeze around me, and I could have sworn I heard Bobby whisper, "Waft on, mate; just keep wafting on," like he always used to.

I almost shed a tear, and I gave Nasta a big hug.

"And I have one other piece of news for you, which might influence you in your dealings with that wretched man."

She smiled, and after a few seconds, said quietly, "I'm pregnant."

I guess we learn to understand ourselves slowly as we go through life. While my children with Debbie had given me no pleasure of any kind, I adored Chloe. The thought of another child with Nasta filled me with delight.

I hugged her.

"That's amazing, Nasta. I am so happy. We'll call him Bobby."

"What if it's a girl?" she laughed.

"Then it's Bobbie with 'ie', but I know it's a boy, and he's Bobby."

Nasta nodded her head and kissed me. "Bobby Junior it is then. It has a perfect ring to it."

"Just look after him well, and keep him out of Yusupov's clutches."

104

The memorial service for Sashenka Stiepel was a big society affair. Show business was out in force, together with the fashion world, so there was a lot of air-kissing, and whispering behind delicately manicured hands.

"Jesus, this bunch is more duplicitous than my lot at the bank," I whispered to Nasta.

She raised her eyebrow at me with a smile. "It takes one to know one."

Yusupov was there, along with much of 'modern' Kuikbakh society. The old aristocracy didn't go for such vulgar displays.

He made a bee-line for me, and in spite of the revulsion that immediately boiled up inside, I couldn't stop an illicit smile stealing across my face. The last vestiges of affection in our contradictory relationship hung on manfully, and refused to let go.

He even hugged me.

"Nick, how good of you to come."

Yusupov just couldn't stop himself hijacking anyone else's celebration. It was the way he was made and, having kissed Nasta on both cheeks, he insisted on introducing us to a couple of his cronies.

Nasta gave me a disapproving look but, in some strange way, this actually was his party. Sure as hell, he had been responsible for disposing of Sashenka when she had outlived her usefulness, but she was only a small bit-part in his overall production.

"Sad way for her to go," I murmured, looking directly at Yusupov as he introduced a devious-looking Kuikbakh.

The rattlesnake lids came down immediately, but he carried on the charade.

"Our Sashenka was a good friend of Nick's, and I expect he is feeling her loss," he responded, putting an arm on my shoulder and winking crudely at Nasta.

My wife had never been one to be cowed by the likes of Tselmeg Yusupov.

"I think the poor girl was just an insignificant pawn on your vile chessboard, Mr Yusupov. When my husband finally did resist her advances, she had outlived her use to you."

Our group became suddenly quiet.

"So, you had her drugged and killed."

Yusupov shot her a venomous glance, but he was, as always, the first to recover.

"I am sorry you think that. I can assure you I had nothing to do with her sad demise."

The look on his face did not reflect the contrite words issuing from his lips. He could not resist adding, "I have to say, Anastasia, you are beginning to sound like a cuckold. You need to look after your husband better."

The exchange was brought to a timely close by Chopin's *Funeral March*.

We moved to our seats.

105

The service was a good one, and there was fine music along with many tears.

Three of her fellow thespians (including two Kuikbakhs) gave heartfelt eulogies. I could see they all really loved her as a person. Many of them seemed to have no time for Yusupov and his regime. You could understand that he would not be very friendly towards their liberal brand of artistic socialism.

Her family were sat at the front, keeping to themselves and nodding tearfully at the homage from the pulpit, and from those who approached them after the service. Her mother wore a black veil.

Just when Nasta and I were ready to leave, she approached us.

"I am so sorry," I murmured, and Nasta put her hand on the woman's shoulder.

She stared at me, and I could see an intensity that I recognised from my brief time spent with her daughter.

"You are Nick de Carteret," she said accusingly, but without harshness.

I nodded.

"She liked you, Nick. Did you know that?"

Sashenka had made that pretty clear, but I was not too sure whether to acknowledge the extent of her predilection, under these circumstances.

No matter. This lady was a straight talker and wasn't taking any prisoners.

"She said you were very like her, Nick. Driven to succeed," she paused, before whispering, "but so vulnerable."

A tear appeared, and I put a consoling hand out, but she pushed it away.

"You both succeeded." She waved her hand disapprovingly round the assembled company. "If this is what you call success. You, and my Sashenka, both became rich and famous."

A sad look fluttered across her face, and she scrutinised me mournfully.

The room seemed to go quiet, although nobody else was listening to us.

"You sold your souls, Nick, you and my lovely Sasha."

She looked in the direction of Yusupov, who was suddenly watching us warily.

"To the Devil."

Now she was crying openly, and some guests eyed us uncomfortably.

"Be very careful, Nick. Sashenka wanted to warn you, but you wouldn't listen."

The look on my face probably told her that her daughter's message hadn't got through.

"Having fallen in with evil, she only knew how to employ its weapons. Lust and greed."

So, she obviously knew her daughter wasn't an angel. I could only nod.

"Be careful, Nick. You also are equipped with all those weapons. Money, looks, greed, charm." She turned to Nasta.

"Take care of him. Bring him back to his senses, or he will end up like my Sasha; Dead." She looked angrily in the direction of Yusupov, who was now laughing with his cronies.

"With the Devil himself, dancing on her grave."

At that moment Yusupov put his head back and roared with laughter.

106

"I need you to come with me, Nick. Tomorrow is Monday, and they have reduced shifts at Mersea Island."

Angie was insistent.

She had summoned me to her office and had just spent half an hour pouring out her worries about developments at the Yusupov-financed infrastructure plants; in particular, the nuclear power station in Essex.

I knew she was seriously troubled because she kept repeating herself.

"My guys are doing an unbelievable job countering the virus. The patch is almost complete. They have even managed to get right into the fundamental operating system and counter the alterations to the control rod schedules."

"Almost complete?" I queried.

She hesitated.

"Every time we shut down one infection, another one seems to pop up somewhere else. It's like the Hydra's heads. And my guys are running out of hatchets. I think they have someone down there in the plant who is interfering with the systems manually. It's the only way I can think that they are able to counter our repair work."

"You mean one of Yusupov's people is running interference there? I don't imagine that would be difficult, would it? Isn't the place full of his stooges?"

"Absolutely not. We deal with the workers down there the whole time, and most of them are a wonderful bunch. Yusupov built it with the Chinese, but it's run by an international consortium, Orchid Environmental Services."

"Never heard of them," I replied. "It sounds like a garden centre."

"In the power production business, sounding environmentally friendly is all-important. They're falling over themselves to appear clean and wholesome."

She laughed, but her anxiety quickly smothered it.

"Yusupov's technical team at head office must be nearly as good as we are. That virus triggered a whole range of alterations, for many of which we simply don't understand the rationale."

She looked pensive.

"Some of the modifications seem to be designed to cause a massive spike in power output."

"What could that do?" I asked.

"It would produce an explosion of steam with some leakage of radioactivity."

"On a Chernobyl scale?" I asked, trying to get a feel for the dimensions of the problem.

"Not as bad as that, as we could probably contain it better."

We eyed each other pensively.

"What's worrying you?"

She hesitated.

"A surge in power could be damaging, but not catastrophic. I can't help thinking that the complexity of the system alterations we are countering would hardly be worthwhile, if that was all they could achieve."

I saw her point.

"That's why you asked me if Yusupov was hellbent on destroying us," I muttered.

She nodded, and spoke quietly.

"A nuclear plant like this uses between three and five per cent enriched uranium. A nuclear bomb is completely different. It needs ninety per cent enrichment."

I was with her, although I wished I hadn't been.

"And you're worried that if, by some unhappy configuration of events, they have managed to introduce some highly enriched stuff into the plant, the power surges they seem to be working towards just might turn Mersea Island into a nuclear bomb."

She nodded. "A big one."

We looked at each other, and I can only assume that the look on my face mirrored the horror on hers.

"But nobody's going to just walk into the plant with some enriched uranium, whack it together and blow us all up," I whispered. "Are they?"

"Unless that enriched fuel is already on site," she replied.

That silenced me.

"That's why I need you to come with me, Nick."

"Yusupov was very clear that he didn't want anybody wandering about on the restricted parts of his projects," I reminded her. "Especially me."

"Then he's definitely hiding something, and we need to find out what it is. But it's alright, I'll book you on a public guided tour round the plant."

"They let the general public in?"

She smiled. "It's all good PR for the nuclear lobby. Obviously, the security to join those tours is minimal, as you won't get to see anything much, but I'll divert you into our control room."

She saw the concern on my face.

"Don't worry, I have reprogrammed the security cameras. He won't see you anywhere you're not supposed to be."

I admired her confidence, but couldn't bring myself to share it.

107

At home that evening, I did a bit of background research on the orchid-loving power company OES. Angie had worried me. That had been her intention, and she had succeeded.

I wasn't reassured by what I could find. I couldn't see exactly how the ownership structure worked, but it was complex.

I did notice that their law firm was Featherstone's, and that got my alarm bells ringing.

I called James Gough first thing in the morning.

"If those crooks are representing them, then these OES people have got money to burn and an integrity bypass," he muttered. "We just heard that Featherstone's are working for two of the four London-based Russian oligarchs who, between them, have syphoned off $20 billion from pension funds run by state-owned utilities." He paused for effect. "Including the KGB." He snorted. "You have to admire their courage, I suppose – or their stupidity."

I could detect a tiny hint of professional resentment elbowing in, alongside his high-principled disapproval.

"Hold the line one second, while I ask one of my partners who just mentioned OES to me."

I was briefly subjected to a passable rendition of Pachelbel's *Canon in D*. It was calming, as I am sure was intended. I imagined myself as a client, in shock at the latest fee note they had received, or a divorcee who has just been screwed out of their settlement. The music had been chosen with them in mind.

The line clicked back on.

"You just can't seem to get away from him, can you, Nick?" laughed James without humour.

I knew immediately what he meant.

"Your environmental friends OES are indeed an international consortium. Liechtenstein-registered, but ultimately owned by Chinese interests." There was a brief pause. "And Kuikbakh ones."

I let out a deep breath. "So not only did Yusupov build the plant with Chinese help and set it all up; he's also running it."

"That's about the sum of it," he answered quietly.

"But let me play devil's advocate, Nick. Is that the end of the world? The man has backed, and helped build, a lot of our infrastructure. His people seem to have both the finance and a lot of the expertise that we need. He may be a pariah to you and me, and I wouldn't want to get on the wrong side of him, but our leaders see him as a veritable saviour."

"I know," I murmured, as neutrally as I could, my personal ambiguities concerning both Yusupov and my government struggling to stay below the surface.

"You could say that we are giving him a rough deal, taking all his munificence on the one hand and persistently hammering him on the other for failings which are merely typical of any fast-growing resource-rich country like his."

While appreciating James' reasoning, I thought it was time to shut him up.

"We think that he may be about to blow up the Essex nuclear plant."

There was a long, shocked silence.

"Can he do that?" he asked incredulously.

"We're not sure. But if by any chance he can, we are doing our damnedest to make sure he doesn't."

"Who is 'we'?" asked James.

"Angie's team who maintain the IT systems for the plant," I replied. "And me."

After another pause, he came back quietly with, "Do you think you need help, Nick?"

"The truth is, I don't really know," I responded, and before he could cut in, I continued, "Angie and I are going down there today. Her team is doing a great job of counteracting the computer virus that Yusupov's people have apparently introduced to all his UK infrastructure systems, including the nuclear plant. We need to see if there is any enriched uranium on site. If not, then Angie's team are totally confident they can keep things under control until I can bring Yusupov down to earth."

"And if there is?"

"Then the plant could go up like a nuclear bomb, taking most of London and the south-east with it. I need hardly say, we can't risk that."

"I am extremely relieved to hear you say that, Nick. So, if you find any hint of enriched uranium on site, you will call in the authorities."

"That goes without saying, James. Of course we will. Somewhat against my better judgement, I have to say, as governments do seem to have an uncanny knack of making things worse."

"Hmmm," he muttered. "You do know that one of the minerals that Kuikbakhistan is blessed with is uranium?"

That was news to me, and I said so.

"They also have an enrichment plant out there, run by OES."

"Jesus Christ," I murmured.

"Yes, Nick. Help from on high would certainly be welcome. Failing that, I suggest that the UK government, for all their obvious deficiencies, would be a pretty obvious next port of call."

"I'll tell Angie," I countered.

"That would be a good first step, Nick. Followed rapidly by your connections in government."

"Let us see what is happening at the plant, James. If you don't hear from me in twenty-four hours, call in the authorities."

"Alright, Nick. Good luck. I will be waiting with bated breath."

108

Angie drove me down to the plant that afternoon. She thought Jimmy and the roller were too conspicuous.

She drove fast, and we got there in under two hours.

"I signed you up for admission to the public gallery," she explained. "There's a brief guided tour. As you go from the first gallery, where you get your introductory talk, through a passage to the main one, you will see a door marked 'Danger – Prohibited Access'. Hang back a little and tap gently on that door. I will open it for you and take you to the control room."

"Aren't there any cameras in the high-security areas?" I asked.

She smiled confidently. "I told you, I've got those covered. Trust me, Nick."

There wasn't much else I could do.

We pulled into the main entrance, and Angie waved our passes.

Our reception inside the building couldn't have been more friendly. Angie and her team obviously treated the plant staff well, and the local team reciprocated. But security was tight, and thorough. True to her word, I was indeed cleared as a guest for the viewing gallery, but it took a good fifteen minutes for us to get through all the protocols, before going our separate ways. There were quite a number of guests milling around, waiting to join the public viewing session.

"You will be visiting the control room as usual, Miss Angie?"

"That's right, Jack. Is David there?"

He looked at his records. "It is his shift, but it says here the intern's standing in for him. Sophie Jenkins."

Angie looked surprised. "Haven't heard of her," she muttered. "Have you got a camera there, Jack?"

Jack fiddled with his screen and gestured. "That's her, miss. Been here two weeks. Bright girl; very pleasant."

We both peered at the screen to see a young girl with slicked-back blonde hair staring intensely at her screen.

"She's all cleared by security," he said, holding both hands up as if to say it wasn't his fault.

"Let me go and take a look," said Angie.

"Shall I tell her you're here, miss?"

"No, Jack, I'll introduce myself, thanks." She came over to me and said quietly, "I'll see you later, Nick. Enjoy your tour."

I did my best imitation of a gawping tourist.

The security door slid open, and Angie walked down a long passageway.

Our group included men and women, most of them in business suits, so I blended in well. Some were chatting casually, and I assumed they had arrived together. Knowing that I was going to drop out quickly, I kept my head down. The guide was a small man with a round face that reminded me of a children's show host.

"Good morning, everyone!" He clapped his hands to make sure he had our attention. "I'm delighted to be taking you round Mersea Island today. This is one of the most modern and safety-conscious plants in the world. There is no chance of you glowing in the dark when you get home this evening, so you'll still need all the lights on. You won't be saving any money on our account, I'm afraid."

He gave us a brief but informative rundown on the workings of a nuclear plant. I was actually hooked and, as we followed him to the second gallery, I was disappointed to miss the rest. But I followed Angie's instructions, and hung back behind the others. When I came to the security door she had mentioned, I checked to see that nobody was looking and knocked gently. It opened immediately, and Angie ushered me through, shutting it behind us.

"Follow me," she whispered. "I've reprogrammed the CCTV. As

soon as it sees my face, it plays a loop of a blank wall." She smiled proudly, like a child with a new toy.

With only slight misgivings, I followed her. I trusted Angie implicitly and knew that, in computer security, she was right up there.

I tried not to keep recalling Yusupov's words. 'Keep out of my facilities. And don't let your erstwhile fuckbuddy persuade you otherwise.'

We wended our way through various passages, and Angie swiped her pass a couple of times, opening doors on the way to the control centre. We entered, and the girl we had seen on the security camera looked up from her screen in surprise and jumped up to greet us.

"You must be Angie," she gushed, coming towards us. I could see that she was trying not to look flustered. "I'm Sophie Jenkins. David has told me so much about you," she babbled. She shook Angie's hand firmly, looking uncertainly at me.

"This is my colleague, Robert," responded Angie, rather coldly.

I shook Sophie's hand, and she smiled coyly at me. She was bright, as reception had suggested, with a clean, slightly lopsided mouth. Not a classic beauty in my books, but attractive in a slightly contrived sort of way. I immediately didn't trust her. Not so long ago, I wouldn't have noticed.

I could see that Angie was of the same opinion.

"You're standing in for him?" she asked

The girl quickly suppressed a flicker of embarrassment.

"He had a family crisis and asked me to cover for him," she claimed, as if it had been a great sacrifice.

"How long have you been here?" asked Angie quietly.

"Six months, and I've learned so much. It's wonderful here," she began to prattle. My antennae went up, and I watched her carefully.

"I actually meant today," interrupted Angie, peering over the girl's shoulder at her screen. "What exactly are you working on?"

"Just routine maintenance."

"You're into the control rod schedules." Angie nodded towards the screen. "How do you have access to that?"

The girl didn't hesitate for a second. "David asked me to look at it. I think he is worried about some anomalies which keep occurring. They cropped up again last night. I don't have access to the Gynox operating system, but I think I see what happened. I'm putting in a patch."

They then carried on a long and, to me, unintelligible exchange about the various systems and the general working of the plant.

I was lost. I could see that Angie was trying to put the girl at her ease, and also that she wasn't wholly succeeding.

"OK, thank you, Sophie," she finished up. "That's really helpful. Keep up the good work. We have to go and look at some other things. Give my best to David."

109

As soon as we were outside the control room, Angie took out her mobile and pressed a speed-dial on her phone.

"Shit," she muttered. "David, please ring me immediately. It's Angie."

"Not answering?"

"Busy. That little bitch beat me to it. She must be warning him that we've rumbled him." Angie sounded really angry.

"I don't trust that Sophie," I said, proud of my detective work.

"Well done, Sherlock," said Angie caustically, just as her phone rang.

"David, what's happening?"

There followed a long, mostly one-way conversation, which didn't involve much more than a few grunts from Angie.

"I thought you had a family crisis?" she asked quietly.

There was another long diatribe.

"OK, I'll meet you at 2 p m. in our usual café down the road."

She looked accusingly at her phone.

I knew better than to ask stupid questions.

"I think I am beginning to see what has been putting back our efforts to counter the virus," she whispered.

"Sophie Jenkins?"

She nodded.

"Sounds like David is in trouble," she added with a strong tinge of regret.

"We've got two hours before we meet him. They're in the middle of a refuelling outage, and I need to find out exactly what's going on here. I can't risk taking you through to where I'm going now, Nick, so I'm going to ask you to ride shotgun for me and watch that Sophie girl, until her shift ends in about half an hour."

"No problem. Although I would have no idea what she's doing, even if she did decide to blow the whole place up right in front of me."

Angie chuckled. "One thing you really are good at, Nick, is giving off totally unwarranted confidence. She'll think you know what she's doing."

It was my turn to laugh.

"Just keep watching her screen. Take some notes if you like. She won't dare pull anything while you are in there with her."

"OK, whatever you say. But don't I need to rejoin my tour? And won't everyone be able to see I'm in the control room?"

"I've done the same disappearing trick with your face as for mine, so don't worry on that count. Yusupov won't have any idea you're here."

She looked at her watch. "And as for the tour, it takes about ninety minutes, so we've got plenty of time. Don't worry, I'll slip you back in there without them being any the wiser." Angie wasn't too bad at exhibiting unwarranted confidence herself, and I told her so.

"Learned it from you," she retorted.

"What are you going to do?"

"I'm going down into the basement." She frowned. "I need to see what they've got brewing down there."

"Could be nothing at all," I suggested.

"I sincerely hope that's the case. But if not, we need to find out exactly what the situation is, and do something about it."

"Good luck, girl," I said, feeling pretty useless. "I'll be here for you."

"Thanks, Nick." She nodded. "I mean it. Moral support is partly why I brought you down here. Just remember, you're Robert in there."

She opened the control room door and ushered me in.

Sophie Jenkins tried to look happy to see me, but she wasn't much of an actress.

For about twenty minutes she fiddled around, not apparently doing much, before getting up ostentatiously.

"That's me finished."

"Where are you from?" I asked as she grabbed her jacket.

"Devonshire," she said, slightly too sharply.

"Lovely part of the world. Where did you go to school?" I put on as friendly a voice as I could muster.

"Comprehensive in Exeter." I was sure that was a well-practised lie.

She turned, and pressed four digits on the wall-mounted security panel.

The door slid open.

"*Prostchoy*," I said quietly, as she walked out. My grasp of the Kuikbakh language was limited, but I could just about manage 'goodbye'.

"*Prostchoy*," she replied without hesitation, and I don't think she even realised her mistake.

110

After Sophie left, I could see myself almost as a spectator, pacing round the control room, trying to avoid the security cameras in case Angie's programming wasn't quite as good as she thought.

What started as mild anxiety soon turned into ludicrous fantasy, as one by one, all the worst outcomes paraded themselves across my consciousness. Angie had been caught; she had tricked me into coming, and was leaving me here alone to pay me back for my previous treatment of her; my siblings were alive and well and were actually watching my demise on the other end of the CCTV system; Yusupov had seen through my subterfuge, and was now going to destroy me before I could bring him down and avenge Bobby.

As these scenarios played out, each more apocalyptic than the last, I realised that the only common factor in any feasible outcome was a final reckoning with Yusupov, entirely on his terms.

I steadily built myself up into a blind panic.

So, it was probably inevitable that, when Angie opened the door, I jumped sufficiently sharply that I hit my head hard, on a low buttress.

She smiled, but could not conceal her anxiety.

I rubbed my forehead and looked questioningly at her.

"Well?"

"There is a full set of replacement fuel rods in the basement," she whispered in my ear.

"Is that normal practice?" I asked.

"It would be if they weren't filled with enriched uranium pellets."

"How can you tell that?" I was both genuinely interested and seriously frightened now.

"I saw some technicians I had never seen before, in full emergency kit, feeding pellets into the fuel rods."

"Isn't that just normal refuelling?" I suggested hopefully, remembering her comment about a refuelling outage.

She was calm, and completely focused and explained slowly, as if dealing with a backward child, which in the circumstances was pretty much what I was.

"They wouldn't need to use their full emergency gear for normal five per cent pellets. It's unbelievably cumbersome and time-consuming to put on, and you need to decontaminate it after every use. Its use is strictly controlled, and they would need to inform the CNC."

"CNC?" I asked.

"Civil Nuclear Constabulary," she reeled off. "They're the guys who are supposed to be responsible for the security of all nuclear sites, and especially anything related to the transportation of nuclear fuel."

"Could you be jumping to conclusions?" I asked, hoping she was wrong.

"If there was a real emergency, and assuming they could get close enough, even in those suits, they would certainly not be feeding more fuel pellets into the assemblies. They might be trying to regain control by extracting fuel pellets, but most likely remotely via my operating systems, rather than manually."

I could see her point, and nodded.

"What's more, those guys just threw me out of the whole assembly area, as soon as they realised I was watching them. They checked my pass, which shows I actually do have clearance to be there. Said they were carrying out emergency repairs, and they needed the area clear."

She looked at me to see if I was with her.

"So, should we be getting out of here?" I asked, trying not to panic.

I looked nervously around, and she pointed at the door.

"Don't worry, Armageddon's not happening right now. They are just preparing the enriched rods for future refuelling."

I relaxed slightly.

"But I am sure now, that if we don't stop them, it's going to be coming soon."

We retraced our steps, and it was with some relief that I rejoined my tour. Our timing could not have been better and, while I would not have been able to answer any questions about the guide's well-informed spiel, I think the group had been so well entertained that they hadn't even noticed my absence.

For once in my life, I was happy about that.

111

David Yates was not at all my idea of a computer whiz-kid. He was tall, rugged and a bit battered, like he'd played rugby, or been in a lot of fights. He was obviously super-intelligent, but I could see immediately that he had no sense of humour. Right now, he didn't have much to laugh about.

As he wandered tentatively into the café, he was close to tears.

Angie and I had been there for five minutes already. I had been filling her in on my time with Sophie Jenkins.

"I think she's from Kuikbakhistan."

Angie looked shocked. "How on earth can you tell?"

"*Prostchov*," I said, enunciating carefully.

"Sorry?"

"It's Kuikbakh for 'goodbye', or 'see you later'. Sophie returned my greeting as I was walking out."

"So, she's a Yusupov plant," muttered Angie. "I guess that much should have been obvious." She looked anxiously at me. "And now she knows we're onto her."

"I'm not sure," I replied. "I don't think she even realised she had said it. Sometimes we trot out routine greetings in our mother tongue, and barely realise it."

"Or perhaps she was making clear that she doesn't give a damn whether we know or not," said Angie.

We looked at each other with a mixture of alarm and bafflement at the way this shit-show was turning out.

Yusupov's words came back to me again. 'Keep out of my facilities, Nick.'

"If they really are going for broke, wouldn't OES just have taken Enigma Analytics off the job, and replaced them with Yusupov's own guys?"

Angie shook her head. "That would have alerted the authorities. They wouldn't want to do that."

Angie waved David over to our table, but he still hovered anxiously, as if not sure whether to sit or stand. I stood up and shook his hand. Angie almost pushed him onto the bench seat.

"I am sorry, Angie," he whined. "My marriage hasn't been good recently, and that Sophie has been very helpful."

"What has she been helping you with, David?" asked Angie, with no hint of compassion. That was unlike her, and I could see she was pissed. "Your work, or your sex-life?"

David was completely flummoxed by these options, and decided to sniffle.

"She was fiddling with the control rod schedules," Angie persisted. "She shouldn't have access to those. Did you give her your passwords?"

At this, he broke down completely.

"She was so nice and comforting," he babbled. "She seemed to understand my situation immediately."

"Did you sleep with her?"

He began to weep uncontrollably at that.

"I take that as a yes," said Angie, and he nodded forlornly.

"She's from Kuikbakhistan, isn't she?" I put in.

The look of total incomprehension on his face told me he had no idea.

"I don't know how it happened," he moaned.

"Probably because it was her intention, from the moment she arrived, to blackmail you into letting her into the operating system."

Angie sighed.

"Please don't tell my wife," he pleaded. "That would finish everything."

Angie looked at me and raised her eyebrows.

"There is a way out for you, David," she said. "Change your passwords immediately, and lock her out."

He shook his head. "She's told me already that if I do that, she'll tell my wife and OES senior management. I just can't risk that."

"Can you monitor exactly what she does, when she's on the system?" asked Angie. "While we work out how to sort out this problem, without ruining your life?"

I was relieved to see the kind-hearted Angie I knew beginning to take over from the gestapo witch.

David jumped at this.

"Of course I can. Our security monitoring programme is designed to do just that. I'll plug you into it remotely as well, so you can see what she's doing and between us we can counter it. Will that work for you?"

Angie thought for a minute, and I could see the terror of anticipation on his face.

The gestapo was back briefly.

"Does she have access to that system?"

He shook his head violently. "Absolutely not, and she knows better than to ask," he babbled.

"And if she refuses to sleep with you, unless you give her access?" She let her voice trail off, but he was adamant, still shaking his head.

"No, no, that was a one-off, I promise you. I promised myself never to repeat that."

He looked genuinely disgusted with himself, and for the first time, we could see some resolve taking over from the fearful wreck which had been in evidence before.

"She has been coming on to me, but I claimed I had a headache." I looked up to see if a trace of humour was also emerging, but his face was deadpan.

Finally, Angie nodded gently.

"OK, David. You do that, while we try and work out how to get out of this mess."

"Thank you, Angie. Thank you, a million times. I promise, I will make this up to you."

"I am relying on you to do that, David," she said quietly, putting her hand on his shoulder. "This is absolutely your last chance."

I thought he was going to kiss her, but, whether it was the look on her face or his own belated sense of self-esteem, he decided against it.

112

"We need help, Nick."

Angie and I stayed on at the café after David had left. She looked shell-shocked.

"I can't believe he did that," she moaned, shaking her head. "He is one of my best managers."

"Can you keep control of the systems, with David monitoring that girl?"

"Yes, probably, while he's online. Trouble is, he can't be on it twenty-four-seven."

I could see that Angie was beginning to lose confidence.

Then I had a brainwave, and I kicked myself that I hadn't come up with it before. I guess my life was getting so complicated that I was subconsciously compartmentalising all the tricky bits.

"Have you ever heard of Soothslayer?"

"*The* Soothslayer?" she asked, with a look that said I was straying into fields which were beyond my paygrade. "On the Dark Web?"

I nodded uncertainly. "I suppose so."

"Never met him, but the guy's a legend. We need someone like him."

"I know him," I said, trying not to sound too blasé.

She opened her eyes wide with horror. "What kind of stuff are you getting into now, Nick? Pornography, drugs, crime?" She looked at me doubtfully.

I explained about my trip to the rebel stronghold, and the unsuccessful assassination attempt on Yusupov.

Her initial disapproval quickly morphed through surprise, concern, and finally elation.

"My god. Would he help us?"

"I imagine he'll do anything to thwart Yusupov. I can only ask him."

I pulled out my mobile and opened Soothslayer's weather app with the bowler hat for an icon. It had a sliding scale of weather conditions, from hot sun, through cloud and rain to blizzard. I pressed blizzard.

Nothing.

I pressed the other buttons in turn, wishing I had asked for some basic operating instructions. Medina had promised it was self-explanatory, and anyway, I hadn't reckoned on having to use it.

Still nothing.

Angie was looking askance at me. "You sure you met the real Soothslayer?" she asked doubtfully. "Or you just ran into him through those porn sites?"

"I'll contact him on Nasta's laptop as soon as I get home," I promised, beginning to doubt my own story.

I paid the bill and was just fastening my seat belt in Angie's car, when my phone rang. It was Bobby's callsign 'Oranges and Lemons'. I hadn't heard that since he rang me just before he died.

I answered, with mixed emotions.

"Hello, gorgeous. Do I detect a damsel in distress?" said Billy Sapito. My phone was on speaker, although I never chose that setting normally.

"Now tell me, Angie, darling," he paused theatrically, "was that little slut any good in the sack?"

I don't think Angie was expecting that, but she took it in her stride.

"Rock'n'roll," she confirmed, grinning broadly, and mouthing 'Soothslayer?' at me.

I nodded, raising my eyebrows.

"But I'm sure Marcus is much better. I always prefer those black hunks, don't you, darling?"

For a few seconds he had managed to take our minds off Armageddon.

We were the better for it.

Angie was opening her mouth to respond, giggling loudly, but he beat her to it.

"So, you're trying to stop our dear president from blowing you all to smithereens." It was a statement.

"I need help," confirmed Angie.

"You do indeed. The trouble is that, while your team at EA is pretty near the top of the class…" there was the sound of clapping, "our friends at Orchid Environmental Services…" he spat the words out with venom, "are sitting at the very head of the table, and I am going to tell you why."

Always the performer, he kept us hanging for a few seconds.

"They are in prime position because they are using the best toolset in the world – the Soothslayer's very own set. The bastards stole various techniques I had been using when they locked me up and had me working for them. That was some of my best work, and they've not done a bad job developing it either."

"So, we've been battling against the Soothslayer," said Angie. "I don't feel too bad that we were finding things so difficult." She looked happier.

"I've been keeping a watchful eye on all the Orchid operations, but I can't say I'm fully up to date. Can you plug me into your monitoring system? I'll need to take a careful look at where we are right now."

Angie pulled into a service station and, while I filled her tank, she texted Soothslayer the details he needed, and she filled him in as far as she could.

"We are interfering with their progress as much as we can, and countermanding their instructions, but there appear to be some deep-sleeping worms which are unbelievably strong. We just can't seem to make much headway against them."

"They're good, aren't they, those little Trojans of mine?" he boasted. "Just depends how they've been using them, as to how quickly I can defuse them."

"Should we get our government involved?" I asked.

One small part of me still wanted to continue to carry on duelling single-handedly with Yusupov, but even I realised we were getting rapidly past that stage.

Billy Sapito agreed. "Given time, I can certainly reverse their work. But, if you say the place is full of enriched uranium, then you'd better get all the help you can muster. It could take me days, and we may not have that much time."

"I'll be back in touch as soon as I have any news. Be good, children."

113

We continued on our way back to London, with Angie at the wheel.

"Soothslayer," she kept saying. "You just can't believe what a reputation he has in my world. The Robin Hood of the Dark Web. He has brought down so many crooks and fraudsters, it's unreal."

"I think Yusupov's his real bête noire, though. Especially after his spell in a Kuikbakh prison." I grinned, remembering Grigor's story. "He changed the prison staff rotas so they were all absent one night, and opened all the doors. The entire contents of one of Yusupov's high-security prisons escaped."

Angie laughed loudly. I hadn't heard her do that for some time. "I suppose that's why he was so keen to help. He's testing himself against some of his own very best work."

"And that's why we need to get the government involved." I picked up my phone. "I'll talk to Petra Marinelli, right now."

I called Petra, but in spite of the importance I managed to impart to her secretary, she was busy, and I left an urgent message.

"I would have thought this warranted an audience with the PM," Angie suggested. "I'll come with you, for the technical backup."

"That would be good," I agreed, "but Petra's my main conduit, and she will know how to get things rolling."

The traffic was sparse, and we made good time back to London.

We went straight to EA, and Angie spoke at length to her leadership team. She explained the remote monitoring that David was setting up, and mentioned Sophie by name. She also told them that Soothslayer was working with them. There were gasps, as if a group of village footballers had been told that Maradona was coming to play for them. She didn't reveal anything about her discovery in the nuclear basement, or why the surveillance was necessary. The fewer who knew what was really going on, the better.

While this was happening, I made sure Jimmy was ready to roll.

Just as I was thinking of ringing her again, Petra Marinelli rang.

I didn't go into any detail over the phone, but simply emphasised the extreme urgency of the situation. So, I was relieved (and a little flattered) that she could see me immediately.

As soon as Angie was happy with her team, I warned Jimmy, and we went downstairs. He was waiting for us with the door open.

London traffic round Westminster is always bad, and today was no exception. Urgency doesn't affect normality. Ask any ambulance driver.

As we reached Horse Guards Road, my phone beeped, with Mother's personal tone.

I whispered into it. "Can't talk now, Mother. I'll call you back. I'm just getting out of the car for an urgent meeting."

"That is exactly why you should listen very carefully to what I have to say, Nick," said Yusupov quietly. "And, please, do not get out of your car."

It took me a couple of seconds for my brain to register why I was talking to Yusupov, on my mother's phone. When it did, I felt sick.

I pulled Angie back into the car, slammed the door and told Jimmy to park where he could.

The urgency in my voice obviously got through to them, and they looked at me strangely. It was only when I continued my conversation, that they began to understand what we were dealing with.

"Where is my mother?" I demanded.

"She is safe, for the moment," he replied neutrally.

"Let me speak to her," I insisted.

He didn't reply, but a second later I heard her voice.

"I am so sorry, darling. I should have been more careful." There was an emptiness to Mother's voice, which I had not heard before.

"You will be alright, Mother. We will get you home safely," I promised her, not knowing if that was a pledge I could actually fulfil.

"I have told your mother my story, Nick," put in Yusupov. "Of how she sold me, like a loaf of bread, to the highest bidder."

"He's as nasty as his father," said Mother plaintively.

Her voice tailed off with a squeak of pain.

That got to me, and I hissed into the phone, "If you harm her, I promise I will kill you."

"I told you that your mother is safe for the moment, Nick," said Yusupov slowly, his tone that of someone who knows he holds all the cards.

"How safe she remains, depends entirely on you. You know what I think of her. Now, calm down and listen to me carefully."

I had no choice, and did my best to control my anger.

"You disobeyed our instructions about the nuclear plant, Nick. I told you not to go there."

I could hardly deny it, but I needed to find out how much he knew about our trip and Angie's work. With Yusupov, flattery was always the key, so I tried it.

"I had heard so much about your state-of-the-art plant. It's all over the news, and Angie had told me everything about it. I just did the public tour. It's very impressive. I was doing no harm to you or to the plant."

I don't think my thespian skills were up to scratch.

But there was silence and he sighed, like an adult dealing with a recalcitrant child. When he spoke, I could hear he was slightly mollified. More importantly, he didn't appear to know what Angie and I had actually been doing there.

"You have always had a tendency to overplay your hand, Nick, as long as I have known you. My negotiations with your government are at a crucial stage at the moment, and we need to be sure that we can rely on you fully, as our intermediary. Past history would indicate that we need to hold a strong bargaining chip to guarantee your compliance."

I started to argue, but he interrupted.

"Your mother is that bargaining chip, Nick. Do not visit the plant again, and continue to represent our cause in your country with your government. If you follow those two simple instructions, your mother will be safe."

"Can I see her?" I asked, more in hope than anticipation.

He ignored me. "If you cross me in this, Nick, she will suffer. Do you understand?"

We were both silent for a few seconds, until he repeated, "Do you understand, Nick?"

I understood, although my reply was barely audible.

Jimmy and Angie were both looking at me. They didn't know what to say, but my predicament was obvious.

I myself, was finding it difficult to think straight. I passed a message to Petra Marinelli, through her secretary, that I couldn't see her at the moment, but would get back to her. I may have been a bit abrupt, and she said rather frostily that she'd pass on the message. I apologised belatedly, and said I would explain when I could. That seemed to appease her somewhat.

"I'll drop you back with Miss Anastasia, boss," said Jimmy, taking things into his own hands. "Then I'll drop Miss Angie at her office."

"Thanks, Jimmy," I muttered.

As we pulled off, Angie whispered, "I guess we're on our own then, Nick?"

I could only nod. "Let me try and think what to do, Angie. In the meantime, do your best. That's all I can ask. I'm convinced that between you and Soothslayer we can come up with something." I smiled at her in an attempt at reassurance. It wasn't wholly convincing.

"I'll get everyone to redouble their efforts," she declared in that no-nonsense way she always had of letting me know that she had things under control.

We looked at each other, and we both knew that this time, she didn't.

114

I rang Anastasia to give her the news and, between outbursts of impotent rage, I explained the situation to her. "I'll be with you in five minutes."

"I'll be here," was all she said. It was all she needed to say, and in my confusion, it was exactly what I needed to hear.

"Good luck," was all I could think to say to Angie when Jimmy dropped me. I tried not to look desperate. "Jimmy will look after you."

True to her word, Anastasia was waiting for me, with the door open.

She saw the look on my face and hugged me, shutting the door behind us.

"Yusupov has your mother? And he's going to blow us all up?"

She led me to a sofa, and I gradually found my tongue. I explained, in a little more detail, the events of the past twelve hours. I ended with an admission that Angie, even with Soothslayer on her side, was probably losing the battle to keep control of the nuclear plant, which was now about to be fully primed with weapons-grade nuclear fuel.

"Jesus," was all she said, shaking her head. "If you get the authorities involved, Yusupov will kill your mother."

I couldn't remain seated, so jumped to my feet and started pacing the room.

"But if you don't, there's a chance he may kill us all. Is that a risk worth taking, Nick?"

She held out her hand to me, but, faced with such a tortuous dilemma, I needed the neutrality of my own space.

Suddenly she said quietly, "What about those ex-army friends of your mother's you met? Swami, something? Didn't they say they'd do anything for your mother?"

My brain wasn't functioning too well, so it took me a few seconds to register. "My god, you're right." I grabbed my phone and looked up his details. I had completely forgotten about Swami Baxter.

"Baxter here," said a gruff voice, suppressing a laugh. I could hear giggles in the background.

"Mr Baxter," I said rather formally, not quite sure how to address him. "This is Nick de Carteret."

"Mr fucking Nicholas de fucking Carteret," he replied. "The last time anyone called me 'Mr Baxter' was when the judge sent me down for manslaughter on my nineteenth birthday. Doesn't bring back happy memories. Just call me Swami, if that's ok with you. What can I do you for, Nick?"

"My mother is in serious trouble. I need your help."

"You've got it," he said, all trace of humour banished. "Meet us at the Old Bell in Mile End in an hour, and fill us in. Can you do that? I'll have the boys there."

"Old Bell in Mile End, in one hour? I'll be there," I confirmed, looking at Anastasia who was grabbing her coat.

115

The Old Bell was full, even though it was a Monday night. If Swami Baxter hadn't suggested meeting there, I wouldn't have gone near the place.

Some people hanker after proper old pubs with wooden floors and character. I have always been in favour of clean ones, with good beer, a fresh feel and all the mod-cons.

The Old Bell was neither. For a start it had a noisy, aggressive atmosphere to it, and Nasta held my hand. Even Snapper kept close to my heels, baring his teeth more out of fear than bravado. The place also smelt bad; an unpleasant mixture of spilt beer and cigarettes, with an additional hard-to-identify blend of bodily fluids. It was dark, and I could barely see my way. As my eyes slowly accustomed themselves, I could see two enormous figures by the bar, waving at us.

We cajoled our way towards them, through the ungiving crowd, prompting a few nasty looks and a couple of expletives. Swami included a beer for me and a ginger ale for Nasta in his order.

We shook hands with Nosey Johnson and Baldy Carruthers. They all looked worried, but on noticing Snapper, Swami bent down and picked him up in his enormous hand. I held my breath. I needn't have worried.

"Hello, precious," he crooned, and Snapper licked his face enthusiastically, as if they were old friends. Swami placed him on the bar next to some pork scratchings which they both tucked into. The barman looked askance, but Swami winked at him. "He's with me." The barman shrugged and smiled.

Swami turned to me. "Your mother's been kidnapped. We think it's Russians." The others nodded.

"It's actually the President of Kuikbakhistan," I replied.

"Who the fuck's that when he's at home?" asked Nosey, wrinkling his namesake. "Excuse my French," he apologised to Nasta.

"Long story, but he's decided to blow up Greater London to pay us all back for the way he believes we've treated him. He's snatched Mother, to stop me warning the authorities."

That brought a stunned silence.

"He's going to blow up London?" asked Baldy incredulously, lowering his voice so I could barely hear above the din.

"How the fuck's he going to do that?" queried Swami. "Sorry," he grinned ruefully at Anastasia, holding his hands up.

I explained about the nuclear plant, and it brought a variety of responses, all along the same, largely xenophobic lines. These boys had spent much of their lives coming up against vicious nationalists, with nasty intentions towards foreigners of any description, and they didn't hold them in very high regard.

"Kuikbakhistan," mused Baldy Carruthers. "That's a new one." I could see his brain racing.

"I think those Somalis we came across, running cocaine and opiates in through the north of Scotland, mentioned something about Kuikbakhs. Nasty bunch was how they put it; and those boys knew all about nasty."

"You're right," muttered Swami. "Remember that guy we managed to turn, what was his name…?"

"Faarax," nodded Baldy. "Faarax Warsame. Horrid little fucker…" He winced contritely at Nasta and touched her shoulder apologetically. "He might point us in the right direction, with a bit of persuasion."

"If he survived, and they never realised he'd filched on them," added Nosey. "Where the hell is he now, I wonder?"

"He had a fling with that bent recruitment tart," mused Baldy. "What the hell was her name?"

"Polly Lightfoot." He answered his own question, nodding to himself.

"Holy shit," burst out Anastasia, to looks of horror from all three of them, who made as if they had never heard a female swear before. Swami crossed himself, grinning widely.

"I knew her a long time ago when I was starting out. She was with Siddley Bancroft Recruitment. Did a lot of government work."

They looked thoroughly impressed now, and Baldy nodded. "That's the one. You still in contact with her?"

Nasta shook her head. "Haven't seen her for ten years, but I'm a head-hunter. I can probably find her. If she's still around."

"I think I've still got a number for her," said Baldy, addressing his mobile as he scrolled through his contacts. He nodded, surprise on his face. "Let me try her."

He fought his way out of the pub and in a few minutes, he returned with a shake of his head. "Not in use."

They all looked at Nasta expectantly.

"You want me to locate her?" she asked, knowing the answer already.

"That would be good," nodded Swami. "Just tell her Swami Baxter wants to get reacquainted."

"Will she be up for that?" asked Nasta doubtfully.

"She won't be too keen at all," he laughed, looking round and lowering his voice. "But if you tell her that Sir Miles is still dead, she'll be very keen to cooperate."

"Do I need to know what that means?" asked Nasta.

"Absolutely not," chorused all three, shaking their heads gravely.

"If you can locate Polly, we can get to Faarax," explained Nosey.

"And if we get to Faarax, we can find your mother," added Swami, looking at me.

"So, let's do it," agreed Anastasia.

"Hold on a minute." I put my hand up. "They've got Mother already. I don't want my wife landing up in their hands as well. Will she be safe?"

Swami looked at me patronisingly. "Don't worry, we're going to look after all of you from now on. We're going to have all your backs, you two both, and Chloe and Bobby Junior as well."

I was about to ask how he knew about Chloe and Bobby, but he put a hand on my shoulder. He nodded at Nasta's bump.

"Tilly told us all about you. She's very proud of you."

That almost brought a tear to my eye, thinking about where she was now, and how I'd repaid her pride by getting her there.

"We need to give that driver of yours, Jimmy, some lessons in evasive driving techniques."

"He'll love that," smiled Nasta.

"I'll warn him," I added.

"How long can your friend Angie keep the nuclear plant in one piece?" asked Baldy.

An uneasy silence enveloped us, somehow keeping out the waves of noise rolling round the bar-room.

'We don't know, but assume days rather than months," I suggested. "Certainly not more than a couple of weeks."

The three of them looked at each other. Swami bit lightly on his bottom lip.

"Then we'd better get moving," he said quietly, sweeping up Snapper who, having just finished the entire bowl of scratchings, gave him a rather abrasive lick.

We explained the situation to Jimmy on the drive back home. He knew bits already, but I felt it was time he was fully prepped.

"Always wanted to do that," he enthused when I told him about the evasive driving techniques. He immediately started to incorporate his interpretation of some evasive moves down the Bayswater Road, throwing Nasta and I across the back seat.

"Hold on, Jimmy," yelled Nasta. "There's nobody chasing us yet, is there?"

"Just practising, Miss Anastasia, can't be too careful, with a couple of prime targets like you two in the back."

The truth of what he had said, half in jest, silenced us all.

"I've given Swami your number, so expect a call any time," I told him, as we got out.

I couldn't stop myself checking over my shoulder before I put the key in our lock.

116

We sat up for a bit, as I vented my spleen at all things Yusupovian.

"Her own son…" I shook my head, feeling punch-drunk. "My brother…"

Nasta stroked my brow.

"First Bobby, and now this. How I ever harboured any positive feelings for the vicious little psychopath, brother or not, I will never know. I want him to suffer hell here on earth." I grasped the arm of the sofa. "And then again, in hell itself. How could I have been such a bad judge of character?"

"Blood is strong, Nick. You know that. You and he are totally different, but at the same time, quite similar." She looked at me without blinking. "In another world, he could have been you." She rubbed my shoulder. "And you could have become him."

I struggled with that for a few moments, but the truth of her unsettling words slowly got through to me.

"We had different fathers," I rationalised.

She nodded. "That's why you are so unalike. As I've said before, you haven't always made the best choices in your life, but you would never do anything like this."

I stood up. I needed the freedom. "Once we have Mother back, I'm going to make sure he dies a miserable death, reliving every foul deed he has perpetrated as he goes down."

"Once we've got your mother back, there will be time for everything, but primarily, I pray, to enjoy the good things that await us in our future," responded Nasta.

"Yes, once we've got her out of his clutches…"

She held my cheeks gently between her palms. "Time to forget all about Tselmeg Yusupov, and all he stands for."

Nasta hugged and soothed me, and slowly the vitriol dissipated. She coaxed me to bed.

Surprisingly, I managed a couple of hours' sleep.

When I woke, it was with such a feeling of pleasure and wellbeing that it took me a little time to reconnect with reality.

"Waft on, mate," I whispered, giving voice to the thought which had been drifting happily around my night-time reveries, like an old, broken, but much-loved record.

Try as I did, I could not recall the dreams that had induced such happiness, but it was almost as though Bobby was still at my side, encouraging and restraining me, in equal measure.

I began to think straight. *What would he do?* I asked myself.

And so it was that, with Bobby's help from beyond the grave, a plan began to take shape; an inkling of a strategy to overcome Tselmeg Yusupov.

I leapt out of bed, waking Nasta in the process.

"What is it?" she asked in panic.

I reassured her. "Nothing bad, in fact all good. I've got it."

She looked at me quizzically.

"It's what Bobby would have done. I have to attack Yusupov's finances. The country's debt stands at nearly two hundred per cent of GDP already. I need to set up a strike on the bond markets. If Kuikbakhistan runs out of cash, with most of it having gone to him, then the people will take it into their own hands and get rid of him. We won't have to bother. We just need to keep wafting on."

Nasta looked at me with concern.

117

I struggled not to keep pestering Swami Baxter, as I knew he was doing all he could.

Anastasia kept trying to contact Polly Lightfoot. It was on the third time of asking that the girl rang back.

I knew Nasta treated everyone she met civilly, even those who didn't return the favour. That is why she had been such a successful head-hunter herself. So, I was relieved that she didn't need to bring up Sir Miles' untimely passing, as Swami had suggested. In fact, Polly sounded happy to hear from her, and they spent a little while catching up and reminiscing about mutual connections. Apparently, she was living in some style out in Herefordshire at a posh-sounding place called Dalston Manor.

When Faarax Warsame's name was mentioned, however, I could see my wife frown. She raised her eyebrows at me, questioningly.

"Solitary confinement?" she whispered. "He must be a tough nut." She smiled at the reply, opening her eyes wide.

Promising to stay in touch, and wishing Polly well, she put the phone down.

"Solitary confinement?" I asked. "Where?"

"Somewhere called the 'Monster Mansion.'"

"Means nothing to me. I'll ask Swami," I replied, dialling his number.

He picked up immediately.

"Anastasia talked to your friend Polly Lightfoot and Faarax Warsame is held in solitary confinement in some place called the 'Monster Mansion'. Do you know it?"

There was a chuckle at the other end.

"Like the back of my hand," came back the reply. "HMP Fucking Wakefield. I spent five miserable years there, quite a bit in solitary. Wouldn't wish that on anyone, even on somebody as nasty as our friend Faarax."

"Can you get to him there?"

"Won't be easy. If someone like that doesn't want to talk, he'll just clam up and bury himself in his nasty little tribe. And friend Faarax won't want to let us anywhere near him, I imagine, unless he's changed his spots a bit."

There was a pause. I couldn't help myself asking fearfully, "So what do we do?"

"Have faith, Nick," retorted Swami. "Trust us to get your mother back for you." He paused theatrically. "We know the prison barber there. Nasty little shit; he runs drugs, as well as everything else in there. All the lags pay him on time, cos if they don't they're liable to lose an ear instead of their hair, and it's pretty fucking obvious who doesn't pay their bills when they're walking round with half an earlobe missing."

He chuckled to himself.

"Little shit was deeply wound up in the 'Sir Miles' fandango, so he'll do what we tell him to. Leave it to me, Nick. I'll get back to you by tomorrow."

"Who was this Sir Miles dude?" I asked again, wearily.

"Don't ask, mate," he advised gently. "You mother wouldn't want you to. Just don't fucking ask."

118

Bill Topping was a character.

He'd made his name at the rougher end of the bond markets, initially as a floor trader; but his nerve and timing (together with his disdain for the finer points of etiquette and regulation) soon propelled him up the ladder, and into his own industry-leading vehicle. With his trademark humility, he named it 'Total Topping'.

"Great to see you, Nick" he beamed. "Thought you'd retired…"

Bill had always been direct. He didn't like to waste time.

"… or died. Glad to see that little fucker from Outer Mongolia hasn't disposed of you, yet."

Bill didn't like Yusupov and while that had sometimes put a barrier between us, I had always admired him and, right now, it made him the obvious go-to man for what I thought of as Bobby's plan.

"Very good to see you too, Bill," I replied. "I have a project for you; a very profitable project."

Bill laughed.

"Ok, Mr de Carteret, what do you need? Your Mongol giving you a hard time?"

We laughed. We had always been on the same wavelength. It wasn't often that a competitor came to either of us with a magnanimous offer to make us richer, without aiming to benefit themselves even more so.

"Let's just say that our paths have diverged," I smiled.

"About time too, if I might say so."

"I think he's overstretching himself," I ventured.

Bill guffawed. "You can say that again. If everyone wasn't so scared of his hoods, he wouldn't be able to finance a fuck-up in a whorehouse. They'd be steering well clear of his bond auctions. As it is, they keep him afloat because they're too scared not to."

He lowered his voice. "Between you and me, I've been gently shorting him." He looked left and right, and I thought I detected an unusual, for him, trace of caution. "Offshore vehicle, of course."

I had not realised the degree of trepidation that even Bill Topping had for Yusupov. If even he was wary of the 'Mongol', as he called him, then the rest of the City must be crapping themselves. I suddenly realised what a claustrophobic little cocoon I had woven for myself. Or perhaps that Yusupov had woven for me, to ensure my opinion of him wasn't tainted.

"I want to orchestrate a bond market strike against him."

Bill's secretary came in, and he gestured at the tray she carried. "Coffee?"

I nodded.

"That could work right now," he said, nodding enthusiastically. "As I said, the rumours are beginning to circulate about your little friend, that he's overstretching himself, as you so politely put it."

His face suddenly took on the laser focus that had made him a billionaire several times over.

"I'll just get a few of my buddies to jump gently on the bandwagon."

"Thanks, Bill. You don't know how much I appreciate that, but I need you to go easy. If he thinks it's all coming from you, he will link it back to me, and that would not be good."

"Don't worry, he won't know what hit him." He smiled, nodding at me. "Or who. But we'll starve the little fucker of funds. He'll be so short, he'll have to sell his own mother, if he's got one."

"Funny you should say that," I muttered. "He's also kidnapped my mother." I left it at that. I didn't think it was the time to divulge any more family secrets.

"I don't believe the little fuck." He banged his fist on the table. "I'll go for his jugular. Leave it with me."

He eyeballed me.

"Do you need help getting her back? I could help with that side of things as well."

Underneath the ego, Bill had a good heart. Not many people recognised it, and even fewer got to see it in action, but I was suddenly admitted to that exclusive club. He didn't give a shit about authority, but he liked an underdog. And in his book, I was now an underdog. Some of his connections had always been referred to as 'colourful', and the offer was genuine.

"Just say the word."

"I have some very well-qualified friends of Mother's on the case," I replied. "If I have any problems they can't deal with, I'll come back to you. But thanks anyway, Bill."

We smiled at each other. He held out his hand, and I took it.

I began to thank him, but he waved me away.

"No thanks required, Nick. That little shyster needs taking off the block, permanently. The fact that he's abducted your mother only makes me realise how overdue his good riddance has become."

He got up.

"How's your friend Bobby?" Bill had always liked Bobby.

I sighed, hesitant to say the words, as if not doing so might alter the truth. "I am afraid that Bobby's dead. The little Mongol, as you put it, had him killed."

"Goddam the creep." He shook his head. "I'm sorry, Nick. I really am. Bobby was a good lad. So, let's get rid of this little Yusupov cockroach for good."

119

"How are you doing?"

Angie had asked me to ring her, and I was frankly, fearful of what she might have to tell me. I was prepared to hear that her team had completely lost control, and the nuclear plant was about to blow.

"Could be worse," was music to my ears.

"How is your mother?" she countered, with obvious concern.

"I believe she is safe for the moment," I pondered, not entirely sure that I really knew. "Some old friends of hers are trying to locate her."

"Can they do that?"

"I trust them," I muttered, tapping my fingers nervously.

"Are you managing to keep control of the fuel rod cooling schedules?"

"Yes, and no," she replied, and my blood pressure soared again.

"How so?"

She paused. "Yes, in that so far we have been able to monitor the alterations Sophie is trying to make to the scheduling, and largely counter them."

That was exactly what I had hoped to hear.

"And no, because they've put EA on notice, and David has today been denied entry to the plant by OES, and blocked from all access to the systems."

"Jesus," I whispered. "What brought that on?"

"Sophie was obviously getting suspicious that all her moves were being countered."

"Does that mean we're screwed?"

"Well, we are about to hand over to some outfit I have never heard of who have persuaded Yusupov they can manage it all."

"Probably some of his cronies," I muttered. "Didn't you say that would alert the authorities?"

"Your friend Yusupov is no fool," she replied. "He told me to sub-contract them so it looks like nothing's changed."

I was about to challenge her, but she beat me to it. "Said your mother's fate depended on my cooperation."

"Fuck." I shook my head. "Do you think this outfit can actually run the show?"

"It won't be easy for them. We have had a hand in almost all the system modifications, and it is basically us who keeps the plant running. It will take them a little time to get fully up to speed."

She paused. "And of course, we'll make it as difficult as possible for them."

"Be careful," I warned her. "You know who you're dealing with."

She nodded pensively. "I'm worried about David."

"Is he ok?"

"They used the excuse that he had been sleeping with Sophie." I could hear the anger in her voice. "That little bitch. It was she who took advantage of his marital troubles." Angie had always been utterly loyal to her team, especially when they got into trouble.

"Does his wife know?" I asked, thinking about the guy's mental state.

"They told me to take him off all duties immediately, or they would tell her. I haven't got much choice. If she ever found out, she would leave him, and I don't think he would survive that. He'd do anything to avoid it, even blow the plant himself."

"How does that leave the rest of your team? Are you still in control?" I asked.

"For the moment. But we're going to need help from on high."

I assumed she was referring to Soothslayer. "I'll talk to Billy," I offered.

"Who's Billy?"

"Billy Sapito. That's Soothslayer's real name, or one of them at least. Sounds like we need him more than ever."

I took her silence as assent, and asked the obvious question. "How long have we got?"

"We will delay as long as we can," she countered.

"How long?" I insisted.

"Ten days maximum. Is that enough to get your mother back, and bring in the authorities?"

"I'm not sure," I told her.

But I was.

And it wasn't.

120

My 'Oranges and Lemons' ringtone had always brought a smile to my face when it had signalled a call from Bobby. Now it had been adopted by Soothslayer, it brought mixed emotions: pleasure at the sound of his cheerful voice, but fear for the bad news he might bring.

He always responded within minutes when I pressed the 'blizzard' button on his weather app.

"Morning, gorgeous," he trilled. "How can I help you this morning?"

"Good afternoon, Billy," I replied, duly respecting his time zone. "Dare I ask how you are doing? Angie is getting worried, as she's been given notice to quit."

"O ye of little faith," he responded, and I could almost feel him shaking his head. "Do you know why it's taking so long?" He giggled. "That toolkit that I created for them all those years ago was just too utterly brilliant." He paused, apparently overcome by his own genius. "But Soothslayer is the best. Better than any of those nasty little worker-drones beavering away for 'The Pig' and his cronies."

I waited for the self-adulation to exhaust itself.

"Does that mean you're succeeding?"

"Soothslayer always wins through in the end."

"And will that end be in time to stop your mate Yusupov annihilating the entire south-east of the United Kingdom?"

He breathed in deeply. "As you know very well, 'The Pig' is no friend of mine. Or yours." I could feel him focus everything into his hatred for Yusupov.

That animosity was our lifeline, so I tugged it.

"That's why we need you, Billy. You're the only game in town who can stop that lunatic from destroying us. You and I have both felt the raw end of his electrodes. We've got to stop him. Can you do that, or are we wasting our time? Is he just too good for you?"

I had a feeling Billy Sapito wouldn't take kindly to the suggestion that he wasn't up to any challenge.

I was right.

"Never, ever disparage the Soothslayer," he muttered angrily. "Trust me, I'll stop him blowing the plant.

"And what's more, I'm arranging for his uranium enrichment plant in Kuikbakhistan to go up in its stead. That's also taking time. When that little shit presses the button, it will be his own pride and joy that goes up in smoke, and I can't wait to see the look on his face when it does."

He signed off with a malicious giggle.

I relayed our conversation to Angie. She had recovered a bit of her mojo. "Sounds like he's more interested in demolishing Yusupov's enrichment plant. But don't worry, Nick. We're on it. We'll keep this end pinned down."

I had no choice but to believe her.

121

"I think I'm being followed."

No sooner had I got off the phone with Angie, than I picked up a voicemail from Anastasia.

I rang her immediately, but only got her answering service. Just as I was beginning to panic, she phoned me.

"What do they look like?"

"Two of them," she replied calmly. "One thug behind me, and a nasty-looking little creep on the other side of the street. I'm trying to lose them in the crowds, but they're sticking like glue."

"Can you find a policeman?" I asked.

"Fat chance, but I'm looking out for anybody in authority. I'm going into the sanctity of Peter Jones to buy a suitcase-full of cosmetics and make a fuss over something. That should keep me out of harm's way for a bit. Can you get here quickly?"

"I will be there in fifteen minutes. Keep shopping until I get there. I'll call Swami also."

Swami's phone went straight through to voicemail, so I left a suitably urgent message.

I texted Jimmy, but there was no time to wait for him, so I hailed a taxi and showed the driver a fifty-pound note.

"This is for you, if you can get me to Peter Jones in ten minutes."

He pulled a flawless U-turn to the sound of various horns, and set off like his life depended on it.

He earned his fifty pounds and dropped me outside the main entrance.

I ran into the perfume section, to see Anastasia with a trolley-full of merchandise, and two excited assistants tending to her every need.

I hugged her thankfully.

"Over there." She nodded her head in the direction of two slightly awkward-looking guys, being attended to by an extremely camp assistant. Their attention was plainly not on the cosmetics he was trying to sell them, and they glanced at us fleetingly.

At that moment my phone rang, and I was relieved to see it was Swami.

"I've sent you a photo of the two guys I assigned to Anastasia," he said calmly. At that moment the WhatsApp on my phone bleeped and I held it up for Nasta to see. Relief swept across her face.

"It's Swami's guys," I sighed, and Nasta breathed out deeply.

"Thanks, Swami," I said. "Let me show you the lengths your guys are going to, in carrying out their surveillance duties."

I took a quick photo, as Nasta laughed. "He's trying to put foundation cream on them."

Swami's boys tried to cover their faces when they saw the camera, but it was too late. I waved and they returned the favour with little enthusiasm.

Swami had not hung up. "We found Faarax," he said quietly. "We're going to need your help. When can you be at the Old Bell?"

122

Jimmy had not been far away, so we were there in half an hour.

Swami was propping up the bar.

"We got to your friend Faarax."

We were all ears.

"He thinks he knows where your mother is being held."

Nasta gripped my hand, and I felt a momentary wave of relief. It passed pretty quickly. I had been trying to carry on as normal, and had almost persuaded myself that the spectre of Mother in the hands of the son who hated her was just a bad dream. But this confirmation of her captivity somehow blew away that charade.

"Where is she?" we whispered, in unison.

"Don't know for certain," said Swami, holding up his hands defensively. "Let's not get ahead of ourselves, but she just may be in an old castle up in the north of Scotland. It's the centre of operations for coordinating all their drug running." He looked distastefully out over the throng of customers. "Faarax and his boys were up to their eyes in it, mainly organising the gangs of mules to distribute the stuff round London and the home counties. But they also went to the castle several times."

"Can we get her out?"

"It won't be easy," confirmed Swami. "It's damn near impregnable."

He could see the disappointment in my face.

"But there is a file on a memory stick, which Faarax's guys put together, in case the Kuikbakhs ever double-crossed them. Apparently, it has the complete layout of the castle, with details of all its security systems, including a couple of weak points."

"That sounds hopeful," nodded Nasta.

"And an old tunnel entrance."

That sounded even better.

"That's where I need your help," he replied. "Your friend Polly Lightfoot has that memory stick. I have a note from Faarax telling her to make a copy for us."

He pulled out a small brown envelope.

"He says she'll do that if you ask her nicely, but she's a suspicious character, so you need to deliver his note to her in person. How was she when you called?"

"Quite friendly, actually. I always liked her, and she was good at her job." Nasta frowned. "Although you tell us that she was bent, and she is obviously in deep with this drugs gang. She lives out in Herefordshire."

"Nothing to lose," said Swami quietly, handing her the envelope. "Go and meet her there and get that memory stick. We can't risk extricating Tilly without it."

"I will," Nasta assured him.

"We both will," I countered.

"Whatever," muttered Swami. "Just get it."

"How long have we got?" he asked, as an afterthought.

I shrugged.

123

Nasta suggested going to meet Polly Lightfoot on her own, but I wouldn't hear of it.

"She will relax more if I'm alone. We can reminisce with some girl chat," she suggested, not unreasonably.

"There is no way you are going alone into the wilds of Herefordshire, to meet a 'bent recruiter', as Baldy put it, who is living in the house of an imprisoned Somali drug-dealer. Especially as Swami says she may well only respond favourably if you threaten her that Sir Miles is still dead, whatever the fuck that means. No way."

"Swami and his boys will look after me," she insisted.

"He'll be on the outside. I'm coming with you, and I'm going to be right beside you, in case she pulls any shit, which she probably will."

Anastasia shrugged. "Ok, if you insist. Thank you. I still think feminine intuition and rapport might work better, but thanks."

We gave Swami the timings and other details of our trip.

"Faarax said not to warn her beforehand about the memory stick. Just drop in on a pretext, and hand her his envelope. Don't worry, we'll be right there with you," he assured us.

We took Snapper and drove down the M4, heading for Belmont Abbey, which was the nearest landmark.

From there, the roads got smaller and windier, until we came to some impressive gates.

"I hope Swami has found it," I fretted, my sense of unease feeding on itself.

"We'll be fine," soothed Nasta in a strange role-reversal. She was normally the worrier.

She got out and pressed the intercom, giving her name and, on prompting, mine and Jimmy's also.

The gates opened slowly, and we drove up an impressive drive, through parkland on which a herd of brown and white Longhorn cattle was grazing peacefully. Those closest to us stared morosely, their long, cream-coloured horns seeming to warn us that we were on alien ground.

We drew up at a rather bleak Victorian mansion.

A bulky, dark-complexioned man was positioned just outside the large door. He didn't move, or even acknowledge our arrival. Snapper growled malevolently and I picked him up before he could do anything stupid. I thought these guys would probably shoot first and not even bother to ask questions.

Then the door opened, and Polly came slowly down the steps to welcome us. She was pretty, in a careworn way. She smiled, and laughed nervously, shaking Nasta's hand with what I felt was slightly contrived pleasure. She quickly turned to me, her hands fluttering, and proffered her cheek with a nervous giggle. I went to kiss her, but Snapper wriggled furiously, his teeth bared, so my efforts to keep him from biting her morphed into a shallow bow. She returned the gesture uncertainly, eyeing him with distaste.

"I'll put him in the car," I said, clamping my hands round his torso and shoving him onto the back seat.

"He hates long car journeys," explained Nasta diplomatically.

Polly clearly didn't buy that, but she clapped her hands together in our general direction. "It's been so long," she simpered, ushering us into the house. She seemed to treat the building with more respect than affection, and I got the impression that it was where she lived, but it was not really her home.

Tea was waiting for us, served by another unsmiling servant who retired, once his work was done, closing the doors behind him.

"We have so much catching up to do, Anastasia," she gushed, slopping her tea in the process, without appearing to notice.

"You are married?" she looked at Nasta and then me. I nodded.

"Yes," replied Nasta, "one child, and another on the way." She felt her tummy, although it barely showed.

"Wonderful." Our hostess clapped her hands again, but her face clouded over. "I have to wait for Faarax to get out for that."

I got the feeling that the prospect of Faarax Warsame regaining his liberty did not fill her with unbridled joy. I suspected her family was going to have to wait a bit. Perhaps until a future reincarnation.

After ten minutes of general catching up, Nasta took the bull by the horns. "Faarax asked me to give you this," she said gently, passing the little brown envelope to her hostess, who took it gingerly and opened it.

A whole host of conflicting emotions seemed to fight their way across her face as she read the brief note.

Finally, she nodded.

"OK," she said, looking at neither of us. "I'm afraid it isn't here, but I'll get it for you. I have it in safekeeping at my bank."

"I know I am pestering you, outrageously," Nasta persisted. "Is there any way we could go and get it now? Faarax knows we are in something of a rush."

That definitely brought on a flicker of fear. It also hardened her stance. She shook her head violently.

"I am afraid I will need to make an appointment with the bank manager." She tried to laugh. "He's such a stickler."

We both looked at her in urgent silence. She got the message.

"I will try him now." She turned and picked up a cordless phone, taking it into an adjoining room.

She was back after a few minutes.

"I am afraid he can't see me this afternoon." The disappointment on our faces must have been obvious.

"He will meet me at 9 a.m. tomorrow morning."

We agreed to return at ten.

There was an awkward silence, and we soon made our excuses, parting on superficially friendly terms.

Her smiles and giggles had returned with a vengeance. Her eyes denied their authenticity. Nor were they reflected on the faces of her employees.

Even the Longhorns seemed happy to see us leave. The largest bull was swinging his pendulous horns from side to side, seemingly shooing us towards the exit.

124

We decided to stay the night in the local village pub, rather than return to London. The Hare and Hounds was a quaint old stone building with a thatched roof.

After checking into our room, we went down, looking for a drink.

It was six thirty, and a small group was huddled deep in conversation, propping up the bar. They eyed us warily.

"Good evening," smiled Nasta. They nodded, although smiles were few and far between.

"Could we have a pint of your local best bitter, and a ginger ale with ice?" I asked the middle-aged woman behind the bar.

"Swan Silver or Ruffled Nectar?" she asked, filling two tasting glasses for me to try.

I tasted them both carefully.

"Ruffled Nectar, please," I decided, nodding appreciatively.

When we both had glasses in our hands, we raised them and toasted, "Cheers," nodding generally at the bar and the group propping it up.

They returned our greeting, with slightly diminished suspicion. I suspected that my choice of a local beer had helped, but it was probably Nasta's sparkle that really did it.

"Lovely place this," she said, half to me, but seeming to include all the assembled company. "Pity we're only here for one night."

Even this brought little reaction, so, with a deep breath, I surreptitiously pushed Snapper towards them with one foot. He hobbled over and I closed my eyes as I saw him sniff a leather handbag on the floor. He liked cocking his leg on anything leather, so I jumped to my feet.

"What a sweet little thing," crooned the owner of the bag, rubbing Snapper's ear, and with that the ice was broken.

Their leader, a grey-haired man with intelligent, sparkling eyes enquired suspiciously, "What brings you to this neck of the woods?"

"Some minor business with Polly Lightfoot at Dalston Manor," Nasta replied breezily.

There was an unmistakeable collective hesitation, and we had lost them. "Good luck with that," he laughed. His team nodded knowingly and seemed to close in on itself again.

"Not big fans of theirs?" I asked, and I could see immediately that I was pushing too hard.

Before they could clam up entirely, Nasta assured them gently but firmly, that we were not any part of the Dalston Manor set.

"I knew Polly years ago and we desperately need her help with some family business," she offered, giving a wonderful impression of a damsel in distress.

It worked, and grey hairs leaned towards her, proffering his hand. "I'm Roger Moffat," he informed her. "And good luck with that, Miss…"

"Anastasia and Nick de Carteret," she filled in for him.

We all shook hands, and they looked at us with renewed interest. Nasta continued, "We've just been talking with her up at the house, and we got the definite impression that we need to be careful."

I was fascinated by Nasta's continuing ability to play, so authentically, the vulnerable heroine. I tried not to look at her in case I put her off.

It worked.

"Nasty crowd," Roger informed us in a whisper, looking round for any sign of intruders. The others nodded resignedly.

"Too many noisy, bloody helicopters," groaned a young woman on a stool.

"Rude bunch," added the landlady, with feeling. "Never say thank you, and not a penny in tips." She turned away in disgust. "I'd be very careful how you deal with them."

They were all nodding, but I could see that their distaste was mixed with a liberal dose of fear.

"Foreigners, mostly, and no respect for the law, I'm afraid," Roger informed us, adding quickly, "Not that there's much law around here to respect."

This met with general agreement, and a rotund, middle-aged man put in, "They beat the crap out of my son last week, just because he gave them some lip. Took him outside and broke his cheekbone and two ribs. The police took a statement, but they just don't want to know anything about it, almost as if they're scared of them, too."

Their head of steam was building, and I tried to help it along.

"Do you think they're into drugs or anything like that?" I asked. As soon as I had said it, I realised I should have left it to Nasta. They looked anxiously at each other, and Roger shook his head.

"Don't know anything about that kind of thing," he declared. "Don't know what they're into." He looked around him at the others. "But I guarantee you, it's nothing very nice."

They were all nodding again, although I could see we really had lost them this time. "You just be careful with those people," counselled Roger.

"There's not much help around these parts if you get in trouble," echoed the landlady "Your dinner's ready," she advised us, pointing to a table in the bow window.

125

We were up early. For my part, I have never needed much sleep, which was just as well under our current circumstances as I was finding it hard to come by. I had always been more of a banker than an accountant, and my sheep-counting was shit.

We had a good breakfast, more to fill in the time than to satisfy any hunger pangs.

Then we read the papers.

"You have to stop looking at your watch," whispered Nasta, putting her hand on my wrist protectively.

We decided to take a walk. I phoned Swami once we were out of hearing range of the pub. Baldy answered his phone.

"We're going to Dalston at ten," I informed him.

"Nick, you have to relax." I heard him chuckle to himself. "You've told us that four times already, between texts and messages. The boys are ready. I promise, we have you covered."

I did relax slightly, hearing him state it so plainly.

"That's great, Baldy. I'm just a bit uptight, what with Mother and everything. Bear with me."

"Understood," he replied.

"Thanks," was all I could manage. "We're going in."

We meandered slowly back to the pub, and paid our bill.

"Thanks, and good luck," said the landlady. "Just don't provoke them," she added, unnecessarily.

"We'll try not to," responded Nasta, "and thanks for everything."

We got slowly into the car and drove the few miles to Dalston Manor.

We were at the gates at five to ten.

I started to get out, but Nasta put her hand on my arm.

"I'll do it." I opened my window, as she walked round to the intercom.

Pulling back her shoulders defiantly, she rang the intercom.

We waited, and after what seemed an eternity, she rang again, more insistently.

"Yes?" said an unfriendly voice.

"Hello, this is Anastasia de Carteret. I have an appointment with Polly Lightfoot at ten o'clock."

"She can't see you," said the voice, without emotion.

Nasta blinked. "But we made this appointment last night and she told us to return at ten this morning."

"Can't help that," said the voice. "She doesn't want to see you."

With that, whoever was behind the voice put down their receiver and, in spite of Anastasia's repeated ringing, refused to pick it up again.

I jumped out of the car. "What the fuck do we do now?" I asked, shaking the gates.

Nasta was on her mobile immediately.

"Swami, its Anastasia," she whispered. "Oh, sorry, Baldy. We are at the gates of Dalston Manor and they won't let us in. What can we do?"

She listened briefly and nodded with a look of resignation.

"Will that work?" she asked.

Baldy obviously felt it would. She killed the call and made another.

"Damn," she muttered, still listening to what was obviously an answerphone message.

Finally, she said slowly into the phone, "Polly, this is Anastasia. We are at the gates, and apparently you don't want to meet us. I am afraid that we need that memory stick. To that end, I am told to tell you that Sir Miles is still dead."

She paused, not quite understanding the significance of what she had just said, and thus unsure what to say next.

Finally, she settled on, "I look forward to hearing from you very soon."

She killed the call, and looked at me questioningly.

.

126

We had little choice but to return to the Hare and Hounds.

I ordered coffees from a waitress we hadn't seen before, and we sipped them despondently.

The question, to which neither of us knew the answer, was avoided by unspoken agreement. We had no idea whether Anastasia's call would have the effect Baldy assured us it would.

After ten tense minutes, Nasta's phone rang, and she reached for it.

"We will come straight there," she said, and put the phone in her bag.

"We're on," she confirmed, rising to go. "She doesn't sound happy. I hope Swami is ready."

Nasta drove, and I called Baldy to tell him our exact movements.

"Is he on full alert?" asked Nasta anxiously.

"Yup," I nodded. "He says everything's completely under control. I hope to God, he's right."

We pulled up at the gates, and this time they opened as we did so. We drove past the Longhorns, who ignored us, and on up to the house.

Drawing ourselves to our full stature, physically and mentally, we walked up to the main door, which again opened for us, as if by magic.

The sullen flunky we had met before ushered us into a large room, which was laid out as an office, with two desks on the far side, and high-backed chairs facing away from us, towards the wall.

Polly was standing near the door, looking nervous, flanked by two heavily-built and suited goons.

She started to smile at Nasta, but thought better of it, and simply pointed to a memory stick, which was on a small, round table in the middle of the room.

"There's your stick," she directed.

"Get it," ordered one of the goons, with a strong accent. He walked over towards us.

Nasta strode over and picked it up.

"Can I check this is what we're looking for?" she asked, but as she turned, one of them pointed a large automatic at her.

"You steal our property," he said, without emotion.

I realised immediately that this was a set-up. Without thinking, I took the fleeting opportunity and chopped my hand across his neck, turning to attempt a kick to his crotch. He parried that, but the first blow had been effective, and had slowed him. He staggered, his gun pointing down.

The other guy turned his gun on Nasta. I launched myself at him, but I was not close enough, and before I could cover half the distance, there were two loud retorts.

Out of the corner of my eye I could see Anastasia hit the ground, and with a ghastly certainty, I remembered where I had heard the killer's accent before.

He was a fucking Kuikbakh.

So, my nemesis, Tselmeg Yusupov, had won.

I sank to my knees in despair, waiting resignedly for the bullet which would reunite us.

"You don't have to pray, Nick," said a familiar voice.

I looked up. Swami Baxter and Nosey Johnson were sitting, guns in hand, in the two office chairs, which were now swivelled to face us.

Polly Lightfoot was crying to herself by the door.

"They forced me to do that," she wailed. "I would never…" she tailed off, sobbing.

Beside her, the two Kuikbakhs lay in pools of blood.

"Didn't think we'd leave you alone with this bunch, did you?"

asked Swami quietly, with an aggrieved smile. "Your mother would never forgive us."

127

Swami and Nosey took control.

I was in shock. I hovered round Nasta, like a dishevelled guardian angel.

Sometimes, it takes a trauma to make you realise what an arsehole you have been. For a second, I thought I had lost my wife and unborn child. That suddenly made me realise how large a part of my life they now were.

Thinking of Mother, in Yusupov's filthy clutches, induced in me a strange, paradoxical calm. Remembering Bobby helped even more. I began to focus.

Nosey had loaded the memory stick on one of the desktop computers, and he and Swami were running through the layout and defences of Yusupov's Scottish stronghold. Some of Swami's boys were making sure all the staff were friendly.

"There's the tunnel entrance," said Nosey, excitedly. "Leads straight to the old dungeons."

"And the cellars where they store the drugs," added Swami, with disgust.

"So, we can get in via the tunnel, extract Tilly, and be off without them even knowing." Baldy looked satisfied that his strategy was simple and relatively risk-free. "Didn't think it would be so easy."

"It won't," said Swami.

The other two looked at him questioningly.

"We're going to put this cesspit out of action for good."

The other two remonstrated with him briefly, but it was clear who was the boss. Baldy sighed.

They immersed themselves, once more, in the layout and security of the castle. I looked at them with a mix of horror and admiration. Horror, that they could so effectively ignore the two mutilated corpses, which were being cleaned up and removed by a group of seemingly indifferent house staff; admiration at their immediate and remorselessly focused concentration on the new task.

"This video is top stuff. That's the boiler room, next to the dungeon, which is perfect. We can take them all out with fentanyl gas, and see what the fuck else they are up to," exclaimed Swami. "Then we torch the place."

That got all our attention.

Baldy was obviously coming round to the idea. "If we're going in after the fentanyl, we'll need protection. Facemasks and gloves should do it." He scrolled through several images on the screen, nodding and pointing out various features, as they all huddled over the computer.

"Assuming, of course, that she's there," put in Nasta.

That brought everyone up short.

"She's there," said Swami quietly. "You're right; we don't know for certain, but I can feel it. She's there."

"We need to move," he said. "Any updates from Angie?"

"She's holding it together," I said. "She doesn't know for how long."

"Then we haven't a second to waste," muttered Baldy who, as the brains of the team, organised all the technical equipment. "We have everything we need and more loaded in a ten-tonner, just out of sight around the corner; fentanyl, surveillance stuff and everything needed to get us in there."

Swami and Nosey looked questioningly at him.

He nodded confidently. "Trust me. Having seen the layout of the castle we're good to go."

"We'll take a helicopter up there with our team this afternoon from RAF Credenhill, the SAS base in Hereford. We're sending this stuff by road. Your Jimmy is a good lad. He's going to be driving it up there for us, with our guys riding shotgun for him."

"That'll be right up his alley," said Nasta with a grin.

"I'm coming with you," I declared.

The three of them looked at each other and shrugged.

"Got hiking gear?" asked Baldy.

I nodded. "Boots."

"Bring them," he ordered.

Nasta started to remonstrate with me, but she saw the look on my face, so just came over and hugged me.

"Take care of him," she commanded them.

"Bring her back safely," she instructed me quietly, understanding the awful dilemma I faced; whether to stay close to my wife and child, or put my mother first. "I'll be at home waiting with Chloe and…" She placed a hand on her stomach.

I kissed her lips, and we stood there tightly entwined. The whole room was quiet. I thought of Bobby, and was sure I could feel his presence.

Even Polly stopped sobbing, as silence reigned.

"OK," said Swami, clapping his hands and in so doing, breaking the spell. "Got your toothbrush? We're leaving now."

They headed for the door and reluctantly disentangling from one of the two women in my life, I went to rescue the other.

128

Jimmy was ecstatic at his new role, and waved at us from the cabin with a grin like a five-year-old with a birthday treat. Three tough-looking heavies climbed in with him, and were obviously infected by his enthusiasm. A partial smile glided across the granite of their self-discipline.

"It says we'll be there at midnight, chief." One of them pointed at the satnav system on his phone, morphing the gesture into a half-salute towards his leader.

"Go for it," said Swami.

"We'll hitch a ride with you." He nodded at me, pointing to Nasta's car. "Anastasia can drop us at Credenhill." He turned to her. "You'll have to drive yourself back home afterwards, love." His tone was filled with sufficient doubt for her to bristle.

"I think I can manage that, thanks. Just don't you worry your pretty little heads about me; concentrate on your job, and get Tilly back, so we can stop that monster blowing us all to kingdom come."

Swami wasn't used to being challenged, and especially not by a female. He blinked uncertainly.

"Sounds about as bossy as your mother, Nick," he smiled. "With those two gorgons running your life for you, you'll need permission to go to the village shop for sweeties." Nosey and Baldy laughed but you could see from the way they looked at her that their laughter was not without respect.

As if to back up her words, Nasta drove fast and competently, and left us at the Credenhill gates. I kissed her, and she held my gaze.

"Take care," she whispered, "and bring her back safely."

I nodded and stroked her head.

"I will."

Snapper opened one eye fleetingly, but went straight back to sleep.

Swami was beckoning, and I ran over to him at the guard post, where a military policeman compared me to my driving licence photo and his records, nodding cursorily and waving me past. "Your colleagues are waiting for you aboard the 'copter, sir," he addressed Swami deferentially.

We ran towards a helicopter, where four men in balaclavas were waving at us to get a move on. They pulled us up the ladder, and as the doors closed the rotors started to turn.

We buckled up and, as the machine lifted off, I could see Nasta blowing me a kiss. I waved back, unsure if she could see me.

I forced myself to turn away and focus on our mission. Nasta would hold her end together. Swami had assured me his team would guard her and Chloe with their lives, and I believed him.

In return, I needed to give him my total concentration. Mother's survival depended on it.

129

The flight lasted just under three hours. The boys spent the entire trip poring over maps and a computer screen, agreeing their plan of attack, and trying to anticipate and counter all conceivable problems. They made sure I knew the overall plan, and as we were getting close, Swami summarised it for me on the map, which was spread out on his lap.

"We will be landing about ten miles from the castle, right here." He pointed with his index finger.

"An old friend of ours lives up here. Johnny Beresford."

The others smiled.

"Silly bugger knocked up some Scottish lassie a few years back, when we were up in these parts. She got pregnant. Johnny decided to stay."

There was obviously more to the story, as their smiles broke into huge grins, but now wasn't the time for story-telling.

He looked at his watch. "Should be there in ten minutes."

He looked at me intently, all humour dispelled. "Johnny'll take us to his house, and we'll start to get ready. Your Jimmy and the boys should be here with the kit in nine hours." He tapped the watch. "That'll be midnight."

"On course," muttered one of the others, looking at his mobile. "They're passing Manchester."

"As soon as they arrive, we'll let Simba loose."

Before I could ask, he continued, "Little remote tracked vehicle, armed with everything you could possibly need to take out these cunts, even at night."

They all nodded.

"We'll rendezvous with the truck at a little sheltered place Johnny uses, about two miles away from the castle, well out of range of their perimeter." Again, he showed me on the map.

"Then we look for any patrols."

"Patrols?" I queried, looking out at the vast expanse of featureless moorland below us. "Will they bother to put out patrols?"

Swami looked at me sharply. "Yes, they will bother."

He shook his head at me. "You still don't seem to get it, Nick. You've obviously got too close to these nasty little people. I'm telling you, they are the foulest sort of bad-arsed, drug-pushing, people-trafficking, whore-mongering motherfuckers from your worst nightmare."

"How you managed to get your little old mother mixed up with a bunch like that, I will never even begin to imagine."

He looked at me, shaking his head.

I was beginning to get the message.

"Yes, they will have patrols, because I am sure your mother is not the only contraband they have holed up there."

He paused briefly, before continuing, "We are going to take out the patrols; then we approach the castle, with Simba deactivating any monitoring systems."

He had the others' attention now, as well.

"We'll go in through the tunnel, and use a small charge to get into the dungeons. It's only a dummy wall at the end of the tunnel."

He saw the concern on my face. "Don't worry, it's a very restricted charge."

"We'll run a hose from Simba, attach it to the air-conditioning system, and wish them all goodnight with a dose of fentanyl gas in the HVAC system," added Baldy.

"The castle's got air-conditioning?" I asked, thinking of the cold, damp piles I had occasionally visited in Scotland.

"Mainly heating and ventilation, in this godforsaken climate," nodded Nosey. "Nothing but the best creature comforts for your buddies."

Baldy traced various lines with his finger on a technical drawing of the building on his lap.

"Total comfort for them, and utter misery for any poor bugger who crosses them," spat Swami. "Like your mother," he frowned at me.

"So, having knocked out your friends, we extract your mother, together with any others they've got holed up there, and take a look round for what else needs sorting," he continued.

"Then we make sure the whole shit heap can never be used again."

"Bad fire," muttered Baldy, shaking his head disapprovingly. "They really shouldn't keep all that explosive down in the basement near the oil tanks."

"Why do they keep it there?" I asked.

"They don't," stated Swami, now smiling and nodding slowly. "Yet."

"There's Johnny," said Nosey, pointing down, as the helicopter prepared to land.

130

I could see that Johnny Beresford had known Swami and his guys for a long time.

He embraced each of them in turn, Swami last.

"How the fuck are you, Baxter?" he asked fondly.

"Good, Johnny, good. How's Daphne?"

"She's well," beamed Johnny happily. "She can't wait to see you."

"Let's get going."

The four of us piled our kit into the back of an old pickup.

The other four, who had come with us in the helicopter, packed what they could of theirs on top of ours, and with a shrug, hoisted the rest onto their shoulders.

"See you at Johnny's," they said, turning on their heels and setting off at a sharp trot.

"How far is your house?" I asked, shaking Johnny's hand.

"So, you're Tilly's long-lost son," he declared, ignoring my question and looking me over curiously, without letting go of my hand. "Glad to see you've come to rescue her from those bastards."

I immediately liked him.

"I probably got her there in the first place," I admitted, ruefully.

"What's done is done," he replied. "It's about six miles."

I watched the quartet of heavily-laden runners with admiration.

"They do that in their sleep," laughed Swami, following my gaze.

We squeezed in, and Johnny took the wheel, as we bounced over the rough track, before joining a very secondary road. We arrived in thirty minutes.

"The speed you drive, Johnny, the boys will be there before us," laughed Swami.

"You always were an impatient sod," replied Johnny. "I'm trying to give Daphne a break; lessen the time that she has to put up with you."

At that moment he turned into his drive, and we could see a small figure waiting outside an open front door, with a broad, infectious smile. I could not help myself wondering what had persuaded Johnny to give up everything to come to these wild parts.

I soon found out.

Once she had welcomed the others with hugs and questions, she embraced me warmly.

"You must be so worried, having only just found your mother again, to have her snatched from you like this."

Swami started to tell her that it was me who was responsible for the mess, but she stopped him in his tracks.

"Don't you listen to these morons. I'm just so glad you came along, to make sure they don't screw up completely."

They all laughed at that, and I found myself apologising again. Something which would have been wholly out of character, only a few days ago.

"I'm afraid Swami's right. It's my fault she's where she is, and I'm really just trying to keep out of their way, while they rescue Mother."

"Nonsense," she retorted. "You just keep an eye on them. You'll probably have to dig them out of some hole or other."

She turned, and with a 'come hither' flick of her hips, ushered us into her home.

131

Daphne had prepared an enormous stew for us, with a pile of potatoes which dwarfed the table.

I was amazed to see the speed with which Swami's team demolished it all. She was delighted, clucking round them attentively, and urging her two young boys to follow suit.

After coffee, Swami went over all the plans again, in detail. Johnny listened attentively and threw in pertinent comments. He knew the locality and the castle well, and they made a few revisions as a result.

"Time for a kip," suggested Swami, looking at his watch. "All the kit ready and prepped, Jody?" he asked one of the runners, who appeared to be in charge.

"Good to go," Jody nodded. "I'll take a quick walk round. You go ahead and rest."

The others all headed off, and Johnny showed them to their makeshift quarters.

Daphne looked quizzically at Jody.

"How's my namesake?" she asked quietly.

"Daphne's great," he smiled. "Megan's nearly two, and we have a boy on the way."

A wistful look swept across his face and for a second I thought he might shed a tear. But these guys didn't cry, and he pulled back his shoulders and grinned at her.

"Your boys look well. You should have more," he suggested, his train of thought following the family theme.

It was Daphne's turn to look sad.

Jody realised he had strayed too far and held up his hand in apology.

Changing the subject elegantly, she admonished him. "You shouldn't still be doing this, Jody."

"I promised my Daphne this would be the last sortie," he agreed, but that forlorn expression flashed back briefly. They looked at each other, but as Daphne opened her mouth, he put his hand out.

"I'm doing this last one for Swami," he stated, in a way that did not brook argument. "And for your mother," he added, smiling at me.

"Had a bad dream last night, that's all. Dreamed I took one in the leg," he muttered. "Didn't make it."

He laughed. "I don't believe in dreams, do you, Daphne?" I could see that it wasn't a rhetorical question. He wanted her opinion.

Daphne took his hand, watching him closely.

"I don't either, Jody," she assured him. "But sometimes people do believe them, and actually help them come true." She looked at him with concern. "For instance, by putting themselves unnecessarily in harm's way. Don't do that, Jody, my love."

He laughed, and I could feel the awkward spell was broken. "I bloody won't do that," he assured her, giving her a hug.

I could see that there was a strong bond between Daphne and these tough young men. I determined to ask Swami about it when we were back home.

Jody pulled out an envelope.

"Just in case, could you give this to my Daphne and Megan, if I don't make it."

He handed it to her.

She shied away from it, as if it was booby-trapped, but eventually took it and held both his hands in hers.

"Jody, if you have any doubts, you owe it to your family to give this one a miss. Swami and the boys will be fine without you. They'll understand completely."

But Jody was back under control and laughed, giving her cheek a pinch.

"Just humour me," he grinned. "I'll be fine. The world needs these fucking parasites out of the way. Wouldn't miss this one last shindig with the boys for all the bread in heaven."

I thought it was a strange turn of phrase.

"Here, I took some blood, just in case." He handed her a large plastic bottle with a drip feed hanging from it. "Just stick it in the fridge for me. I won't be needing it; just feel happier knowing it's there. I'm AB negative," he explained. "Not very common."

Daphne took the bottle and placed the letter carefully in her desk drawer. We watched as he lit a cigarette, and wandered outside.

"What do you think?" she asked me, and I felt flattered that she should value my opinion, when she herself obviously knew Jody and his family so well.

"Funny turn of phrase."

"I agree," she said. "And I wonder if he really thinks he won't be needing that blood."

"Should we tell Swami?" I asked.

"Definitely. He's quite emotional is Jody. Tougher than nails, but soft inside, and his family's growing." She shook her head. "This is no business for a family man. I can see his heart's not in it."

There was little I could add.

"But you try telling that to these nutters." She smiled, nodding towards the bedrooms.

132

I managed a couple of hours' sleep and, before I knew it, we were ready to go.

Jody seemed to have put his misgivings behind him and his efficiency was ruthless, prompting and encouraging his three colleagues. He was in charge of the small group of commandos. We were all camouflaged up, and I had been decked up in some army fatigues they had found for me. Only my underwear and hiking boots had passed muster.

Jody smiled at me confidently, and I put any worries to the back of my mind. It was time to get Mother out of Yusupov's clutches.

This time we had two vehicles, and Daphne drove one of them, an old Land Rover. She dumped us with a "Good luck, boys; do your bit," and retraced her path.

Jimmy and the three heavies in the truck were already at the rendezvous, at a clearing in the middle of a small, but dense forest of Scots pine trees. It was a cloudy night, with a half-moon giving some occasional light between the rolling Caledonian clouds.

They were silently unloading a small camouflaged tracked vehicle. To my untrained eye it looked like something out of *Star Wars*. Armed with a heavy machine gun, two satellite dishes with antennae peered out from each side. At the back were three large compressed-gas cylinders.

"Fentanyl," said Baldy proudly. "Battery-powered electric motor, with solar backup. Silent."

He looked at me with a grin.

"Until you decide to kill any local vermin." He tapped the

barrel of the gun, and stroked two much larger diameter tubes beside it.

He set to work at the controls and manoeuvred Simba to the edge of the forest.

The others waited patiently and, in a few minutes, he murmured, "Two patrol groups."

He called out bearings and distances quietly, and a voice above us replied, "Roger. In range. Nosey's two should be in sight from ground level."

I looked up to see one of the guys attached firmly by a three-way harness, near the top of a pine tree, his rifle dangling beside him. He was pointing across the moor, directly towards the moon.

Nosey set himself up on a small bank and looked through his telescopic sight.

After a few seconds adjusting his aim, he murmured, "Bingo," almost to himself. "You onto yours, Smokes?" he asked.

Smokes settled himself carefully, and after a pause, whispered, "Got them."

"Any chatter on the radios, Baldy?"

"All quiet," confirmed Baldy. "We'll wait for them to check in before we take them."

A tense silence reigned.

Eventually I could stand it no longer. "What the hell are we waiting for?" I whispered to Swami.

"Baldy's been monitoring them, and they check in every half hour. Should be sometime about now. Simba will record their voices, so we can respond to any queries after the kill."

Before I could add anything, Baldy whispered, "Yours, whenever you're ready."

"Swami, count us down," directed Nosey.

I could just make out the visible patrol, which he was targeting.

"Three… two… one…" counted Swami quietly. "Fire," and two shots rang out almost simultaneously.

I could see one of the figures in Nosey's patrol fall to the ground.

Before the other target could even react, two more shots rang out, these not quite so well synchronised.

"Targets down," echoed Nosey and Smokes.

"Any chatter?" asked Swami.

Baldy paused a while before replying, "Negative. I'll keep listening."

"Hopefully, they're over-confident and sloppy," muttered Swami.

"Johnny said they get a lot of poachers on the moors," whispered Nosey. "If the others did hear the shots, chances are they won't worry."

Smokes was down the tree in seconds and Simba began to roll silently forward, with Jody leading the way, Baldy on board and the others fanned out in close formation. Jimmy and one of his travelling companions stayed with the truck.

I was put firmly in the middle, directly behind the vehicle, and we moved off as a thick bank of cloud took away most of the light.

133

Not a word was spoken in the twenty minutes it took us to get in sight of the castle.

We took no chances, skirting round the little hillocks, using them as cover, while Jody guided us away from any treacherous boggy patches. Baldy kept his earphones on, and he and Swami scanned the horizon with night-glasses every few minutes, searching for any activity. There was none.

Baldy drew up at what looked like any other peat hag, and ran a detector across it. He nodded, pointing at a spot on the side. Jody took a spade from Simba and carefully prodded, until he found solid resistance. He scraped round it and soon exposed a rustic door, which he prised open. He shone his torch in and beckoned Swami.

"Just like it said, the tunnel's not in bad shape." He poked the sides. "We can even get Simba in, some of the way."

"Take her in first," directed Swami quietly, motioning to Baldy.

"She'll light the way and we'll keep all the sensors on, in case of any booby traps," he explained, largely, I think, for my benefit.

We followed the vehicle, which drove slowly downhill into what was a well-formed tunnel. It would originally have had solid wooden walls, but most of them had rotted and were hard to discern from the peat and mud. Some sections had obviously been repaired more recently, I assumed by Faarax and his Somali gang.

I reckoned the castle was about half a mile from the tunnel entrance, and we were making good progress although it was hard to tell in the gloom.

After perhaps ten minutes, Baldy held up his hand and halted.

He pointed forward, and we could just make out what appeared to be a solid wall. In front of us, the tunnel was shrinking, and he got out to inspect it, carrying a small sensor with him which he used to scan the obstruction, and pulling out a knife, with which he prodded it, seemingly at random. He came back to us and whispered, "It's the dungeon wall."

"Those plans were good," nodded Swami.

"One person inside, lying against the far wall."

"Perfect," nodded Swami. "Will it blow tidily?"

"Should do, the wall's not in great shape."

Baldy placed what I assumed was an explosive charge into a crack in the wall, having enlarged it with his knife. He waved us all back, and reversed Simba to a safe distance.

Checking that everyone was clear, he pressed a button and there was a dull thud. Once the dust had settled, we could see a small hole in the wall. I rushed forward, but Swami held me back, pointing to his weapon and peering gingerly through the newly-formed opening.

"What took you so long?" came a voice from inside, but the angst in my mother's voice belied the composure of her words.

"Where are the guards?" whispered Swami, pulling aside a large stone to clear a path.

"Along the passage," came the reply. "That barely woke me. Those lazy sods will still be fast asleep."

The others helped, and in a few seconds, we had cleared a body-sized gap. This time I didn't wait, and I was the first through it.

The pleasure and surprise on Mother's face was all the reward I needed.

The others quickly checked out the small dungeon cell, and took up defensive positions.

"The boiler room's outside the door and first right; guardroom along to the left?" Baldy checked with Mother. She nodded.

"There are two little children in the next cell past the guardroom. You have to free them, too," she pleaded. "Brother and sister."

"Don't worry," said Swami. "We're going to evacuate any captives, and blow this shithole to kingdom come."

"With all the sewage still in it," added Nosey. "But we need to move quickly."

Baldy was holding a small device close to the door lock. He was totally focused. Every few seconds, and in response to sporadic bleeps, he pressed keys.

After less than a minute the door clicked open. Jody, pistol at the ready, looked both ways before moving out into the passage. He was followed by two of the others, who were similarly armed and carrying a thin hose from Simba.

They signalled for us to wait, and moved down the corridor to the right, while two others covered the opposite passage.

We were all issued with simple facemasks and long-sleeved gloves.

"In case you're exposed to fentanyl," he explained to Mother, rolling down her sleeves and making sure she was fully covered.

He looked quickly round at the rest of us, to make sure we did the same.

"What's fentanyl?" asked Mother.

"We're running it though the heating system. It will knock them all out, so they don't give us problems."

"Will it kill them?" she asked.

"Usually," shrugged Swami.

"It had better," she said quietly, to my surprise, shaking her head. "They traffic both drugs and people, like those two up the corridor, poor little dears."

A look of anger flashed across her face.

"They cater to the worst kind of disgusting pervert. Like the one who abducted me, Maxim something-or-other." I thought for a moment she was going to spit.

"Maxim Omarov," I sighed. "One of Yusupov's sidekicks."

"We'll get them out," nodded Swami reassuringly.

Baldy reappeared. "We're all hooked up and pumping." He

looked at his watch. "Give it five minutes and everywhere except the cells down here will be full of fentanyl. Remember to keep your masks on, and skin covered just in case.

134

Swami delegated two of his men with Mother to rescue the children. I insisted on going with them.

With one commando leading and one behind us, we moved out of the circular hallway and crept up the passageway, which led off it. We went up a short staircase. As we passed the guardroom, the lead guy poked his head carefully round the door and held up his thumb to us.

"Somalis," he whispered, "out cold." The fentanyl had obviously done its business. He closed the door quietly.

Going carefully down a similar set of stairs on the other side, Mother guided us to the children's cell, and she went in alone, so as not to alarm them. In a couple of minutes, she reappeared, leading by the hand a terrified little boy and girl, who could not have been more than six. They held each other's hands tightly, and looked nervously at us, through their newly-donned masks.

We all smiled and gestured for them to follow and, looking at Mother for reassurance, they did so.

We retraced our steps in tight formation, past the guardroom and back into the hallway outside Mother's cell.

"Welcome," said a voice behind us, and a shot rang out. One of our guides dropped to the ground, groaning and holding his shoulder.

"Do not be brave," advised the voice. As I turned round gingerly, I could see three of the Somalis, who had supposedly been asleep in the guardroom, now fully alert and covering us. The other commando dropped his weapon and kicked it over to them.

Swami, Nosey, Baldy, Jody and the other squaddie were kneeling on the ground disarmed, but apparently otherwise healthy.

"The guardroom doesn't have HVAC," muttered Swami. "They were just asleep. Until you woke them," he shrugged. I was beginning to admire his stoic acceptance of fate, although I could see his brain was working overtime to find a solution.

"You've got a problem, skinny," he said to one of our captors. "All your mates are dead."

As if in confirmation, one of the other Somalis took his mobile away from his ear and shook his head. "No answer."

"Then you will all follow them," said the tallest, who appeared to be their leader.

"You first," he said quietly, pointing his automatic at Mother, but looking at me.

"President Yusupov told us to kill your mother in front of you, if you showed your face here."

The mention of Yusupov brought on a feeling of infuriatingly impotent rage. He had killed my oldest friend, and was now going to dispatch my mother.

Time seemed to stand still, and perhaps for the first time in my life, I realised that there were other things in the world more critical than my own success and wealth.

As that revelation slowly sank in, I understood what I had to do.

I sank to my knees, sobbing. "Please don't kill us," I begged. "I will give you everything. I am very rich. Mr Yusupov will vouch for that. Please don't kill me," I babbled on, as I moved slowly towards him.

He laughed, as did the other two. "The president said you would prove yourself a coward."

Swami looked at me with such a look of contempt, that I could only redouble my efforts.

"What a pitiful little man," spat Baldy, waving his hands at me, although I thought I could see a flash of comprehension. The guards turned their guns towards his movement.

That was all I needed. I grabbed the leader's automatic and wrestled with him, holding on with all the strength that I could muster, and splintering his nose with my elbow.

I could see, out of the corner of my eye, Jody launching himself at one of them who raised his weapon and fired without aiming. Jody staggered and almost collapsed, a red splodge appearing on his trouser leg. He forced himself on, and tackled his target to the ground. I could hear a crack which, I was horrified to realise, was the man's neck snapping.

Havoc reigned, as Swami and his boys took full advantage of the diversion.

There was no time for feelings. My opponent was strong, and his gun was turning back towards me. He had his arm round my throat and was slowly throttling me. I bit his arm and kicked what I hoped was his crotch, as I began to lose consciousness, but he knew his business, and I realised I was going under.

I gave one last desperate struggle, which managed to loosen his grip on the weapon, before I passed out.

135

When I regained consciousness, Swami and Baldy were tightening a belt around the unconscious Jody's leg.

"Bastards got his femoral, just like he dreamt," muttered Baldy. "Think he'll make it, though." He gave the belt a final tug, and looked at me with what I decided to interpret as respect. Jody stirred slightly and groaned.

"We need to get out of here," ordered Swami. "This place gives me the creeps."

"I've put a charge under the oil tank," said Baldy. "There's enough crap in this place to burn for a week."

At that moment, two of the squaddies reappeared.

One of them made a cutting motion across his neck.

"All cleaned up, chief. No survivors."

Swami put his thumb up.

"There must be two tons of cocaine, and God knows how many pills, in a large storeroom off the guardhouse. Christ knows what it's worth."

"Or how much suffering it would have caused," muttered Swami.

"I put an incendiary there, and we spread a few others round in strategic spots. The whole place should go up like a …"

"Nuclear plant?" suggested Baldy, reminding us all of the reason for our being here.

I checked my mobile, but there was no signal, not even for an emergency call.

Swami nodded. "Grab Jody, and let's get out of here." They picked him up, and Baldy checked the tourniquet.

"We need to get him home."

Mother swept up the two petrified children, and we retraced our steps rapidly out to the tunnel. They clambered onto Simba. Jody was draped across the front, and Baldy reversed the vehicle slowly back up the tunnel.

It was with a sense of utmost relief, as we reached the entrance, that I breathed in a cool lungful of clean Highland air. We discarded our masks and protective gloves.

When we were all in the open, we moved well away from the tunnel entrance.

Baldy held up his hand and said, "Watch this."

He pressed a button and there was the satisfying thud of an explosion. We could see the flash in the basement where we had been, only a few moments before. Flames leapt out of several windows and there was a blast of hot air from the tunnel entrance.

"Good riddance," said Swami and the others nodded as flames began to appear from all the ground and first-floor windows, and some secondary explosions followed at intervals.

"I need to talk to the prime minister," I said, half to myself, looking at my phone. The liberation of my mother would, no doubt, prompt Yusupov to accelerate his nuclear plans. He might even be in a position to blow the plant right now. But there was no reception, and I realised I would have to wait for that. I tried not to think the worst.

"Oh fuck me," muttered Swami. "Now he reckons he saved us all back there, young Nicky thinks he's God-all-bloody-mighty." They all laughed and he shook his head at me. "Now you've got a hotline to him…" he pointed at the stars, "… why don't you just tell him to sort it all out for you?"

The others sniggered quietly. But, behind the banter, I could feel a modicum of respect. They understood the urgency only too well.

"Perhaps you need to tell your friend President Yusupov as well," suggested Mother quietly but firmly, bringing me back down to earth.

136

Swami radioed Johnny, but his old buddy wasn't one to wait on orders. As soon as he had heard the explosion, he'd made for the rendezvous. By the time we got there, he was waiting for us with Daphne, who supervised the operation to get Jody into a vehicle. They laid him flat on the back seat, took his blood pressure, and Daphne pushed a small syringe into his forearm. She attached the plastic bottle of blood that the commando-turned-family-man had so presciently made ready.

"Reckon he'll make it?" asked Swami anxiously.

"I think so, God willing," murmured Daphne, giving me a knowing look. "I don't want to have to give that letter to his wife and children."

She also tended to the only other casualty, a shoulder wound.

"You got her then, boss," said Jimmy to me, seeing Mother in the flesh and giving her a hug.

"You gave us a fright there, Mrs Bloomfield," he said, shaking his head.

"It would take more than a bunch of half-arsed Mongol Mafiosi to dispose of our Tilly," laughed Swami.

Jimmy and the remaining commandoes loaded Simba and the other kit onto the truck, and then clambered up themselves.

"Mission accomplished, chief." One of them smiled at his boss with a relaxed salute. "We should get out of here."

"Great job, guys," replied Swami, saluting them smartly and clicking his heels, in a show of respect. "Go safely. See you at the Old Bell tomorrow for a debrief."

"Look after Jody," one of the others said from inside the cab.

"Don't worry, we will," replied Johnny.

Mother shepherded the two fearful young children into Johnny's vehicle, and we set off.

Dawn was breaking as we arrived and at five thirty I could restrain myself no longer. I rang Angie first, on Johnny's landline, so that I could understand the urgency I would need to impart to Petra Marinelli.

Angie's phone rang and I was just beginning to think she wouldn't answer when she did. Unsurprisingly, she sounded sleepy, but she soon kicked in.

"How long have we got?" I asked, bypassing the pleasantries.

"I'm afraid I just don't know," she replied.

A nasty thought struck me that perhaps she or her team had been compromised by Yusupov.

"Are you ok?" I asked more gently.

"Yup," she assured me. "But I'm not sure the plant is."

"How so?" I retorted, immediately apprehensive.

"They've banned us from the site completely. We'd been procrastinating as long as we could."

"Are they ready to blow it?" I was trying not to panic.

There was a long pause.

"Nick, I honestly don't know. I wouldn't think so, and one of Soothslayer's Trojan bugs is still giving us partial access, so we can slow their progress a tiny bit."

She paused. "They could probably have a go at blowing it in a crisis," she said quietly. "Soothslayer assures me he has it all under control. I just can't be sure he isn't more interested in blowing up the enrichment plant in Kuikbakhistan. In any event, they wouldn't get full power." She was silent again, and I could sense her anxiety. "But in an emergency…" she tailed off.

"I think we've just provided that emergency for them," I responded.

She was wide awake now. "How so?"

"We just recovered my mother from their main operating base, and we blew it all to hell for good measure."

"Christ," she muttered, and as an afterthought, "Thank God you got your mother back. Now we need to pray that doesn't piss him off enough to set off Armageddon."

137

I wanted to ring Anastasia, to tell her we were ok, but Angie had scared me.

Petra Marinelli was always in to work early, and sure enough she answered right away.

"Nick, what the hell are you playing at?" she asked immediately. "You're really worrying me."

"I'm afraid I'm not going to make that any better now," I responded. "The nuclear plant at Mersea Island is about to explode."

"Like Chernobyl?" she asked incredulously.

"No, much worse than that, more like Hiroshima." That silenced her completely, so I continued.

"Yusupov's people have been introducing enriched uranium into the plant, and they have now taken over complete control of the operating schedules. We think they may be in a position to blow it at any minute."

"Christ," was all she said, followed by, "How can you possibly know for certain?"

I explained Angie's role there, and her sudden exclusion from the plant. "She doesn't know for certain, but she thinks that Yusupov might just be able to detonate the plant. You need to take the facility back under physical control and let Angie and her team on site immediately to restore operational normality."

A short silence was followed by a series of expletives, and she obviously put her phone down, as I could hear terse instructions being issued.

After a few minutes, she was back with me. I could feel her

anger, and not unreasonably, her first question was, "For God's sake, Nick, why the hell didn't you tell me before? You were coming to talk with me before the weekend. Did you know about this then?"

I explained briefly about Mother.

"I can understand your concern for your mother, Nick." She paused, I assumed to recover her equilibrium. "But did you ever stop to consider the other sixty-plus million people in the UK? CNC were getting really concerned about Mersea Island. They have been looking for any pretext to go in there. We would have closed it down by now if you had been thinking of anyone other than yourself."

I could understand her vitriol, but only rapid action was going to avoid this catastrophe.

"You need to take over the plant immediately," I repeated. "I don't want to tell you how to do your job, but Yusupov will be aware that we liberated my mother, and destroyed their Scottish base, and he will have armed heavies on site. If I were you, I would send some SAS in first and let Angie's people, with a fully qualified CNC team, get the plant functioning normally again. How quickly can you get them there?"

I realised I could be accused of suddenly trying to manage my country's deliverance from peril when arguably I had been the one to put it there.

Petra, however, was back in the driving seat. "I'll talk to the PM immediately and call Cobra. Leave it with me. They're pretty much ready to go."

There was little else I could do.

"We need you available, Nick, for that Cobra meeting. Where are you?"

"I'm in Scotland, on a friend's landline at the moment, as there's no mobile connection."

"Stay exactly where you are until I get back to you," she ordered. "I'm going to talk to the PM."

She rang off.

I explained the situation to Swami and Johnny. "Stay here as long as you need," said Johnny.

Then I called Nasta quickly, to let her know Mother was ok.

"Coffee and bacon sandwiches for everyone." A smiling Daphne came in with a large tray.

I could see through into the kitchen, where her two children were showing their toys to Mother and the little hostages from the castle. The latter seemingly looked at Mother as their guardian angel, from their time together in captivity.

"Poor little dears," said Daphne. "All they need is a bit of love and attention. God knows what they've been through but, in spite of all the trauma, they can still enjoy new toys." She looked at me with a smile. "Your mother did a good job. They seem to trust her completely. If not for her, I think they would be in a much worse state." She looked wistfully at them, and I could see a maternal spark igniting.

"Where do you think the kids are from?" asked Johnny, who saw his wife's look.

"Tilly says they're orphaned siblings from some place in Asia," replied Daphne. She looked at me again, this time more doubtfully. "She said you'd know, Nick."

"Kuikbakhistan?" I asked incredulously.

"That's the one," she agreed.

My mouth fell open. If that were the case, then Yusupov was showing a cynicism that even I had not thought him capable of.

The man who claimed to have been abused by his stepfather, and to abhor paedophiles above all other mortal beings, had actually been trafficking his own young people for profit.

My mouth hung open. I could not close it, and sat there like a goldfish in its own constricted little bowl.

And that, I realised, is exactly what I had been all these years for Tselmeg Yusupov. His own little brother in a goldfish bowl entirely of his making, swimming slowly round in semi-sentient circles.

I felt a severing of the last vestiges of any kind of bond between us. When he executed Bobby and Marina I vowed to bring him down, to let him know that his own demise, when it came, was Bobby's payback. Now, my goal was simple; urgent. No more mixed emotions. I had to destroy him.

Petra rang back almost immediately. "Nick, MI6 use a clean room at Aberdeen Airport. The PM won't allow a connection into a Cobra meeting without proper security. How quickly can you get there?"

I swallowed my anxiety, and asked Swami.

"I can be there in just over an hour."

"They'll meet you at the airport. Call this number to bring you in. We'll start without you. The PM's in favour of sending in the SAS, as you suggested."

She gave me a number, which I noted down. Swami and the boys loaded up their kit with renewed urgency.

"Don't wait for me," I said with rising panic. "He's got my vote. Time is of the essence."

"I'm staying here with the children and Johnny and Daphne," declared Mother, as I tried to herd her towards the door.

I started to remonstrate, but the look on her face told me it was pointless, and I had other wars to wage.

I nodded, and gave her a hug.

I did think to myself in passing that the further she was from Mersea Island, the better her chances of survival.

138

We made good time to Aberdeen Airport. The pilot understood the rush. Swami made sure of that.

Even so, I could not stop myself looking to the south for a nuclear mushroom, which would tell me Yusupov had won.

During the flight, I took the opportunity to talk to Nasta at more length, and filled her in on the unfolding events. As always, once I had confirmed that Mother and I were ok, she sounded fine and took everything in her stride. We skirted elegantly round the possibility of a nuclear holocaust.

As our wheels touched the ground at Aberdeen, a small delegation was sprinting towards us, and they waved me to follow them, at a run.

They led me into a brick building off the main terminal and, after a brief security check, I was ushered into a small room with a large video screen.

I recognised the PM, Petra, the Home Secretary, the Chief of General Staff and also the head of MI6, who had impressed me during our recent extraction of the British Ambassador out of Yusupov's clutches. There were various others.

"You know most of those present, Nick, and I have briefed them as far as I could. You may not know the head of our Civil Nuclear Constabulary, who obviously has a particular interest in this."

An angular face looked at me disapprovingly.

"We have been worried about the OES plant for some time," he said accusingly.

I had never been one for diplomatic niceties, and with an

impending nuclear explosion not far from London, now didn't seem like the time to polish them up too much, so I waded in.

"Have you sent in the fucking SAS?"

Petra raised her eyebrows. The CNC guy ignored me, and continued. "It would have been helpful if you had been more open with us. My team had been poised to enter the plant. If you had briefed us before, the plant would have been closed down already. We are now, finally, in close contact with Angie Ross and her team."

He left it at that, which I thought was pretty magnanimous of him.

"Angie and two of her team are on their way there now. They should be there any minute," added Petra.

Before I could respond, she continued, "And yes, Nick, special forces are standing by to enter the plant."

She turned to the others and reminded them that I was there because of my understanding of Yusupov's mindset. She made it clear that was the only reason.

"Nick made it plain to me that he feels the situation warrants armed entry to the plant."

I didn't want to disillusion her about my grasp of Yusupov's increasingly psychotic thought processes, so I laid it on with heavy brushstrokes.

"The guy seems to be becoming increasingly unhinged. His Scottish bastion, from which we have just liberated my mother, was full to the gunwales with drugs, but they were also holding two young Kuikbakh children, who his minions were obviously trafficking." I looked at Petra, who immediately got my drift. The anger and horror on her face mirrored mine at the time of first hearing.

"So, his outrage about Matthew Abbott's admittedly disgusting performance was all feigned; just political posturing," she murmured, shaking her head. "He really is a nasty piece of work." She looked at me disdainfully.

"Did the children come as a surprise to you, Nick?" she asked quietly.

There was silence round the room.

"I think I was about as horrified as you. I feel totally betrayed and having recovered my mother from his filthy clutches, I want to see this sickening little bloodsucker removed from the face of the earth."

There was silence, and Petra finally said, "I'm very glad to hear that, Nick. There have been times when I have wondered whether you were fully committed to that strategy."

She was right, of course.

"You need to get things moving," I pleaded. "Yusupov will know Mother is free, and will therefore understand that he is facing the full resources of the UK government. I am afraid that will not deter him, in fact quite the opposite. He will do everything in his power to stop you gaining entry, until he can fire up the enriched uranium."

"He has declared war," said George Watkins Bt, who had been offscreen until now (the Foreign Secretary's Macavity-like tendencies remaining intact even in this emergency.)

That took us all back.

"You certainly need to treat Mersea Island as an enemy target that will defend itself," I said.

"Should we lock down the entire south-east?" asked the PM to the others.

"That would cause major panic," suggested MI6.

"And may not help much," added the head of CNC.

"Just take back the plant before it's too late," I implored.

The PM nodded to CNC, who passed on the order to his onsite team. They had obviously agreed the procedure to follow.

The PM then turned to the Chief of General Staff. "Send in your SAS team, Mike, and keep me posted on the situation as it unfolds."

Mike saluted and left abruptly.

139

Things were coming rapidly to a head and so, while the PM, Petra and most of the others returned to their day jobs, the heads of CNC and MI6 stayed put with a small group of assistants. Everyone was on full alert in case any rapid decisions needed making.

In only a few minutes, MI6 announced that Angie and her team had arrived at the plant.

The SAS and CNC contingents were already there. "That's Colonel Rigby in charge." I heard someone whisper.

One of the special forces' operatives was equipped with a body camera, and our video had been plugged into the system.

I could see Angie, with two of her team. There were about five others in uniform who I assumed were all CNC. They were looking slightly shocked.

One of them whispered to Colonel Rigby in an aggrieved tone, "Some thugs in there just threw us out. They had guns."

Looking totally unfazed, the SAS moved towards the entrance, the colonel indicating for his men to cover both sides of the door. He whispered to nobody in particular, as far as I could see, "Stun grenades."

One of his team opened the door, standing well to the side, and two others lobbed black canisters into the reception area.

There were a couple of loud explosions, and two balaclava-clad SAS rushed in.

Two solitary shots rang out, and almost immediately one of them came out, put a thumb up, and waved for Angie and the CNC team to enter the building.

One of the SAS stayed outside, but the remainder (including our body cam) fanned out inside, taking control of the large reception area and calming down the receptionists, as they regained consciousness.

There were two corpses sprawled on the floor, bleeding profusely and not moving. They didn't look as though they were going to.

"We need to get to the control room," announced Angie, showing a fearsome calmness. "It's through that door."

I remembered it well.

The leader of the CNC group looked to be in shock, but one of his team rose to the occasion. He showed them all the layout of the plant on an iPad.

"We'll clear the way, miss," said the SAS leader, subliminally acknowledging Angie's leadership. "You and whoever is necessary, follow us as we clear each sector."

A receptionist, who had obviously been in the loo, emerged looking terrified, but slightly less dazed than the others.

"Can you show us, on your screen, the route to the control room?" he asked her.

The girl was shaking, but sat down at her post and, with three SAS section leaders, Angie and the CNC guy all looking over her shoulder, showed them a selection of CCTV shots.

There were armed hoods at various points along the way, and the soldiers noted their positions, the leader allocating targets.

When it came to the control room, we could see various people in there, concentrating on their screens. I could see our friend Sophie, working diligently. There were three more armed goons in there with them.

"I'll take the control room," said the colonel quietly. "Skip, you take the guys in that passageway; George that sector," he ordered, pointing at the screen. "Charlie, you clear the viewing theatre." Their eyes met. "Coordinate with me when you've eliminated the targets up there.

When we're ready to go in, you blow the glass to distract them.

The second you've done that, we'll take out those targets in the control room..." He looked at Angie. "Then, it will be up to you, miss."

The SAS section leaders quickly briefed their teams and, with a nod from Rigby, set off.

The operation was so slick, they made it seem easy. As they entered each sector one would go in, while the others covered him. Forewarned by the CCTV previews, they eliminated any resistance with grenades, and single shots. In less than two minutes they were at the control room.

Waiting outside, the leader spoke into his microphone, while one of his team attached something to the door handle.

There was a shattering explosion from above, in the viewing room, followed by a muffled one, which blew the control room door in.

As before, two stun grenades were pitched into the room, followed immediately by three SAS, who threw themselves to the ground at either side. We heard five shots and, while we could see little, as our body cam was apparently prone on the ground, there was a loud shout of, "Three targets down."

Our view rose up slowly from the floor and panned round the room.

I could see three bodies, and two terrified technicians standing with their hands in the air.

Sophie was still at her desk. She was wearing earphones and had been shielded from the blast by a solid screen. She seemed oblivious to the mayhem around her.

My immediate thought was that she must be too close to her objective to give up now. I wanted to scream at them to get her off the keyboard, but our sound system was one-way only.

Angie had the same thought and rushed at her, only for Sophie to smile in triumph, raising her hand theatrically and bringing her index finger down on one of the keys.

140

I could see Angie cower slightly, looking up at the ceiling as if expecting Armageddon.

But the only sound that came was music from the plant's public address system. 'Oranges and Lemons'.

Nobody but me understood the significance, and it brought a big smile to my face, and a solitary tear to my eye.

Soothslayer was letting me know.

He had won.

Sophie had just detonated the enrichment plant in Kuikbakhistan.

Angie dragged Sophie, struggling, away from the keyboard, assisted by one of the soldiers, who disabled her with handcuffs.

Angie ushered one of the CNC team into the chair at the main console, and stood over him. I assumed he was the technical whizz.

"I believe my team's virus may have slowed down that girl's manipulation of the fuel rod programme. But you need to get it back under complete control and close it down immediately," she directed.

I was impressed that he didn't argue, but plugged in a memory stick, and worked at the keys for some minutes, before inclining his head towards her.

"It was running very hot and there are some strange counter-commands in the system."

"Some of those are put there by my team," admitted Angie.

"I think I've got it under temporary control with our emergency override system," he said. "It was heading for a possible steam explosion the way the fuel rods and the cooling schedule had been manipulated."

"With those rods completely full of enriched uranium, it could have been a lot worse than that."

He looked genuinely shocked. "There's enriched fuel in there?" He appeared dumbfounded, and stared at his boss.

"Afraid that was only on a need-to-know basis, Jim," the latter said. "National emergency."

"Christ Almighty." Jim wiped his brow. "If I'd known that, I'm not sure I could have done what I just did."

He looked genuinely traumatised, and got up from his chair, holding onto the back of it.

"Do we need to check anything else?" asked Angie. "Are you sure it's getting back to normal operations?"

"We're taking over full responsibility for the plant," said the CNC head. "We'll close it down and do a complete review, both physical and technical, together with your team." He smiled uneasily at her.

He looked at the SAS. "Is it all safe? No more lunatics?"

"My teams are doing a full search of the premises," the leader confirmed. "Until I say so, the plant remains in full lockdown."

He pointed at Sophie and asked Angie, "Are the other operatives on our side or theirs?"

"Treat them all with caution," said CNC, taking control. "OES will be stripped of their operating contract."

"They shouldn't be allowed near any infrastructure at all," suggested Angie. "Someone needs to check their credentials bloody carefully. That one's from Kuikbakhistan." She pointed at Sophie.

141

The 'copter had long gone, so I took a scheduled flight down to London.

Nasta met me at the airport with Chloe and Snapper, and our emotions got the better of us. We hugged a lot and some tears flowed. Including mine.

Mother had been in touch with them, and I filled in the details.

"She said you were a hero, darling," cooed my wife, admiringly.

Before I could get too cocky about that, she added, "She also said how very happy that made her, as she realised how your early life with her had led you down the wrong path in life. She was only now coming to understand just how wrong that path had been."

I had come to accept that Mother's compliments were always sprinkled with little IEDs, designed to constantly remind me of my deficiencies. She was taking over Bobby's role.

"She's been talking to the wrong people," I laughed.

"Apparently Daphne and Johnny are going to adopt the two little Kuikbakh hostages," added Nasta, changing the subject. "Poor little things."

She looked at me disparagingly. "Your brother," she muttered, shaking her head. "Does he have no boundaries?"

"My nemesis, President Yusupov," I corrected her. "I don't think he does boundaries. But his time has come."

In the car back, I phoned Bill Topping.

"Bill, it's time to turn the screws," I told him.

"Your timing's good, buddy," he replied. "Lot of rumours going round, about how he's seriously over-extending himself. The market's beginning to do your work for you. I've been piling in myself. No comeback from his heavies yet."

"They've got their work cut out, I think." I hoped I was right. "Can you short Kuikbakh government bonds for me openly in my name, Bill?"

"How much?"

"A billion."

"You sure, Nick?" he queried. "You'll need the margin on that."

"No problem, and make sure my name's on it. This is personal. His head's going to roll, and I want him to know who's wielding the axe."

"Be careful, Nick. The guy may be down, but he's not out yet. You know what they say about wounded animals."

"I've got my end covered. You watch your back too, Bill. He'll know that you control this market."

"Good on you, Nick. I think you've finally seen the light."

142

For the next few days, I watched the markets more closely than ever, even when I had been fighting my way up the bank. I was specifically watching the appetite for Kuikbakh government bonds.

Finally, that appetite disappeared completely, and the buyers (along with all foreign investment) went comprehensively on strike. Yusupov had already been paying ridiculously high interest rates for the finance he so desperately needed to keep his country afloat. His oil reserves were running out, and he had sprayed his country's largesse so generously round the world, while skimming a generous froth off the top into his own pocket, that he was even finding it hard to pay his own security forces. Everyone else had been on short rations for some time, and inflation was heading into triple figures.

But the man was no fool. He knew that the day he stopped paying his army, was the day he signed his own death warrant.

So, I should not have been surprised or shocked when my mobile rang one morning.

"Good morning, Nick. Congratulations on rescuing your mother."

The man had never lacked audacity, but his bipolarity completely floored me this time, and I could find no immediate words to acknowledge it, as anger slowly overtook me.

"I knew you were resourceful, and I trained you well, so I was not surprised," he continued. "But after all I have done for you, is this the way you repay your brother, by trying to bankrupt my poor country?"

Words finally began to pass my lips. Fuelled exclusively by rage, they seemed to come from somewhere deep inside.

"You killed Bobby. Now you are selling your country's own little children to the highest bidder."

There was silence.

"After all you suffered in your youth, and your protestations of disgust when Matthew Abbott abused that poor little boy…" my voice tailed off into a low hiss. "I didn't believe that even you could sink so low."

I paused. "You provided Matthew with that young boy, didn't you?"

He exploded. "How dare you accuse me of that, Nick. You know that is not true."

"I accuse you, because you show yourself capable of the lowest, most perverted depravity. How could you do that?"

I felt forlorn, at how utterly and comprehensively the man had led me down his own hell-bound path.

Forlorn, as I understood that if Anastasia had not come into my life, and if she had not found my mother, then I, too, would have trodden that same sad path myself.

"How could you do that?" I asked again.

At length, he murmured without conviction, "Sometimes the end justifies the means, Nick."

I could only shake my head.

"And that end is so close."

It was then that I realised how delusional he was.

I was about to tell him so, but should have realised that delusion takes many desperate and dangerous forms.

He spoke quietly, and his voice suddenly took on all its former control and focus.

"I rang you, Nick, to invite you to reverse your large trade against my country, and to persuade your friends and colleagues to do the same, and especially that Bill Topping." He sounded angry.

I was tempted to laugh, but managed to resist. My thoughts

of laughter soon took flight, as he said quietly, "You have no idea how vulnerable your wife and family are, Nick. Even with your new mercenary friends." He spat out the words with venom. "That Topping man as well.

"You have one hour."

143

As soon as Yusupov rang off, I called Swami. I couldn't get through, which sent me into something of a frenzy. To add to it, the traffic was diabolical.

Finally, he rang back.

"Yusupov's going to try to pull some more shit," I babbled. "He could be targeting Anastasia and Chloe."

"Or your mother," suggested Swami, as always, ahead of me.

At Mother's mention, I realised how unprotected she was in the wilds of Scotland, close to Yusupov's operational base.

"Don't worry, Nick, we have them all covered. I'd have thought you'd be able to trust us by now," he said reproachfully. "My boys are watching your house, and Johnny has your mother."

"Sorry, Swami, of course I trust you," I confirmed. "It's just that…"

I swallowed and proceeded to repeat my conversation with Yusupov.

Swami was quiet for a few seconds.

"Come back to your house, Nick, and stay here with Anastasia and Chloe. It will make it easier for us if you're all in one place."

I ran out into the street and hailed a taxi. I pleaded for him to hurry, and couldn't help myself from back-seat driving.

We drew up as near as he could to my house.

I paid him off and, pulling out my key, walked quickly towards the front door.

I didn't think anything of the raucous buzz, as a noisy scooter roared down the street past my taxi, towards me. I finally turned to see two black-helmeted youths on it. One of them threw a large canister.

A man in trainers ran at me and I looked desperately for my escape, opting for a basement stairwell.

He was too quick for me. With a "Get down, Nick," he tackled me to the ground and, in an expert variation of a parachute roll, bundled us both down the stairs.

At that moment a cacophony of automatic gunfire rang out, peppering the wall above our heads. I tried to bury myself in the flagstones, such was my desire to hide, but the parachutist was actually on top of me, protecting me as I now realised, his handgun drawn and ready.

There was an almighty explosion, and the whole building shook.

"Not a cricketer," he said, as if commentating at a sports festival. "Wrong stairwell. Lucky."

The shooting wasn't all one-way traffic, and there was suddenly a crash of metal on metal, followed by the sound of screeching tyres and the thud of dead meat.

"Get in the house," ordered my protector. "We'll clear this up." He pulled me roughly up the stairs.

With a shaking hand I opened my front door, to be greeted by Swami.

"You've really pissed him off, haven't you, Nick?" he said, taking a quick look up and down the street, where I could see a number of running figures, before closing the door.

I peered out of the window and saw a large white van draw up quickly. They loaded the mangled remains of the scooter and two bodies into it.

The street was suddenly quiet again.

"Where's my family?" I asked.

"They're upstairs," he replied, pointing to the next floor.

I pelted up and ran into Nasta who had obviously also been given the all-clear. I held her and Chloe tightly.

"What's happening?" cried Chloe. "Are we all going to die?" I could see the same question in Nasta's eyes.

"We're going to be fine," I assured them. "Swami and his boys are on top of everything. This is just Yusupov's death throes."

Nasta twigged, as I assumed Swami had relayed parts of my phone call.

Chloe did not and understandably burst into floods of tears.

"What are death throes?" she wailed.

Nasta tried her best to calm her. It wasn't a total success.

144

Swami decided to move us to one of his safe houses.

"We're a bit of a sitting duck here," he declared, which I didn't find very comforting.

"Will he try again?" asked Nasta.

"Who knows?" he replied, ushering us towards a blacked-out four-by-four which drew up outside the door.

"But just in case, let's get you guys out of here while we deal with the police."

"What will you tell them?" I asked, hesitantly.

"Don't worry, a lot of those guys are friends of ours. Some were on 'ops' with us in Ireland and Iraq. They'll cut us a bit of slack," he smiled. "Give us a bit of time before the fucking media gets here." He held up his hand in apology to Chloe and Anastasia. He needn't have bothered. Nasta could take it, and Chloe hadn't heard.

There wasn't much we could do, so we climbed into the vehicle. Chloe clung to Snapper.

They drove us out into the suburbs, and we decamped into a functional terraced house.

"I've put together a little snack for you," said a lovely smile attached to a weather-beaten face with sparse white hair. "You poor dears. I'm going to look after you here." She swept Chloe up in her arms, unusually without any resistance. Chloe normally took her time with strangers, but this one won her over immediately. Snapper also seemed totally at ease, and curled up in a large armchair.

"I'll bring it in for you," she said, setting Chloe down in pride of place, in front of a big screen.

We snuggled up close on the sofa, and Chloe started to flip through the channels, when I saw a headline, 'Riots in Kuikbakhistan'. I took the remote. "Just let Daddy look at this for a minute."

After brief coverage of rioting in Szchymkent, there was the inevitable interview with Yusupov. He was ranting that it was all instigated by 'foreign subversives and terrorists', and that 'criminal elements in foreign banks were taking advantage of the situation to make illicit profits'.

"He's really feeling the heat," I said to nobody in particular, nodding with satisfaction.

Snapper jumped off his seat, barking manically. "He doesn't like that man," said Chloe approvingly, at which point Snapper launched himself at the screen, which teetered before regaining its balance. I grabbed him before he could do any more damage. In his younger days he had actually broken a screen when Elbows had appeared on it.

"That's the man who tried to kill Daddy," explained Nasta to our daughter.

"He's evil," whispered Chloe.

"Out of the mouths of babes," said Nasta, smiling at her.

They cut quickly to an interview with Bill Topping.

The interviewer was obviously on Yusupov's side. I wondered fleetingly, if he had been paid off.

"Why are you shorting Kuikbakh government bonds, Mr Topping? Can't you see the damage you are doing to their struggling economy?"

Bill Topping didn't like journalists. He had suffered a few run-ins with them over the course of his career.

"The only damage being done to the Kuikbakh nation, is by the corrupt bastard who rules it. Just ask him where he got all his houses, boats, planes and investments, if the country is so poor and suffering."

I was glad to see that Bill had lost all his previous inhibitions, and was now openly criticising Yusupov. He had obviously come to the conclusion that the Mongol's powers were on the wane. I felt I should warn him that, while that was probably true, his 'corrupt bastard' was lashing out, and wasn't going to go down without a struggle.

I tried to phone him, but he didn't answer, so I left a short message to that effect, finishing with, "Thanks for your support, Bill. I owe you. Watch your back, though, the guy just tried to kill me."

Chloe took the remote back, and just as she changed the channel, I saw a newsflash.

I grabbed it back from her. "Sorry, honey, just give me one more minute." I turned back to the news.

The same journalist was explaining that the interview we had just seen with Bill Topping had been recorded an hour previously.

"Since then, Mr Topping has been shot," he said, with what looked and sounded remarkably like satisfaction. I immediately disliked him.

They showed the front of a hospital.

"We understand that his injuries are serious, but not life-threatening."

They ran some pictures, which were obviously library shots, of an ambulance drawing up, and an emergency team running a trolley into the building.

"Mr Topping's security guards…". The man couldn't hide his distaste, "…killed one of the alleged attackers."

I realised that Bill Topping didn't need me to look after him, but I was glad I had warned him anyway.

I handed the remote back to Chloe.

"The good guys are winning," I smiled at her and gave her a hug.

"Who are the good guys?" she asked innocently.

Nasta raised her eyebrows at me questioningly and replied for me. "Good question."

145

Bill Topping rang me a few hours later, from his hospital bed.

"That little fucker," he blazed, but I could tell he was scared, and Bill didn't scare easily.

"If my boys hadn't been quick, I wouldn't be here."

Bill was very openly atheist, but he believed in the forces of good and evil, and paradoxically, in some form of afterlife. He was fearful of death. "With all the shit I've pulled in my life," he would say with a shiver, "someone down there is just gagging to pull my eyes and nails out, and cut off my dick with a blunt carving knife." He would laugh, but you could see that he believed it.

"We need to keep the pressure on him," I insisted. "His people are rioting in the streets. If we keep starving him of funding, they'll get rid of him for us, and save us the trouble."

There was silence.

"Bill…?"

"That was too close for my liking, Nick," he muttered. "I can't risk not being at his bond auction this afternoon."

"Bill, you have to stay strong. Get some more security. You can afford it." I was almost pleading. Bill Topping had been the main driving force behind the Kuikbakh bond strike. That, of course, was why Yusupov had targeted him. If he backed down, then the market would follow, and Yusupov would live to fight another day.

"Don't worry, Nick, the finance I'll offer him will barely move the ticker, and I'll keep shorting him behind his back." He paused. "I just don't want to meet my Maker quite yet, if that's ok with you."

"You don't believe in any 'Maker'," I reminded him.

"Whatever," he muttered, and I realised I'd lost him.

"Get well quick," I encouraged him.

I quickly rang round my contacts in the bond markets. They had all heard the news.

"Shit, Nick," one of them almost whispered to me. "They got Bill Topping, and I heard they had a pop at you too, didn't they?"

"That was nothing," I countered, not wholly truthfully. "And Bill's fine."

I could see I was losing this battle. The markets were fickle. I should know; I had made a lot of money myself out of that very flaw. They only answered to two drivers: fear and greed. And right now, fear was winning. Not the usual fear, of losing money. That could cause sudden rash decisions. The players in this market were running scared that someone was going to take them out. That put a whole new façade on their behaviour. Suddenly, it was as if they were motivated entirely by altruism.

"President Yusupov has done so much for his little country," confided one of the larger bond dealers on the evening news. To my certain knowledge, he had held one of the biggest short positions on Kuikbakh bonds prior to Bill Topping's shooting. "We owe it to him this afternoon, to make sure he has the finance to continue doing so," he simpered.

"Thanks a million, buddy," I muttered despondently to myself, changing the channel.

"Talking to yourself, now?" asked Nasta, popping her head anxiously round my door.

"The bond strike's falling apart, after Bill Topping's little incident," I informed her gloomily. "That means Yusupov is getting a lifeline of more finance, which will probably enable him to survive."

"And I don't suppose Swami will let us out of this safe house, until Yusupov stops breathing," she mused, looking apprehensively in the direction of Chloe's room. Our daughter had gone to her room and was moping, alone with her computer, whether out of shock, or boredom we could not tell.

"Can't you get the government in on this campaign?" asked Nasta. "We are virtually at war with him after that fiasco at the nuclear plant, aren't we?"

"We'd already cut all diplomatic ties with him before that," I replied.

"Couldn't they put an embargo on any form of financing for him, including purchasing his government bonds?" she asked.

"That wouldn't work. Most of the big trading houses are outside British government domain. They just do what makes the most money for them and in this case, whatever puts the least threat to their life and livelihood." I shook my head.

"But there are things we can do. I'll have a word with Petra. It's worth a try," I said. I had reached that stage when almost anything was.

146

I rang Petra. She wasn't available. I left a message for her to ring me urgently.

In the meantime, Yusupov's bond auction went 'swimmingly' well. That's what he told me, in a jubilant text message, which arrived shortly after I refused to pick up his call. I couldn't face talking to him. His voicemail said the same thing, thanking me moreover for 'rallying my friends to his cause'. The irony was clear.

He had always been adept at rubbing his adversaries' noses in his success, or in their own failure. I had every intention of doing the same to him.

The truth was, he had obtained nearly three billion dollars at pretty much investment-grade rates.

I had no idea how far that would get him in the context of his current financial dilemma, but it was a very unwelcome development, and would give him the confidence to continue with all his nefarious operations.

Including, no doubt, trying to get rid of me.

I realised that Chloe's boredom at being locked up in our safe house was the least of our worries.

We spent a despondent evening together, and Chloe refused to sleep in her own room. We put a mattress down on our bedroom floor.

I slept fitfully.

In the morning I tried Petra again, and to my considerable relief, she answered straight away.

I set out Nasta's strategy, and she was moderately receptive.

"We've been looking for a suitable response to the Mersea Island saga," she said.

"Surely that's an act of war, isn't it?" I asked.

"If we could prove, beyond all reasonable doubt, that he was intending to detonate the plant, it would be."

"Can't you?" I asked. "Angie and her team were in no doubt."

"I know," she responded, and I could feel political risk assessment taking over. "But we're a long way from being able to prove that in a court of law. We may well get there, but not yet. He would refute everything, blame it on OES and indeed, on Angie and her team."

Just as I was about to explode, she continued, "But it's a fact that OES did introduce enriched uranium at the plant in large quantities."

"OES is controlled by Yusupov," I informed her.

"We know," she agreed. "I understand their enrichment plant in Kuikbakhistan exploded. Do you know anything about that, Nick?"

"No idea," I lied. "But that sounds like good news to me. And even if you can't prove he was trying to eradicate the entire southeast of the United Kingdom, introducing enriched uranium must be illegal, mustn't it?" I couldn't see how there could be any problem in throwing the book at him.

"Absolutely," she agreed. "Especially as the uranium actually came from Kuikbakhistan itself."

"You could make public also that he has no hesitation in kidnapping old ladies and trafficking young children for sex."

"I'm not sure we want to draw attention to criminal acts which you have personally been involved in, Nick, and which could conceivably be connected back to the government," came the inevitable reply. "And, of course, your friends did manage to destroy all the evidence."

I was beginning to tire of these devious machinations. I even preferred the recent physical violence, to the labyrinthine twists of Petra's political manoeuvrings.

"But the prime minister is going to make an announcement this morning."

I realised, with a mixture of relief and annoyance, that she had been playing me along, and that the politico-diplomatic machinery had actually been whirring into action as we spoke.

Unsurprisingly, Petra and the powers that be were trying to distance themselves from my financial and physical battles. The value of my relationship with Yusupov was rapidly diminishing, as his own usefulness to my country petered out.

"We are pulling together an international accord, in response to these latest incidents. As part of that, we are freezing all assets belonging to President Yusupov, and a number of his colleagues."

That sounded positive, but I could hear that Petra was not finished and I was keen to hear her out.

"We are also embargoing all Kuikbakh exports of uranium and oil, and suspending all payments of capital and interest on his infrastructure finance, until such time as President Yusupov is able to explain himself."

Bingo, I said to myself. That would make clear his status as an international pariah, and I had little doubt that the bond markets would have no hesitation in treating him as such.

"You know that there are criminal gangs operating here, under his control?" I wanted to make sure she was aware of the power that he still exerted in the UK.

"The police are conscious of that, Nick," she stonewalled. I could feel my influence in her circle wilting rapidly. As long as Yusupov went down, that really didn't worry me at all. In fact, I relished it.

"You do manage to ally yourself with some unsavoury characters, Nick. First Yusupov himself, and now these criminal elements, who seem to be making themselves felt rather loudly around the country."

I was damned if I was going to let that go without comment.

"Those 'criminal elements' as you describe them, Petra, secured the release of my mother, and eliminated the centre of operations for all Yusupov's trafficking in drugs and young children. I understand they have good connections into the law enforcement bodies, and are actually cooperating fully with them."

To be fair to her, she was not slow to acknowledge what I said.

"We are mindful of that, Nick, and we are grateful, both to you and your friends, although you will never hear that from official sources."

There was a slight pause, and I could feel her marshalling herself.

"My colleagues and I feel that the time has now come for us to sever all ties with President Yusupov. It is time for democracy to take its turn in Kuikbakhistan."

I could see what was coming.

"As such, Nick, I have been asked by the prime minister to thank you for your help over the past few years."

She was too diplomatic to say what she meant, so I said it for her.

"Goodbye, Petra. It has been fun working with you."

147

It was all over the news.

First, the Foreign Secretary spoke at length in the House of Commons about the sequence of events at Mersea Island.

It was all pleasingly undiplomatic.

He categorically accused OES of introducing enriched uranium to the plant, sourced out of Kuikbakhistan.

He pointed out that OES was controlled by 'interests based in Kuikbakhistan'.

He alluded to drugs and children, sourced in Kuikbakhistan, being trafficked internationally, including in the UK.

His case was so strong that he barely needed to mention the Kuikbakh criminal gangs targeting Bill Topping. I had mixed feelings about not being cited personally. I was glad to be out of the limelight, but at the same time, I missed the thrill of being at the centre of things.

When he went on to explain how they were freezing Yusupov's assets, as well as those of his cronies, and suspending all payments of interest and capital on his infrastructure finance until further notice, there was a standing ovation in the House of Commons.

And in the house of de Carteret.

I rang Bill Topping.

"You heard the news, Bill?"

"Sure did," he replied. "Thank God I'm way short on Kuikbakh bonds, even after my little foray into the market yesterday."

"Don't think you need to worry about retribution anymore, Bill," I suggested, giving a dig at his reluctance to participate in the latest auction.

"Self-preservation is a strong human instinct," he laughed. "You, of all people, should know that, Nick."

Touché, I smiled to myself.

"The other guys will take a bit of a beating, though. Hope they don't blame you for putting Kuikbakhistan on the map and getting them involved."

"The sanctimonious crap they were coming up with about 'Saint Yusupov' yesterday, made me sick," I replied with feeling. "I was doing my level best to keep them out of trouble. Frankly they deserve everything they get."

Bill laughed. "The next time he comes to market, he'll get pretty short shrift. Any idea when that might be?"

He couldn't stop himself from tapping any source for useful information, and he believed that I was privy to the inner workings of Yusupov's financial strategy.

I didn't disabuse him. "He'll be back soon. The country is bleeding cash and with these new embargoes, inflation will take off, and things are likely to turn nasty for him. I reckon he won't last a week."

I had no real evidence for that view, but I intended to do everything I could to turn conjecture into reality.

I could feel Bill analysing my position, with the wisdom of a long-time freewheeler.

"I think I'll juice up my short position," he murmured. "Do me a favour, Nick," he continued. "I know you want to destroy him. Just hold off telling your buddies he's going down, until I've got all my options in place."

Bill Topping was a key player in this game of life-poker we were all playing, and in that game, you always want to keep a few favours up your sleeve. You never know when you might need them.

"No problem, Bill. Just tell me when you're ready."

148

Sure enough, the Kuikbakh finance ministry announced an auction the next day. There were some fifty-two-week bills being offered, but they knew there wouldn't be much appetite for anything remotely long-term, and most were only four- or eight-week maturities.

Nevertheless, it was a complete disaster.

The Bank of Kuikbakhistan tried to drum up enthusiasm, and bid for some of the shorter bills. However, rumours had been circulating about its own finances for some time, and it was only a token transaction. Most people agreed it was a circular one, which would not add one cent to overall Kuikbakh liquidity.

There was an almost total publicity blackout from the Kuikbakh capital. The international news agencies tried their best, and there were a couple of satellite shots of disturbances and rioting, but they were relying mostly on rumour.

I was sure that the UK government was still receiving intelligence, but I was now completely out of that loop.

We were sitting in our safe house, watching what passed for the news.

Swami wandered in.

"I think we can get you back home," he declared.

"Yeessss!" shouted Chloe, pumping her fist, and jumping up and down.

The beaming grin on Nasta's face was, if possible, even more revealing.

"Yusupov's hoods are keeping a low profile. Our boys in blue are now targeting them openly, but even more than that, it looks like their financing and sponsorship has pretty much dried up. So, there are a few scores being settled against them. I don't think they offer a credible threat anymore. Those that can, are getting the hell out."

Nasta gave me a hug, just as my phone rang with that slow, stuttering FaceTime drawl.

I answered it, without thinking.

"Nick, you have to help me."

It was Yusupov.

I had never heard him plead before.

The chairman of BOK was there with him in his government office together with another bureaucrat, who I remembered from the finance ministry. I recognised it all from that other life when I had been an integral part of their regime. There were a dozen uniformed goons, heavily armed.

"You have to help me get some finance. The market will do what you tell them. I know you have influence. You control the bond markets." He was looking nervously towards the door, and there were shouts, and a couple of shots. The soldiers pointed their weapons towards the danger; the civilians looked alarmed.

The moment had arrived. "You murdered Bobby."

He looked startled, but his eyes told me the truth, even though his mouth denied it. His normally belligerent tone was plaintive as he shook his head.

"You know that isn't true," he lied.

"I know for certain that it is. I saw them die."

"Get me the finance, Nick, before it's too late." There were more shots.

"Admit you killed him and Marina," I insisted.

"They were rogue troops, completely out of my control." As always, he was using whatever subterfuge might be available. "I made you rich," he whined.

A tiny grain of compassion fought its way to the surface. Pity for the man whose birth and childhood had, like mine, made him what he was, and who had in turn helped to make me what I had become. If not for Anastasia and Mother, I could have mirrored, and who knows, even exceeded his plummet into the abyss.

For Bobby's sake I pushed the thought back down.

We stared at each other.

"My friend, Bobby, was always your nemesis, Tselmeg, you should know that; and when you executed him, together with his wife, and unborn child, you sealed your own fate."

Our eyes met, and I believe that he finally understood.

"The end always justifies the means, Nick," he repeated his mantra, looking over his shoulder and nodding frantically to himself. Even at the gates of hell, the man continued to delude himself.

Tselmeg Yusupov's time had finally come. He could not accept it, but I was there to see it all unfold.

I looked into my brother's eyes. "And while I could indeed persuade the bond markets to open up and save your skin, I will not do so."

"Save me, Nick, I beg you, for all I have done for you."

"You tried to kill me, Tselmeg, you kidnapped my mother, you trafficked your own country's little children, you killed and slaughtered your people, all to make you richer still."

He was finally speechless.

"But when you killed Bobby, you signed your death warrant."

I hesitated briefly, looking at the man I had tried to emulate, had even admired, for all these years.

"I am going to ring Bill Topping now, and tell him to double my short call on Kuikbakh bonds. He, and the whole market, will follow my lead."

"Please don't do that, Nick. Think of all I gave you. I am your brother."

I shook my head. "You told me, some time ago, Tselmeg: that whore can never be your mother."

I smiled at him. "So, in the same way, you can never be my brother. Because that woman who you so despise was indeed the one who gave me life."

There were scuffles behind him, and he looked desperately over his shoulder. I held his gaze.

"And when I take out those contracts to short your country's bonds, I'm going to tell Bill Topping to put Bobby's name on them. He liked Bobby. He'll understand."

Tselmeg Yusupov's bodyguard spirited him away, just before the rabble could reach him, the mob scything down the others who would protect him.

I watched mesmerised, as our connection stuttered and faded out.

I raised my eyes to the heavens. "Keep wafting on," I whispered. I felt a warm glow.

"Keep wafting on," came the reply. "Just keep bloody wafting on."

This book is printed on paper from sustainable sources managed under the Forest Stewardship Council (FSC) scheme.

It has been printed in the UK to reduce transportation miles and their impact upon the environment.

For every new title that Matador publishes, we plant a tree to offset CO_2, partnering with the More Trees scheme.

For more about how Matador offsets its environmental impact, see www.troubador.co.uk/about/